BASE Status: Online

Also by E. Engberts

As Emmy Engberts
Her Elysium

As Skylar Heart
Hunter/Shattered
Blaze/Unraveled

As Rosa Swann
Lunar Pack Serial
Mated to the Alpha Serial
The Baby Pact Trilogy
Second Chance Mates Serial
Making a Family Serial
Omegas' Destined Alpha Serial
The Vampire's Past Trilogy

BASE

Status: Online

E. Engberts

© 2018 E. Engberts
All rights reserved.
Cover design by Easily Distracted Media
Formatting by Easily Distracted Media

© 5 Times Chaos / Easily Distracted Media
ISBN 978-90-825832-8-1
NUR 285

20190221

I

Departure

1
Ordinary World

You are now logged into Destruction of Elysium

The message appeared in the middle of Willow's line of sight as the world around her started to materialise. The low houses gave the feeling that they were about to burst out a whole family of ghosts and a dense fog fuzzied the edges of her surroundings, making the lights at the end of the street look creepy and haunted.

Willow's 'low sensory' settings muted all of the voice announcements in the game, instead showing them as notifications in the middle of her view. It also influenced the background music, keeping it fairly quiet, the light effects, dampening their brightness a tad, and even her experiences of scent and taste in the virtual world. She always thought it was one of the best inventions ever, being able to decide on your own world settings and not having to deal with the harshness of sensory experiences that others seemed to have no problems with.

As she walked down the street, it occurred to her, not for the first time, that the real world would be a much better place for her to live in if they could get the sensory settings in augmented reality as advanced as they were in virtual reality.

The thing was, the muting option in AR was just an imperfect rendering of what they already had running in VR. Since it was just not as easy to mute impulses inside a brain as it was when they could just send her brain a lower setting in the first place. Though, she hoped that the AR settings would get more advanced soon. There were places outside of the building she lived in that she'd love to visit for real, like the beach or going skiing in the mountains, but for now, she just couldn't. It would send her into sensory overload and probably trigger a panic attack. *Bummer.*

Willow looked around, quickly locating where she was as she saw the name of the city listed over the almost translucent map in the top right side of her vision. *Araepolis*, city of the cursed spirits, and she was in the residential district.

Okay, good. She quickly tried to recall what she had been up to before she'd logged off yesterday.

A red exclamation mark slowly pulsed in the lower right edge of her view. She moved her eyes in that direction and a screen popped up in front of her.

NOTIFICATIONS
√ 300 XP for daily logging in
√ New message from Violet
√ Update on Guild Ship Items List
√ Quest update for 1 quest
√ 150 items have been sold in the marketplace

As she read the list, the top message's faint glow disappeared, and the XP message slowly faded away, the others moving up a row.

She focused on the update of her items list, and a new list appeared.

Guild Ship Item List
Gather:
    □ Cedar Wood: 490/500
    √ Linseeds: 250/250
    □ Ghost Leaves: 189/200
    □ Juicy Olives: 276/300
    √ Titanic Cassava: 100/100
Craft:
    □ Cedar Lumber: 75/100
    □ Titanic Varnish: 37/50

The numbers for cedar lumber and titanic varnish glowed as the game registered her most recent crafting attempts as successful, even though she hadn't actually collected them yet.

Her guild was building a guild trading ship so that they could directly trade with other guilds, cutting out the fees of the marketplace, but it also allowed trade of rarer items that couldn't be sold through the regular market. If they completed it before Helheim Fallen Online came out, and used it to run a couple of trading missions, it could give them a significant boost in in-game income which meant that buying the new game would be a lot easier.

Willow switched back to the notifications list, the items list update row now also gone. She ignored the message from the marketplace. There was no use checking that until she was actually going to invest time in it and could set up new items to sell, which probably wouldn't be until later.

She took a quick peek at the updated quest log, but it was only for the quest to open a new raid. The dungeon she'd finished last night had finally registered at the main quest registry, and now she just had to do three more dungeons until she could enter the new raid. She didn't know why the updates on dungeons had to be so slow to register, though it probably had something to do with giving people enough time to recover from doing a dungeon or event before going onto the new one. Dungeons and raids were pretty exhausting, mostly mentally, so there were certain barriers in place to make sure people didn't overdo it.

Then she focused on the notification of a message from Violet, and a new screen showed up.

> Hi Willow,
> Good morning!
> Did you hear it yet? They're sending out the
> new batch of beta keys for Helheim Fallen
> today.
> I'm so excited.
> I sooo hope we both get one, but if only one
> of us gets it, we have to tell the other what
> it's like.
> Promise me!
> Okay. Off to bed.
> Night!
> Love, Violet

Most people these days would send voice or video messages, but Willow preferred to do things old school, just typed notes. She liked it better because it was calmer and quieter, voice or video messages just tended to be loud and obnoxious.

A keyboard appeared in the air in front of her, and she quickly typed a message back to Violet. They sometimes missed each other when they were both on different sleep schedules, though it didn't matter much. Time had become almost meaningless these days.

The economy, the games, it all ran 24/7. Day and night had become merely words referencing to it being light or dark outside, nothing more.

About twenty years ago, before Willow had even been born, a device called a BASE unit, Bioelectrical Augmented Synapse Enhancement unit, had been invented. This small device was implanted at the base of the skull and could read but also create and send neuro-electrical pulses to the brain. The BASE unit was able to adjust pulses from different parts of the body and this way it could create a very realistic augmented reality experience. The BASE unit also came with its own software platform called the BASE platform, which did away with most people's needs for old school computers as it could directly interface the internet with their brain. The most popular use of the BASE platform was the virtual reality option where people could walk around a game, or any virtual world, like they were really there.

When almost everyone in the world switched to the BASE implant and lived their lives either in AR or VR, it opened up a world of possibilities. For example, it allowed Willow to set her own sensory setting for things like volume or light, which was such a blessing to her because those were the main areas she had problems with because of her autism. But it also allowed the world to run 24/7. The BASE platform would read people's 'biological clock' and then notify them when they should go to sleep, or get something to eat and things like that. Because no matter how realistic BASE was, those bodily functions still needed to happen in the real world.

There had even been reports of people getting suspended from the BASE platform for hours or days at a time when they ignored the BASE messages for too long. And if that kept going on, they could even get visits from a doctor and be sent to a specialised hospital unit that would teach them to take better care of their bodily needs. *Scary.*

The BASE unit used to be this *big dangerous thing* and people would warn against, giving companies such easy access to their brains. But these days, most kids had it implanted within a couple of months of being born. It was a normal procedure. That, and the battery of tests that would determine so much of a kid's future.

When kids got their implant, doctors would also use that time to test how they responded to sensory stimulation, how well they reacted to social interactions, if their body had any physical deformities or if their build could potentially make them athletic stars. There was a whole list of tests. And in the end, all the results were ranked almost like they were 'stats' about a human being.

Or, that's how Willow imagined it anyway, that there was a stats sheet on her on some system or in some drawer like she had for her character in DoE.

Intelligence: Average
Social Skills: Very low
Physical Skills: Average

**Sensory Processing: Problematic
Class: Autistic**

The tests were what got her an autism diagnosis, and that had influenced the rest of her life since. From going to a tiny preschool class, to private lessons at primary and secondary school, to the 'low sensory housing' she lived in right now.

Or, as she liked to call it, 'the rollercoaster of going absolutely nowhere in life'. She was autistic, so she'd been put into a system that was basically designed to keep her busy and somewhat healthy until the day she died. Because she was never expected to amount to anything anyway, so why bother?

Through the BASE implant, the AR side enhanced daily life around the house. From things like ordering groceries or anything else a person needed right from where they were standing, to being read a story, or even calling friends. It was all done in the BASE's AR system, right there through the BASE unit in their brain.

And when someone wanted to go to the virtual world, they'd put on a VR headset and be transported to the BASE platform, from where they could choose from any game or program they owned or browse new games and programs. The BASE platform worked all around the world, so no matter where someone logged on they would always be connected to the same system. When playing multiplayer games, they could be playing with someone from the other side of the world and not even know.

Willow moved her head slowly side to side, letting her eyes go over the empty windows of the houses around her, trying to decide if she wanted to dive into a dungeon or if it would be better to get to crafting the items for the guild boat first.

Crafting, probably, especially if they were going to get the guild boat done before Helheim Fallen Online, the new VRMMORPG, came out.

A message popped up in the chat box on the lower left side of her vision.

> **Sage:** Where are you at?

Willow smiled. Sage was another one of her friends from the guild. It wasn't a big guild, but they'd all been friends for years and had gotten to know each other pretty well.

> **Willow:** Just logged on, going to set up the next round of items for the boat, and then going to queue for a dungeon. I'd like to open the next raid before the weekend. Get it out of the way and stuff.

Her fingers flew over the projected keyboard. She'd seen real keyboards when she was little, and since she preferred to play in mostly quiet or silence, this was actually a great way to communicate with others.

> **Sage:** Cool. I'm about 80% done with my part. Do you have some flax in your inventory?

Oops!

> **Willow:** Sold it last night. Sorry!
> **Sage:** No problem, can go grab it myself. You need the money more than me anyway.

That was true. Willow lived on benefits because she was deemed 'unemployable' because of her 'autism issue' and the money she got each month was... well... not that much. 'Experts' said it was enough to live on, but that was only if you never bought any new games or wanted to drink more than water all day. It totally depended on your definition of 'living'.

Luckily, she could make some extra money by selling items in the marketplace in games. The exchange rate from game-currency to real world-credits in DoE was crap, but that didn't really matter. Some games, like most RTS games or hardcore puzzle games, had a better exchange rate, but she didn't enjoy those as much, and there was little use playing them against her own preference when she would enjoy DoE much more. Right now, she was saving up for buy Helheim Fallen Online, which would set her savings back quite a bit.

She opened the game menu with a swipe of her hand and scrolled through the locations she could transport to until she hit 'Guild House'. She clicked on the button and a new screen popped up.

Are you sure you want to teleport to Guild House?

'Yeah, yeah,' she thought, and the system interpreted it.

The next moment she felt the insistent pull on her whole body as she was transported to the housing area, spawning in the middle of her own room in the guild house. The room was filled with plush toys, cute trinkets she'd collected and everything that made her happy. Plus, of course, two crafting benches, one for alchemy and one for carpentering.

Willow opened a chest near the crafting tables and grabbed the supplies she needed. Then she went over to the alchemy table and collected the bottle of titanic varnish from it.

You have collected Titanic Varnish.
Alchemy +250 XP

Then she put an empty bottle at the end of the distiller and grabbed the three other ingredients she needed from her inventory, juicy olives, ghost leaves and titanic cassava. She first carefully peeled the cassava root, making sure to take all the skin off, as this was the base of the varnish and leaving any of the skin on would mean certain failure of the recipe. Then she cut up the cassava root into small pieces and put it in the bowl at the start of the distiller.

Cooking +10 XP

Then she finely tore up the ghost leaves. They were meant to stabilise the mixture, before throwing them into the bowl too.

Cooking +1 XP

Finally, she took the juicy olives, throwing them into the small centrifuge Violet had made her, before throwing in a couple of marbles and closing the lid.

She turned the lever, spinning the centrifuge, and the oil from the olives collected in the outside bowl, slowly seeping into a beaker at the base of the centrifuge. When no more oil came out, she stopped, catching her breath for a moment. That thing really needed an improvement or something, it was still too much of a hassle to handle.

Cooking +25 XP

She poured the oil into the bowl at the start of the distiller and with a flick of her wrist put a fire under the bowl, the upside of being an elemental mage. She was mostly specialised in nature and some ice magic, but that one skill point into firebolt came in really handy for cooking and a range of other uses.

She kept a close look on the mixture as it was starting to heat up, the root slowly dissolving and, as she saw the first of the leaves shrivel as they browned, she put the top of the bowl on and opened the distiller valve.

Now the recipe was set up, and she just had to wait. The game would turn the fire off automatically when the recipe was done and she didn't have to wait around for it. Titanic varnish took about two to three hours to finish. There were better things she could do with that time.

She went over to the carpenter table and took the cedar lumber from it.

Carpentry +300 XP

Then she took the cedar wood from her inventory. It was always funny how these big items could fit in her inventory all tiny and still become this huge thing when it hit the table or when she crafted with it. *Game mechanics, right?*

She placed the cedar wood on the table and grabbed the small bag of linseeds. Then she slowly poured the linseeds into the funnel on top of the machine. The addition of the linseeds meant that there was a greater chance of the end product being of extra high quality. Which would mean a better boat once it was finished.

It wasn't useful on all the items they were using, but it was good to try and get extra quality where it wouldn't add extra time or money. Getting the best quality while staying sensible about time and cost constraints was always the best.

She turned the machine on and watched the wood slowly go towards the rotating saws.

Carpentry +100 XP

The best thing about doing this in VR? She didn't have to worry about the noise or the dust that would normally go everywhere with one of these machines. It was nice and quiet and clean.

Willow quickly took another look at the varnish in the distiller and then left her room, walking into the rest of the house.

She loved having a house with the guild, it was cosy and she felt at home here, much more so than the place she actually lived in.

They were only a small guild, five people in total, her, Violet, Sage, Juniper and Opal. Enough for queueing up for dungeons and as a small part of a bigger group when doing raids, but not much else. Which was fine with her, they didn't need much else.

They just needed each other.

2
Nature and Biology

Willow walked down the stairs, finding Sage in the living room on the couch.

"Morning." She sat down next to Sage, pulling up her inventory and taking a plush hippogriff toy from it, hugging it close. She had the exact same one in the real world, a birthday gift from Violet.

"Morn," Sage yawned. "Anything interesting going on today?"

"Hoping to do some dungeons and get some more items for the boat. And, of course, Violet is excited about the Helheim Fallen Online beta keys being handed out today. What are you up to?" Willow didn't really feel like moving though, she'd rather veg out on the couch than go do anything. Luckily, she could.

"I should be getting some items for the boat too." Sage shrugged. "But I've got to get to work in three hours..." They looked around the place. "Do you want to run a quick dungeon together?"

Willow shrugged too, a little too comfortable where she was. "We could just go do some gathering." Right now, that would probably be better spending of her time. She wasn't as far along with the gathering of the items she needed for her crafting as the others were. Not that she could really do things any faster, since she only had the crafting tables in her room to use most of the time. "Hey." She looked at Sage, at their odd eyes and their weathered skin. Sage was a satyr, a wood and mountain creature of Greek mythology, who were known for their close connection to nature and their love of drinking and parties.

Willow had always found it so interesting, the different races that a player could choose from and how it related to who they were. She was a dryad herself, a forest nymph with flowers for hair, green-tinted skin and gear that looked like plants had just grown around her. It fit the type of mage she usually played, someone who was more connected to the lighter sides of nature and who got most of their powers from being surrounded by trees. Violet was a Naiad, a water nymph. Which she explained was because it was cool to play and somehow the race perks made her a better rogue, but Willow always suspected it was because Violet liked looking at herself in every reflective surface she passed and the race kind of... They were beautiful and didn't wear too much.

"Yes?" Sage smiled, reaching up to tap the tip of her nose. "You got distracted again."

"Eh. Yes." Willow blinked, coming back to this world. "I'm going to set up the crafting tables in the basement, if there are any empty right now. Do you want to go gather some things from the garden after that?" She wasn't up for doing anything big yet, but gathering was fun and didn't require too much of her energy.

Sage pulled a face. "You're going to have to wait. Violet and Juniper filled them up this morning before they logged off."

"I guessed as much." Willow sat up more, putting the plush hippogriff back into her inventory. "Was worth a try, though." Even in their basement they only had a limited number of crafting tables since the house was so small.

"True," Sage said as they stood up. "You want to go out back now?"

"Yeah." Willow also stood up. The guild house also had its own garden, and they'd been farming a lot of things that were either great for selling off or were used in making the boat. Or, at least, the items that wouldn't take too long to grow. Trees for the wood for the boat were too much of a hassle, they took two weeks just to fully mature and then they had to be lucky that they were of a high enough quality. But the flax only took 48 hours, so they'd been planting them in 6-hour increments so that they could often harvest a couple of them at a time.

As soon as Willow stepped out the door, Mira was pushing her beak against her leg. Willow grinned and petted the small hippogriff, ruffling her feathers. "Hi, sweetie. Did Violet lock you out of the house again?"

Violet tended to do that. Since the coding for baby creatures, especially hippogriffs, actually included strings of code that allowed them to 'eat' things they found around them or 'trample' it which would break items. It had been fun when Mira was still in her baby phase, but she was now in her third stage, almost getting to juvenile, and the skills she'd unlocked had been... a little bit more annoying sometimes.

Willow pulled up Mira's stats screen.

Name: Mira
Creature: Hippogriff
Age: 4 weeks
Stage: Child
Time to next stage: 56 hours
Attack: 10
Toughness: 8
Sleep: Low
Hunger: High
Parents: Violet & Willow

"Ah, you just woke up, didn't you?" Willow reached into her inventory and pulled out a piece of raw rabbit meat. How these things didn't go bad in her inventory... She didn't question it. "Time for breakfast!"

Mira stepped back a little, her head bobbed up and down, her eyes on the piece of meat, her beak wide open, but her screeching quieted because of Willow's settings.

Then Willow threw the piece as far as she could. It made a nice arch, but Mira caught it easily, happily munching. Willow and Violet were both 'parents' to Mira. They'd raised her together from when she was an egg and once Mira was big enough, they'd be able to fly her together. Which was awesome. More than awesome, really. There weren't many hippogriff parents in Destruction of Elysium, as taking care of the egg before it hatched was such a hard job. But between the two of them, they'd managed it.

As Mira was eating, and tumbling around, playing, Willow

turned to the fenced-off patch of garden. They'd put the fence in after Mira destroyed part of their crops one night.

Sage was already looking at the flax, running their fingers through the tops as it waved in the computer-generated wind. They looked her way. "How much do you need?"

Willow checked her list. "No more linseeds, but I do need olives." She pointed to the trees at the back. She had to pick out just the right ones. Not all the olives would be 'juicy' ones, no matter how much she'd helped the trees grow as strong as possible. It had been a hassle, growing a high-quality tree from nothing. But it was definitely worth it over having to go out into the woods and search for olives in the wild, surrounded by mobs.

"Cool. I'll just get these done then." Sage pulled a big fork-like tool out of their bag and started pushing it into the ground to loosen the flax roots for harvesting.

Willow went over to the olive trees, running her fingers over the leaves, letting them play against her skin. She loved trees and the feeling of leaves and flowers. It was one of her 'things'.

She reached up, putting her fingers around an olive and pulled carefully. The ring around the olive turned yellow, and a status bar appeared over it.

Almost ready.
Do you want to harvest it?

She let the olive go, it was a little too early for that one. She'd still get the XP for harvesting it, but it wasn't worth it if she wouldn't be able to get the right items from it.

She reached out to another one, this time, as she wrapped her hand around it, it blinked green for a moment and then fell into her hand.

Olive

Ingredient which can be used in food or can be turned into oil for a range of uses.

Bummer. She really needed the high-quality juicy olives for this the recipe, or it would be too much of a hassle to make the olive oil.

She reached out to another olive, with her other hand this time. It also blinked green, and then fell into her hand. Another regular olive. With the quality of the trees and her skill level, she could get a juicy olive about one in five or six gathering attempts. And it was really worth it. But that still meant she had a lot of normal olives in her inventory too.

Willow harvested another twenty olives, getting four juicy olives from it. The tree now no longer had any ripe olives on it, so she could try again in six to seven hours and there would hopefully be new ones ready by then.

That put her at 280 juicy olives gathered for the titanic varnish. She was almost there now.

She looked around and found Sage planting new flax in the patch, the space empty after their harvest. The guild had a pretty good system going here, planting, gathering, making sure to always have stock to sell while they also had enough items to use themselves.

She walked up to Sage, who looked up.

"Do you want to go into the forest for a while? I need to get some pelts and a few other items for the boat." Sage cleaned their hands on their shirt as they stood up.

Willow looked out over the area behind the house and the garden, there was a forest not too far off, and she didn't have anything else to do right now. "Sure. Let's go."

"Cool." Sage swapped out their gear, going from a farming specialised gear set to an 'adventuring' gear set, which had a couple of attack skills but mostly had good stats for gathering items.

Willow also swapped out her gear. DoE made it really easy to keep multiple gear sets on them at the same time and that way they didn't have to sacrifice stats for convenience.

They took off to the forest out back, it was only a short walk. The guild house was built in a mid-level zone, so while they were definitely overpowered for the creatures roaming here, that didn't mean that the loot they dropped wasn't useful.

By mid-level, most people would have already specialised their crafting and gathering skills, choosing just a handful of them to focus on. Trying to get all the skills levelled up at the same time was not only time-consuming but also not very practical. So, instead, people either focussed on keeping three to four skills up high enough to gather and craft everything themselves, or they would be dependent on the marketplace.

And that's where players like Willow, Sage and Violet came in. Their gathering skills were the highest level skills they had, because that allowed them to sell stuff off. Their crafting skills always lagged behind the rest because crafting often cost more than they could make selling items off, especially at the lower levels. Which is why Willow was only now getting close to the max level for alchemy.

As they walked into the forest, most mobs and critters

didn't even seem to realise that they were there. Their coding told them that attacking players who were so much stronger than them would be a stupid choice. Which made these trips a lot simpler, really.

Then they spotted a clearing with some rabbits hopping around in it and at the edges were blackberries that Willow had her eyes on.

Sage grabbed their bow and seconds after they aimed it at one of the rabbits, an arrow flew out, and the rabbit was killed instantly. Then Sage shot a handful of other rabbits in quick succession, aiming the bow and the attack happened almost automatically, just by activating the skill.

Then Sage walked up to the first rabbit, took out their butchering knife, and as soon as the knife touched the rabbit it fell apart into rabbit meat, rabbit pelt and some sinews. The butchering left behind an almost clean carcass that would fade away in a couple of seconds.

Willow walked up to some of the bushes with the blackberries and reached out to them, tugging on them carefully, waiting for the indicators go blink green before harvesting. Blackberries sold pretty well on the marketplace because they were used for some strength and speed potions and in some food that enhanced speed, HP and strength, perfect for warrior type classes and even some tanks, depending on setup.

You have collected 2 Blackberries
Gathering +4 XP

Then, Willow saw a deer from the corner of her eyes, it seemed to have a golden glow around it, making her heart beat faster. If that was what she thought it was… It would be a very rare mob. Mythical deer barely ever spawned. Their fur and meat would definitely get her some nice coins.

She held out her hand to the deer, palm forward, and her hand started to glow, a notification of the ability to use one of her attacks blinked before she 'pushed' and the firebolt flew from the palm of her hand towards the deer.

You hit the Mythical Deer for 658 damage
+40 XP

It was dead instantly, a forty level difference did that.

She walked up to the deer, pulling out her butchering knife, and as she touched it to the dead animal, it automatically triggered the butchering skill and the deer fell apart.

You have collected 1 Mythical Venison
You have collected 2 Mythical Hide
You have collected 1 Mythical Bone

"Lucky," Sage said from behind her. "I haven't seen one of those in months."

Willow turned around, winking. "Well, it's good that I did see it, then."

They strolled back to the clearing. Some of the rabbits had already respawned, so Sage killed them off again swiftly for their drops. And Willow gathered more blackberries, getting a good stack of them to sell.

This was simple and easy, but game economy depended on it and so did her own finances. It was mindnumbing work, but that often meant that it was even more rewarding than if it had been too easy.

After a while, Willow stood up straight and stretched her in-game muscles, even in the game you could move wrong for too long and get stiff. Then she looked over to Sage. "I'm going to log off for a bit. I think I need some more sleep." She'd been up quite late last night, searching guides on how to complete the final quests she was still working on for DoE and looking at pre-release footage for Helheim Fallen Online.

Sage smiled at her. "I guessed as much. I'll be off soon too." Sage reached out and a trade screen popped up in front of Willow.

She accepted the trade invite and a whole bag of linseed and a stack of raw rabbit meat appeared in front of her.

"I don't need all of this. I've got all the seeds for the boat and I've got enough meat for Mira too." She felt bad to just take items and not give anything back.

"These are left over from today and I don't need all of them myself. They're of more use to you, for cooking or selling." Sage shrugged, still smiling.

"Thanks." Willow smiled back. "I really don't have anything to trade though."

"No problem. These are just for you."

"Okay." Willow accepted the trade and the linseed and rabbit meat appeared in her inventory. That would make her some money. Even if it weren't that much, anything helped. Then she turned back to the house. "I'm logging off. See you later!"

"Later," Sage called after her.

Willow went back to the guild house, going up to her room. This was a better place to log off, and she wouldn't be as disoriented when she logged back in than she was this morning.

She quickly pulled up her character screen, letting her eyes skim over the stats until she found what she needed.

She was almost another level up for her alchemy. That was good, because it would unlock the final recipes, which included a health potion that could make her quite a lot of money. The recipe required a lot of hard to find ingredients, but she'd been collecting those for weeks already, so it would definitely be worth it. Not everyone could be bothered to get their alchemy skill up this high, because it took a lot of mind-numbing work, but working on the guild boat really helped with levelling the skill slowly but steadily and she didn't even have to spend extra time on it.

And after they'd finished the boat, she could sell the potions at a much higher price directly to other guilds with their trade boat. Which would make all the work with it.

Time to log off.

Willow pulled up the gaming menu and hit the very last button on the popup.

You are now logged out of Destruction of Elysium

Two blinks later, Willow opened her eyes to the white ceiling of her room. She took the VR headset off and stretched her arms and legs, rolling her shoulders. She put the headset on the table next to her bed, and stood up.

Her bedroom was... pastel coloured. Pastel green, pastel blue... The 'experts' on sensory overload issues insisted that pastel colours in the bedroom was the highest level of 'stimulation' that people with sensory issues should be exposed to when they woke up. It was this or white, and Willow really didn't want white walls to go with the white ceiling and the white chair and the white bedside table. It was... too hospital-like.

She took a deep breath and went to the window, putting her fingers to the 'glass' in front of her. Currently, it was showing a beautifully rendered image of a sun coming up, since her biological clock assumed that it was morning.

Tapping on the window twice, the glass turned into a menu, showing her all the different 'safe' options she had that she could turn the window to. But she scrolled all the way down, hitting the very last button, unlocking the 'unsafe' options with her fingerprint, and then scrolled all the way down again, past storms and lava and space stations, until she found the setting she was looking for.

Turn window projection off

She clicked on it.

Are you sure?

'Yes.'

**This will turn off the safety settings on
your account**

Are you sure?

'Yes.' What was it with all the stupid questions about things she'd already decided on? Sometimes it felt like the system wasn't helping her, instead, it felt like it was trying to keep her locked in a box. A box called 'safety'. 'Sensory safe' or 'autistic specialised' software or settings or even food. It was ridiculous. Like she hadn't lived in a mostly 'normal' world for sixteen years when she lived with her parents.

But this was the world she lived in now. As soon as she turned sixteen, 'experts' had insisted that she move her out of her parents' house and into this 'sensory low' building. All the people living here had different levels of 'sensory issues', and the whole building was set up to support them so that they could be 'the best they could be'. Basically, it meant constant check-ins and the system coddling them. Not just that, everyone was in their own little apartment and from the start she'd felt like she was discouraged from even talking to the other people living here.

It was ridiculous. For all the cool things the world had gotten because of the BASE implant and the globally connected system... They were still hiding people away who they felt were 'different' and instead of trying to understand them, 'experts' insisted that they always knew better. And parents *always* seemed to fall for it.

The window in front of Willow faded dark and then slowly came to life again. Even when she turned the 'safe' options off, some were just too hardcoded, like the fading in and out thing.

In front of her, the world was illuminated in grey, the sky in the east was lighter than in the west. From her room, she could see over the wall surrounding the building and glance at the streets and neighbourhoods beyond it. They were was mostly stupid grey blocks lined up, all nice and neat, with windows on them that never actually showed what was going on behind them. The 'real' world had become unreal and impersonal now everyone lived in VR or used AR when they were out and about.

It was right before sunrise. She loved this time of day best. Maybe because her biological clock worked like that, or just because it was the most serene moment of the day.

Would it be warm enough outside to go check it out?

Temperature -2°C

Okay, that was cold.

Willow went to her closet and put on warmer jeans and a sweater and then grabbed her thick jacket. Cold or warm, she just had to go outside.

She had to go outside to greet the rising of the sun.

3
Call to Adventure

Willow's breath came out in small puffs, like the breathing of a dragon, as she stepped out the front doors of the building into the walled-off garden. The world around her illuminated in grey, it felt almost ethereal, unreal, like it didn't really belong in this world.

She slowly turned down the settings on her BASE unit, letting the real world take over. The sounds around her grew louder. The humming from the AC units on the outside of the building. The water running through pipes somewhere not too far off. And there was the sounds of birds, awakening at dawn, singing as they started their day. She hadn't heard the songs of real birds in a very long time. Although, standing in this walled-off garden, the birds could just as well be simulated too, to give the place some extra 'authenticity of nature'.

She walked over to the fountain, which stood in front of the building, all nice and attractive for visitors. Now, in the winter, it wasn't turned on, but that didn't take away from how magnificent it was. The fountain was made out of a white stone, which would almost glitter in rainbow colours in the sun, and it portrayed two dolphins spraying water into the air. It could have looked tacky, but, instead, it looked serene.

Willow sat down on the edge, letting her eyes go over the rest of the garden. The trees, lining the sides, hiding most of the wall, the grass, so soft in the summer that it made for a great place to fall asleep, the park benches, scattered around in a way to appear almost random, but in reality made for easy visibility for the cameras that kept an eye on them. This was all designed to be as 'safe' as possible. To be as 'calming' and 'comforting' as possible.

Those weren't her own descriptions. She'd read the leaflet that her parents got before she was taken here. This place was described as the 'perfect oasis' in the 'overwhelming' and 'fear-inducing' outside world, a place to 'encourage the best out of autistic minds'. In reality, it was a prison more than anything. In the months since she'd moved in here, she'd not been outside the walls again... She was locked in here, by design, her freedom taken from her, supposedly to 'protect' her, but more so that the rest of society didn't have to deal with her 'peculiarities'.

She didn't know why, but the ways in which people, especially 'experts', dealt with her felt so fake. Everything supposedly 'good' coming out of their mouths sounded more like it should have sarcasm quotes around it. So much of it was just hiding the truth behind pretty words.

'Serene', the lack of original details and design of the building and the surroundings made into a virtue instead of a flaw or a failing. 'Calm', nothing ever happened. 'Encourage the best out of overwhelmed autistic minds', put them into their own box, read: apartment, and only give them enough stimulation that the company can't be sued for neglect. 'Teach new kills to encourage independence', put people into VR classes that only superficially appear useful, even though there is no plan to ever let them out of the system again.

Of course, there were actual people who helped them out with things on a more daily base. There were the people who delivered her food. The woman who would check if she kept her apartment clean enough. The man who picked up dirty dishes and laundry. But they all looked at her with that same pity in their eyes. Every last one of them.

She took a deep breath and stood up again, walking over to the bare trees. The winter rid them of their beautiful leaves, the trees and the ground below all totally bare and frozen solid. She played with her fingers over the bark, touching every tree, enjoying the differences in structure. Until a slight blinking on the lower right side of her view told her that something or someone wanted her attention.

The next moment, as she focused on it, a message popped up in front of her.

New results for search: Helheim Fallen, Helheim Fallen Online

Oh, of course, it was Sunday, did they send out the new batch of beta codes yet?

Willow opened the notification, but it wasn't exactly what she'd expected to find, it was a topic from the HF forums.

My friend logged onto the beta for Helheim Fallen a week ago, they haven't responded to any messages since.

This wasn't the first time she's seen a message like this, this wasn't even the first time she'd heard of people closing themselves off from their friends like that either. But, like always, the replies to the topic were a lot of people laughing at the original poster, telling them it was probably because the friend enjoyed the game more than their company. People didn't take it seriously.

But, really, it was getting a little strange. In all the years she'd been playing online games, she'd not heard about not being able to reach friends at all, at least not this often. And definitely not that all the instances of this happening were connected to a single game. Sure, people 'disappeared' from time to time, usually because they logged out or took a break 'from all the digital in the world'. You know, the usual stuff. But this was more odd, that people would get a beta key and then suddenly go radio silent to all their friends for a week or more? That wasn't normal.

Then her eyes fell on one of the replies.

The same happened to my friend, two weeks ago.

The reply was timestamped an hour ago, but it seemed like the account of the person who posted it was now wiped, or at least empty. Again... not strange, per se. Sometimes people made fake accounts just to post ridiculous lies, but it was a little unsettling that someone would post something like that and then they'd have an empty account not even an hour later. Especially since it wasn't the first time she'd seen this happen.

In the other replies, the original poster was accused of lying and of trying to spread fear, and that they must be working for a company who wanted to bring Helheim Fallen Online down before it could be released. All the usual obsessed fan accusations, really.

Willow closed all the messages, a strange feeling in her stomach. The first few times she'd seen the messages, she tended to agree with some of what the posters had said, 'it must be a cry for attention,' or 'just someone trying to make a new company look bad'. But she'd started to doubt that lately, especially now there were more and more of them showing up. It had started to become too strange for it to just be a hoax anymore.

Willow turned around, ready to go back inside, into the warmth, until she saw someone at the gates, looking through the reinforced glass doors, staring right at her. A shiver went down her spine. She didn't know how visible she was right now, the garden didn't really have any lights, but the sky was already getting lighter and everything around her became more visible.

But as she looked at the person at the gates again, they turned around and walked away.

Strange, really strange.

She shook her head, some people just had weird hobbies, or something.

If the person at the gates had any bad intentions, the gate security would have captured who they were and the security was directly linked to the police system. So it wasn't like she had anything to worry about. This place was safe, secure.

And a prison...

Yeah...

Upsides and downsides, sometimes they were the exact same thing...

Willow leaned back onto her couch, her VR headset snug, and dove into her memories, playing them like movies.

She especially liked the memory from Destruction of Elysium where she was together with Violet as their hippogriff Mira hatched from her egg a couple of weeks ago. It was so adorable to watch, and she felt such a rush as Mira broke away the shell and stepped out of the confinement she'd been in for so long.

Willow had never felt closer to another person than she did that day. She'd never felt closer to Violet or anyone in the world before that moment. Sharing such an intimate but at the same time amazing experience, it had warmed her up inside, made her feel more welcome and loved than she'd ever felt.

And it was all real, the feelings were anyway. It didn't matter that it happened in VR. Though, these days, most people lived in VR almost full-time, so it wasn't exactly strange to experience new things for the first time in VR. But she never thought that she'd ever feel so close to another person, ever. It had been somewhat of a magical experience.

Although, maybe she enjoyed watching old movies too much and that clouded her idea of what was real and what was magical. Movies from back when people lived in the 'real world', as some people call it now, when augmentation was just a dream and VR was still this strange happening and something only people who were really into computers even did anything with. But the experience had almost been romantic, in an old-school kind of way.

A purple notification started to blink at the edge of her view. *Violet!* She focused on it and a message appeared.

Willow laughed, her fingers going over her augmented keyboard.

The next moment, a phone sign appeared in front of her and after she'd accepted the call, Violet's voice rang out like she was sitting right across from Willow on the couch, though she wasn't actually there. There was a possibility to add video to the calls, but no matter how advanced it was, it just never felt right to Willow.

"Hey," Violet yawned. "Morning."

"Morning." Willow let out a laugh and curled up on the couch. She smiled as she wrapped her arms around the hippogriff plushie, the same one as she had in DoE, just real this time.

"Done anything interesting yet?" Violet still sounded a little sleepy, her voice a bit rough. Willow imagined that she was probably still in bed, just having woken up.

"Crafted and gathered in DoE, and then went outside for a while. Watched the sky come to life. Just normal stuff, you know?" She loved their easy banter, it always made her feel so much better.

Violet laughed deeply. "Sounds like you. Why'd you even go outside? It's like... crazy cold right now, right?"

Willow shrugged. "It's not that cold. I was wearing warm clothes. It's just... the air is so fresh when the sun is almost coming up. The coldest time of the night, all clean and stuff." It made sense in her head.

She could still hear Violet's joy. "Yeah, not around here

that doesn't happen. That's just because they keep the air so clean in your little bubble and all." Violet always said things like that, she always mentioned how Willow lived in a bubble, how lucky she was. But it didn't feel like that, it felt smothering, what she'd heard of Violet's life sounded so much more interesting.

"Okay, so... tell me something." Willow glared at nothing in particular in the room, since she couldn't glare at Violet.

"Hmm?" That got Violet's attention. "What do you want to know, bubble-girl?"

"If I live in this clean bubble, then where do you live?" She'd asked this before, but Violet somehow never answered, always changing the subject. And Willow didn't expect today to be any different, but she still asked because she really wanted to know. "If I'm bubble-girl, then who are you?"

Violet stayed quiet for a while, Willow almost expected her not to answer today either. "Do you really want to know?" There was something different about Violet's voice.

"Yeah." Willow needed to know. Maybe it was the rumours of people going missing, or just feeling extra lonely, but she had to know.

"Okay." She could hear Violet take a breath. "If you're bubble-girl, I'm mud-girl. Sewer-girl."

"Vio—"

"No, let me explain." Violet was serious, something Willow didn't hear often. "You grew up well. Loving parents, always protecting you, always trying to do what's best for you. Enough money to live on. A good education. You said so yourself. You may hate living in that bubble, and I don't envy you for that, but you're protected, sheltered from the real bad things. And that's important." Something was off about Violet's voice. "That's really important to remember."

"Violet." Willow's heart was beating like crazy, tears in her eyes. Had Violet really grown up that unsafe? She hated thinking of her friend as being unsafe and unloved. Violet was such a friendly and loving person, to think that her past wasn't happy made her sad.

"I'm the middle kid, out of five. My parents worked two full-time jobs, just to make sure we were able to have a roof over our head and to keep us online and..." She stopped for a while. "It wasn't easy. Growing up wasn't easy. And when I got caught stealing food out of the garbage from a store for my younger brother when he was really ill... He just had to have something with vitamins in it, fresh fruit. He needed it so badly. My parents couldn't afford to take him to the hospital."

Willow was quiet, not sure what to say.

"I don't live with my parents anymore. After I got caught and everything... I got sent to one of those 'deserted kids' places. I still live there. I just..." Violet let out a deep breath. "Don't pity me." Her voice harsher now. "I'm strong. I'm getting out of here. I promise you. But if you're bubble-girl, I'm sewers-girl. I live in the filth and waste of society."

Willow shook her head, trying to process what she'd just heard. "*No.* No, you're not. You're fighter-girl. You're..." She didn't know how to word it. She could feel what she wanted to say, but couldn't find the right words to express it. "You're like metal, you bend. You're strong, but you don't break. You're metal-girl."

Violet burst out laughing, the sound surprising. "That makes me sound like I should be in some kind of band or something. With black and white faces, wearing old ratty band shirts and screaming at people all the time."

Willow smiled too, glad to have her friend laughing again. "Maybe you should be. Maybe we should both be in a band. Metal and bubble girl, taking over the world."

"Mebugi, metal-bubble girls. We rock your world and do it quietly from behind our VR systems because we're too scared to show up at venues." Violet's voice still sounded like she was smiling, though she'd calmed down again.

"Maybe we should. It sounds like a cool idea." Even though Willow had no idea how to play an instrument or how to even start a band.

"Could make us money too, you know. Probably more than we make right now, if we become popular enough." Violet still sounded happy, but there was an edge to it again. Something strange was going on with her today, something really strange.

"Probably." It wasn't hard to make more money than they did now. She knew Violet worked some dead-end data-computing job, but like Willow, she also mostly made extra money by buying and selling things on the marketplace in DoE or some of the other games she played.

"Okay, we've been serious enough. I didn't mean to make it all strange like that." Willow could almost feel, more than hear, that Violet had started to move around. "I just... I don't know. I guess I wanted you to know."

"Why?" The word was barely above a whisper, and for a while she thought that Violet hadn't heard it.

"Because..." Violet stopped. "Because it matters. Who we are matters. And I wanted you to know about me. I wanted to be honest with you."

"Thank you."

"Don't expect me to talk about my crappy life more though. I'm playing to get away from that, not to talk about it even more." There was the fierceness in Violet that she knew.

"I wouldn't expect you to." Violet sharing this much had been a surprise in and of itself. But now she knew just a little bit more about her friend, just a little bit more.

"Change of topic." Violet got excited again. "Did you see the countdown on the Helheim Fallen Online website? They're sending out new keys in a couple of hours."

"Really?" That was new. They hadn't done that with previous batches. Maybe it was because the release date of the game was so close now. Willow blinked, then pulled up the website, wanting to see it for herself.

There, in the middle of the page was a timer.

2:03:46 until the new beta keys are sent

The seconds kept going down, counting until the new batch would be released into the world.

"Cool. I *so* hope we'll both get one." Willow grinned.

She really wanted to try the game. She hadn't seen much of the gameplay yet, apart from what the creators had shared in videos and press releases. And of course some illegal short clips and screenshots that people who already had beta keys were sharing online. Mostly in private spaces because they weren't allowed to actually share anything.

But what she'd seen had looked so cool. Helheim Fallen Online was a Norse mythology based game where players fought off invasions of monsters that were trying to take over the world of Helheim, one of the realms existing on the world tree Yggdrasil.

The starter zone was all frozen over, and players had to fight wolves and other creatures to get to the next zone. It was promised as 'the next generation in full immersion VR gaming' with 'hyper-realistic gameplay'. It sounded really cool, especially since Willow had been playing DoE for so long and she was ready for a new VRMMORPG in a fantasy setting.

The realistic gameplay sounded interesting and had her intrigued. No more hitting buttons or skills to get stuff done, but actually interacting with the world. She could only imagine what that would feel like.

But as she thought about the game, her mind also went to the messages from this morning.

Cool and interesting, sure, but apparently also dangerous for some people…

4
Beta Keys

Willow wandered around her apartment, trying to kill some time before the new beta keys were sent out for Helheim Fallen Online. She looked in her fridge, finding some cheese and sausages, but not something to make a full meal with. Not that she really needed to worry about that. She'd get some food dropped off at her door soon enough, it was getting close to one of the 'meal times', but she'd just like a snack. Another one of those strange things that they did here in the building, private dinner times based on each person's biological clock. While it made sense, she imagined that it could be annoying too, especially for the people who made the meals, or those who delivered them.

She let out a sigh, grabbing a slice of cheese and nibbling on it as she got back to her bedroom, to the VR system. She didn't really want to get away from the system, just in case she may actually get a key. But she also couldn't seem to focus on anything else, just on the possibility that she could get the key… Her brain wouldn't let the 'maybe key soon' idea go.

And as soon as she got the key, she could then download the game and log on. HF couldn't be pre-downloaded, it could only be downloaded by someone who already had a key. A form of protection or something like that. Annoying.

She flopped onto her bed, putting the VR headset on, logging onto VRHome, which was basically a digital living room. In her VRHome she had a few soft and plush couches, a couple of windows, all showing different areas that she loved in DoE, and shelves all around with toys and other cool items she'd collected and found in a variation of games. It was a hundred times more 'her' than her actual apartment.

A couple of moments later, Violet also came in. They both looked like their DoE characters, probably their favourite characters to play.

"You nervous yet?" Violet grinned, then she pulled the website countdown from a viewer in front of her onto the wall. The wall was now basically one big screen showing the numbers slowly going down, way too slow.

0:02:34 until new beta keys are sent

They had a couple of minutes left, and Willow's stomach was all in knots.

"Of course." Willow grinned a little, letting out a tense breath. "What are you going to play as? Have you thought about it yet?"

Violet shrugged, appearing much calmer, but Willow could still see the excitement in her eyes. "Something rogue or hunter like or something. That probably works best in HF. You?"

"I'm thinking about getting a mage again. Something that makes things go *boom*." She put her hands together and moved

46

them as if she was mimicking an explosion and then grinned. Helheim Fallen Online had been handing out beta keys every week for the last two months. The release date was only ten days away now, and everyone was getting excited to play it. Like, really excited. The net was full of people talking about it, trying to find out extra information or simply trying to speculate what the game could be like. Because the creators of HF were not showing a lot, they were 'keeping it all a surprise'.

Willow and Violet had been trying not to get too invested in it all, especially since they were still playing DoE and still hadn't finished all of the end-game content. Plus, they knew that HF probably wouldn't be better than what DoE was now, especially since the game was so new and nobody had really heard of the people who were creating it. But now that the hype was getting so high everywhere, it was hard to stay neutral about it. Especially when the things that were coming out, official and illegal screenshots and videos, looked so cool.

0:01:45 until new beta keys are sent

"Almost." Violet grinned as she stared at the wall with the countdown.

Willow's stomach was trying to eat itself, not from hunger, just from nerves. What would she do if she got a key but Violet didn't get one? Or what would happen if Violet did get one, but Willow didn't get one?

Why were her final thoughts while waiting on the counter such negative ones? The biggest chance was that they both wouldn't get it anyway.

0:00:29 until new beta keys are sent

Willow crossed her fingers, locking her jaw down way too

hard, but she was just too focused, bouncing her leg up and down at high speed, the sound almost like a motor.

0:00:01 until new beta keys are sent

They looked at each other, before the text on the screen changed.

Beta keys are sent! See you next week for the final batch!

She waited, hoping for a sign or anything. Hoping that there would be something to tell her that she got one. But nothing happened.

"Whoa!" Violet's mouth dropped open as she stared at Willow before moving her hand in front of her, sharing whatever she was seeing. "I got one." Violet's voice was barely audible. "I got one."

> Congratulations Violet!
> You have won a beta key for Helheim Fallen
> Online!
> You can find the key in your BASE platform
> inbox when you reach the store.
> Happy exploring!
> Daryl Hill
> Creator of Helheim Fallen Online

Willow's stomach dropped, disappointment overtaking her for a moment. Disappointment about not getting in, disappointment for being left behind. The largest chance would have been neither of them getting it, but just one of them had always been a possibility too.

"Willow." Violet reached out to her and Willow took her hands, squeezing a little.

"Congrats." She tried to smile, but she knew that Violet could see right through it. They'd known each other too long to not know how to easily read each other.

"Thanks. And don't worry. I'll send you private pictures as soon as I can, maybe even videos. Maybe I can live stream it." Violet's eyes grew, her grin getting bigger. "I promise. I'll share as much as I can. And I'm not staying there all the time, I'll be back later today. We still need to finish the guild boat. I'm not going to leave you guys hanging on that one."

Willow hugged Violet. "Don't make promises you can't keep." She knew that Violet could get so wrapped up in a game that she'd lose all sense of time and then reappear two days later, totally obsessed with a new game and having no idea how long she'd been gone at all.

"I know." Violet hugged her tighter. "They really don't allow live streaming there though, people have tried. Sorry."

Willow laughed. Of course, there was that part too. "Just tell me everything when you get back, will you? I'm going to live vicariously through you until I get in myself. Promise me?"

"I promise." Violet tightened her arms around Willow, then let her go. "Now, I'm going to have to jump. I want to download the game and then quickly do some stuff in DoE before I get into HF, making sure that I keep crafting for that boat of ours."

"Go. Go." Willow smiled, enjoying her friend's excitement. "I'm happy you got the key. Just, don't do anything stupid."

"I won't." Violet smiled back. "You, don't go sulking around. Mira won't like that, and I'm pretty sure you're behind the rest of us with your parts for the boat. Maybe you can now get ahead of me."

"I know, I know." Willow shrugged. "I'll get on it." She

would. It wasn't like there was much else she could do right now. It wasn't like she didn't have a whole list of things to do in DoE before she could start playing HF, especially things that would mean she'd be able to afford to play HF in the first place. "See you later."

"Later." Violet waved at her and her character dissolved into digital glitter as she left the room.

Willow sighed. She was happy for her friend, but it was also kind of disappointing that she didn't get a beta key too. They'd signed up at the same time. But there wasn't anything she could do about it now, not apart from waiting for the new batch that would be sent out next week.

It was probably a good idea if she would go play DoE right now, at least that would distract her from sulking too much.

Probably. Maybe?

You're selling 99 Flax for 339 coins each, 33.561 coins in
total

Willow was going through her inventory as she checked out the marketplace, trying to see what she could sell at a profit right now.

You're selling 99 Flax for 339 coins each, 33.561 coins in
total

Currently, the lowest selling stack of 99 flax was 342 coins per item, but smaller stacks of 1 to 15 flax were selling as low as 325 coins per item. Only, there weren't enough small stacks to get almost a hundred items in one go. So selling them just a few coins lower than the cheapest large stack would make her the most profit. Just a few days ago, the best price for a large stack was closer to 319 coins each, so this was definitely an improvement.

Also, selling in stacks of 99 items made things easier to move around. It was a lot of flax, while at the same time not too much that the stack would seem too expensive to buy for most players. The game of buying and selling in the marketplace, knowing when to buy and when to sell, it was something that she loved doing.

The repetitiveness of the task made it comfortable, but it also made her feel good when she knew that she was making a higher profit than other players. Of course, there would always be new people who would underprice from her pricing, but that was the chance everyone who did this always took.

She searched the marketplace for regular olives, since she had a lot of them from harvesting for the juicy olives. They weren't selling for much, the lowest stack was just 189 coins each for 24 olives, but it was also the cheapest stack by far. The next cheapest stack was 274 coins per olive and was a large 99 item stack, and the next cheapest after that was 281 coins per item.

She could chance that, 274 coins was pretty low for olives in the marketplace anyway, so she could sell it up.

She quickly bought both the stacks of olives and they appeared in her inventory, adding to what she already had.

773 olives

She created a stack of 99 olives and put it into the marketplace system screen. Then she priced it at 279, just two coins under the lowest one currently selling. This was two fold, because people perceived a price ending in 9 to be much lower than the next round number, so it was more attractive, but it also meant that, without pulling down the price too much, she'd still be the best option to buy.

> *You're selling 99 Olives for 279 coins each, 27.621 coins in total*

Then she put up a second stack.

> *You're selling 99 Olives for 279 coins each, 27.621 coins in total*

Willow checked the time. By now, Violet had been in Helheim Fallen for four hours. She'd not heard from her yet, but that wasn't too unexpected, Violet was probably just having a good time.

She put another 99 olive stack in the marketplace, this time pricing at 299 coins each, if the lower stacks sold out, then she'd be making a little bit more money from these stacks than the lowest price she was pricing at, and it cleared out space in her inventory. The only reason she didn't just throw the regular olives away was because this was more profitable.

She put two more stacks in the marketplace and then left the rest in her inventory. It wasn't like she really needed to sell everything off in one go. If she put up too much too soon, she'd be flooding the market, which would lead to lower prices, which was bad. And if the price of the flax or olives changed in the next couple of days, she could make more profits by keeping a couple of stacks at hand to sell then.

Willow checked her other offers on the marketplace, changing the pricing on some of them when they were too far above the current optimal pricing for the items, and then closed the window. Enough of that.

It had been a really good sales day. Just her marketplace sales got her at least 100 credits into her BASE account. Which wasn't much considering most games cost about 2400 to 4000 credits, lower price for games which had been out a while and higher price for new games, and getting actual nice food delivered to her place, okay, junk food, but it was often still nicer than most meals she got, cost her 200 credits every time. It was 250 credits for a pizza, just one medium pizza, and not even a fancy one.

Anything she wanted that was 'above basic', as decided by the government department that oversaw food and other regulations for people who didn't have income or high enough income, she had to pay for herself. And selling things in the game was the easiest way to do that, for her anyway.

She went over to her crafting tables, the titanic varnish and the cedar lumber were going to take at least another thirty minutes before she could make the next items.

Waiting around sucked.

She opened a new message.

> Hi Violet!
> Hope you're having fun!
> Send me some screenshots!
> Love,
> Willow

Okay, so, maybe she was just bored because she really didn't know what to do when Violet was off doing something cool and she was just here waiting. Violet being at work was one thing, but waiting on Violet when she was playing a new game that Willow also would like to play, that was something else.

A notification told her that she had a new message. For a

moment, she hoped it was from Violet, but it was from Opal instead.

Willow!
Come to the minotaur dungeon entrance.
I have something really strange to show you!
Opal

She blinked. What would Opal want to show her? Although, maybe he was just trying to distract her, which was a possibility.

Sure, on my way.
Willow

She sent the message back. Opal could have said something in the guild chat, but somehow, he sent it through the message system instead, which would have also given her a notification of the message if she hadn't been in DoE.

Willow pulled up the transportation screen and transported herself to the hub nearest to the minotaur dungeon. From here, it would take her a couple of minutes of walking to actually get to the dungeon entrance, but she couldn't get any closer. This was one of those times that having a flying pet like Mira would have come in handy.

She opened a private chat with Opal.

Willow: *What did you want to show me?*

She was getting a little curious now. Especially since there were a lot of players around her, lots of people heading to the same dungeon. That wasn't normal. What was going on?

Opal: *You'll just have to see it.*

There was nothing around her that gave any clues to what was going on. And as far as she knew, there wasn't a special event in the game either.

She turned her volume of DoE up a little, maybe she could

catch something in the chatter from players around her. First the sounds were little more than mumbling, but as she raised the volume more and more, she could understand actual words.

"I heard they caught someone who stole an account."

"I heard that they got someone to talk about Helheim Fallen."

"It's about the beta keys."

"It's about cheating players."

Apparently, nobody had any clue about what was going on.

Well, that wasn't unexpected. She turned the sound lower again, she didn't need to keep hearing random people talk.

But no matter what, something big was going on, that was for sure. She hadn't been the only one called here, and that made her feel out of the loop once again.

When they got to the minotaur dungeon entrance, she looked around, trying to find Opal. When she spotted him, she walked over to him.

"What's going on?" She opened a private voice chat with him.

Opal blinked for a moment, then he frowned. "We don't know exactly what it is. But... it's strange. I thought you may want to see it, it's over there."

People were crowding in the area that Opal pointed at, but she didn't feel like being all pushy-pushy with them. "Can you show me?"

The BASE platform had built in 'memory' systems, most of it was saved gameplay from the last couple of hours. If someone wanted, they could save certain bits to their account, if not it would be wiped after seven hours. The best part was that saved memories could be shared with other people.

"Sure. Just... don't freak out." Opal didn't look too happy.

"Why?" This kind of started to scare Willow.

"Just... Whatever, I'll show you."

An invite popped up in her view and she accepted it. The next moment, a video started playing in front of her, seeing exactly what Opal had seen. This was probably from earlier, though there weren't many people around back then.

The video was only short, it showed Opal walking into the area before he suddenly looked from side to side, and then focused on a single... thing.

"There was an actual player there, just seconds before. Play it back." Opal sounded almost scared.

She did as he asked, going back to the start of the video. He was right. At the start of the video, someone was mining a node at a rock formation, and just seconds later, that same player lay on the floor, their avatar... bleached almost. It looked strange, more unreal than anything in this game, almost cartoonish. And before her eyes, the player turned into a blob of black and white, strings of code running through it, like something broke the graphics of the game or something. Like she could see into the code instead of the graphics that would normally be a person.

Like the outside of the character was stripped, their insides all reduced to nothing and having turned into a blob of goo, deposited right there on the ground. Their digital insides visible, their code visible.

A bad feeling settled in Willow's stomach. This was bad, this was really really bad.

It almost looked like a player got erased, right as they were playing. Like they were there one moment and then disappeared the next. Gone.

What was going on? Who did this?

5

Refusal of the Call

Willow still couldn't believe what she just saw in Opal's video. Did a player really just disappear from the game?

"Do we know who it is?" Her voice didn't even sound like her own, almost ghostly.

"No." Opal's voice was tense. "No idea. Looking back through the video, their name was already gone before I even noticed that they were there, that something was wrong. I know it was there before, I think anyway. But when you look at it again, it's gone. It's not in the video, or my memory."

Willow nodded. "Let's go." She didn't want to stay here. It was getting really crowded in the area in front of the minotaur dungeon and it wasn't like other people had any more idea about what happened than she did. It was only triggering her anxiety to see so many people so close together. People who were worried or panicked tended to act in irrational and unpredictable ways, she hated that.

"Where are we going to go? Do you have any idea what

just happened?" Opal stared at her, like she had the answers. Like she somehow had more answers than he did.

"Someone disappeared." Willow tried to come up with more than that, but her hands were shaking and she felt a little sick. "Someone just got wiped from the game, or something. I don't know."

Opal nodded, looking uncomfortable. "I don't know if I want to be in DoE right now." Opal wasn't wrong, it didn't feel safe here.

"Let's go to my VRHome room." VRHome was an app that was part of the standard software of the BASE platform. That had to be safer than a 3rd party game, right?

"Okay." Opal nodded, and then disappeared from the game.

Willow took one last look at the people huddling around the where someone had just disappeared. Everyone looked confused and scared. Nobody had any idea what they'd just seen, nobody. And that scared her even more.

What *had* just happened?

"Blitzing," Sage said, their eyes serious as they looked at each person in the room. "It looks like blitzing."

"What's blitzing?" Willow had never heard the term before, and she did tend to hang out in tech places that she shouldn't...

"Blitzing is just a hoax. An urban legend." Juniper shook her head, scowling. "It doesn't exist."

They'd all come to Willow's VRHome, all of them, apart from Violet. Violet still hadn't replied to any messages Willow had sent her.

"Hush." Opal glared at Juniper. "I want to hear this. Urban legend or not, a player just disappearing and their avatar being reduced to code... that's not normal."

"Blitzing is when someone scrambles the connection between your personal and your BASE ID, usually all but destroying your BASE ID data. When I say all your data, I mean all of it, from your saved memories, to your games, to being able to call someone. So you basically lose your account. You won't be able to log onto it anymore, or use it." Sage looked really serious. "And without a BASE ID, you can't connect to the BASE unit to the BASE platform. So you're locked out of everything you know."

"What?" Willow felt sick. That wasn't possible. Without their BASE IDs, they couldn't do anything in BASE but if it even broke the connection with the personal ID... How would people even know how to get their data back? Everything was connected to their personal ID.

It was like a fingerprint, or like... an old-school IP address for computers. Their personal ID was connected to their bank account, to their BASE platform, to their... their *everything*. It was how everyone was identified in the world. And within the BASE platform, the BASE ID took that same role.

The BASE ID was what allowed players to have a single login for games but could have multiple characters. That way they weren't stuck with just one name and could choose their own name in games and such if they wanted to. And outside games but within the BASE platform they weren't just stuck with the name their parents gave them at birth, they could choose any name that they wanted.

But losing connection to their personal ID... Yeah... That was a lot more important, that was the one thing that kept all of their information gathered in one place. Doctors used the personal ID of people, government agencies used it, banks used it, all the important stuff. But nobody knew their own personal ID, at least, most people didn't. So if they were locked out of their BASE ID and didn't know their personal ID... how would they be able to do things?

Willow didn't want to think about the implications of that.

Sage shrugged. "It's just what I heard. I don't know for sure. It's just what's been going around the net." They looked really serious now. "I've never heard of someone actually being logged in and playing when it happened though... Usually, the stories are about how someone is hacked while they're asleep..."

"Both are bad." Willow shuddered. "How can someone... Why would...?" She didn't get it. Why would someone do this?

"I don't know." Sage looked over to her, reaching out. "I really have no idea."

Willow stepped into Sage's embrace, their touch calming her down a little. "What else do you know?" She had to figure this out, or it would keep spinning through her head.

"Nothing. I'm sorry." Sage looked so disappointed that she believed them. "I wish I knew more."

Willow nodded. "What are we going to do?" They should be able to do something, right? Do something about this?

"Make sure you're safe. Don't go places you don't trust, games or on the new. Don't download things you don't know are going to be totally safe. Just... you know, smart stuff." Sage shrugged, pulling a face.

"And DoE?" Juniper looked up to them.

"I don't know."

Opal nodded, his eyes dark. "Is logging into DoE safe?"

"It should be. But like Juniper said... this is supposed to be an urban legend, not reality." Sage shrugged. "If this *is* blitzing, it's done on your BASE platform account, not on your DoE account. So it doesn't really matter what you're doing. They could always get to you." That was not a comforting thought.

"Thanks for the pep talk." Juniper rolled her eyes. "I'm just gonna... I'm gonna go offline for a while. Maybe I'll feel safer there." She had her arms wrapped around herself.

"Juniper." Sage looked at her. "Can you... Can we all stay in a text chat? That way we're sure nobody gets scrambled. At least..." They shrugged. At least they would see it happen, or something.

Juniper nodded, and the next moment Willow got a chat invite. She accepted it and saw just the four of them online. While an invite had been sent out to Violet, it didn't automatically show her as connected to the BASE platform. Strange.

Juniper nodded. "I'm going. See you all later. I just need to... not be here." And she disappeared.

"I'm out too." Opal disappeared from where he was sitting.

Now it was just Willow and Sage left.

"Sage..." She didn't know if she should ask them, but maybe sharing her worry would make it ease a little.

"Yeah?" Sage swayed side to side a little, soothing Willow as they held her.

"Have you heard from Violet yet?" She swallowed hard.

62

"No. She got an invite to HF, didn't she?"

"Yeah."

"She's probably too busy playing." Sage's voice sounded mostly calming, but there was an edge to it too, and Willow knew that they were worried also.

"Probably." Willow nodded. It would have just been easier if she'd been sure. If Violet would just respond to messages, or at least show up as 'online' in the chat. It wouldn't make her so worried.

What was going on? First people saying their friends disappeared while playing Helheim Fallen Online, and now someone in DoE being 'blitzed'?

What was going on?

Willow knew that she shouldn't be doing this. She knew that she really shouldn't be snooping around the Helheim Fallen Online forums like this. But she just had to see if there was a connection between everything going on in DoE and what had happened in HF and the HF forums were her only real source of information.

She didn't really want to ask Sage where they got their knowledge about blitzing, Sage was a little bit more... advanced, when it came to computer stuff than she was.

Willow pulled up the thread she'd seen about the poster's missing friend this morning. Checking the profile of the original poster, but it looked perfectly normal. It didn't look like there was anything interesting on it and they didn't seem like a troll or someone who was out for attention. Which made their plea for help seem at least more real.

Then she scrolled through the replies, trying to find the one from the empty profile she'd seen. But it wasn't there anymore. The reply was gone. Though the responses to it were still intact, they were now responding to some stupid senseless comment that definitely wasn't the one she'd seen before.

Did she remember it wrong? Or was there something else going on?

She scrolled down, trying to find more replies from others who had missing friends, but there weren't *any* of them. She closed the topic and then went back to the main forums, trying to find older posts like this, people looking for their friends.

She knew there had been more of them. She'd seen them pop up before and was sure that she'd seen some with replies from others who were in the same situation. But even though she found the older threads, there were no replies from people whose friends had also gone missing. Right now, it just looked like a handful of random people ranting about their friends no longer liking them.

It was strange, uncanny.

But the video Opal showed her was still clear in her mind. No matter if people were calling the thread starters losers and crazy, she knew that something was going on, something serious. And maybe it wasn't connected to just Helheim Fallen Online, but there was definitely something going wrong in the BASE platform or some of their games.

Willow pulled up a new screen, putting 'Helheim Fallen blitzing' into the search bar, and it immediately gave her some results. But, like the posts on the forums, they lacked any real information, just some people complaining about their friends not being online and others mocking them for being such lozers. This was no use.

She pulled up the guild chat screen, but Violet's name was still showing as not having accepted the invitation, and all the messages she'd sent Violet were also unread.

It wasn't strange for Violet to disappear for a couple of hours or days when she found a new game, that was pretty normal for her, but at least the messages would get through and the chat would connect to her account, even if she hadn't accepted the invite yet.

With everything going on, Willow just wanted to know that Violet was safe. She just needed to know, no matter how needy it made her sound. They were friends, and she was worried. Violet could at least accept the guild chat invite, no matter how busy she was playing a new game.

A new chat tab opened out of nowhere. Willow hadn't gotten an invite for it. And even though she remembered Sage's warning about staying safe, she was also curious, too curious, and clicked on it.

> ***You are in a chat with Rotnem***
> **Rotnem:** You've seen it, haven't you?
> **Willow:** Who are you?
> **Rotnem:** You've seen the person in DoE, right?
> **Willow:** I need to know who you are.

How would they know this? Who were they? And why were they talking to her?

The person stayed quiet for a while, and Willow almost closed the screen again. Probably just a prank.

> **Rotnem:** Who I am is not important. It's not about me.
> **Rotnem:** You already know me, we've talked before. You
> were learning to code the old-school way.

'The old-school way', it rang a bell for her, especially the way this person was talking. But it was a fuzzy memory, from years ago.

She'd been interested in learning old-school coding, C++ specifically, mostly because she was bored and didn't know what else to do with her time. She'd learned it from a paper book, one she'd found in her parents' attic.

She'd loved doing it. But with the BASE platform being universal and big computers being totally out of fashion, it hadn't been easy to find a way to properly code. Not the way they used to do it back in the day, anyway. So she'd found some online groups that could explain things better. Was this person from one of those groups?

> **Willow:** Why are you talking to me?
> **Rotnem:** You've seen it, right?

What was it with that question? What had she seen? The blitzing? She'd seen too much today, and she didn't really know what the 'it' was that Rotnem referred to right now, though she could guess.

> **Willow:** Why do you want to know?
> **Rotnem:** I need your help. I need your skills, I can't do
>   this on my own.
> **Willow:** Why me?
> **Rotnem:** Because you can see through things. You can
>   see things that nobody else sees.

Cryptic again... Great. This was getting annoying now.

> **Willow:** How do I know I can trust you?
> **Rotnem:** You don't. Just like I don't know if I can trust
>   you.

She had to stay safe. She couldn't just listen to some random stranger, no matter how interesting they sounded. No matter how much they seemed to know about her, it wasn't exactly a secret that she'd dabbled in some old-school coding back in the day. It was on her list of 'skills' on her profile. They could have just gotten the information from there.

Willow: I can't do this.
Rotnem: I'm sorry. I get it.
Rotnem: I would really like your help, but I get that you can't just trust me.
Rotnem: You should keep yourself safe. That's good.

Willow frowned at the screen, not sure exactly what to reply now.

Rotnem: If you want to talk to me, if you change your mind. Find me in the first game you played in BASE, look for Ilana.
Rotnem left the chat

What the…? What just happened? Was that someone who had real information for her, or were they just trying to get her to trust them with some stupid questions?

And how could her old coding skills be of any use to anyone? She'd not coded in years, at least not for anything more useful than making some quick calculators for market prices and selling points for items in DoE, but that didn't really count.

And how did this person know where to find her? How did they know she'd seen anything at all? How were they able to get into her chat without an invite?

Was her system compromised?

Was her system already bugged? Was that how they knew?

Was that how they got to other people too? Was this how a person got blitzed? Try to get them to trust them and then steal and break their accounts?

Was this how they operated?

Willow quickly closed all the programs she had opened. Even though she couldn't disconnect from the BASE platform itself, she could at least try to close as many open apps as possible, at least close as many programs that could be sending someone information on her that she didn't want to share.

Then she grabbed her jacket and left the apartment, left the building. She stood in the gardens again, like this morning. Only, right now, it was dark, night had already fallen, and the air felt suffocating, not cleansing.

Like her brain, suffocating, scared.

What was going on?

6
Missing information

Willow leaned her back against the building, turning her BASE settings off, letting the normal sounds surround her. Letting in the real world around her, as much as it was really real…

Her eyes burned and her throat felt almost closed up. She needed to talk to someone but didn't have anyone she could reach out to right now. She needed someone to comfort her. She needed someone to hold her, touch her, but didn't know where to do that.

On impulse, she opened her contacts lists, it was only a short list, and then called her mum. If she couldn't get a hug, she could at least hear a comforting voice now, someone she could feel more connected to.

"Willow?" Mum's voice sounded slow and sleepy, and a little surprised too.

"Mum, did I wake you?" She already felt guilty. She hadn't really considered the time or at what part of the day her mum could be right now. And now she woke her mum up with her selfish request even though she'd been trying not to disturb people. "I'm so sorry. I shouldn't..." She disturbed someone and shouldn't have done that. It wasn't right.

"Sweetie, what's wrong?" Mum sounded more awake now, more alert too. "Are you okay?"

"I'm..." She was lonely, but how did she explain that to her mum?

How did she explain her loneliness to someone who believed the 'experts' when they said that because Willow was autistic, she'd never be able to make real emotional connections with friends or family and that any show of it would be Willow mimicking what she saw around her. Just because she had a hard time communicating with people didn't mean she wasn't making social or emotional connections with people, she just had a harder time expressing them.

"I'm okay. I just wanted to know how you were doing." *Mimicking, pretending...* Those were the words people used to describe autistics in social situations, totally ignoring that autistics often had the exact same social and emotional needs as people who weren't autistic, they just showed it differently. And right now, she needed connections, she needed her mum, she needed someone to talk to.

"I'm doing well. The company is growing fast, we just opened another office in the city, and your dad got a promotion at work too. And he's hoping that they'll have another promotion lined up for him soon, something about a new development department that they're going to open. How is the apartment? Are they taking good care of you?"

If there was anything Willow knew how to spot, it was disinterest hidden behind questions that looked like actual

70

interest, like her mum was doing now. It often made her wonder who the one without the ability to make real emotional connections actually was.

How was it that Willow was accused of being the one who didn't have empathy, when people treated her horribly because of perceived notions of what she could and couldn't do. Notions based on 'evidence' from 'experts' who had no real living experience with autistic life, just horrid flawed tests based around their own idea of what 'normal' looked like. Just because Willow's 'normal' was different didn't mean it was wrong.

"They're really good to us. The food is good too." That's what her mum wanted to hear, right? She wasn't interested in hearing about how the food was bland and uninspired, that would show that Willow didn't actually enjoy how strict this place was… Which was what her parents liked so much about it.

"And are you still taking classes?" Polite chit-chat, no real connection. Distanced words from someone who had no idea how to really connect with someone as 'different' as Willow, because she'd never really tried, always believing the 'experts' because they knew best, supposedly.

Classes… Right. Because if Willow couldn't work, the government still wanted her to do something 'useful', so they shoved classes at her to keep her busy. 'Self-improvement' classes they were called, like learning how to pay her bills on time, even though that was already taken care of for her by the system, or how to cook, even though they made all her meals for her. She'd not really paid much attention to the classes, they weren't that useful. They even made her take one on how to do job interviews, even though she had a 0% chance of ever being invited to one because the system listed her as 'autistic and in care' which automatically meant 'unemployable'. It was ridiculous on so many levels.

"Classes are going well. I'm learning how to cook." That was actually the class she enjoyed the most, even though it wasn't useful. There was just something about the idea of being able to make cakes or pies herself someday, even though most of it was currently in the VR space only…

"Oh." That surprised her mum, Willow could hear the slight change in pitch in her voice at the short word. "That's… interesting. They said that they'd prepare all your meals for you, they still do that, right?"

"Yeah, yeah," she quickly answered, not wanting to worry her mum. Willow didn't need her to go and complain with the people who oversaw this place.

"So, learning to cook is just for fun?" Her mum sounded relieved.

"Yes, just for fun. They're teaching us how to make pies and cakes and things like that." And pasta and actual normal dinner food, but right now, she thought that it may not actually comfort her mum if she found out what they were teaching her exactly. Keeping it to 'fun' food things was always safer. 'Self-improvement' classes were not very useful in the situation she was in right now, but realistically, they could be useful if they ever let her out of here. Even if the chance of that was minuscule, she still hoped somewhere that they would let her out.

"Oh, how *fun*." Yeah, definitely disinterest from her mum. That strange voice pitch was only reserved when she really thought she should be excited about something.

Then she remembered something, something the Rotnem person had mentioned in the chat. "Mum, do you remember that old computer I had for a while? Do you know what happened to it? Or the books I had to learn how to code?"

Her mum was quiet for a bit, probably thinking. "I don't know, you're going to have to ask your dad. He helped you clean out your room back then. If he didn't sell it off, it's probably in the attic. Do you want me to ask him?"

"Yes, please." Even if she didn't know if she should trust or believe Rotnem, that didn't mean that she couldn't get back to her hobby.

Coding had always been fun back in the day, it was a way to escape the restrictions put on her. Although she didn't know if she could get the old computer to work at her apartment, if there were connection sockets for it to connect it to the net or any of the other things she was going to need for it. But the idea still excited her, having her old trusty computer back felt comforting somehow, even just the idea of it. And if she did need cables and such, well, she could probably find those online.

Getting back into coding, that would actually be fun, even to just make time pass by faster. Coding had always made sense to her, if she put the words and operators in the right order, then everything just fell into place and would work. If it didn't work, she probably hadn't done it right.

"Willow?" Her mum pulled her from her thoughts. "Was there something else you needed?"

"No, thanks. I just..." She shrugged, admitting to needing to hear her mother's voice wouldn't get her anywhere. It would just make things more complicated. "Thanks. I'm sorry if I woke you up." Because of the different biological clocks for everyone, which were based on calculations of brain chemistry and things like that, it wasn't always easy to know when someone was supposed to be asleep or awake. This was even truer when not everyone seemed to make the same hours of asleep and awake and stuff like that.

"It's okay. I had to get up anyway, time to get to work. Have a good evening. Bye."

"Bye." But her mum had already disconnected the line. Of course. No gooey 'love you' or 'take good care of yourself' because they'd given up on doing that years ago.

Willow should go to bed though, she really should. But everything that happened today kept going through her head, spinning and twisting, and she had no idea what to even expect tomorrow when she woke up again.

Would her friends still be here? Would Violet be back?

Violet!

She opened the guild chat screen. Everyone had left a couple of messages, just joking stuff, but Violet's account still hadn't connected to it. Her chest tightened, and she closed the screen.

She had to try.

Willow opened her contact list again, this time scrolling to Violet's name and calling her. The connection tune kept going and going, until a message appeared in her view.

This account is not currently connected to the BASE call system, contact the user another way or call the operator if you think this is in error

What?! What the...?

That had never happened to Willow before.

Where was Violet? Where did she go? Was she really gone?

It had been a full day since Violet got the Helheim Fallen Online beta key and went into the game, a full day without any contact from her at all.

The net was now full of people talking about the 'blitzed' person in DoE, though nobody knew the name of the person yet, and there had been two more reports of people going missing after getting Helheim Fallen Online beta keys. But even as there were more and more reports of missing friends, others were still treating it like nothing was wrong, like this was *normal*, like people's accounts not being reachable through the BASE system, like not being able to contact them at all, was normal...

Willow didn't know what world those people lived in, but friends going missing was definitely *not* normal to her.

She opened the guild chat, though it had been quiet for the last couple of hours. Violet's account was still not connected to it.

> **Willow:** I'm starting to get worried about Violet.

She had to share her bad feeling with someone, had to.

> **Sage:** Yeah, it's not like her.
> **Willow:** I tried calling her.
> **Willow:** Her account is not connected to the call system anymore.
> **Opal:** Really? That's definitely not right.

Tears formed in her eyes, she was tired, she was so tired of being scared, of not being able to contact her best friend. Violet was always at her side, just a click away, but now she only felt this loss, this emptiness.

> **Sage:** Have you sent her a message?
> **Willow:** Yeah, it's not been delivered yet.
> **Sage:** Okay…

The chat fell quiet, and she tried to come up with something else to say, but it was all a blur in her head. She had no idea what to do next.

> **Willow:** I'm going into my VRHome.

She stood up from her couch, going over to her bed, and grabbed the VR headset.

Then her eyes fell on a different notification from the chat, and curiosity got the better of her. It wasn't the guild chat, she could see it from the notification colour, it was the one with the person who asked if she could help.

> ***Rotnem joined the chat***
> **Rotnem:** A second person in DoE has been blitzed.

They hadn't left the chat yet, probably waiting for her answer.

> **Willow:** I don't know how I can help you.
> **Willow:** You're better off contacting someone who
>   actually knows about these things, someone from
>   BASE or DoE.
> **Willow:** Or the police.

She hit a couple of buttons.

> ***You have left the chat***

Now she didn't have to worry about that anymore.

It wasn't like she could help them. Finding people who hacked accounts and things like that was the job of the police, not just some random girl who wasn't even able to have a normal life. It really wasn't up to her or random strangers on the net.

She put on her VR headset and immediately went to the VRHome, curling up on the couch there, a much more comfortable couch than the one she had in her real apartment.

Sage came into the room soon after her, their face serious. Then they came over to the couch, putting a hand on her shoulder, carefully touching her. One advantage of VR, they could touch each other, and it triggered the exact same things in her brain as touch in real life did.

"I can't find her." Willow's voice was rough, almost hollow, she was just so tired.

"I know." Sage nodded, kneeling to her level.

"This has never happened before." She couldn't remember a time where Violet, Sage, Juniper and Opal weren't just a click away.

"I know." Sage came closer, carefully wrapping their arms around Willow, holding her. "I've tried too, I tried to call Violet. I got the same message as you did. She's not connected anymore."

"Where *is* she?" Willow tried to come up with a different way to contact Violet, but for all she knew Violet lived on the other side of the world. It was entirely possible that Violet wasn't even anywhere near her time zone, just that their sleeping patterns sort of matched up on a regular basis.

Sage rocked her side to side slowly. "I have no idea. I wish I knew. I wish." They shook their head, sighing. "It's only been a day, officially she's not even 'missing' yet. She could just have an issue with her BASE device, or she got locked out of the system for pushing her limits too far." Both of which had happened before.

But they also knew that even if that was the case, they

should still be able to connect to Violet's account, it should give them a 'timeout' message, not a 'not connected' message.

What were they going to do if something serious was going on? If this was really as bad as Willow was starting to suspect?

"She'll be back. She won't leave you all alone. Especially not with Mira going into her next stage just over a day away." But Willow could hear how Sage didn't even believe their own words.

They were right about one thing though, Violet wouldn't want to miss Mira's growing up for the world. She loved Mira, even if she was a pet in a videogame, not an actual real-life one, but Violet loved Mira just the same. She wouldn't not be there when Mira reached the juvenile stage, just one stage away from becoming a proper two person mount. But there was no sign that Violet would be able to get into DoE on time. That she'd somehow be able to be there, if she wasn't even connected to the BASE platform right now.

"Violet wouldn't want to miss it." Willow nodded. But not wanting to not be there and actually showing up were two different things and right now, it seemed like they both had the same result, no Violet.

"Did you do your crafting for the boat yet today?" Sage moved, but kept holding her close.

Willow shook her head. "I should probably check in."

"You should." There was a smile in Sage's voice that she didn't quite understand.

"What did you do?" Sage sounded like they were up to something again.

"Nothing much, but if my calculations are right, we should be able to have all the supplies and craft the boat in the next few days. And then the waters will be wide open for us, we'll be able to actually do better trades in just a couple of days time. I do hope you stocked up on things to trade." Their voice was full of mischief now.

"A little." She smiled too. Better trades, more money. And right in time to be able to buy Helheim Fallen Online at full price on release instead of having to depend on the beta keys to be able to play the game. "At least that's good news."

"Yes, but it requires you to finish your items for the boat too." Sage frowned a little. It wasn't just Willow who needed to finish her items, Violet too.

Unless they wanted to source the final items some other way, which would probably require a lot of extra money, they needed Violet's items, and they had no way to contact her right now...

And like that, her mood fell again.

They needed Violet, not just in the guild, but as a friend. It wasn't the same without her.

They all needed her.

They needed to find her.

7
Meeting the Mentor

Willow walked over to the delivery box near her door, the green light for a new delivery was on, but she couldn't see anything inside the box. Probably a blip or something. Even in a world so advanced, bugs and hiccups of code still happened.

She'd mention it to one of the people who ran this place if it was still on tomorrow. It was a little annoying, but it wasn't like the light was very obvious, and it wouldn't interfere with her receiving any deliveries either, so it was pretty low on the list of priorities.

She walked around her apartment, running her fingers over each surface, trying to calm herself down with the familiar structures.

She shouldn't freak out over Violet not responding to messages yet. There was no use in freaking out when she couldn't actually do anything, so why did her brain go over everything she'd seen and read on the net over and over again?

The messages from people saying that their friends had

gone missing after getting a beta key for Helheim Fallen Online, the video of the blitzed person in DoE, and now Violet not responding to any messages sent her way… It didn't have to be connected, though it seemed less and less likely that it wasn't.

It felt connected, and that wasn't a good thing. Someone was messing with people's accounts, and she had no idea why they did it or how she could protect herself, or her friends.

Willow opened the chat screen from Rotnem, but apart from the messages she'd already received there wasn't anything else in it that could tell her how much this person knew about her or who they were. Even a quick query of their information didn't give anything. It actually gave her literally nothing. Just the name the account was using and that was it.

Could she trust this person?

Just then, a call came in, overtaking her view and breaking her chain of thought, it was her dad.

Willow connected the call, a little surprised. "Hi, Dad."

"Hi, sweetie. How are you?" He sounded upbeat, happy, she thought.

"I'm good. How are you?"

"I'm good too. Your mum told me that you asked for your old computer?"

"Yeah. I'd like to play around with it a little. Do you still have it?" It was her dad's old computer, technically. He was a software engineer back in the day, before everything went onto the BASE platform and creating software and games became something much simpler. He now worked for the BASE platform main company, overseeing the department that worked on office apps and general use apps and things like that. It was kind of cool, in a nerdy way.

"It should be in the attic. Why do you want it? Do you want to get back into coding?" Unlike her mum, her dad did sound interested, as long as it was something he knew about, like computers or coding. He'd actually show genuine interest from time to time.

"Yeah, I was thinking of doing that. Spending some time doing something interesting instead of just playing videogames." Sort of, close enough.

"Smart. Yeah. I'm pretty sure it's up here somewhere. Do you also want the books with it?"

"Yes, please. There aren't that many tutorials around anymore, not with BASE and stuff, and constantly looking things up online isn't always so simple." Very few people had an interest in the more complicated and 'old school' coding languages when they could create anything with just a couple of simple building blocks from one of the hundreds of program or gaming engines these days.

"Of course. Yes, I can imagine that guides and help aren't that easy to find, not like back in the day." She heard him move some things around. "I think I just found it. Do you want me to send everything over? I think it should fit in a box."

'Send them over'... Of course, he wasn't going to bring them over himself. Everything could be delivered in no-time, and this way he didn't have to go out of his way, this way he didn't have to take the time to see his daughter... This way he didn't have to see her... Her heart sank, reality kicking in.

These thoughts weren't going to help her.

"Sure. Just send them over." Because how important was personal contact anyway, you know? It's not like she hadn't seen him in months, maybe even over a year. It's not like that mattered, because she was *autistic*, so personal interactions was something that scared her, not comforted her, according to 'experts' anyway.

"Will do. I'm glad to see you taking up something useful again, maybe this will help you get ahead. Do something productive with your days." He sounded so upbeat when he said it. Like he wasn't insulting her or diminishing all the hard work she was putting into simply staying alive and not turning into a depressed mess. Which wasn't easy with the way everything around her was built to hold any ambitions she may have had back, to make sure that she would never be able to get out of this system.

Her throat closed up with tears, and she shook her head, she had to go now. "Thanks. Talk to you soon." She quickly disconnected the line, before he'd hear her tears. Before he found out she was crying because she wanted to see her father. But actually asking to see her parents would go against everything her parents had been taught about her autism and would make them ask ridiculous questions about where she'd learned about how to model emotional behaviours towards her parents.

It wasn't like it hadn't happened before.

She'd been eight or nine years old, and after her parents had both been away from home for work for over a week, she'd been so happy to see them return. She'd missed them so much. She'd cried, she'd wanted to hug them. She needed to be close to them, feel them and make sure they really were back. And they'd looked at her like she was an alien and had asked her where she'd 'mirrored' that response from, where she'd learned to behave like that. That it wasn't 'normal' for her to miss them, or for her to need their touch or physical contact so much.

Of course she'd missed them, she'd not seen them for over a week. And the only response she'd gotten was that her behaviour was 'not right for an autistic, too emotional', that she 'was just feeling happy because her routine would be back to normal, that it didn't have anything to do with them' and that she 'should behave normally *for her* and not try to copy what she saw in the media, because that *wasn't her*'. It broke her heart, she'd felt so lost, so lonely, and she'd still been so young.

That was the moment she learned that her parents only saw her as her autism, not as a person, and it was also the moment that she learned that if she wanted any connection to her parents, it had to be in what they saw as 'autistic appropriate' ways. She had to mask her real feelings, her real personality, and show them what they wanted to see, what they'd expected from her and nothing more than that. As long as she behaved in 'appropriate' ways, they would be happy with her and would be happy for her, but that meant not showing who she really way, not to her parents or the therapists or the 'experts' in any way.

So, to try and get a closer connection with her dad, she decided to learn how to code, which delighted him. And she was finally able to have some relationship with her father, which she needed so much.

Not long after that, she'd met Sage online, immediately getting along well with them. Sage understood her, they got her, and they were there for her when her parents couldn't or wouldn't be. Sage was her first friend, her very first friend.

It said something about the way she was brought up that the first time she remembered having more than a fleeting social connection with someone around her age was when she was about nine years old. That she'd had no friends before that time, no way to even learn how to do it, because her parents had raised her so sheltered, even though she'd often craved more social relationships than she had.

Her second friend had been Violet. Who had saved her when she was just a DoE noobie and had gotten herself in trouble in some dungeon. Violet came in, all swords and arrows and killing everything in her path until she'd reached Willow. Violet had been her second friend, her saviour and the person she told her darkest thoughts, her deepest secrets and her most painful memories. Violet had always been there for her.

And now Violet was in trouble.

Willow berated herself. *What was she doing?*

Of course!

She knew what she had to do. She already knew. There was no doubt in her mind, just fear of the unknown.

Willow wasn't going to get Violet back by hiding, by ignoring all the things going on. All the little connections, no matter how fleeting, they mattered, and they were going to show where to go.

Violet saved her when she was little, Violet had always been there to save her. And now Willow had to save Violet.

When Willow had realised that her parents weren't going to come to her birthday a couple of weeks ago, Violet had sent her a plush toy of their DoE pet Mira. She'd sent her a beautiful plush hippogriff that she could always hug and hold close. It had been the sweetest thing, straight from her heart.

Violet had always been there for Willow and now she needed to be there for Violet. Because no matter what, something bad was going on and she had to do something about it.

She opened the chat with Rotnem and looked through it again. To get in touch with them, she had to find Ilana in the first BASE game she'd ever played.

The first game she'd played on the full BASE platform had been a long time ago, but it was pretty easy to remember what the game was. The first game she'd played without her parents sitting at her side the whole time, or the system not letting her interact with other players, was actually DoE.

Telling her to go to the first game that she'd played had been a very simple and maybe even a little lazy clue. Willow had been a fan of DoE from the start and she'd always played it. As soon as she was old enough, she'd gotten herself an account and she'd started playing.

Willow went over to her bed and put on the VR headset.

Then she logged on.

You are now logged into Destruction of Elysium

She spawned in the middle of the garden next to the guild house. Mira quickly came over to her, pushing her head to Willow's hand.

"I know. You miss your other mummy too. I know." She ruffled her fingers through the feathers on Mira's head. "I'm going to try and find her. I promise."

Mira let out squawking sounds, running around her a few times before she leaned against Willow.

"I know. I'll be back. I promise." She leaned in, kissing

Mira's beak. "I'll be back."

Then she pulled up a player search and put in the name Ilana.

There weren't many Ilanas, but she found one who was just level one and was still in the starter area.

She didn't know why, but it felt like that was probably the right player. Something about the first game she played and this Ilana being in the starter zone made sense, also, it was the easiest player to reach.

Instead of sending a message, she transported to the zone. It was strange, being back here, none of the mobs paid any attention to her.

She walked around until she found the Ilana player near a pond, not doing anything, just staring into nothingness.

"Hi?" She stepped in front of Ilana.

Instead of speaking, a message appeared in the chat.

> **Ilana:** You came.
> **Willow:** Yes.
> **Ilana:** Why? What made you decide?
> **Willow:** I don't know.

What was the harm? This was just some person, and it wasn't like they probably didn't know everything about her already. They could probably get into other parts of her account too if they could get into her chat.

> **Willow:** My best friend is missing. She logged onto HF
>   and her account can't be reached anymore.
> **Ilana:** Right.
> **Ilana:** I was afraid that was the case. I'm sorry.
> **Ilana:** I'll be outside the Metropolis Dome in two hours.
>   Meet me there if you really want to help and solve
>   this.
> **Willow:** Metropolis Dome?

Meeting someone outside the game. Heck, going outside the walls... That was definitely stupid behaviour according to Sage's 'stay safe' rules, so why was she considering it? Why was she considering going?

But before she could give an answer, Ilana logged out and when Willow searched for her again, the whole avatar didn't exist. It was like she'd never even been there. That was definitely strange.

Was she going to meet this person? Was she really going?

That wasn't really a question.

The Metropolis Dome. It was about twenty minutes by bus to get there. It was one of the few places in the city where you couldn't use the BASE platform. It was a 'BASE-free' zone, as they called it. They didn't disconnect it or anything, and the platform still collected your vitals and things like that, but AR wasn't possible, and neither was logging into VR there. They built this beautiful park just so people could experience the 'real world' but in a safe way. It was built inside a dome, and it was always good weather there. Depending on the area you went to, you could experience all the different seasons as much as you wanted.

Willow had been there a couple of times. Not a lot of people went there anymore after the novelty had worn off, so it was always nice and quiet, and it allowed her to relax in ways that she just couldn't do at home or in the VR.

She was going, there was no question about it. If Ilana or Rotnem or whoever turned out to be some creep, she could always leave.

But if they knew something about what was going on, if

they knew something about Violet going missing... She had to take this chance.

She had to save Violet.

Willow got off the bus. She hated going out into the world, even with her BASE system muting as much of the surroundings as possible, there were always advertisements and things rushing around her, always trying to sell her new things. It was too much on her senses, so she rather stayed within the walls of the building she lived. Even now, after just a short bus ride, she felt raw from all the impulses that being out in the world gave her and she really wanted to curl up in a quiet place as soon as possible. But she had to stay strong, there were more important things going on.

She looked up at the huge dome in front of her. It always looked spectacular, even in the middle of winter. It was late in the day, and it was already getting dark, but there was enough light to see that there were a handful of people milling around outside. Some were talking to each other, others were just standing there, probably waiting on someone.

A notification showed for a moment, and then the chat opened.

> ***You are in a chat with Rotnem***
> **Rotnem:** By the door, I'm standing on the left side of the doors.

Willow looked up, spotting a figure in the shadows near the doors. She carefully walked over, her heart beating loudly and she didn't know what she'd do when she finally met this mysterious person. But she had to hear them out, if they could help her with finding Violet, she'd do anything. Maybe. Mostly.

Within reason.

But as she came closer, she realised that the person waiting for her was a girl. Well, more a woman. She was probably a couple of years older than Willow, and she was wearing fancy shoes, a pencil skirt and was hiding most of the rest of herself inside a much too big, dark hoodie. She was also carrying a small, nondescript briefcase.

She looked... Willow looked the woman over again. She somehow looked familiar, not just like Willow had seen this woman before but also like this was probably how Willow would dress if she had to show up in nice clothes for her job.

If she'd ever get a job, or a normal life.

"Let's get inside," Rotnem/Ilana spoke.

8
Accepting the Quest

Willow followed Rotnem/Ilana into the Metropolis Dome, the system registering them both and a message flashed in front of her.

All BASE functions like AR and social contacts are disabled after this point

Even if she wanted to contact anyone, she couldn't. That was a scary thought.

On the other hand, it would be hard to spy on them through the BASE system here. Someone had to actually get really close to them if they wanted to listen in on what they were saying. It made for a pretty safe place to meet up if you didn't want people to overhear you.

And who would look twice at two young women meeting up in the Metropolis Dome?

"What is your favourite season?" Rotnem/Ilana turned to Willow, taking off her hoodie and revealing a woman who probably wouldn't stand out in the corporate culture. Her dark brown hair was pulled back into a ponytail, she was wearing some light eyeshadow that matched her grey-blue eyes and she smiled in a non-descript way.

Willow thought for a moment. "Summer." It wasn't technically her favourite season, but the summer area in theome was one of the best ones. It had a sloping hill and projected mountains and fields around the outside. It was calm and beautiful, exactly what she needed right now.

"Good choice." Rotnem/Ilana smiled. "I could use some warmth right about now." She nodded to one of the hallways deeper into the building. "Let's go there so we can talk." She started walking again and Willow followed her.

Willow felt so small, so young, so unknowing next to Rotnem/Ilana. The woman looked like she really knew things, like she'd been out there in the world and knew everything about it, while Willow had been locked in her bubble all this time.

But then she remembered the way Ilana could make her whole avatar in DoE disappear into nothing, and she got a little nervous. She may be a worldly woman, but she was a worldly woman with a high level of technological knowledge.

Rotnem/Ilana opened the door to the summer area and they stepped inside. As Willow followed her, R/I grabbed a picnic basket and a blanket from the pile next to the door and walked on, going up the slope. Then she looked around.

"Where would you like to sit?" R/I seemed genuinely interested in making Willow feel comfortable.

Willow pointed to the top of the hill, next to a tree, the area covered in flowers.

R/I walked to it and put the basket and her briefcase down

before spreading the blanket out. Then she took her shoes off and sat down on the blanket, looking up at Willow. "Are you joining me?"

Willow nodded, taking off her own shoes and sitting down too, on the other side of the blanket from R/I.

R/I looked at her hands. "I know that you have no reason to trust me. I know that there are many reasons as to why you shouldn't trust me at all, especially right now, but I'm here because I need you. I need your skills."

"Why? I'm just an autistic girl with no future." Wasn't that what everyone had been trying to teach her her whole life? So why was this woman so interested in her suddenly?

R/I jolted a little, looking up, her eyes filled with some pain that Willow didn't know how to understand. "Don't think of yourself like that. Please... Don't. Just because you're different doesn't mean you're broken or bad. Or that you won't have a better future."

Willow didn't know what to say. R/I's words touched something inside her. Something she'd always been trying to squash, or that others had been trying to squash for her, but ignoring that feeling had always been her safest option. "Why me?"

"Do you know how many people can program in C++ in this world?" R/I opened her briefcase, pulling out some papers and pens.

"No idea." Why would she? There had never been a reason to wonder something like that. Coding wasn't for everyone, and with BASE there had been even less of a reason to learn it. She could do it, and her father could, but outside of them, she had no clue.

"I know that *you* can." R/I looked up. "And I can count the others in this country that can at the level that you are able to on two hands. At least, those are the ones that I know of, there may be some underground hackers who can, but just the ones that are known and in some cases registered... There are very few of them. There will, of course, be more in the whole wide world, but people who can program in C++ are rare these days." She spread the papers out between them. "Take a look."

R/I had spread pages and pages of code between them. It was written in C++, and Willow quickly recognised pieces of the code. Some were variables for things like settings that influenced AR opacity for menus, others were code that influenced how for example the BASE platform connected with a social media application for sending messages back and forth. They were just small pieces of code, nothing major.

But as her eyes fell on a different page, she stopped and got a bad feeling in her stomach. The code didn't look like the rest of the official code of the BASE platform itself. It looked off, like it was created by someone or something that shouldn't have been messing with the code.

She picked up the page.

It was a code sequence that let a program read out someone's personal ID, but something wasn't right with it. It wasn't meant for the BASE platform mainframe, it was meant for some other program. A program which likely wasn't supposed to use those variables, a program which wasn't supposed to have access to someone's personal ID.

"What is this?" She held out the page to R/I.

"That's why I need you." R/I took the page, looking troubled. "I found this piece of code in a program that shouldn't have it. I caught it and took it out, but I know they've been popping up more recently." Then she looked up for a moment. "I know that you saw the 'blitzed' avatar in DoE."

"How?" There it was again, R/I knowing things about Willow that nobody else was supposed to know.

R/I closed her eyes for a moment. "I was there in DoE. I saw you come into the area when your friend called you over. I know that that boy showed you his memory. I was there when the account got blitzed." Her eyes were filled with pain, her voice rough. "I saw the avatar go down, I saw him disappear. And when you came into the area... I knew it was meant to be."

"Who *are* you?" Willow now really had to know, she couldn't keep doing this without knowing the identity of who was asking for her help.

R/I licked her lips. "I'm Soleil. We've met once before. Just once."

"When?" Why would she remember meeting Soleil? But more importantly, why would Soleil remember her?

"You were really young. You came to work with your father one day. I was an intern back then. A 'child genius' working at BASE, in the same department as your father. He taught me a lot, but not too long after, I was moved onto another department where my skills were 'better suited' for the work they were doing there. At least, that is what they kept telling me."

Soleil? Willow could remember something about going to work with her dad once, but it was mostly a blur. The place had been way too busy for her to feel comfortable. People everywhere, screens blinking, people projecting AR things all over the place. It had been loud, smelly and she'd felt really overwhelmed.

"You had your first try at coding while you were sitting in my lap, behind my computer, and pecking at the keys one by one. You loved it, and your father was glad that you'd found something to do while he went into a meeting. I've kept my eyes on you ever since. Your hyperfocus as you were learning a new skill, it intrigued me. And..." Soleil shrugged. "I was on the boards you frequented when you were learning to code, I saw it all."

"Why?" This sounded insane. Someone would find her that interesting that she'd keep track of her? Yeah. Definitely sounded insane. "Why would you do that?"

"Autism doesn't have to be bad. I wish I could have shown you that when you were little, when you were growing up." Were those tears in Soleil's eyes? She met Willow's eyes fully, but then looked away. "*I'm* autistic. It's not in my medical files, my parents were very careful to keep that out of my files. But I still am. I'm no 'child genius', I've just got an obsessive knowledge of some programming languages. And when I saw you that first time, I knew that you were like me. I knew it."

"I don't get it. Why would you..." Something bubbled up inside her, and she didn't know how to handle it, it was too strong. Her hands started to shake, and she had to do something with them or she'd start to try and pluck at every imperfection on her hands.

"Here." Soleil handed her a small toy. It had different types of fabrics and surfaces, and Willow's fingers automatically found the smooth ribbon and ran it through her fingers a couple of times. It flowed so easily. Then she found the spot with a fluffy fabric and ran the top of her hand over it, it felt like a plush toy.

"Why didn't you say anything? Why didn't you tell me who you were?" Maybe she would have felt less alone.

"I didn't want to involve you in things if I didn't have to. You were safe and you were well taken care of. But the things I kept doing, they weren't safe. But now, bad things are happening right, and I can't do this on my own. I need your help. I need *you*."

"With what?"

"I need you to go into Helheim Fallen Online and find out what happens to the people who 'disappear'. I need someone on the inside who can help out." Soleil looked almost desperate now. "I can't do this on my own, and I need someone on my side. I need someone who also knows about what I'm doing. Who also takes the missing people seriously."

"Violet got a beta key to HF, and I can't reach her anymore. Her BASE account seems like it's gone or something." Willow felt a panic come on, but she also felt a certain calm come over her. Maybe she could really save Violet? Maybe Soleil was how she was going to save Violet?

"I know." Soleil nodded. "It's the same as the other people who've gone missing. This is the same every time. They go in, and suddenly their account disappears. I think they get blitzed when they're in there."

"And you want to send *me* in there? You want *me* to get in danger for some idea you have about how to fix this?" Willow wasn't entirely sure that she understood it right.

"Basically, yes. But you're not going in without protection. If you decide to do this, I will give you an item that lets you control the world like a game developer can. It will let you strip back the VR and get right into the code behind it. You can see exactly what happens at any time." Soleil sounded like she was so sure this would actually work.

"How sure are you that this is safe? How sure are you that Violet disappearing and the blitzing that happened in DoE and the other account disappearances are connected?" Willow wasn't entirely sure herself.

"One-hundred percent." Soleil looked at her with a steady gaze. "I know they are, I just don't know how or why. Or how the victims are chosen."

"And you want my help to figure it out?" Willow still felt like this was too much like a weird joke or a dream or something.

"Yes." Soleil nodded. "You don't have to decide right now. You can think it over. But I really need your help, it would really help me out."

Willow nodded. "I'll have to think about it." Could she put herself in danger for the chance that it would help Violet? For the chance that it would help the other missing people? Could she really do that?

"Of course." Soleil nodded, then handed her an envelope. "The information on how to contact me is in here. Plus some extra things. Please consider this carefully. There are risks to doing this, I can't deny that, but there are people going missing and I think you can help out trying to find them. I think that you can help with figuring out what's going on."

Willow accepted the envelope, it was pretty heavy for looking so small.

She didn't know if she could trust Soleil yet. She could just be lying to make Willow trust her. But after the story Soleil told, Willow remembered the moment she talked about. She remembered sitting behind that computer. It was how she got so interested in learning how to code in the first place. It was how her interest in it really got started. Her father had taken her to his office for some reason, she couldn't remember exactly why anymore, but that first time doing some small coding and making things happen on the screen was what got her interested in it.

But was that enough to risk everything? As far as she knew, if she got blitzed herself, she would basically be wiped from this world. She would stop existing in the way she'd always known.

Was that risk worth it?

Willow closed the door to her apartment behind her, locking the icy weather outside as she took her jacket off. It had started to rain as she walked through the garden and it had made everything feel even more surreal. She couldn't remember the last time she'd been outside while it was raining. It felt strange. And she'd totally forgotten how bad near-freezing rain was too.

Her delivery box was still showing that she had a delivery and as she walked over to it, she saw a huge box sitting inside. Since it wasn't yet time for dinner, it could be her father's computer.

After talking to Soleil and remembering how she got into coding and why she got so interested in it in the first place, getting the computer now felt different. Willow had started coding to feel closer to her father, to have some relationship with him. But incidentally, she also made friends through it, friends she could rely on, friends who would always help her out. And, apparently, friends, or people, who were always trying to protect her. People like Soleil.

Willow pulled the big box out of the delivery box, slowly pushing it to her table, looking it over. She didn't remember the computer to be this heavy.

Then something dark blue caught her eye. A dark blue square in front of the delivery box. It must have fallen out as she took the big box out of it.

She went over to it, picking it up.

On the front of the note was one word, 'Mebugi'.

Willow's heart started beating loudly. Mebugi. That was what Violet had called them. Mebugi, metal bubble girls.

Then she realised two things.

Firstly, there was only one other person who knew about that conversation, Violet.

Secondly, this note wasn't addressed to anyone. It just had that one word on it. That meant that Violet had dropped this note into her delivery box by hand.

Violet was here.

Violet was here and had left her a note.

Violet was nearby!

And she was alive.

9

Crossing the Threshold

Willow opened the note, the handwriting on it strange and loopy. Then she remembered a conversation she'd had with Violet a few years back. Violet loved what she called 'cursive', a handwriting type that was practised a lot in the last century, but with everyone going digital and especially with how easy it was to just send voice messages these days, nobody used it anymore. It was rare enough to find someone with legible handwriting in this world, let alone finding someone who could write in something as special as cursive handwriting.

It took her a bit of focus, but she could decipher the message.

> Dear Willow,
> When you find this note, please don't worry
> about me anymore and tell the others not
> to worry either.
> Better yet, tell them that I'm fine, that I'm just
> playing HF and that I'm deep into the game
> or something.

That didn't feel right. Why would Willow lie to their friends? Why would Violet ask her to lie?

> I'm writing you this message to tell you that I'm safe, I'm okay. I'm not in any danger or harm.
> I'll contact you again soon.
> Love,
> Violet

What? Why?

There was nothing in the note that could help her figure out what had happened or where Violet was right now. Nothing.

Then she looked over the small note, trying to find any distinguishing marks. But there didn't seem to be anything on the paper. It was simple dark blue paper, folded a couple of times, and then just dropped into her delivery box. No stained ink, no dirt flecks, nothing.

Wait! Her delivery box!

It had shown that she had a delivery earlier today, she just hadn't seen anything in it at the time so she'd presumed that it was an error. But the note would have been too small to be visible from the top of the delivery box... How long had it been in there? How long ago had Violet been here?

She went over to the delivery box and a menu showed up in her AR vision.

Send Delivery
Last Received Deliveries
Settings

She hovered her eyes over the 'Last Received Deliveries' option and it gave her a list.

Willow checked the time. It was just past nine in the evening now, so that meant that Violet had left her the message nine hours ago...

Nine hours, and she hadn't had a clue. She'd just presumed that the machine was malfunctioning instead of really checking it out. If she'd actually paid attention, maybe she could have found the message sooner and could have met Violet...

Although... The delivery came from an unknown account, while a message from Violet should have come from her account. But if Violet really delivered it herself and her account really was disconnected from the BASE platform... It would make sense.

Willow's head spun. This was crazy. This was not right. How did things get even more confusing? How did it get all so messy?

She opened the envelope from Soleil. If she couldn't get in touch with Violet via the BASE platform and Violet didn't want her to tell any of their friends that she may be in trouble... There was only one other person Willow could reach out to right now. Only one other person who knew about blitzing and that Violet's account was gone.

Inside the envelope was a small plastic stick, square in shape and with a cap on one end. The off-white plastic had some remnants of paint on it, but it wasn't enough to see what logo or message had originally been on it. When she pulled the cap off, a rectangular metal computer plug became visible. A USB Type A drive? It'd been years since she last saw one of these... They were proper old-school technology. *Wow.*

Then she found the note in the envelope.

> Plug the USB into your computer, you'll find
> important files there. Don't connect the
> computer to the net when you do, and don't
> save anything from it onto your computer.
> There is also a list of websites on it, you'll find
> cables and things to connect your
> computer to the net there, if there aren't
> any with your computer, or if they don't
> work at your place.

With everything going on, Willow still smiled a little. It was like Soleil really did know her dad. Or maybe Willow getting her old computer back and needing the supplies for it was just an obvious thing for her to do. If Soleil really had been keeping an eye on her for so long, that could easily be true too.

> If you want to talk privately, pull up a
> command prompt on your AR and put in
> the code below. That will open a secure
> link to me and we can chat there privately.
> Thank you for helping out!
> Soleil

That was quite a big leap to make for Soleil, to just assume that Willow would be able to do these things, especially since Soleil had put this together before they'd even met face to face. To assume that Willow would know how to get to the command prompt in the BASE platform in AR and be able to put in the code, was a pretty big leap. Not that she couldn't. But Soleil probably expected at least some level of competence from the people she worked with...

Willow read the code at the bottom, it was fairly straightforward. Then she pulled up a command prompt, something she wasn't supposed to be able to reach this easily just as a normal user, but with the number of times she overrode her 'low sensory protection protocol' settings, it was almost a reflex by now.

You are now in a chat with Rotnem

No invitations that were being sent. Just a direct chat to someone without any questions or hurdles or privacy protections. Interesting.

Willow: What happens when an account is blitzed?

She looked at the chat, waiting for an answer, almost holding her breath.

Rotnem: The ID is scrambled, all your data is basically unusable.

She knew that part. Sage had already explained that part of it.

Willow: But what if you're supposed to be clocked by a system? What would you show up as?
Rotnem: Show up as?
Willow: The name or account, what would show?
Rotnem: I have no idea. Sorry.
Rotnem: Do you have an idea?

An idea was a little too much for the small inkling that she had, but at least she now knew that there was very little known about what happened when people had blitzed accounts. And that there wasn't a standard way to find out if the blitzes had taken place or not. She only suspected that Violet's account had been blitzed. With everything she knew right now, that seemed to be the simplest explanation.

> **Willow:** Maybe. I don't know yet for sure.
> **Willow:** My missing friend delivered a note to my place,
> and the delivery box didn't register a name.
> Literally, no name.
> **Rotnem:** Okay. Interesting.
> **Rotnem:** I've not been able to talk to someone who's
> been in contact with someone who's been blitzed.
> At least not in a way where I could get information
> about their accounts showing up in the system.
> **Rotnem:** I've been having to rely on assumptions about
> the BASE platform code and how things should
> and would work within it.
> **Rotnem:** But this is interesting and new...
> **Rotnem:** Thanks.

Willow looked over at the box with her old computer. Trying to decide if she should set it up now.

Then a notification blinked at her, and her heart jumped. Was she now really going to get jumpy at every notification she got?

It opened without her input, that only happened when the system thought the notification was too important to ignore for her.

New Results for Search: Helheim Fallen + missing

New Results for Search: Destruction of Elysium + blitzed

Oh, no. Not good.

She selected the first search and a short list of topics opened. In the last couple of hours, three more people had posted about friends going missing, all of them got beta keys at the same time as Violet and all of their accounts had become unreachable immediately. This could be three different people talking about a single friend or three people talking about three totally different friends. Still... Some people, like Violet, went into HF and their accounts were gone soon after, that much was obvious.

Violet had gone into HF, all happy, her account fully intact, and now her whole BASE account seemed to be missing. It took moments for it to happen, but would impact them a lot. The connection between the codes being sent out, people logging on, and then a handful of them going missing was… alarming.

Then she opened the second search and there were ten topics talking about people being blitzed in DoE. Though, it wasn't exactly obvious how many different people had been blitzed or if they were just asking and worrying about the same two or three people constantly. It was obvious that they were much more worried about the openly blitzed accounts in DoE than the people disappearing when they logged onto HF…

> **Willow:** How many DoE blitzes have been reported?
> **Rotnem:** From just the videos and screenshots I've seen... Three at least. I'm not sure about the fourth yet.

Wow. No way. That was definitely adding up.

> **Rotnem:** And I've also seen videos and screenshots of at least two more blitzed accounts in Bullet Pack Online and another three in Biome Defender IV in the last three days.

Crap. What the hell? Those were the three largest multiplayer games in BASE, Destruction of Elysium, Bullet Pack Online and Biome Defender IV. So there definitely would have been more people who got hit by blitzing, they just wouldn't be found if they mostly played single player games or when it happened in smaller games where fewer people hung out.

> **Willow:** You think that HF is at the heart of this?

Because this was hitting a lot of games at the same time.

> **Rotnem:** Yes. It didn't start happening until after they started sending out more beta keys for HF, and every player hit by the blitzing had been on the beta key waiting list.

Willow didn't even want to know how Soleil knew that.

> **Rotnem:** Also, we don't exactly know what happens in HF to the people who go missing.
> **Rotnem:** We're assuming that they're also blitzed but we're not so sure.
> **Rotnem:** You can't reach those accounts anymore. There isn't a way to contact them. And any posts on the HF forums about this are getting deleted and accounts banned and otherwise preventing people from talking about this.
> **Rotnem:** So whatever is happening, people in HF don't want the players to find out.
> **Willow:** Could it be a bug or accident?

Because thinking that something on this scale was intentional was scary. Accidentally messing something up was one thing, but purposefully ruin people's lives like this... that was a whole other level of evil.

> **Rotnem:** Even if it's a bug, we kind of need to find out what the bug is so that we can fix it, you know?

Yeah... That was kind of important. They couldn't fix this or help people when they had no idea what was actually going on.

> **Rotnem:** I know I'm asking a lot of you. But I really believe that you would be the right person. You're

     also in a very unusual situation which can really
     help me.
Willow: Unusual?
Rotnem: Don't get angry, yeah?

Why?

     Rotnem: You being officially diagnosed as autistic
     means that people don't pay attention to you.
     You're smart, you know a lot of things about
     coding and nobody is looking at you. You don't
     have a job to show up at, you don't have to worry
     about people wondering where you are or what
     you're doing most of the time.

Right... So far, that was true, even if depressing to think about in these terms.

     Rotnem: We can use that to our advantage. You're
     invisible in the best way possible.
Willow: You're sure-sure that going into HF is the only
     way that we can figure this out?
Rotnem: Yes. Nobody but the developers know what's
     really going on in there. Nobody seems to be able
     to get into the code of the game from the outside.
Rotnem: I can't even get in from the outside as a BASE
     developer and we can get into almost everything.
     They've been really strict about closing the game
     off. The only way in is by the front door.
Rotnem: You need to go into the game itself as a player
     to see what's going on.
Willow: You can't do it yourself?

Because trusting her with such a task seemed kinda silly with Soleil's expertise.

     Rotnem: No. They know my account, they won't let me
     in.

That sounded strange, and didn't make her feel any safer.

     Willow: Why?

Rotnem: I've had a run in with some of their developers
in the past. They've got a search out for my BASE
account.
Willow: But I can get in safely?
Rotnem: Yes. I promise. I've...
Rotnem: Someone else is helping us out and they got
us in. I just can't do it myself because of the flag
on my account and you're the only one I know who
has the right expertise to pull this off. To get us the
information that we need.

Did Willow want to put herself in danger? For people who were basically strangers? Was that going to be worth it? And wouldn't she be putting her own account in danger too?

But she couldn't help herself. The messages about people going missing tugged at her. She could imagine the fear the posters were going through, their missing friends, not being able to reach them. It really sucked. And also, there was the fear of the people who'd gotten blitzed, who were now without friends or family, or a way to get in touch with other people. They were all alone, no way to get to their finances or anything like that. That was even more scary.

Willow had to do this. If there was one feeling she knew well, it was loneliness. Loneliness and fear of being alone all the time.

There was no other thing she could do, she had to do this.

Willow: I'll do it. What do you need from me?
Rotnem: Thanks. Thank you so much!
Willow: What do I need to do?
Rotnem: If you log onto your VR system, you should see
a code in your store cart soon. That code gets you
into HF, there will be an item in your inventory
which will help you to see through the game and
into the code behind it, letting you explore what's
really happening.

110

Rotnem: But as soon as you're in, you're on your own.
Rotnem: I won't be able to contact you anymore because of the rules set into place by the HF creators, you're going to have to abide by the same rules as the beta players.

Right. She'd be on her own until she logged back out.

If she'd be able to log out and didn't get blitzed when she stepped into the game instead.

Willow: If I don't log back out and check in with you in twelve hours, meet me at the Dome at noon tomorrow.

That way she'd at least be able to get in touch with Soleil somehow, even if stuff went wrong. Safety first and all... Although, this was far from safe. This was definitely a 'nope' when it came to safety.

Rotnem: Will do.

Willow sat down on her bed, taking a deep breath.

Willow: I'm going in.

She closed the chat window and pulled the VR headset on, then she let herself fall back on her bed and checked into the BASE platform store.

The world around her changed, and she was standing in the store area of the platform, the white nothingness spreading to all sides, the games and programs she owned spinning slowly around her.

Then she opened the store menu and Soleil had been right, there was a code in her cart, giving her access to Helheim Fallen Online.

She accepted the 'purchase' of the game and watched it download. It was pretty fast, but then again, the connection in her apartment was really good.

The icon for Helheim Fallen Online appeared in front of her and she took another breath.

Now or never.

She hit the button and was sucked into the game's icon.

The world around her went dark, until a small light in front of her appeared, growing bigger.

"Helheim is the realm of the underworld, of the darkness, underground. It is ruled over by the goddess Hel, daughter of Loki, but where once this world was hidden, now the veil between worlds has thinned and the creatures of other worlds are invading it. Hel begs every person to help her protect her world from falling any further."

II
Initiation

10
Character Creation

Willow blinked again and again as the fully immersive video ended and she actually formed in the game, the disjoint between the two disorienting. The intro video to Helheim Fallen Online showed her shown her frozen fields with creatures fighting for survival, dark dungeons where monsters were hiding out and creatures all over trying to stay alive. The final scene had been a closeup of a beautiful woman in a dark throne room, Hel, the Norse Goddess and ruler of Helheim, furious about the other worlds invading hers.

Now, Willow was standing in a room which was more of a wooden hut, really. The lights in here were muted, although she couldn't find an actual light source and it was sparsely decorated with a rack of weapons at her side and a mirror on the other side of the space.

***You are now logged into Helheim
Fallen Online***

***This game is in beta and allows limited
contact through outside chat systems***

The second message didn't come as a surprise to her, she'd known that having contact with the BASE platform while inside HF was prohibited because the creators of the game feared that people would 'spoil the surprise' or something like that. But it also meant that she really couldn't reach out to her friends while inside the game, or to Soleil, which wasn't so good.

The creators of Helheim Fallen were really strict about how much of the game they were showing to the world before release. Being unable to make screenshots or videos in the game and the limited contact with the outside world helped with that.

Willow looked down at herself, or, where she expected to exist. But she had no physical body yet in the game. She could feel her hands as she moved them, she could feel the air as she moved her hands through it, but she couldn't see any part of her body.

A window popped up in front of her.

Welcome traveller.
*This is the character creation room, you can choose your look at
the mirror and your first choice of weapon at the weapon rack.*

Okay, simple enough, right?

Also, *first* choice of weapon? That's an interesting choice of words. But, since she didn't see any real way to interact with the game around her without a physical body, she turned to the mirror.

As she stepped in front of the mirror, a human female appeared, who looked quite similar to what Willow looked like in real life. She was wearing a set of a simple top and trousers from a rough fabric in some dull brown-ish colour. Hmm… Yeah, no. Not to her taste at all.

As she looked to the top of the mirror, she saw five symbols appear, and as she looked at each one of them a word appeared under it.

Human

Dwarf

Elf

Jötunn

Draugr

The first races were easy enough to understand, those were the most basic races that appeared in nearly any fantasy game. As she looked at the symbols closer, she first turned into a short and blocky version of herself as a dwarf and then a slightly taller version of herself with much skinnier limbs as an elf. But the last two races she didn't recognise.

As she focused on the Jötunn she went back to her normal size, but her features distorted and she was suddenly hunched over. It reminded her of what trolls were supposed to look like in stories she'd seen as a kid. Kind of an interesting choice to add to the game, but not her thing.

Then she focused on the Draugr and stumbled back in surprise.

She'd suddenly turned skeletal thin, her face like all the life had been sucked out of it and she was sure that some of her skin was missing in places. Undead. Cool. *Really cool.*

Okay, while not exactly one of her usual choices, this was definitely odd and strange enough to get her interest. When she could look like this, she didn't care about potential stat boosts or whatever, she just cared about looking awesome.

'Yes,' she thought. The game would interpret her thoughts as easily as it would interpret if she'd actually spoken the word.

The mirror in front of her changed, some menus appeared along the edges, and she could now choose the basic options like hair colour and select facial and body features. But most interesting of all, she could select the level of 'undead' look she had. Though none of the options were very outrageous, as BASE liked to keep some of the player's looks in the avatar they played, giving them more 'human' features, that apparently would improve the connection that people would feel towards each other in the game.

Willow didn't want to look too decayed, she liked having some physical body for her character, so she chose a middle stage between 'decaying and bloated a couple of days after death' and 'flesh almost fully fallen from the bones'. That would do.

She didn't really feel like changing much else about her avatar. The game was pretty good at mixing what Willow looked like in the real world with this fantasy race that she now played. She didn't need to do much else.

Then she turned, her body now feeling different from before. It felt both heavier and lighter at the same time, like she was really strong but also kind of big, and every joint in her body appeared to creak. Strange and interesting, but she'd probably get used to it.

The weapon rack now had fewer weapon choices on it than before, probably because those other options weren't available for her race. But, luckily, there was still a staff available, and that likely meant that she didn't need any other options anyway. She really was at her best as a mage, or a caster in general. The other options were a large sword, a sword and shield and a huge axe.

Willow grabbed for the staff, her almost skeletal hands surprising her for a moment as they came into view, but then she wrapped her fingers around the weapon, and it started glowing with a blue tint.

Seidhr

*Are you ready to cast fear into your enemies with a single look
or raise trouble from the earth and elements around you? Then
the Seidhr is the right choice for you.
Fight with the elements, illness, a companion or your own
enhanced strength. The choice is yours.*

A companion? Elemental magic? Yeah, that sounded right up her alley.

Willow didn't even look at the other classes. What would be the use when this one sounded exactly like what she liked to play?

*You chose the Seidhr as your first class.
Do you confirm this choice?*

'Yes.' Again with those stupid confirmation questions.

Then the game changed, new elements showing up in her view. A map appeared at the top right of her vision, though it was black apart from the small hut she was in right now. A row of buttons under it, though they didn't seem to be interactable right now. At the bottom of her view was now a long bar. There were a selection of slots in the middle of it, probably spell slots or things like that. On the right side of the slots was a tree, and when she looked at it a bar of text hovered over it.

XP to next level 0/400

Okay, interesting.

On the other side of the bar was a darkened shape of an animal, a bear or something, but as she looked at that, nothing showed up. Probably something that would appear later.

She didn't have any 'spells' yet and also couldn't get to an inventory or anything. She was just in the character creation mode right now.

As she looked up, she saw a door she hadn't realised was there before. Or maybe it hadn't been there before at all. Had this only appeared after she'd chosen her race and class?

She walked over to it, touching the handle.

Are you ready to choose your name, leave the character creation
room and start playing?

'Yes.'

Please fill out your name below.

A screen popped up.

Name:
Race: Draugr
Class: Seidhr

She smiled a little, it'd been a long time since she saw one of these short character breakdown screens in a game. Old school but interesting.

She pulled up a keyboard and typed her name.

Willow

That name has already been taken.
Please choose a different name.

What? Okay...

Willow sighed, next try.

\/\/1770\/\/

It was a little overboard, but she could try it.

No punctuation can be used in names. Only the Latin alphabet. Please choose a different name.

Frustrating, though, '\/\/1770\/\/' would have been annoying anyway.

She tried to come up with another name. Most games didn't care much about a unique character name, as every account had a unique identifier within the BASE platform anyway and that was what the system remembered, not just the name of a character.

Meadow

It was the other name that her parents were thinking of giving her. And it was a little more uncommon as far as names went.

Are you sure you want to take the name 'Meadow'?

'Yes.'

If you are sure about your choices, touch the door handle again and you will be transported into the game.

Name: Meadow
Race: Draugr
Class: Seidhr

Willow looked around one last time, not sure what would be waiting for her on the other side, but she couldn't stay here. She had to find out what was going on and she needed to be in the actual game to do that.

She reached out to the door handle, touching it again.

It was all or nothing now.

The world around her came back into view. She was standing in the middle of a village. Although, it was more of an encampment kind of setting.

The huts around her looked similar to the one she was in during the character creation. The low walls were made of rough wooden beams. The roofs were made of branches and mud, some even had grass growing on them. Around her, in the streets, there were piles of snow, and everything had that blue tint that signalled 'winter' or 'snowy setting' in most games.

There was no question that she was in a game that took place in an old Norse setting. This definitely looked like the old pictures she'd seen in books about old Nose mythology.

The area she spawned in was quiet, very quiet. But that wasn't unexpected, most people with beta keys would probably already have left this zone, since it'd been more than two days since the new batch of players had arrived here. Starter towns usually didn't keep players there for more than a couple of hours, a day at most.

But that could potentially be a good thing. This way she could explore the area more easily, and not get all overwhelmed by all the other players and nobody would question her checking every little corner of the game.

A creature appeared at her side, like a ghost or helper or something. It looked a lot like a fairy, but not the ethereal type that was so common on other games, this one seemed more down to earth. It had wings like a dragonfly and the body of a tall almost goblin-like creature. *Eek.*

"Welcome hero, we are so glad that you have chosen to join us in our fight against the invasion." The creature started blabbing at her about the village needing more heroes and things like that, but Willow zoned it out. Instead, she reached at her side where she suspected her 'bag' would be and her inventory appeared in front of her.

The inventory had sixteen slots, which was pretty common when it came to starter inventory sizes in most games. In her inventory she already had two health potions, two mana potions and a potato.

Wait, what?

Soleil had said that she would get some item that she could use to get more in-depth access to the game. Where was it? Did she have to pull up another screen for it or something?

She grabbed the health potion, and the creepy creature started a new sequence about the use of health potions. That wasn't it, obviously. Then she grabbed the mana potion, and again the creature changed tracks to explain the use of mana potions. Still not it.

Finally, she grabbed the potato and the creature shut up. *Good.*

Potato

You better not eat this one, it doesn't taste that nice.

Okay... She frowned, then interacted with it, and a menu appeared.

Player Rights
Bug Catchers

She focused on the X-ray Vision and a screen popped up in front of her. Not a screen like one where you can put text in, but more like a viewer, like it was doing an x-ray scan of the area around her as she looked through it.

Willow could see some of the code that controlled the creature in front of her. The helper was pretty limited in what it could do. Just a couple of set sequences of explanations and it would try to guide her to the first quests, at which point it would despawn. *Neat.*

This must be the item that Soleil talked about.

Then she put it back into her inventory. That was enough playing around. She probably wouldn't be able to find anything in just the starter village, at least, there wasn't anything around her that looked off.

And what was it with her skills bar? Why hadn't she gotten any spells yet?

"If you're ready for your first adventure, please follow me." The creature floated up and down in the middle of her face, getting really annoying and she wished she could just reach out and break the code for it…

Well, it wasn't like she had much of a choice but to follow what the creature wanted her to do.

Willow sighed and looked at the ugly creature. "Sure. Show me where I need to go."

The creature slowly started floating ahead of her. "As a Seidhr, you control the elements and can use natural curses…"

Willow zoned out the voice of the creature again as she followed it. Why did this stupid game not have a setting to turn the spoken words into text pop-ups? And where *was* her normal settings menu?

What was it with this game? Why did it have to be so annoying and closed off?

She'd been looking forward to playing this 'innovative' and 'revolutionary' game, but right now, it felt more like a watered down version of basically any VRMMORPG fantasy game out there. And that wasn't what she'd been promised…

11
Tests

Willow walked up to a group of elves, humans and draugar standing around in what was probably the 'town square' of the encampment. They were just standing there, waiting around for players to start talking to them, pretty static so far.

For a game saying that it was the 'next generation' in VRMMORPG games, it had been a pretty strong disappointment for her yet. It looked a lot more like it was 'two generations ago' and never bothered to improve or even look at how newer games were structuring their starter zones. Even Destruction of Elysium, which had been a really popular game in the normal version before VR took off had moved to a much more natural and dynamic way of presenting and grouping NPCs.

This looked more like HF was trying to look old-school while also lauding itself as 'next generation in gaming', and it was failing at both ideas spectacularly. It felt like a weird mix of both elements, and then there was the issue of most of the game not being accessible while starting in the first location.

As she tried to pull up the main menu to see how long she'd been in HF, nothing happened. No menu, not even an error message, just nothing. She was still locked in this story mode that didn't let her do anything outside of the set steps. *Fine.*

She couldn't get to her menus, she couldn't see what skills she had or how to even interact with most of the world. So, she was going to have to follow whatever the creature wanted her to do. She would go through the starter quests and if that didn't open up anything else, she could use the potato to force herself out of here. This was starting to feel a little claustrophobic.

As she came near the group, the starter creature floated in front of her. "Before we accept you into our ranks to fight off this invasion, we need to make sure that you're strong enough to handle it. The captains overseeing this encampment have come up with some tests they want you to complete to that end. Talk to each one of the captains and fulfil their trials to join our mission." Then the creature moved to the side as a sort of glowing path appeared between her and the group of people.

Too linear, definitely too linear. Who even designed games like this anymore? Normally, players would at least get a handful of skills immediately, so that if they didn't feel like going questing, they could just start killing creatures immediately.

The group of captains all wore similar uniforms, though some wore plate armour and other just cloth robes, but the colour schemes on all were the same. A base colour of black with blue rims and accents and even white details. They would definitely not blend in well with their surroundings, looking like that, but at least they stood out, which made it easy enough to find them for questing…

Willow first walked up to the draugr, appreciating how it looked more gore-y than her character did and it was quite a bit taller. Its dark skin was blackened from decay and its hair was missing pieces where the scalp was visible. Where the skin was split open, maggots and other crawly thingies were coming out of it, and other patches were covered in a white-green-blue-grey dusting that looked a lot like it was rotting. *Ick!*

The draugr captain looked at her, but didn't say anything and no quest invitation or whatever showed up.

"Talk to each of our captains and accept their trials." The starter creature repeated again right next to her ear and it made her jump and swat at it, but her hand went right through the creature, the sensation cold and damp, like a ghost but not quite the same. *Oh! Ugh again!*

Fine. So she had to actually speak to it then.

"Hello." Her voice felt weird, and sounded strange too with how raspy it was. But since she was undead, that probably influenced the voice in this game.

"Hello, stranger. What are you here for?" The draugr looked at her, but it didn't seem very impressed.

"I would like for you to test me." What else was she supposed to say?

"Ah! You're a new hero. Welcome here. New heroes need to be able to find their way around this world. I want you to go to the training grounds and get a flask from the trainer there, then I need you to go to the apothecary and get a basket with some items, and then to the butcher and get a parcel from him too. After that, report to the guard at the gate and show your items to him.”

“I will.” And as she said the words, something pinged and a red glow in the lower corner of her view told her she had a notification. She focused on it and a screen popped up.

Quest Accepted: *Find Your Way Around The World*

Great, one down.

Then she looked at the human next to the draugr. “Hello, I’d like for you to give me a trial to complete.”

“Would you like *any* trial, or are you looking for something in particular?” Apparently, this game had at least considered people trying to be a smartass and trying to get through this exchange faster.

“I’m a new hero, I’d like to fulfil a trial to help fight off the invasion.” Trials. Tests. No. She never liked to be tested or having to complete stupid trials, but the game insisted on this language apparently. Tests usually meant more annoying things for her down the line when she had to do them in real life, though, in this case, it wasn’t like she had much of a choice in the matter, she couldn’t even log out of the game yet.

“Ah! Welcome, new hero. There are wolves outside the gates, they’re from the other world and they’re a pest to our critters. I want you to fight ten of them to make it easier for our own critters to survive and fight back.”

Simple enough. “I will.” And, with a ping, a new notification showed up.

She talked to the other captains and got four more quests. They ranged from fighting even more monsters to butcher them and collect their meat to gathering some herbs and berries and things like that. For now, this game was being very basic and standard.

The visuals of the game were great. There was so much detail in the buildings around her, and the NPCs also looked very realistic and all just that little bit different. But the thing she loved the most, the actual playing of the game left a lot to be desired.

Then the floaty creature showed up in front of her again. "Here our alliance ends. You're on your way to becoming a fine hero and will find many people and creatures along the way to help you on your path to glory. I bid you farewell." And with a pop, it disappeared. Just, into nothing.

What the…?

Okay. Usually, games were a little more helpful at the start. At least, more helpful than simply guiding a new player to the first quests and then disappear. But, whatever.

As she looked around the game's layout again, the buttons that had been uncooperative before were now active and it seemed that the game finally unlocked the rest of the user interface. Good. About time.

She focused on the buttons under the map. The first one was labelled Menu, the second one Social, the third one Progress and the final one Character. She focused on the first button and the game menu popped up.

Menu
Return to Game
Sensory Settings
Options
Leave Helheim Fallen
Play Time: 00:46

Simple and short, but that didn't matter much. Willow had

been inside the game for almost an hour, that was a lot of time for how little she had accomplished.

She focused on the Sensory Settings and a new screen popped up. Here, she could finally change the in-game dialogue from 'voice and audio' to 'text only' and lower the sounds of the things going on around her, just as a precaution. Then she looked through the rest of the settings, but in the sensory menu there wasn't a lot she could do. Most of it was just the same as always, and her special 'autism' settings were already put into this game. As was the reach of how much her life was influenced by that diagnosis... Great.

She left the menu and instead opened the character screen.

Name: Meadow
Race: Draugr
Class: Seidhr
Level: 1
Health: 69/69
Mana: 45/45
Armour: 0
Strength: 15
Dexterity: 6
Intelligence: 12
Wisdom: 10
Endurance: 12

So, maybe her choice of playing a seidhr wasn't the best choice for the starter stats for this race, but then again... It had a strangely high amount of strength *and* intelligence at the same time. Maybe she should look into what a draugr actually was when she got out of the game again. There had to be some explanation for those stats.

She closed all the menus. Enough fooling around. She just had to try the game out to see what would happen next.

Willow looked around the encampment, trying to see if there was some way to figure out how her attacks and everything actually worked. Because, right now, she couldn't find a way to actually kill all those wolves it wanted her to kill. Unless she was supposed to go in with her bare hands and that didn't really seem like the correct plan for a mage-like class.

Anyway, one of the first quests she got talked about a training ground or something like that. She could probably go and see what would happen there.

Training grounds. Where were they? She checked her map, but nothing showed up, the only visible area was what she'd actually seen in the game itself, nothing out of that reach.

Okay, so that meant that she had to explore this encampment to figure out where everything was first.

Some games…

Trainer: Attack the training dummy three times. Show me your strength, and I'll give you the item the captain wants.

Okay, three attacks, Willow could do that, *if she knew how to*.

Trainer: The first attack is a special draugr racial attack. Collect your fury and grow to double your size, then attack the dummy.

Wait, *what?* How did she do that? How the…?

She took a couple of steps back, it felt weird to have to execute an attack like that, it felt wrong for her class. But the game was designed like this, so it should work, right?

Willow looked at her bony hands, tensing them, they

creaked as she put pressure on them. Then she took a couple of deep breaths and let out a yell. Her body changed for a moment, just a flash, she felt the shifting of her body mass and she lashed out to the dummy. But as she hit it, she'd already returned to her normal form. Okay, almost. But the idea on how to do it was right.

What could she do to keep that other form? How would this work?

She moved her body, jumping up and down a couple of times. Then she felt it inside, the way the muscles of the creature were wound tight. She mentally reached for the ball of tension, grabbing hold. It felt strong, powerful.

As she mentally kept hold of the source of power inside the draugr, she stepped back again, reaching one arm behind her and she growled, at the same time she activated the source of energy and the world changed. Suddenly it was in grey tones, like night in the day, like undead. When her hand hit the dummy again, it had transformed into a claw.

You hit the Training Dummy for 53 damage

She let go of the source inside her again and stepped back.

Wow. That was strange. Was that some other form of the draugr? Like a shape-shifting thing?

> **Trainer**: Great job! That's your racial attack. It can really come in handy when you're in a tight spot. Not only does it do damage, it also has a chance to fear the target.

Oh, that was definitely a cool ability then.

> **Trainer**: The second attack I want you to do is an elemental attack. You have two choices for this, you can use a fire-based attack or an ice-based attack.

Wait, there was a difference? She could actually choose? Okay, that was interesting and somewhat unique…

> **Meadow**: How do I choose?
> **Trainer**: Focus on the element of the attack as you cast a spell, either fire or ice. But remember, this choice will influence the attacks you will receive for the next fifteen levels, at which point you can learn to specialise in the other element too.

Okay. This was really all-involved kind of gaming. It was interesting, but she didn't know if she'd enjoy playing it for long stretches of time if it was all going to be taking this much energy to get the most basic things done.

She held out her hand, like most mages in other games did, turning at the wrist and facing her palm up. A basic attack was usually just a bolt of some sort. Focused energy in the palm of her hand, but she had to choose between ice and fire here instead of it being pre-decided. She just had to see what came naturally.

Willow focused on her hand, mentally creating a ball of energy, letting the element come on its own, not influencing it. The palm of her hand started to glow, feeling hot and then cold and then hot again, cycling between the two.

Hmm.

Then it became stronger and suddenly she was holding a ball of energy that was both red and light blue, the two elements rolling over each other, coming together, forcing against each other, but never mixing.

Ehhh… She was pretty sure that this wasn't what she was supposed to do. Was this even possible in the game? It was happening, that was obvious, but she wasn't sure this was a bug or intended use.

Okay. She took a breath, keeping the energy in the palm of her hand and then threw it in the direction of the training dummy.

The attack missed.

Hmm. This game apparently didn't auto-target. The other attack had been easy enough to hit what with the range being limited but the reach of it pretty broad, but she had to really focus this one.

Right. *Again.*

She turned her arm again, her palm up, and like she did in Destruction of Elysium, where she used a small flick of her wrist to create the tiny firebolt, the movement easily let her pull on the magic attack in this game. The fire-icebolt appeared in her hand, and this time she focused on targetting the dummy as well as she could as she threw the bolt, trying to get it as close to the dummy as possible.

This time, it did hit the dummy. Blue and red flames spew away from it.

Wow.

You hit the Training Dummy for 16 damage

Just 16 damage? The other attack had been much stronger.

Trainer: Great! That was a fantastic example of an %elementbolt.

Ehh…

She was pretty sure that it had to actually name the element she used. If she could do this combined bolt within the constraints of the game, it should have an official element name, right?

Trainer: Are you good with having %element as your first element to master?

Even though she wasn't exactly sure that it wouldn't be breaking the game or cause strange things to happen later, she couldn't resist the temptation of having a unique type of attack.

> **Meadow**: Sure.

Choosing one element, fire or ice, would probably be a better idea, but this looked too cool and it did show her a little of the coding behind the game, constantly reminding her about why she was here.

> **Trainer**: Your third attack is not really yours. I have a
> special present for you. As a seidhr, you are able to
> summon your own fylgja. This creature will also
> fight for you.
> **Meadow**: Fylgja?

A pet? Maybe? The class description did say something about there being a pet for this class.

> **Trainer**: A fylgja is a creature of fate and destiny, and it
> will accompany you on your journey ahead. The
> fylgja will present as a creature that is most
> closely connected to your personality. Try calling it,
> and it will appear.

Try calling it? What now?

> **Meadow**: How do I call it?
> **Trainer**: To call your fylgja, you reach into your
> innermost feelings and it will come to you.

No help there then. She flicked her wrist again, pulling up her magic ball attack, looking at it as she thought about how to solve this riddle.

How was she going to call her own *fylgja*, when she had no idea how to summon anything from nothing, especially not a creature which was supposed to help her?

The other two attacks seemed obvious enough after a moment, but this one was a little more confusing.

Well, that was a strange hurdle for the game to throw at her... Summon her companion when there were no real clues on how to do that.

What kind of test was this?

12
Allies

Willow had just been given the most impossible task that she could imagine by the trainer. She had to somehow summon her fylgja, her companion, her pet, and she had no idea how to do that.

Frustrated by this strange request, she threw the %Elementbolt at the training dummy again, just for the heck of it.

You hit the Training Dummy for 14 damage

> **Trainer**: You've already shown me your %Element attack. Now I want to see your fylgja attack the dummy.
>
> **Trainer**: You can summon your fylgja by reaching into your innermost being and connect to the animal side of who you are.

Great...

And with the lack of an actual game guide for this game, she couldn't just search for what the game was actually asking from her and get another clue or, preferably, a step-by-step guide of what she had to do.

Willow sighed. *Fine.*

'Reach into your innermost being', that was what the trainer kept telling her. No other clues, just that strange touchy-feely stuff.

But just imagining having any pet after having raised Mira in Destruction of Elysium, after knowing that she wouldn't be able to celebrate Mira growing to her next stage together with Violet at her side in just a couple more hours, she didn't really feel like summoning some random creature in this game too. Why would she do that when she knew that he'd probably lose the pet again soon anyway? What was the use of that?

She wanted Violet back. She wanted to go back to DoE and play with her friends. She wanted to feel safe again. She didn't want this constant fear running through her and feeling so lost. She wanted to go back to how it used to be.

Maybe she should just tell Soleil to find someone else. She wasn't cut out for this. This exploring and finding out things, finding missing people, constantly being aware that this could be her last moments in this game too. It wasn't for her. It was…

A small sound pulled Willow's attention. It was in the game, but it hadn't been there before and somehow it didn't seem to be affected much by the sound settings. This was something new.

Willow opened her eyes, not even realising she'd closed them, and in front of her was a dragon. Well, dragon may not be the correct word, really. When people thought of dragons, they thought of big and majestic creatures. This dragon… It was small, maybe the size of a large cat, but it was definitely built like a dragon, and it was looking up at her.

The little creature opened its mouth and let out a cry. Like it was asking for help, like it was asking for something, anything, and she was the one who had to give it to them.

Willow knelt in the frozen grass, her knees creaking, and reached out to the small creature. "Hello, little one." She didn't know why she spoke to it, she really didn't like talking in games, but it felt right. She then put her hand on the small, scaly head.

The dragon's scales were a deep black with a purple shine when the light hit it just right. It had a sturdy body, a narrow snout, sharp claws, a spiky tail and something that looked like folded wings on its back. It was as cute as as it looked fierce and Willow couldn't help smiling at it.

The dragon put its head on her hand, a low rumbling from its throat vibrating against her skin. It was purring? This seemed a lot like purring.

"Are you my fylgja?" The word felt strange in her mouth, the sound unusual. She ran her hands over the rest of the dragon. Its scales were warm. Not hot or cold, just warm, like a human body kind of temperature.

The dragon let out a happier sound this time, walking closer, pushing its snout against her legs.

"I guess you are. And how am I supposed to make you attack that dummy? You look way too cute for that." She stared at the dragon some more, then she stood up. "You're not cuddly and soft, like I normally prefer, but you're cute and warm. I like that too. Now, to complete this quest, I need you to attack that dummy." She pointed at it. No clue if this was even going to work.

The dragon looked at the dummy and then at her.

"Attack the dummy." She pointed at it again.

How was a baby dragon the size of a cat going to be helpful in this game?

The dragon took a couple of steps towards the dummy, opened its mouth and let out a fire blast that engulfed the whole thing.

Fylgja hit the Training Dummy for 43 damage

Oh, wow. Okay... That was a lot more effective than she expected, especially from such a small creature.

> **Trainer**: Great job! Your fylgja has a very powerful attack. Do you want to name your fylgja?
> **Meadow**: Sure.

She couldn't keep calling it 'dragon' or 'little dragon', and fylgja was kind of weird too.

A small screen popped up.

Name:
Race: Dreki
Level: 1

That was the level 1 attack? Wow. She couldn't wait to see the damage output at higher levels.

What would be a cool name for the dragon? This was always the hard part. Naming things.

"What do you think of Iris? Your scales have a similar colour to a very dark iris."

The dragon walked back up to her, rubbing against her, like Mira did a lot in DoE. It was so cute.

"I guess Iris is a good name. Yes." She knelt down, wrapping her arms around Iris's neck. "And you're so nice and warm." Which was a given really, with such a strong fire attack. But in this cold world, the heat from Iris's body was a welcome change.

The small screen reloaded.

Name: Iris
Race: Dreki
Level: 1

And then it disappeared.

Trainer: Congratulations! You've passed my three tests, here is the flask that the captain asked for.

+ 100 XP
You receive Captain's Flask

A small victory sound played, but she no longer paid attention to it because as the quest completed, the bar at the bottom of the screen also filled up, the buttons finally showing things in them. There were now three buttons on the bar.

Ravage
Draugr racial ability
You lash out in a rage, putting fear into your enemies.

%Elementbolt
Seidhr ability
You shoot a bolt of %Element at your enemy, %Effecting them.

Summon Fylgja
Seidhr ability
Summon your very own Fylgja to fight at your side.

Interesting... Now she was both able to attack things and could actually see what those attacks were. But as with most of this game, it was so linear and frustrating to get to the next step. At least this part was done now.

She was pretty sure that the next step would be to go fight some wolves or something, or one of the other collecting quests that the captains asked for. For all the 'innovative gameplay' she'd been promised, she wasn't seeing much of it yet.

Willow was getting kind of tired of Helheim Fallen Online now. Having Iris at her side made her miss her friends in DoE even more and missing her friends was a constant reminder that Violet had been in HF too and had disappeared.

Willow wasn't here just for fun, she was here because she had a goal, she had to figure out what happened to the people who logged onto HF and then suddenly stopped responding to messages from their friends. And with more and more people reporting friends going missing and the official release of HF getting closer and closer, she had to figure things out fast too.

She opened the menu again, trying to decide what to do next. She could go back to the normal world, but what was she going to tell Soleil about what she'd found here? Helheim Fallen Online was just a game, much too linear for her taste, but there seemed to be nothing else odd going on? She couldn't do that. She had to bring something back with her, no matter how small.

Willow tried to figure out where she could find the time of the outside world, since the play time timer didn't really help her if she couldn't remember at what time she came into the game. But nothing seemed to show up in any of the menus.

She sighed and pulled up a virtual keyboard in front of her, which seemed to work in this game too. Good. Then she punched in a couple of keys and it pulled up a small command screen, showing the stats from the BASE platform.

Global time: '42 - 05 - 25 00:27

Local time: '42 - 03 - 25 01:27

System: Sleep impending

This was her own little program within the BASE platform, her own way to get a quick view of the time and what type of system messages her BASE account was going to throw at her. She had to go to bed, or the BASE platform was going to be annoying, soon-ish.

Right.

She didn't have much of a choice then, did she? She was up well past her normal bedtime and would be a wreck tomorrow if she kept going. But she hadn't gotten anything interesting to show Soleil from playing HF or any clue as to how she could find Violet or the other missing people.

But that would have to wait until she woke up again.

Willow closed the time stats screen and knelt down, running her hand over Iris' head.

"I'll be back tomorrow. I promise. But I've got to go now." She looked at the cute little creature.

Was Iris going to grow up like Mira did in DoE, or was this the final size of the dragon? She thought she remembered that Norse dragons tended to be bigger than this. But maybe it would grow as it gained levels or something. Which would be cool.

"See you later."

She pulled up the main menu of HF and logged out, everything around her going black and fading away.

Willow squinted at the brightness of her bedroom as she slowly tried to open her eyes. Her whole body felt heavy with sleep, which she hadn't felt while she was in the game but it became obvious now she was back in the real world. The room around her was much too bright for her liking. And, just as she thought it, the lights dimmed to a more tolerable intensity. The BASE implant sensed her feelings and emotions and adapted the world around her to it.

She really should go to sleep, but after everything that happened in HF, she felt like had to check in on her friends first and talk to Soleil. She opened the guild chat.

> **Opal**: Willow? Where are you?
> **Opal**: Willow?
> **Sage**: Willow? Please respond to messages.
> **Sage**: Come on. Please?

Sage's last message was from twenty minutes ago.

> **Willow**: I'm here.

She scrolled up the chat, seeing what they had been talking about while she was away, but nothing stood out as to why Sage would be worried about her.

> **Opal**: Good! Don't scare us like that, please.
> **Willow**: What's going on?
> **Sage**: I think it's better if we talk in VRHome...

That didn't sound good.

> **Willow**: Why?

She kind of wanted to go to sleep, and she still had to talk to Soleil, check in with her too.

Opal: Just, please?
Willow: Sure, give me 10 minutes. I need to get a drink
before I go in.
Sage: Okay. See you in a moment.

What was going on? Why were her friend so worried? And why didn't Sage want to talk about it in the chat?

But, as she stood up, she realised that she really did have to get something to drink, she was thirsty. Which made sense, as she'd been in the game for hours.

As Willow left her bedroom, she pulled up Soleil's chat.

Willow: I'm back.

She walked over to the kitchen and poured herself a glass of water.

Rotnem: Good. Glad you're back out safely. Did you find
anything?

Willow shook her head, unhappy that she didn't have much to share.

Willow: Not really. Just that the game is really
restrictive in what you can and can't do while
you're in the beginning area. It's really annoying.
Rotnem: Yeah, they like the whole 'fully immersive
experience' where you don't get to open things up
until you're 'ready' for them.
Rotnem: At least their idea of 'fully immersive', anyway.

Willow smiled at Soleil's use of quotes around words. It looked a lot like her own use of them, sarcasm quotes.

Willow: 'Fully immersive'? More like 'forced on a set
path'.
Willow: You can't even log out of the game until you've
accepted all the starter quests. You can't even log
out from the character creation area as far as I
could see.
Willow: That's just... Bad design?

She'd been frustrated with it while in the game, but the way Soleil was talking, this seemed to be normal behaviour? From the creators or just in general? She had no idea, but this didn't seem like the right time to ask about that.

> **Rotnem**: Wow. That's a lot more severe than I thought it would be. Maybe that's why...
> **Willow**: What?
> **Rotnem**: People can't take screenshots or video in Helheim Fallen, so they can't share anything visually. But nobody has talked about finding blitzed accounts inside the game either.
> **Rotnem**: You'd think that people would see those blitzed accounts, though. And they would talk, screenshots or not.
> **Willow**: You think that people are getting blitzed in the character creation or other instanced areas, instead of the open world?
> **Rotnem**: Basically. Yes.
> **Willow**: Makes sense.

It would explain the lack of HF players talking about blitzed players in the starter areas. And since most people who did go missing or radio silent or anything like that did so within an hour of starting the game, that's where those players should have been.

> **Willow**: But if it's like that, is it even any use that I keep playing? I won't be able to see anything anyway.
> **Willow**: They'd be gone before we can see them.
> **Rotnem**: I wish. I wish I could pull you out there right now. I would do it in a heartbeat.
> **Willow**: But?

There seemed to be a but at the end of that sentence.

> **Rotnem**: While you were in the game, there have been some... reports.

Willow's heart started beating loudly. 'Reports' and 'I wish

I could' never went well together, that combination always meant problems.

> **Willow**: Reports about?
> **Rotnem**: There has been some leak in the media about HF players going missing.
> **Rotnem**: And they found a body, about half an hour ago... A young woman. In one of the slums. Her BASE account was blitzed. She'd frozen to death after she couldn't get back into her house. They haven't identified her yet.

Willow gasped, feeling like her heart had stopped, the sudden pain in her chest overwhelming.

No way. This couldn't be true.

She put her hand over her mouth, trying not to cry out, and felt her cheeks wet with tears.

"No." Her voice shook as she dropped the glass of water on the floor. The glass shattered and a combination of glass and water went everywhere.

This couldn't be true, she couldn't believe that this could happen. This *wasn't* happening.

> **Rotnem**: Willow!
> **Willow**: jio

Her fingers on the keys felt strange, unreal, her movements choppy. She couldn't get anything into words. The feelings so strong that she had no way to express them.

> **Rotnem**: I don't know if it's your friend. I will find out for you. I promise. I'm only telling you because I want you to know, because I need you to know the reality.
> **Rotnem**: We need to find out if HF is the real cause of these blitzes and you will need to keep playing to get to the bottom of it. Between now and when the game releases, many more people could go missing. Please.

Willow saw the words, but couldn't think anymore.

The young woman the police found could be Violet. Violet could be gone. *Dead.*

> **Willow**: I need to
> **Willow**: My friends are waiting for me. I'll be back.
> **Rotnem**: You can't tell them about what we're doing.
> **Willow**: I won't.

But she had to be with her friends. She stared down, at the broken glass on the floor. She should clean it up, she really should, but then she carefully stepped back.

She could do it later, not now.

Willow padded over to her bed and put the VR headset back on. This must have been why Opal and Sage had been worried and trying to get a hold of her.

And she needed them with her, she needed her friends now.

No matter if the girl they found really was Violet or not, the fact that it very well could be was what scared her most.

She needed her friends, she needed to make sure that they were okay. She needed the comfort of their friendship. She needed her allies.

13
Enemies

As Willow appeared in her VRHome, she immediately realised that everyone was here, all waiting on her. Opal and Juniper were sitting on the couch, and Sage was walking from one end of the room to the other, looking really worried.

It was good to see her friends all here, but the look in their eyes made that feeling disappear quickly.

"Willow!" Juniper stood up, going over to her, but then she frowned. "What's wrong?" Juniper reached up, and Willow could feel Juniper's soft touch on her cheeks.

"I always forget even tears appear in VR." Willow wiped at her cheeks, hoping to dry her tears, but it didn't help the way her chest was hurting. "Opal and Sage told me to come here. What's going on?" She cleared her throat, the tears making her voice sound strange. She may be upset, but they had been the ones asking her to come here, so whatever was going on, that went first.

Sage came over too, their face worried. "We couldn't get a

hold of you, you were ignoring our messages."

"I was just... too focused on a game. I'm sorry. I lost track of time." The others apparently couldn't see that she'd been in Helheim Fallen Online, unlike when beta players were in there. Which meant that even though she was in the game, there was something on her account that showed her as being in a totally different place. Interesting, and good, for now. "Why?"

"Have you seen the news?" Sage looked at her.

"I've heard some stuff." Just what Soleil had told her, but Willow wasn't sure that that was the same thing her friends were talking about or if there was even more going on in the world right now.

Sage nodded. "The police found someone whose account was blitzed. They don't know who it is yet. But..." Sage shook their head and Willow could see the tears appearing in their eyes. "The person they found couldn't get back into their house because the door lock couldn't recognise their ID. This is... scary stuff. Being locked out of your own home, not able to get back in or contact anyone..."

"Where is Violet?" Opal's voice from the couch was harsh, he'd not moved since she'd come in. And when Willow looked at him, his eyes on her were hard. "Where is she?"

Could she lie? Could she lie to her friends, after news like that broke? But the look on everyone's faces made her go against Violet's wishes of keeping what was going on a secret, because their friends deserved to know the truth, at least part of it. "She can't get into BASE."

"Why not?" Opal's voice was angry. "Why?"

Willow felt her tears come back, get vision going all blurry. She couldn't do this. She really couldn't.

"Violet has been blitzed?" Sage sounded surprised, and a little scared.

Willow didn't want to say anything more, she couldn't find the words anyway. Even just nodding or shaking her head felt like it would be too much.

"That's why you were crying. You think Violet..." Juniper stared at her, her face paling. "It may have been Violet they found?"

Willow dropped her head, not able to look at her friends any longer, pulling her sleeves over her hands and covering her face. Her breathing hitched, her shoulders tightened.

"Are you sure?" That was Sage, wrapping their arms around her.

She shook her head. Then she focused and started mentally sounding out words for the chat. She couldn't talk now, her voice wouldn't work, her throat all closed up, her body shutting down.

But her mind still made words, and she needed to tell them things, she couldn't wait until she'd calmed down again to tell them this.

> **Willow**: The person they found was a young woman.
> Violet lives in the slums, though I don't know
> exactly where. And she was outside yesterday
> afternoon.
> **Sage**: How do you know?
> **Willow**: She was at my place, gave me a message. She
> was out there, in the cold.

In the freezing cold, the weather having turned pretty bad in the last couple of days. Violet had been out there, with a blitzed account, in the freezing cold.

> **Willow**: It could be her.

Soleil had told her, but if that hadn't been officially on the news, then Soleil must have found out some other way. And that meant that Soleil was getting her information from a lot of interesting places, so why was she depending on Willow for such sensitive things as gathering information inside a game?

It was strange, feeling Sage's arms around her while talking in the chat. But it was also good, she needed it, she needed the comfort. She was falling apart inside, and Sage was keeping her together, for now.

The one thing she often needed most but couldn't get in the real world, a hug, closeness. When everything went wrong around her, went she felt so scattered and raw, all she really ever wanted was someone to put their arms around her and keep her close, keep her from falling apart.

She felt Juniper coming closer too, wrapping her arms around them. "I can't believe it. I don't want to," Juniper whispered, her breathing moving Willow's hair at her neck even in the game.

"I know." Willow's voice was a whisper too. "I don't want it either. But it's just..."

It was too coincidental to ignore. And she had no way to get in contact with Violet right now to confirm otherwise. Until

Violet contacted her again, she wouldn't know if Violet was safe or not.

> **Opal**: Did you read the other parts of the articles too? Do you know about the other things?
> **Willow**: Other parts?
> **Opal**: They're saying that it's connected to HF. That people have started going missing when they log into HF and that the person they found had probably had their account blitzed that way too.
> **Willow**: If they don't know who they found, how do they know that it's connected to HF?

He wasn't wrong, but she needed to know how much was actually out there in the news. How had these connections been made? Were they onto something?

> **Opal**: It's just conjecture. They found the messages that people are going missing in HF on the HF forums and combined it with the reports of people in other games getting blitzed.
> **Juniper**: But they haven't found any blitzed people in HF, people would tell. If they saw a blitzed account in HF, they would tell, wouldn't they?
> **Juniper**: They would post it on the forums? Especially now?
> **Opal**: Maybe. I don't know. Just, word out there is that it's connected to HF.
> **Sage**: Why would it be?
> **Opal**: They're saying it started after the HF beta codes were getting sent out and it's gotten worse leading up to the release of the game.
> **Sage**: 'They're saying'? Maybe don't pay as much attention to conjecture. Right, Willow?

What her friends were saying wasn't wrong, and they were the exact same questions she'd been wondering about herself, and had asked Soleil previously. But to see her friends worry about this, these things, it made it all too real.

She got a little lost in her own head, trying to stay calm, storing everything she knew about what was going on away and trying to find more connections. But like Opal said, and Soleil too, so many of these connections led directly or indirectly to HF and their beta codes, no matter what way she turned it.

> **Willow**: I have to go. I need to sleep. The system will start bugging me soon.
> **Sage**: Right. Don't worry too much, I bet Violet is out there, doing her own thing. Nothing wrong.

That snagged onto something in her head that turned her frustration, her fear, into anger.

> **Willow**: Everything is wrong if some user got blitzed and has now frozen to death because of some bastard who did that to them.
> **Willow**: Everything is wrong if Violet can't use her BASE account.
> **Willow**: People without BASE accounts have no way to buy food, to pay their rent, to open the security to their homes.
> **Willow**: Violet got blitzed. That much I know for sure. They may or may not have found Violet's body, but that doesn't take away that someone who got blitzed was found, frozen to death.
> **Willow**: Does it really matter if that person was Violet or someone else? Someone else's close friend?
> **Willow**: Do you not even care about that?

She couldn't do this. All the emotions inside her were getting too strong. She logged out of her VRHome, getting out of the VR system. No, she couldn't keep doing this. She wasn't made for this, this wasn't for her.

Willow put the VR headset to the side and changed into her sleeping clothes. When she crawled into bed, she opened the chat with Soleil again.

> **Willow**: I want to meet tomorrow.

Then she closed the chat and silenced the notifications. She had to sleep, she couldn't deal with this anymore, she just couldn't.

The world had become so much scarier and she didn't know how to deal with that.

And maybe that was the scariest part of all. She'd lost grip on the world, she'd lost grip on what was going on and now she felt like she was losing everything that mattered to her.

Panic crawled at the edges of her mind, ready to invade her brain as soon as she fell asleep, and she had no way to stop it.

Willow dressed up as warm as she could before she left for the Dome. Mira, the hippogriff pet she shared with Violet in DoE, would grow to her next stage the exact moment Willow met up with Soleil. But, in light of everything, she had more important things to worry about than a creature in a game, no matter how attached she'd gotten to it. Important things like making sure Violet was alive and safe.

None of this was going to be worth it if Violet wasn't there with her. All her friends should be there to play games together, including Violet. She couldn't just let this go, she couldn't let this happen anymore. She had to do something.

Willow's notifications slowly began to blink red, and she opened them as she looked around the area in front of the Dome.

The chat had been quiet all night after she left the VRHome, which was strange, but maybe she had been too harsh on them... She'd been too wrapped up in the moment, and had lashed out at her friends, they hadn't deserved it.

> **Willow**: I'm okay.
> **Sage**: You're not in DoE? Mira is going to level up soon.
> **Willow**: What's the use when Violet isn't there?

> **Willow**: I'll be going out of range for a while. I need to
>   clear my head.

She couldn't tell Sage that she was going to meet Soleil or what they were up to, but a warning that she couldn't be reached would probably be good.

> **Sage**: Okay. Stay safe, please.
> **Willow**: I will.

Sage and their 'stay safe' line. She hadn't been safe for days, none of them had been. And as much as she wanted to believe that things would be okay again, that was getting harder and harder. How could this ever turn out okay again?

She spotted Soleil near the doors and walked up to her. Soleil was dressed in jeans and a warm jacket this time, not dressed up all proper like last time. She looked younger like this, a lot less intimidating too.

"Hey." Willow's voice was rough, she hadn't used it since last night, and she always had a raspy voice after she cried, which she had, for most of the night. She'd been going between crying, being wrapped up in the panic in her head, and restlessly sleeping for a handful of hours.

"Hey." Soleil looked at her, then stepped closer. "Do you want a hug?"

Tears sprung to her eyes as she nodded, and the next

moment, Soleil took her into a tight hug, holding her close. Willow also reached out to Soleil and held her too, taking a deep breath, something inside of her falling into place. This felt good. With everything going on, this felt like it kept her grounded, even if just a little.

Then Soleil let her go again. "Let's go inside. Where do you want to go?"

"Autumn." She didn't want the winter area, too cold, and it was already way too cold out here anyway, but everything else felt like it would be too bright for her mood.

"Okay." Soleil started walking, and Willow followed her.

When they reached the autumn part inside the Dome, the air was heavy with the scent of fallen leaves and they walked right through the trees to a clearing they apparently both knew how to find easily. It was a little out of the way for most people who came here, but it was quiet and there were some simulated sounds of small forest creatures scattering and scrambling around.

They sat down on the trunk of a fallen tree and were quiet for a while, then Soleil moved.

"I don't have any news yet about the woman they found. I wish I had. For now, I don't know if it's your friend or not." She sounded so sorry, so filled with regrets.

"Violet." Willow pulled a face, her voice was rough, and her throat hurt a little.

"Violet," Soleil repeated the name. "I don't know if it's her. I'm sorry."

Willow nodded. She hadn't really expected anything else, though she had hoped that Soleil had known more by now. "I don't know if I can keep doing this. It's... too scary." Her mind kept going between needing to do this because she wanted to help other people and feeling like she couldn't because it was too scary and she couldn't deal with it.

"I know." Soleil's voice was quiet, and she let out a deep breath. "I know. I wish that I didn't have to ask this of you. I know very well the dangers that I'm asking you to put yourself in. Very well."

Willow looked at Soleil, something in her voice off, but Soleil was looking away from her. "Why?"

Soleil shook her head a little. "It's not easy to explain. But I need you to be strong. I need you to keep going."

"Why?" She knew that she kept asking the same things, but she hated that she didn't know things and that she was working from nothing here, everything strange and unfamiliar.

Soleil sighed and then looked her way. "It's the only way we can find out what happened inside the program itself. We need to find out why they're doing this, how they're doing this. How they're choosing their victims." Soleil looked around, her eyes scared. "What I'm about to tell you, you can't tell anyone. Nobody. Promise."

Her chest tightened, and Willow acutely wondered how much danger Soleil was putting herself in by doing all of this. How many chances Soleil was taking by being here, talking to Willow, trying to find out all these things. The one in the most danger here wasn't Willow, it was Soleil. "I promise."

Soleil leaned in closer, tugging on her shoulder until Soleil's lips nearly touched Willow's ear. "The person inside HF who is helping us out, they told me that the higher-ups in HF are aware of the blitzing and that they're doing everything to hide this from the public. They're scared. They're really scared, and they're running around trying to do damage control. If it comes out that the blitzed people were all on the beta list for HF, that could ruin the game in an instant. They don't want that."

Willow nodded. The people in charge in HF had every reason to try and keep this quiet.

"They're aware of what's going on and instead of fixing whatever it is that's doing this or causing this, they're trying to cover it up. They're silencing anyone who even steps a little out of line. If they find out what you're doing... What we're doing…"

"They'll come after me too," Willow whispered. "After us."

"Yeah."

Willow's blood began to boil. "But they're fine with people getting blitzed, as long as it doesn't harm the reputation of the game. They're fine with people going missing, with people dying, as long as it doesn't harm their game."

Every hero needed an enemy, someone or something to defeat. And covering up how their game was ruining the lives of ordinary people was a pretty evil plan and a pretty good motive for an enemy. If they weren't the ones causing all of this to happen in the first place.

But Soleil was right, if she was going to find out what was happening, she needed to find others, she needed to progress in the game and find other players. She had to keep going, because if there was one thing she was good at, it was videogames, and with the tools Soleil had given her, she could maybe even defeat these people at their own game.

She may be a girl and autistic on top of that, but that didn't mean that she couldn't find what was going on. That didn't mean that she couldn't go out there and figure out exactly where things were going wrong. Because people were very keen on underestimating her, and that could be her one advantage here. Not just that, she could ruin this game from the inside out, keeping going until she found out what was happening and solving the problem.

She had to do it. For Violet, for others like Violet, those who were blitzed and had no way to defend themselves. She had to be the one doing this.

Every hero needed an enemy, and she had just found hers.

14
New Experiences

Willow logged in to Destruction of Elysium, the world around her bright, much brighter than she expected it to be. She was standing in the middle of her room in the guild house, everything around her the same as it always had been, everything familiar. But she felt totally different now, and that was strange.

As she went downstairs, nobody was around, the house totally quiet. It was a little unsettling, to have it be this quiet, but at the same time, it calmed her down. Then she walked out the back door to the garden.

Mira came up to her immediately, now much bigger than before. Mira was a juvenile hippogriff now, her shoulders reaching to Willow's shoulders and her beak bigger than both of Willow's hands side by side. "Hello, beautiful. I'm so sorry I couldn't be there when you grew up." She slowly reached out and then wrapped her arms around Mira's neck as best as she could, she felt warm and comforting, comfortable.

Mira let out some happy sounds, which were luckily mostly muted by the game's system, because she really couldn't do loud noises right now.

"I'm sorry. I was looking for your other Mum. I know she hasn't been around for a while, but I'm trying to get her back." She hid her face in Mira's feathers, loving the sensation of the soft feathers against her skin. This felt so good, it was so fluffy. "I will get her back for you. I promise." She tightened her arms around Mira, wishing she could make that promise come true.

Mira nudged her shoulder, and Willow stepped back. Then Mira kneeled a little, looking at her intently.

"You want me to get on your back? Are you sure?" She'd never done this before.

Mira was finally big enough to carry one rider at a time. In her adult form she would be able to carry two riders at the same time. But that was going to take a couple of weeks longer. Weeks that Willow didn't know if she could even take care of Mira, weeks that could pass and none of the plans she had with Violet of going cool places could come true. When it came to Mira, she was on her own now, and she didn't even know if she could do this…

"Okay." Willow smiled a little, then she tried to figure out what would be the best way to get on top. "I'm sorry if I pull out any feathers." She reached up into Mira's neck and grabbed a hand full of them. Then she lifted herself up, and the game did the rest, effortlessly putting her on Mira's back, between her shoulders and her majestic wings.

It felt strange, so different from the horse mount that she sometimes rented when she wanted to go places quickly that the teleportation couldn't get her.

The next moment, Mira pushed off the ground and they were flying, everything quickly shrinking under them, falling away as they shot up into the air.

Willow wrapped her arms around Mira's neck as she looked down. There was this tightness in her stomach at the height. She wasn't scared of the height specifically, but she was definitely scared of falling, which was now making her a little dizzy as she saw the ground disappear under them. She knew she was safe, the game wouldn't even let her fall off, under no circumstances, but that fear of falling and getting hurt still peaked panic in her head.

Then Mira stopped rising and just flew ahead. The wind in their hair and feathers, the great view in front of them. It was amazing, and she could barely believe this was in a game and not real life. She could see the forest in front of them, the fields, and on one side, she could even see mountains at the horizon, the mountains that indicated where this zone ended and the next one started.

They were on top of the world, and it was amazing, in so many ways.

"Thank you," she yelled at Mira over the sound of the wind. "Thank you so much." This had been exactly what she needed. A small escape from the world, just letting go and being away from it all for a while.

Nothing pulling her down, nothing that could dampen her mood here. Just them, the wind, and the world as far as the eye could see.

Then a message in the chat popped up.

> **Juniper**: Willow, you there?
> **Willow**: Yeah.

Juniper: Good. Just... needed to know you were really
  here.
Willow: I'm here. Just checking in on Mira.
Juniper: Yeah. She's so big now.

Mira slowly started descending. A calm movement, nothing like falling, luckily. They were slowly coming back to the real worls, the real world with real problems and real problems she was going to have to solve…

Juniper: Where were you yesterday? When Sage and
  Opal were looking for you?

She had to lie, but she couldn't figure out what to say. She didn't want to lie to her friends, and she didn't want to constantly have to remember what lies she told who.

Willow: I can't tell you. I'm sorry.
Juniper: Were you trying to find Violet?
Willow: Something like that.
Juniper: Okay.

And then the chat fell quiet again.

Willow: Are you okay with that? Just that?
Juniper: Yes. It's not the same without her, and if she
  got in trouble... I don't want to get you into more
  trouble when you're trying to help her.
Willow: Thank you.

Mira was now low enough that she could see Juniper sitting on the roof of the guild house. She waved at Juniper as Mira landed.

Willow climbed off Mira, her legs a bit wobbly as she hit the ground. This was strange, but it was also really cool. The flight still kept her mood up, even though it was slowly falling now.

But no matter how much she wanted to stay here, she had to go, there were things she had to do and take care of.

Willow: Can you tell the others not to worry?
Juniper: I'll try.
Juniper: Don't do anything stupid.
Willow: Do I ever?
Juniper: Listen when people tell you that? No. But I can
    try.

Juniper had a point, but that wasn't going to stop her.

Willow: I'm not on my own. I promise. I've got people
    who're helping me, they're keeping an eye on me.

Well, she was the one helping others... But that was the same, for practical purposes here.

Juniper: Okay. See you soon.
Juniper: Please, do check in at least once or twice a
    day.
Willow: Will do.

Willow would do anything to make her friends feel safe again and not like Willow would also just disappeared on them, just like Violet had done. She would check in on them any time that she would remember to, just so they'd know she was still there. That she hadn't gone missing too.

Willow: See you later.

She swiped the menu.

You are now logged out of Destruction of Elysium

The words appeared in her view for a few moments before the world around her went white. She was in the 'store' area of the BASE platform. This way she could jump into Helheim Fallen Online without much trouble. But, before she did, she opened the chat she had with Soleil.

Willow: I'm going back into HF. I'm going to figure this
    'going missing right at logging in' thing out, one
    way or another.

Soleil: Okay.
Willow: My friends are worried.

She'd already told Soleil this when they met just a couple of hours ago, but seeing Juniper reminded her how much her friends really did worry about her and how much she worried about them.

Soleil: I promise I'll try to keep them safe and I'm still
      looking into the Violet thing.
Willow: Thanks.
Willow: I'm going in.

She looked around and focused on the Helheim Fallen Online logo. The white world around her disappeared, and she was standing in a new place she hadn't been before.

***You are now logged into Helheim
Fallen Online***

When she looked around, she realised that she was standing in the middle of what looked like a galaxy of some sort. It was beautiful, the dark blue and purple hues and the stars all around her. At the side of her view, the stats of her character were visible.

Name: Meadow
Race: Draugr
Class: Seidhr
Level: 1

If she was going to get anywhere, she had to get a move on and raise that level. That was the goal for today, get as far as she could. And, of course, keep her eyes open for any clues about strange things going on in this game.

Anything stranger than the weird world she was in anyway...

Willow turned her wrist again, the ball of elemental energy appearing in it easily.

You cast %Elementbolt

The bolt flew from her hand at the wolf standing a little away from her.

You hit the Dire Wolf for 25 damage

Then, as she waited for her mana to refill a little, Iris attacked the wolf too.

Iris hit the Dire Wolf for 57 damage

The wolf went down to the ground, curling up like it was in pain and Willow cringed. Of all the things they made 'realistic' in this game, it of course had to be the creatures dying...

+ 35 XP
You've reached level 3!
+4 Strength
+1 Dexterity
+6 Intelligence
+4 Wisdom
+3 Endurance

Nice!

Iris has reached level 3!
+6 Strength
+4 Intelligence
+6 Toughness

It was pretty obvious that Willow was playing a pet class, as Iris was doing a lot more damage than she did, and her mana regeneration was a little on the slow side too, although, Iris' attacks weren't the fastest either.

Willow was getting more and more frustrated that she couldn't just check a guide to see how to optimise her class or Iris' stats. But for now, she could deal with this, it wasn't too bad, yet. She just didn't enjoy going in blind with these things, especially not when she didn't know what stats combinations were the most important for her.

She opened the main menu, and it showed her that she'd been in HF for almost two hours now. Two hours to gain two levels...

That wasn't the fastest levelling, especially not this early on in the game. But of course, she'd been having a couple of problems figuring out how to do her attacks between the actual physical movements and the buttons on her bar, and how other mechanics like gathering and butchering worked.

She'd found out that at least for the bolt, it was easiest to just conjure it with a hand movement, even if her wrist was going to hurt from the repetitive movements later on. Which, yeah, was a real thing…

Willow walked up to the wolf, taking her butchering knife and sat behind the wolf, reaching over and cutting open its belly. The knife was resisted for a moment, the thick skin of the wolf stopping her, but when she put more pressure behind it, it pierced the skin. Then she dragged the knife through the skin at the belly of the wolf, gutting it.

It made her shiver as she felt the blood and gore flood over her hand. Luckily, that was the exact moment the game took over.

You loot Fur
You loot Wolf Meat
You loot Leftover Animal Pieces

All that was left over now was a simple carcass.

Apparently the 'leftover animal pieces' were for her dragon to snack on, which was cool. Although, the text on it also made it seem like if she gained enough levels in butchering, she'd be able to find more useful items from them.

+25 XP Butchering

She was finally halfway through the wolves she had to kill for one of the captains, and had collected half of the pieces of wolf meat she needed for the butcher in the encampment. This game was definitely slow going in places. She needed the pieces of meat before the butcher would give her the parcel for the quest from the other captain. All fun things...

Although, apart from these quests being pretty generic, they hadn't been too bad in the way of the type of quests she had to do. 'Gather X', 'Kill Y' and 'Talk to Z' they were all pretty standard. But that was also comfortable. It made the game feel a little less scary now she was doing things that she already knew how to do and that she knew she was pretty good at. It made understanding the game easier.

Well, comforting apart from the gory parts that the game somehow loved to be very explicit about. From the decay on draugr characters, to the way mobs curled up in pain as they died, to the actual act of butchering... The game's focus on the pain, torture and gore was a little off-putting.

Sure, she'd been promised the 'hyper-realistic' elements, but she felt more like most of the game had been very bland and anything torture or pain related wasn't just 'hyper-realistic' it had been turned into a way to show off how cool they were for showing blood and gore and torture. Because the details on those things were very out of proportion when compared to the other elements of the game.

In the two hours Willow had been playing, she hadn't seen any other players yet, so she was going to really have to step up her game if she wanted to see anyone any time soon. She was pretty sure that she was in the normal player areas now and no longer in the instanced parts. But with people already a couple of days ahead of her, she had to do some catching up.

"Okay, Iris. Next wolf." She pointed at a wolf standing in the forest a little off to the side. It was just out of range to trigger aggro on her, so it hadn't attacked her yet, but she had kept her eye on it all the same. She didn't want to accidentally pull a second wolf while fighting the first, that had been a mistake she'd made earlier on...

And dying and then having to respawn and run all the way back to her corpse was as little fun here as it was in any game she'd played before. Luckily, she hadn't lost any items or gear or anything like that, but she had lost quite a bit of time…

As Iris ran for the wolf, Willow pulled up a bolt, throwing it just as Iris let out her own colossal flame attack.

You cast %Elementbolt
Iris hit the Dire Wolf for 58 damage
You hit the Dire Wolf for 28 damage

The wolf looked at her, and she knew that the aggro was going to be on her. She hated that, Iris was a lot more sturdy, generally. But sometimes the game would not focus on the pet, who did much more damage and was a lot less squishy, but it would focus on her instead.

You cast %Elementbolt
You hit the Dire Wolf for 31 damage
The Dire Wolf hit you for 15 damage

Ah! No!

And the wolf went down in a burst of flames, she could feel the heat of them on her skin. Jikes!

Fighting in this game was fine, but she was really going to have to do something about those notifications. She could guesstimate how much HP the mobs had left with the health indicator above them, she didn't need to constantly see the actual damage she was doing to them, especially since it was so distracting in the way it kept popping up.

She grabbed the skinning knife again and reached over the slightly scorched wolf, putting the tip of the blade to its belly.

And, again...

There was some resistance, then the blade went through the skin, before she cut the wolf open and blood and guts spilled over her hand.

She was also going to have to see about maybe changing the settings on the gore in the game too or she would have to stop being a butcher, because she really hated the feeling of the blood and guts of the fresh kill spilling all over her hands... The texture and feel it it was bad enough, but the guts were also still warm, like it really was a freshly killed real wolf. Ick!

After six wolves, she still hadn't gotten used to it, and thinking ahead, she probably didn't even want to consider what other creatures she was going to have to feel the insides of. If possible, herbalism and mining were probably going to be more of her thing... Maybe, depending on how realistic the gathering of more prickly plants would be and if this game implemented blisters from using a pickaxe for too long, which wouldn't surprise her.

The whole gross butchering thing had been the other part that was keeping her up from levelling faster. She first hadn't wanted to believe what she had to do and then she had to overcome her own queasiness every time she had to butcher a wolf. Fun was different…

She checked her inventory and then looked around. She had no idea how long it took for mobs to respawn, she hadn't been bothered to time it, but she probably wanted to move out of this spot before they did...

Probably...

15
Preparing for Battle

Willow stared at her quest log, a little overwhelmed by everything on it. She had to kill 15 of some bird, then gather 20 clusters of lingonberries, but the most daunting one was the new quest that the main captain, at least he seemed to be the main one, the draugr captain, had given her.

Quest: Explore the North

There are rumours that some of our allies have gone missing north of this encampment and we can't seem to get in contact with them.

Explore the area north of the encampment and find out what happened to them.

North. She'd looked that way when she went back to the encampment after the wolf quests, and she'd seem some new mobs there, including some birds, and it hadn't looked that welcoming. But, of course, it made sense that she would be sent there next. Game mechanics and all.

She looked down at Iris. "Are you ready? Let's fry some

birds and see if we can save some poor lost people."

Then a message appeared right in front of her, startling her.

Time to eat!

It was a BASE platform message, and considering how long she'd been playing, it was probably time for dinner.

"Okay. Too bad. Going to have to wait then." Willow knelt down, running her bony hands over Iris' scales.

It was interesting how she could feel the warmth of Iris's body, even though the flesh on her hands, and thus her nerve endings which should be sensing this stuff, was mostly gone. Game logic again. The BASE implant would still send signals to her brain that she should feel certain things in the game, but the character she was playing would probably not even experience them. Game logic or just lazy coding, either worked.

"I'll be back soon."

Iris let out a couple of squeaks and Willow threw her a piece of 'leftover meat' which Iris downed easily, happily munching on it, walking in small circles.

"I'll be right back, stay here." Not that Iris could really go anywhere. Unlike Mira, who was part of the game environment and was more like an NPC, Iris was connected to her character, it was her specific pet, so when Willow wasn't in the game, neither was Iris. But it was still more fun to pretend that she was an actual living pet instead of just some game coding which only existed while she was in the game and then disappeared again when she left too.

Willow swiped at the menu.

You are now logged out of Helheim Fallen Online

Then she opened her eyes and sat up, taking off the VR headset.

She'd been in VR ever since she came back from meeting Soleil at noon. It helped to not be locked in this apartment, because in HF she at least felt like she was doing something, like there was progress, even when in reality, she was mostly just waiting around for news.

Willow went over to her delivery box and found a box of food in it. It was still hot, which was normal, considering that the BASE message usually appeared at the same moment as the food arrived. She'd ignored the previous messages about it being dinner time 'soon', those were just there to remind people to find a place to log out and that they should probably try to finish the dungeon or whatever thing they were in so that they could go eat.

As she picked up the food, she checked the rest of the delivery box to see if she maybe had gotten a message from Violet too, but there wasn't anything she could find. *Bummer.*

Somewhere, Willow still had hope that maybe it wasn't Violet they found and that Violet would come out here again and leave her a message to let her know this. Anything would be good now, really. Some part of her even hoped that the news about the woman the police had found was fake and that there wasn't anyone. But she was realistic enough to know that that wasn't true.

She opened the box at the table, sitting down as she stared at it. It was a pretty standard meal, pasta with some red sauce and a salad, all packed into their own little containers. None of the food was 'touching' other food.

This was another one of those 'autism things' that experts

insisted on. Apparently, it was common for autistics to hate it when 'food touched', aka when food wasn't divided into specific little areas all on their own. But instead of listening to the needs of individual people, organisations just applied these 'preferences' to all autistics.

She'd fought her parents on this thing a couple of times. They'd insisted that her mixing her foods was 'just another way to try and be normal', while she really just hated plain pasta or rice and wanted all the flavours and textures together, not separate.

It might have been true for some autistics that they hated the 'food touching' thing, but since she didn't know many, if any, autistics, it wasn't something she could ask the opinion of others on. And to ask Soleil about this would just be odd. Right?

Willow stood up and went over to one of the cupboards, taking one of the two plates in there and then sat down at the table again. She grabbed the container with pasta and dumped it on her plate. Then she poured the sauce all over it, spreading it out as well as she could. Finally, she hunted down the small packet of cheese and sprinkled it all on top, hoping that everything was still hot enough to make it melt. If there was one thing she really didn't like with food it was not fully melted cheese over her pasta. It often had this weird almost gritty texture to it, so not fun. Then she grabbed a fork and started mixing everything together.

She didn't hate it when food touched, she hated it when the sauce wasn't properly mixed into all the pieces of pasta. When things weren't mixed evenly. Maybe that was same problem in her brain, just manifesting the other way around...

No food touching at all or all the food touching all over and evenly distributed. Hmm.

She looked through the game forums as she ate her dinner. She hadn't seen any new messages about people getting blitzed or going missing on the DoE or HF forums today, but that didn't mean that it wasn't happening.

If Soleil was right, then the messages about people going missing in HF were probably getting deleted or changed pretty quickly after getting posted onto the forums... So she couldn't trust the forums anymore, that had become very clear in the last days. If anything negative or potentially negative was getting deleted, then she couldn't trust anything posted on there anymore.

Willow pulled up a document in front of her, and the AR keyboard appeared next to her plate. She let the fingers of her right hand hover over the keys as she thought about what she wanted to write down.

Everything was getting messed up in her head, she couldn't put her finger on exactly where she was having to focus her attention right now. So, she needed to organise things, and writing down was the only way she knew how to organise things. Lists.

WHO ARE BLITZING THE ACCOUNTS?
- Creators of HF?
- People working for HF?

Those were the most obvious options. There could be more, but currently, HF seemed to be involved somewhere along the chain of people going missing.

WHY ARE THEY BLITZING ACCOUNTS?
-

She had no idea, nothing to write down. There didn't seem to be any reason as to why Violet's account would be blitzed. And since she had no clue where any of the other victims lived, or who they were, she didn't know if it could potentially even be geographically linked. Maybe they all lived in the same area and it was simply an error with the BASE platform there? Although, by now, that had started to look unlikely…

WHERE ARE THEY FINDING THE ACCOUNTS?
- HF beta list (according to Soleil)
- Forums?
- Some other list?

WHAT DO THEY NEED TO BLITZ ACCOUNTS?
- Personal ID, not BASE ID

So whoever did it had to have pretty detailed insider knowledge of how the BASE IDs were linked to people's real personal IDs, because companies weren't supposed to have that information.

The government had that information, and a very select group of people working at BASE who were responsible for the coding to keep these systems working together had that information. But nobody else should.

WHEN ARE THE ACCOUNTS BLITZED?
- Early on in the game in HF?
    - - Day 1 of playing?
    - - ??

It did appear to be very early on, from what she'd seen on the forums and everything, almost instantly from the moment someone logged on for the first time. At least, that's what it had looked like with Violet.

- In other games?

-- ??

The blitzes in other games seemed to be random and not really based on any time or state of the account, they happened when they happened.

The worst part of it was that it was all so random. Some people went missing as they logged onto HF, and the number of people this happened to went up over time, but probably because more beta keys were being handed out each week. But in the other games, it never seemed to make any sense.

Why was the account from the person in DoE blitzed when it was mining some ore? It wasn't even doing something interesting or odd, the player was just doing their thing.

Why did it happen?

That was the most important question for her. *Why?*

Why were people blitzing accounts and what were they getting out of it? Because that was very hard to understand right now. It made no sense, and that made trying to make any sense of all the other questions she had or the information she'd found even harder.

She looked at the time, it was ten in the evening. She could play HF for a while longer, but she wasn't exactly sure she should. She'd done enough gross things in HF for one day, and the next quests she had to do were all big quests that took a lot of time.

Maybe she should try to get some sleep first, get back to all of this with a clear head tomorrow. If that was even possible...

How could she come up with a plan when she knew that her best friend was missing and she was potentially no longer alive?

How was a 'clear head' even possible?

Name: Meadow
Race: Draugr
Class: Seidhr
Level: 5

Willow materialised in the middle of the encampment, the captains were all still standing around waiting for new players to talk to them. At her side, Iris came into being with a soft 'pop', and she let out a happy squeak as Willow reached out and patted her head.

"Yep, I'm back. Are you ready for another day of levelling?" She looked at the little dragon. Was it just her imagination, or had Iris grown since she appeared to her at the start of the game?

Willow checked her inventory, making sure she had all the items with her that she needed, and then walked to the area with the merchants. Not that there were many here, apart from of course the butcher and the other ones she had to do quests for before, there were also a general supplies seller and a gear and weapon seller.

"Hi." She waved at the general supplies seller.

"Welcome. Do you need potions, food or anything else for your dangerous travels? I'm the man you'll need. Take a look at my wares and let me know what you're interested in." The general supplies seller bowed a little as he moved his arm over the items that were laid out in front of him.

The game really didn't seem to be able to keep everything to text-only, but she guessed she was going to have to get used to the audio thing at some point. Most people playing would have their voice chat on almost at all times, and she didn't have any of her friends here who knew how much she hated doing voice chat, especially in a game.

"I'm in need of supplies, and would like to barter for my own wares." Hey, she had to stay in-character somewhat, this game liked that. It seemed that it had pretty specific keywords that it responded to.

"I'm happy to trade." A screen popped up and showed her all the items she could buy from the seller. First, she sold off a couple of pieces of the meat that she couldn't identify anyway, and then some items that didn't seem to have much use. She didn't tend to throw out 'useless' items, since most games gave some coins for them, but the different types of rocks, sticks and other bits and pieces she got from mobs were just taking up space in her inventory. Time to exchange them.

Then she bought a few more health potions, those could come in handy, and looked through the rest of the items on offer. But she didn't think she needed 'cooking ingredients' right now, not when she was going to kill mobs and apparently try and find some lost heroes or explorers or whatever later. Training her cooking skill wasn't on her list of things to do.

"Thank you." Then she looked at the gear and weapon seller. "Hi, I'd like to browse your wares."

"I have the finest wares. Take a look." A new screen popped up.

She skimmed through most of the top list of the items, those were for classes who needed some actual protection, like leather and chain-mail gear. Her gear was further down the list. She was still wearing the same equipment as she did when she first spawned. None of the mobs had dropped anything, and she hadn't gotten anything from quests yet. But it seemed like the right time to get herself a little geared up now.

Initiate's Robe
*It looks like someone left a cheat sheet on the
inside of the sleeve.
Armour: 3
Intelligence: 2
Wisdom: 1*

Right. Willow smiled. Cheat sheet sounded fun, even when it probably wasn't something she could actually use. What could the game come up with to make something like that useful?

Soft Boots
*At least your feet won't hurt as much walking
over those rocks and stones anymore.
Armour: 2
Endurance: 1*

Well, she had been walking around barefoot for now, though, looking down, it didn't seem to hurt her character too much. But gear was useful anyway.

Initiate's Slacks
*Walking around gets less windy this way.
Armour: 2
Intelligence: 1*

Okay, the makers of HF at least had some humour. Now, what else could she get?

Initiate's Staff
*Not for hitting people on the head, this is a
magical item, not a club.
Intelligence: 2*

She had no idea why she had to use a staff when her magic came from within herself. Until now, she mostly had the original staff she'd picked up just on her belt so it was equipped, since even the starter staff had an extra point for intelligence. But maybe most people did actually use them during casting?

She equipped her new gear and her health and mana points both went up. Good. She'd been in desperate need of more mana to fight those mobs. Now she had it.

Then she looked through the rest of the items to see if there was any gear for Iris too, but couldn't find anything.

Hmmm.

She opened her inventory and took out her old robe and the butchering knife. Then she cut out a large square and held it next to Iris.

"Yeah, that will do." She used the knife to make the ends at the front pointier and easier to tie. Then she sat down next to Iris and motioned for her to come over. "I can't be the only one with upgraded gear."

Willow put the cloth over Iris' back and tied it at the front.

"Now you have a cape. You're a superhero."

Iris ran off and then came back, letting out little happy squeaks as the cape fluttered after her and Willow smiled. For a game with such lazy programming in some places, it seemed pretty advanced in what it could handle in other parts. It was cool to see that HF did allow at least some modifications that weren't built into the game itself. Some personalisation of things was always good.

Now, if she could only find a place where she could get

cooler gear, that would definitely make her time here a lot better. The Initiate's clothes set were all a dull grey-brown that she really didn't enjoy. But she probably needed to get to the first real town or city to find someone who could do that for her, and for that, she had to get a move on with her quests.

Right, time to go.

Time to face the rest of the game.

16
Approach to the Inmost Cave

The second large bird at her feet disintegrated as Willow took the loot from butchering it. These large goshawks were annoying. It made her glad she had ranged attacks and not just melee weapons. The goshawks kept shooting up and then swooping down to attack her, the moment they were within melee range was only short, so these were easier to get rid off with ranged attacks, as they never got out of range to those.

Just now, while she had been fighting one goshawk, she'd stepped back into range of a second one, which of course had started attacking her right as she'd finally managed to get the first one at about half of its health. That had not been a good move. She'd seen her HP go down, bit by bit, as she managed to kill the first one, while she'd stuck Iris on the second one, hoping that it would stop attacking her. Which it didn't. Her health had gotten precariously low before she'd finally managed to kill the second goshawk.

Luckily, there hadn't been another one around as she

butchered both of the birds, not wanting to miss out on the loot. She had to get some reward for getting her heart racing like that. She really didn't want to get killed and then having to run back here when she was so close to done with the quest for the birds.

Willow grabbed a health potion from her bag and drank it. She was still surprised by the flavour. The potion itself was red, like most health potions in games tended to be, but the flavour wasn't something she immediately recognised. She'd expected something like generic red berries just like in DoE or just strawberry or raspberry as in some of the other games she'd played, but this one was much more sour and a little tangy. It was a curious flavour, but she didn't dislike it. It was simply different.

Iris let out a soft low growl, a warning that a mob was getting within range of them soon and that it would be able to trigger aggro on one of them. This little warning mechanism was very handy, and it had saved her a couple of times, although, it totally didn't help when she was already in battle and something else would attack her from the back.

Willow looked around the field, but didn't see anything even close to being within range, then she looked up and spotted another large goshawk up high, probably ready to swoop down to 'spawn' right around where she was standing.

Mobs didn't just spawn in Helheim, at least not in the location where they would be roaming around. A mob would spawn somewhere that was out of view of most players, and it would be invulnerable to attacks, and then it would go over to their roaming area, at which time they finally became targetable. This way it wasn't so much 'spawning' as 'mobs who walk up to the location where they roam around'. But apparently, fylgjur like Iris would still detect the mobs as they spawned but before they reached their roaming area.

She should probably get a move on, she still had three of the goshawks to kill, but she was also getting near a forest area that looked a lot like it could hide the next part of her main quest. That was, if this game really was as predictable as it appeared to be... After she finished the next part of the main quest, she'd probably have to get back to the encampment anyway so she could kill the final birds on her way back.

Willow sprinted the short distance to the trees, the air moving heavier against her the longer she did it. While there didn't seem to be a countdown timer or something for sprinting, as most games had, there obviously were some mechanics that prevented her from sprinting for too long, one of them being the air getting heavier or 'thicker' the longer she did it.

You've reached sprinting level 1!

Oh, wow! So there was a sprinting skill? Interesting. She wondered what other hidden skills there were like this. Most of the skills had been pretty obvious, like gathering or crafting, but there seemed to be a couple of hidden skills too. Cool!

Then she walked past the group of trees, ready to fight whatever mob the main quest would throw at her for reaching this specific area where some soldiers had gone to but never returned from.

What she hadn't expected was to find an area littered with corpses. Sure, it fit the overall focus on death and decay of this game, but she still hadn't expected this…

In front of her were the lifeless bodies of multiple NPCs,

dressed in what looked like soldier gear that seemed to match the type of things the captains back at the encampment had been wearing. Her stomach lurched as she looked around.

The corpses were thrown about the area, their bodies at odd angles, and it was deadly quiet here, not even in-game bird or other animal sounds were coming through. She'd expected the quest to be a rescue or an escort mission, not a... What was this? A retrieval mission? And of what? What was she supposed to get from here? Did she have to get some insignia off them or carry a corpse back to the encampment?

That would fit the humour of the game as she'd found it up to now, but it didn't feel like that was what she was supposed to do here either.

Willow carefully walked past a couple of the bodies and reached out to one that appeared to be some sort of ranger, a broken bow still at his side. She put her fingers to the guy's throat, but there was no heartbeat. Not that she knew if there should be in this game, she was undead herself, so she couldn't really test it on her own body and there weren't any other players around to test it out on either. But with the way they were lying here, that wasn't a good sign, right?

As she looked around, she saw some elves, some humans, dwarves and other creatures, and even some fylgjur. The corpses ranged in classes too, warrior types, mage types, ranger types, all sorts of things.

Then she stopped in front of a body that gave her shivers. It was a draugr, and a severely decomposed one too. It was supposedly wearing some warrior or tank gear before, as it was still dressed in it. But the body inside the gear was much much smaller than the gear it was wearing. Was this what she'd look like if her character died? Would she decompose like that too? That was a strange thought, and a little creepy too.

She looked over the area, but didn't see any mobs around, or anything that would guide her as to what she had to do next. Neither did there seem to be any reason for these corpses to just be lying here…

Okay?

She opened her quest log, checking out the main quest.

Explore the area… Sort of, check?

Find out what happened? Well, they seem to be killed by something… What it was? She had no idea. But it didn't seem to be lurking around anymore, which was a relief.

The quest in her quest log didn't change or spark anything new, and she didn't feel like killing more birds just yet, the butchering still hadn't grown on her. So, instead of going back, she would rather just explore the area more, see if she could find any interesting clues at all. She walked to the edge of the area, sticking close to the treeline on the right side, and followed the edge, letting her eyes go over everything, hoping something would stand out.

Then, as she passed a densely grown area, Iris let out a low growl. There were mobs nearby, but Willow didn't see any.

She took a couple more steps, but Iris growled again, louder this time. There had to be something nearby. There was no other explanation. She pushed at some of the leaves and found herself looking at rock behind it.

A rock formation?

She walked further on, one hand on the rock as she followed it and an %Elementbolt in her other, in case she needed it.

The rock fell away sharply and Willow walked around a small row of trees, trying to get to the other side, as she rounded the corner, she found herself standing in front of an entrance to a cave.

She couldn't see far into it, the cave was very dark, but she could hear things move around inside and Iris kept making that low growling sound. Mobs, there were mobs in that cave, somewhere.

Willow took another step forward, trying to see inside. Was this what the game wanted her to find? Were those NPCs supposedly killed by the creatures in this cave?

Likely. Right?

She slowly crept into the cave, trying to stay as quiet as possible, ready to attack whatever she'd encounter. The sounds at the start of the cave were odd, she couldn't figure out exactly what they were, just general 'creatures live here' sounds. But she kept going.

As she went further into the cave, the darkness around her disorienting, the sounds grew and after a good couple of minutes, the area started to become lighter again. She could see some torches high on the walls of the cave, giving off just enough light that she could see things again. And as the light grew, the sounds did too. There were what looked like voices, things moving around, smaller and bigger things.

Willow rounded a corner, and suddenly there was a wall in front of her. A beam of light came from a square hole in the wall and there were torches near what looked like a door. It wasn't just any sized door, it was more than six times her size, it was huge. Which fit with the cave, as it was only a third of the height of this part of the cave.

She motioned for Iris to stay where she was, Willow didn't want her to get hurt, or get aggro from one of the creatures inside.

Then she climbed the rocks in front of what could be explained as a window of some sorts. It took her a while, there weren't many places where she could hold onto, but then she was able to look inside.

She almost let out a squeak. In the room were trolls. Huge ones. Big huge ones. They were talking to each other, seemingly just doing their thing. It almost looked like a living room or something. There were chairs and tables, and one of the trolls was standing at what could be considered a stove, probably. It was a homely scene. Two trolls making dinner, like it was the most normal thing in the world. Which, to be fair, it was, to them.

Then her eyes fell on something on the table, a brightly coloured pile of something. As she looked at it better she realised that it was a pile of meat of some sort. Meat wrapped in the same cloth as what the soldiers outside were wearing. Her stomach rolled. This wasn't just any meat, this was people meat. These trolls were eating people.

Well, there was the answer to that question, the trolls definitely killed those NPCs outside.

She focused on one of the trolls, trying to find its level, but that didn't turn out as useful as she'd hoped.

Mountain Troll

But where normally there would be the HP, Mana and level of it, there wasn't anything. The HP and mana bars were greyed out and where it normally showed the level there was a skull instead.

So, nothing there. But she also definitely didn't want the trolls to come after her. Not now, maybe not ever.

Willow slowly slid down the wall, carefully walking away again, out of the cave, making Iris follow her.

Well, that was one quest around here done, probably. Now she just had to get back to the captain to tell him that he really should watch out that he didn't send any of his men to a place where trolls lived again. It wasn't good for numbers or morale and trolls didn't like intruders.

They would quite literally eat the intruders so that they couldn't do it again. A pretty harsh punishment, she thought, but it was what it was.

As she was leaving the cave, a flicker pulled her attention. There was something to the side of the cave, something that would give some light from time to time. Blinking, flickering.

She went over to it, not sure what to expect. But as she got near, fear gripped her. This was a worse feeling than seeing the dead NPCs outside or the trolls further down the cave. Much, much worse.

In the darkness of the cave, she could barely distinguish a black shape, but what she could see was something she'd only seen on video before now. A black blob with pieces of white code running through it from time to time.

A blitzed account. Right here in HF! Right in the middle of the starter area.

She didn't know if this person hadn't been targeted until later for some reason or if people hadn't seen it because they were too busy with the rest of the game around them and didn't pay enough attention to things like this. But it was right there in front of her.

Willow took the potato out of her inventory and selected the X-ray Vision setting. A screen popped up and she directed it to the black blob.

First, she saw the outlines of how the area was shaped. The places where structures were strung together. Where 3D modelling bones were covered in textures and things like that, the first layer. And in that layer, she couldn't even see the blob, even though she could see it with her own eyes in front of her.

Then she focused on the blob more, hitting the zoom button, and now she saw the code behind the outside architecture.

While the rest of the code was static, which made sense, since this was just a cave, walls weren't supposed to move, the area of the blob and around it were moving. Rows of code recalling the stats of the player, the race, the class, everything about it, but it wasn't the way it was supposed to be. Character code was supposed to be fairly static, a standardised way to represent it so that the program could easily read it, this code was moving over itself, like snakes coiling in a pile. The pieces of code kept moving and moving, not stopping, like it was on some loop that it couldn't break out of, like there was supposed to be something keeping them together. It was like unravelled fabric, there was supposed to be structure, but it was now gone, the treads in a heap on the floor.

It seemed like the structure of the code had been compromised. Like the thing that was supposed to keep it together, the backbone, the main thread, was ripped out of it.

She reached out, her own hand now visible in the view too. Her own code moving, but only slowly as it was needed for her movements and reaction to the world around her.

When she came close to the blob, her own code started moving faster too and she could feel a pressure stopping her from touching the blob, even though she hadn't been that close to it. Strange.

She pulled her hand back, taking a couple of steps away.

She'd found a blitzed account, right here in HF, and it wasn't hidden inside some instance, it was here, right out in the open, sort of.

She knew this was good news and bad news at the same time. Good news because she'd found the first proof of a blitzed account inside HF. Bad news in that there were still people getting blitzed in HF and making it out of the starter instance didn't mean that a player was safe.

How was she going to show this to Soleil? How was she going to give her this evidence? There was no way to record in this game, that option had been turned off.

Although... was it really?

A normal player couldn't record because the creators of HF wanted to keep the game a secret, but there had to be some option for mods and other people running this game, right? Or they wouldn't be able to actually *see* how things were working and what bugs there were. They had to be able to record video evidence of bugs, right?

She looked through the other options that the potato gave her, but couldn't find much. Plus, if she put this on the bugs list or whatever, she probably wouldn't be able to get to the recording herself anymore, since she couldn't get to that outside of the game.

Great... Now what?

How was she going to show the broken code to Soleil so

that they could look at it and figure out what made a blitzed account look like that?

Willow had to get out of the game, but then what would happen? If she logged out here, would she respawn in the middle of a special 'trolls coming out of their cave' event or something?

No good.

She had to get back to a safe zone before she logged out, she didn't want to take any chances.

She could find this place again when she logged back in, she knew where it was, so that was enough. But for now, she had to get back to the encampment before she logged out.

Just to be safe.

Because even though there wasn't really a heartbeat in her character, she could feel her own heart beating way too fast from fear.

This was scary, way too scary!

17

Contact with the Civilized World

Willow gasped as she pulled the VR headset off, trying to collect her thoughts. She'd just found a blitzed player in HF and she'd seen the way that the code was broken.

She now also knew what the black 'blobs' were, the broken inside of characters but with all the textures stripped away from their structure and the code that could be seen running through was actually character-based code but without any account-based information on it. Anything that would normally keep the character up, like the actual polygons inside the mesh, were somehow affected and now the mesh had dissolved into a puddle on the ground. The link between the character someone had played and the account they were playing it on had been severed somehow. This wasn't just a glitch, the blobs weren't glitches, this was something much more sophisticated.

But the fact that she'd seen it at all, it could mean that the creators of HF didn't know that it existed or that they simply hadn't gotten to cleaning it up yet, as most of the other games did after they'd become aware of the blitzed blobs.

She opened the chat with Soleil.

Willow: I found a blitzed account in HF.

Her heart was still beating way too fast, drowning out the sounds around her and she kept fiddling her fingers over another, to keep her hands moving, to get some of this nervous energy out. She waited impatiently for Soleil to respond, but when it took more than a couple of seconds, she stood up, walking around her bedroom.

Willow looked through her desk, which she never used because she was much more comfortable sitting on the couch when she was doing whatever, and found an old notebook and some pens in a drawer. She'd put them in there when she moved into this place but hadn't seen the need to pick them up again. They could be useful now, at least to keep her hands and her brain busy.

Willow began drawing what she'd seen in HF on the paper. The broad lines making up the framework of the terrain, of the rocks, and then the way the blitzed account's code was sort of slithering right next to it, the contrast between the two stark.

After a couple of minutes, she leaned back and looked at her drawing. It looked nothing like what she'd seen in the game, but at least it made sense to her. Her drawing skills weren't that good, and she'd given up on trying a long time ago, but it was good enough as a visual representation to make sure she'd remember things later. And that should be good enough for explaining things to Soleil, she didn't need a real and detailed drawing for that.

A new message popped up in the chat.

Rotnem: Really? Where?
Willow: Some cave in the starter zone, around the level
    five or six area.
Rotnem: Are you sure it's a blitzed account?
Willow: Yes. I've seen it, it was easy enough to
    recognise.
Rotnem: Wow. I hadn't expected an account to show up
    there. Not so early in the game anyway.
Rotnem: Do you have an idea of the code behind it or
    something? Something we can work with?
Willow: Just a sketch of what it looks like, but nothing
    too useful.

Yeah, no. That sketch wouldn't be useful for anyone but Willow, they wouldn't be able to get anything from it that would be real usable data.

Willow: It mostly looked like there was structure
    missing from the code.
Rotnem: Structure?
Willow: Yeah, like it just fell apart right there, nothing
    holding it up anymore, no skeleton.
Rotnem: Okay. Interesting.
Rotnem: Seems to be the same as the other games
    then.
Rotnem: Any idea who it is?

Willow tried to think back, but while she could see the code for the player's race and class and stats in her mind, there wasn't any other identifying information in it.

Willow: No clue.
Willow: Unless we can find out who it is based on class,
    race and level? Maybe last location?

Most games would have databases of that type of information, and if Soleil had someone on the inside, they could probably look at it. Right?

Willow: Your source inside the game, would they be
    able to find the person if I gave them the info?

That way they could directly link a player to the blitzed account, hopefully. Even if the rest of the data was now corrupted, they could go back into earlier versions of the database to find out, right? That's why backups exist. That's why games often backed up information, so that if something went wrong, it wouldn't mean that someone had to start over from scratch.

> **Rotnem:** Probably. I'm just not sure...
> **Willow:** Why not?
> **Rotnem:** My source may not want to expose
>   themselves like that.
> **Willow:** But they could help. They could help us figure
>   out who this player is. They could help us save
>   other people from getting blitzed.
> **Willow:** They don't want that?

Why was this so hard to understand? Why was this so hard to get through to people?

> **Rotnem:** It's not just about that.
> **Rotnem:** I've asked for that information about blitzed
>   accounts from other games too. It was no use. The
>   accounts were gone.
> **Rotnem:** All the data from those accounts was gone. All
>   of it. Going back to the start of the character
>   someone played.
> **Willow:** How? That makes no sense. Backups should
>   still hold that information.

How was that possible? That's why backups existed. That was their sole purpose, keep information from getting totally lost after a glitch, or in this case a blitz.

> **Rotnem:** They probably could have, or should have.
> **Rotnem:** And in normal cases of blitzing they would
>   have. But this blitzing is different. It seems to
>   corrupt a whole account, and as soon as the game

database does a backup, the data on that backup
also gets corrupted, going back and back.
Rotnem: Normally, in cases of blitzing, as long as
people can get their BASE account unscrambled
and get it connected back to their personal ID, they
should be able to just keep going as before. But
this blitzing is different, it introduces a bug or
something into the system that is really persistent
in destroying all the account data, even in backup
servers.
Willow: Why hasn't anyone stopped it from happening?

A blitz introducing a bug which would wipe out all she'd
ever done? She couldn't even imagine something like that. That
was, too severe.

Rotnem: I only found out about this blitzing being
different this morning. I'm sorry.
Rotnem: It's not easy to get access to data like that, to
get people to help you when they think you're just
some freak with too much of an imagination.
Rotnem: So I hadn't realised the backwards corrupting
thing until I got someone to finally help me this
morning.

Willow sighed as she sat down on her bed, her head
spinning.

Willow: So we need a freshly blitzed account, find out
their character details and then get a copy of the
backup data before the game makes another
backup and can corrupt the whole system. All so
we could maybe find out what BASE account the
character belong too?
Rotnem: Yeah. That would be the most desirable thing
to happen now.

Well, that was a plan, at least part of a plan.

Willow: I think I can make that happen, but we're going
to have to trust some other people.
Rotnem: Your friends?

Willow: Yeah. My guild.
Willow: They can keep an eye on things in DoE. They
        can get to any place in the game that they may
        need to get to in moments. If they can get you or
        someone else to a recently blitzed account to grab
        the character data, would that work?

She crossed her fingers, hoping that Soleil would accept her plan because she had no other ideas on how to get to that information otherwise at least not without having to be in a hundred places at the same time herself.

Rotnem: They can't know about what we're doing.
Willow: They won't have to, they only have to know to
        look out for a blitz and to contact someone when
        they find one. That's all.

Soleil was quiet for a while and Willow bit on the inside of her lip as she waited, nervous.

Rotnem: Okay. Do it.
Rotnem: It's the best we've got.

It really was. If the blitz also backwardly corrupted data, then they had to get to the data before it could get damaged and that wasn't an easy task. Systems hadn't been designed for this type of corruption, obviously.

It had to work. If they could find people after they were blitzed and could still contact them without the need for BASE, then they could help those people. It was only partially preventive, but it was help, that was the most important part.

If they could find blitzed players they could help them and find out what the connection between all these accounts was.

Sage, Juniper and Opal didn't ask any questions about why they were doing what Willow asked them to do and didn't ask her to explain more. They all knew that she couldn't tell, but also that whatever they were doing, it would help them get closer to finding Violet, and prevent more people from getting blitzed, and that was the most important thing, really.

Willow thought about going into DoE for a while, play a game she actually knew she enjoyed and which she could play comfortably. But instead, she went back into HF. It wasn't just her friends who could find a blitzed account. If she kept playing and got into areas with more people who were also playing the game, she'd also be able to record data from any blitzed accounts she may run into herself. And in the meantime, maybe she could find out information from other players about the people who went missing as soon as they logged onto HF, see if they knew more.

It was a long shot, but now that she'd found one blitzed account, she knew that it was possible for people to get blitzed later in HF. And that meant that she could potentially find more blitzed accounts later on in the game too. Finding people and hoping to be able to do good was a much bigger drive for Willow right now than playing something comfortable.

If they could identify the people who got blitzed, if they could find them in the real world, they could figure out why those people were getting blitzed. If they could talk to those players, they could ask them what happened, they could ask them what was going on. And that was information that they desperately needed. If they could find out the 'why' they could prevent this from going on any longer. Hopefully.

After she'd handed her quest in with the 'main captain', telling him it was trolls who'd probably killed those NPCs, she got a new quest from him to go and report to a different captain in a new place. Probably the next town that she could play in, which meant that there was a bigger chance of actually running into players, unlike in this small corner of the game. She'd not been that far behind the beta player batch, so she should be able to catch up with some of them in a next town.

Before she left the area around the encampment, she killed the final three goshawks and finished all the other small quests, she hated leaving quests unfinished. *Hated it.*

Just as she handed in the last of the quests, she gained another level.

+100 XP
You've reached level 9!
+4 Strength
+1 Dexterity
+6 Intelligence
+4 Wisdom
+3 Endurance
Iris has reached level 9!
+6 Strength
+4 Intelligence
+6 Toughness

This game was really pretty slow when it came to levelling. The XP she got from kills or as quest rewards were low but the XP needed to get to the next level was also quite high. Both of which didn't help. It slowed the game down significantly when you had to do so much work in the same small zones before you could move on.

But after all the killing and questing, she was finally able to get to the next area, to the first real village or city or whatever it was.

Willow quickly sold off the useless items which were only taking up inventory space at the general supplies seller, and then walked to the gate of the encampment. There, she looked back one last time, looking at the town-ish she'd been in for way too much time. And she was pretty glad to actually be out of here, it was depression how much she wanted to get to the next area.

She started walking down the road, Iris following her, past the wolves and the forest where she had been to collect herbs and skin some rabbits, then she crossed a small bridge. This was where the previous area ended, but as she stepped over it, the map around her filled up with new things.

To her left, she saw more wolves, though, these looked a quite a bit more dangerous, and bigger, than the previous ones.

Rabid Wolf
HP: 453
Mana: 168
Level: 14

They were a few levels above her, and she didn't want to find out what 'rabid' implied in this game. With the cruel sense of humour of HF, it could just as easily mean that a bite from those wolves really gave you rabies in this game, even for a short amount of time, or it would just put an annoying bleed debuff for 10 seconds, or just nothing at all. Not anything she was keen on testing.

The right side of the path was mostly empty fields, though she did see something in the distance, probably more mobs to fight.

She kept following the road, trusting that it would get her to the city she had to get to. The area around her changed some, a thick forest now on her left side and on her right side she could see a lake. A huge frozen lake.

Willow stopped, looking over the surface of it. It was beautiful. Most of the lake was frozen over, especially around the edges and it reflected the light, creating a rainbow of beautiful colours everywhere. It was so amazing to see.

She could barely believe it. For a game that seemed to enjoy death and torture so much, they would also put in something so stunningly beautiful.

Then, as she followed the edge of the lake with her eyes, she could see a city in the distance. It was going to be quite a walk, but instead of following the road, which seemed to go through some mountains next, she stepped off the path and went down to the lake.

She could walk over the edge of the lake, it would probably be faster than taking the road since it was more of a straight line, but it would definitely be more beautiful than the inside of caves.

When her feet hit the ice, she could feel how slippery it was under her 'shoes'. She grinned, this was great.

Willow pushed off and then slid over the ice, trying to stay up straight and not fall flat on her face. Next to her, Iris didn't seem to have as much trouble staying up, she just put her claws into the ice to get a better grip.

At the very edge of the lake, she could see the plants trapped under the clear ice. She could see the mud and the plants growing under it. The ice had frozen all the way to the bottom, not leaving any water.

But as she got away from the edge, she could see the bottom fall away and the layer of water grow, and with it came moving plants under the ice. She kept going, the bottom of the lake no longer visible, the water under the ice now a black hole with nothing in it. It was even too far away for plants to get close enough to the surface to be visible.

She stopped, not sure if she should keep going... She didn't like it when she couldn't see what was happening beneath her and she started to get a bad feeling about this.

Games tended to put creepy things in lakes, really creepy things with big jaws and sharp teeth that she didn't really feel like encountering right now. Especially not since she was in a higher level zone and she had no idea if she would even be able to fight off whatever could find her.

Willow carefully slid back towards the edge of the lake in the direction of the city. She wasn't going to tempt fate here. Sure, Iris would warn her if she was getting close to a mob, no matter the size or level difference, but she didn't feel like escaping from a big evil creature on this ice and slipping away and then... Yeah, that was not an image she liked.

As she got closer to the city, she could see people moving around it. She wasn't sure if they were NPCs or players, both would make just as much sense.

But she felt excited and scared at the prospect of both of those. She was so done with being the only player in the area, but she also didn't really feel like meeting new people... Especially players who were going to be all loud and over excited and everything, as tended to happen with new games.

She wanted there to be more players around, so she didn't feel so alone, but she also didn't want to have to play with or talk to those other players...

Willow approached the city, conflict still going on inside her and she didn't know what she wanted or dreaded more.

She was going to have to find that out by actually getting

there.

Sooner, rather than later…

18

Strangers Among People

It became very clear to Willow as she climbed onto the docks that this wasn't the usual way for people to enter the city. Around her were NPCs carrying things from one location to another, some bartering for goods while yet others seemed to be simply hanging around. This dock was very busy even though the lake next to it was frozen over and there shouldn't be any ships that could reach it. Curious.

She looked up at the high stone walls of the city and then stepped through the large wooden gate in front of her. Wooden buildings were lining the street, in front of most of them were stalls with a variety of wares on display. She saw some NPCs selling potions and food items and a range of other things that people living in this world would need. Though, some stalls didn't seem to be interactable by players as she walked past them but some of the NPCs still stopped at them. Maybe they were just for show and for NPCs, or maybe for a future expansion.

She walked on through the street as the scent of fresh and not-so-fresh fish and other foods got stronger. This was definitely the trade district.

It took her a couple of moments before she realised that she was seeing other players between the NPCs. There was little distinction between players and NPCs, they both seemed to have name tags and the NPCs were pretty natural in their movements. It was mostly the more erratic behaviours of the players that tipped her off to the ones who weren't NPCs.

There was so much going on around her, it was hard to take it all in, but she tried anyway. The city was beautifully designed, the houses behind the stalls were each unique and had the feel of having been there for decades at least. NPCs were walking in and out of the houses and she could even catch glimpses of things going on inside them.

After almost ten minutes, she reached the end of the street and it opened up into a large and bright city square. She stopped straight in her tracks, unable to fully grasp what she was seeing.

The square was brightly coloured, from the pale stones on the ground to the colourful doors and shutters of the houses lining it and then the fabric on some of the stalls standing in the middle. It was all light and bright, something she definitely hadn't expected in this setting. This world had been mostly dark and moody until now, but it seemed there was a spot of brightness in it all, a spot where things didn't seem so bad after all.

Someone bumped into her back, and she stumbled a couple of steps forward. She turned around, glaring at whoever was stupid enough to not watch out, but she didn't get very far.

The guy who'd bumped into her wore a long black coat, his black hair up in spikes. He carried two long swords on his back and walked with the confidence or stupidity of a guy who wasn't afraid of anyone. On his arm was a girl with long red-blond hair and in a white and red outfit who was leaning into him, laughing, giggling, a small female elf-like creature was fluttering around them. Behind the couple were more girls, all just as beautiful and each one of them was grinning and laughing with the others. At the end two guys were trailing the group, one of them had one of those bandana things around his head, his light hair sticking up above it in spikes, like he was some kind of anime character or something. Had she just walked into a different game or something? Why were these people so… shiny?

Willow looked after the group, too stunned to even call them out. How did people look this happy in a game that made people disappear? She couldn't understand it. But, of course, apart from her, not a lot of people knew about the players going missing anyway, or weren't taking it seriously, and she had to keep it that way for a while longer, sadly enough.

She didn't know how to react now. She hated people bumping into her and everything, but she also never really knew what to say when it happened. It was like the words popped up in her head, but never left her mouth. Sometimes the right words wouldn't even come until hours later, and she always felt so stupid for not speaking out sooner. She knew the words. She could talk. So why did the words never come out when she needed them? Other people never seemed to have that issue. Which made everything even more frustrating, especially when people would look at her oddly for not responding or for 'suddenly' coming up with a response to something that happened hours before. She hated it. She hated all of that, she hated the way her brain wouldn't let her react fast when it was needed.

Willow stepped into the square, getting out of the way of the other people behind her. It wasn't like she was small or anything, definitely not as a draugr, she could easily look over almost any players or NPCs around, but it still seemed that people were just so focused on other things that they still ran into her, or into other people, probably.

Now, what was she actually supposed to do here?

She pulled up her quest log, her eyes going over the single quest on it. Of course, find a captain, again...

Since she had no idea about the layout of this city and she'd gotten in through the wrong entrance, she should probably try to find the big entrance gate or whatever that road had connected to before first.

She'd probably have a better time finding clues there, or at least get a better idea about where everything was if she started at the 'right' side of this apparently vast city.

Willow looked at the 'letter' in her hand. She was supposed to bring it to some higher up person in this city, only she couldn't read the words on the scroll. The game used its own script and language, supposedly, so of course it made sense that she couldn't read it. But letting her eyes flit over the sentences, she wasn't even sure if they'd really created a language for it or had just put some lorum ipsum into a strange font.

She wasn't entirely sure why it bugged her, but it just

212

seemed lazy for some reason. Really, it didn't even matter if there were real words and sentences on it, it could just as well be all bogus.

As she walked through the streets, amazed at every new detail she discovered in the design of the buildings and the other elements, she received a message in the chat. A chat which had previously been very empty…

> **Dawn:** *You have a dragon fylgja?*
> **Meadow:** *Yeah. Why?*
> **Dawn:** *Those are super rare. I think there is only... one other player with one and he's one of the few almost max level players here.*
> **Meadow:** *Really? Being max level is odd?*

Max level characters happened all the time while a game was still running in earlier versions, how else were they supposed to test it? And with such a long 'beta' period as HF was running, she was expecting there to be at least a good number of them before the game went live, hadn't that been the purpose of it?

> **Dawn:** *Have you even paid attention? Nobody in beta has reached max level yet. There are only a handful who are getting close.*

Well, it wasn't like she'd been here long anyway, and this was her first time seeing other players, or interacting with them, but Dawn didn't need to know that.

> **Meadow:** *Oh. Okay.*
> **Dawn:** *Turn around.*

She stopped, not sure she should, but this player already knew who she was, since they talked to her about Iris and it wasn't like they could do anything really. There was no PvP allowed in the city, that had been very clear with messages all over the place.

Willow turned, looking through the street she'd been walking, at the other characters scuffling on around her, and then spotted an elven guy waving at her.

Dawn: *Hello.*
Meadow: *Hi.*

She waved back at him. She couldn't immediately spot his class, they looked like robes, but some of it also looked like leather. He probably wasn't a warrior type class since he wasn't wearing thick armour or something like that. But anything more than not-warrior she couldn't figure out since she didn't have enough experience to recognise all the other types of armour in this game on sight.

Dawn: *You're pretty low level for someone who joined in the last batch of players.*

That was because she hadn't...

Meadow: *Just been playing slowly, haven't had much time.*
Dawn: *Ah. Yeah. Most players here have a lot of time to dedicate to it. Some are thinking that's how they choose who to let join. But maybe not.*

Dawn came over to her, looking her up and down.

Dawn: *Beginner player, and low on cash, I bet?*

Willow shrugged.

Meadow: *Why?*
Dawn: *Most people buy costume gear to cover up the fact they're low-level players. But it's expensive and you can only use it on one piece of gear, so it gets costly when you're still swapping out gear for something better every couple of levels.*
Meadow: *Just not interested.*

She had been, previously, but now she wasn't anymore. So she would be able to buy better-looking gear, but unless she bought it with real world credits, it probably would still look like crap. That's how these things worked. Thanks, micro-payments...

> ***Dawn:*** *Hardcore.*
> ***Meadow:*** *Why do you only talk in chat?*

Most people would just talk to her with voice chat as soon as they came within talking range, and most people expected her to just prefer to talk verbally anyway, not just typing in the chat.

> ***Dawn:*** *Ah... I'm ehh... I'm deaf, so this is easier.*

He moved his hands a little as he watched what her response would be, like he was used to signing and didn't exactly know how to keep them calm while his brain was coming up with more words to type. Willow felt a little uncomfortable, not knowing how to respond to that new knowledge, usually people didn't offer knowledge like this so easily, usually she'd had to ask more than just about his preference for typed chat. Would she have to offer her own autism in return?

But Dawn apparently didn't wait for an answer as he kept talking.

> ***Dawn:*** *I know that they've made all these great*
> *advancements to make me able to hear in the VR*
> *worlds, and I can, but it's still strange. I don't like it.*
> *I prefer text chat.*
> ***Meadow:*** *Me too. I like chat better.*

Dawn looked at her as he smiled.

> ***Dawn:*** *So, where were you going?*

Willow held up the letter.

> ***Meadow:*** *Handing stuff in.*
> ***Dawn:*** *Want me to join you?*

Meadow: Why?
Dawn: Because you have a cool dragon, play a race not a
lot of people play and seem in need of someone
who knows more about this game than you do? You
seem cool, you may need help? Or friends?

The guy had a point.

Meadow: Fine. What class do you play?

Dawn let out a laugh, though, she couldn't hear much, with the low settings and all. She couldn't imagine not hearing at all. She may always like to turn the volume low, but not hearing things at all... that had to be a totally different experience.

Dawn: Same as you, seidhr.
Meadow: Really? Aren't you supposed to have a pet? Or
fylgja, or whatever?

Dawn laughed again, his eyes twinkling.

Dawn: You're just not seeing her.

He held up his hand and a small bird flew down, perching on his finger. Willow may not know much, but she recognised this bird, it was a bullfinch, a songbird, and Dawn had named her Aya. And the irony of it didn't escape her. Only, the colours of its feathers were a beautiful rainbow instead of the normal red, and it looked at her with interest.

As Dawn lowered his hand, it flew up again, staying a little above them.

Meadow: It has an attack?

Because that thing was tiny, she couldn't imagine it harming anyone.

Dawn nodded.

Dawn: It does something with sounds waves. Makes me
a little glad I'm deaf and can't hear it.
Meadow: Cool.

That at least was a little original in this game. Willow checked Dawn's stats, trying to get an idea of who she was talking to.

Name: Dawn
Race: Elf
Class: Seidhr
Level: 29
Health: 622/622
Mana: 620/620
Armour: 66
Strength: 48
Dexterity: 127
Intelligence: 180
Wisdom: 136
Endurance: 110

Wow. More than twenty levels above her... Yeah, that would be hard to catch up to any time soon, but having someone at her side who was more experienced in the game than her would help.

Meadow: Does this game allow for power levelling, the old-school way?

Power levelling was usually when one or more higher levelled players helped a lower level player to quickly progress in the game. Some games these days didn't make it profitable to do this by making sure there were no advantages to the higher level players, or even make sure they were actively annoyed by the game mechanics so that they would stop. Those games believed that power levelling broke the 'natural' progression of a game. Other games actually encouraged it with things like mentor options, where both the higher and lower level players would get bonuses by playing together, or with special items you could buy with real world credits which would boost the level progression of the lower level player even more.

Willow didn't want to have to use actual money to buy things, especially since she wasn't so sure that doing that may not actually trigger something bad because she wasn't supposed to have a beta code. Not bringing more attention to her account would be the safest option.

> **Dawn:** *Yeah. Are you into that? I'm mostly a healer, so levelling on my own has been slow, but if you're an offensive player, we could make it work.*
> **Meadow:** *Do I unlock healer abilities later on in the game?*

She hadn't seen any of those yet. Eight levels into this game and she was still stuck with the first two attacks that she'd got...

> **Dawn:** *You don't have any new attacks yet?*
> **Meadow:** *No.*

It wasn't supposed to be like this, right? Dawn's reaction kind of clued her in on that. Was she supposed to have more attacks already? When was she supposed to unlock those? Or where?

> **Dawn:** *I'll help.*
> **Dawn:** *Did you not listen to any of the chat going on when you first logged on? Did you ignore it all?*

There hadn't been other players when she logged in...

> **Meadow:** *Not really.*
> **Dawn:** *Okay. You need to unlock new attacks and spells and things by actually doing them. There are a range of things you can unlock at certain levels. Some of us have kind of put together a list of possibilities, but most of them are pretty basic.*

Dawn: *After you've finished bringing that silly letter over to our big leader, we can go to one of the nearby areas and try out some stuff. Maybe even pick up some quests along the way.*
Dawn: *Good idea?*
Meadow: *Sure.*

With the lack of an actual guide website or something else on the net, having a player around who knew a lot of things was second best.

Maybe it would help her feel a little less lost if she knew what was going on, instead of just walking around doing whatever seemed right.

She missed her friends, but making a new friend in HF was probably a good idea too, especially if she was going to stay here for the unforeseeable future. She didn't see another way to find out what was going on here without figuring out what this game was about, what the creators were after.

She had to keep playing, and having someone near her who knew things about the game was going to be useful. And less lonely.

19
Elements of Surprise

Willow eyed the mobs and players around her, this was a new area of the game, the environment was also a little different.

Though, since Dawn had taken her back to the main gate and then they'd just taken the road right outside, she expected that if she had gotten here the 'normal' way she'd probably have seen this place before.

There was still snow on the ground everywhere, like in the previous zone but it wasn't as dense and the trees were also less snow-y and more leaf-y. The mobs that were running around here were lynxes, their descriptions read 'Hungry Lynx', which wasn't exactly creative but definitely got the job done.

> **Dawn:** There is an area with fewer players but enough mobs to try a few things out not far from here. We could go there to practice?
>
> **Meadow:** Sure.

There were quite a lot of other players around here, especially in comparison to how many she'd seen in the actual zones before. They were all killing the lynxes for as far as she could see and she didn't really want to fight the other players over a couple of mobs just to learn how to unlock more spells for her class. Because she was pretty sure that there was no limitation on PVP in this area.

Dawn started walking again, staying close to the edge of the woods on the right side, not going in, although that had probably more to do with the limitations of the game from what she could see on her map. As the woods suddenly fell away, they walked into a clearing with a handful of lynxes, but no other players. It looked kind of perfect to try and kill a few things on your own without being interrupted by other players.

> **Dawn:** A side quest leads you here, but not many people
> will bother with it, so it should give us some space
> to practice. How far to level 10 are you?

Willow eyed the XP tree at the bottom of her view.

> **Meadow:** About 15% left?
> **Dawn:** Good, you unlock an extra skill at level 10
> anyway, so you should have about 7 skills soon.
> **Meadow:** 7? Seven?

She had two skills right now. Going from two to seven... *Wow.*

> **Dawn:** Yeah.

He smiled at her, eyeing the lynxes.

> **Dawn:** Can you kill one of them? I'll explain how to gain
> new skills after that.
> **Meadow:** Sure.

> **Hungry Lynx**
> HP: 392/392
> Mana: 153/153
> Level: 11

It was a little stronger than she was used to, but Dawn was a healer, so he should be able to save her, if needed.

She focused on the lynx, targeting it.

'Go!' She thought the command to Iris, who ran towards the lynx and attacked it first, a large cone of fire going out in front of her.

Iris hit the Hungry Lynx for 120 damage

Willow turned her wrist, pulling up her elemental attack as the lynx now focused on Iris, keeping Willow safe from its attacks. As soon as it felt right, she let the bolt go, throwing it at the lynx.

You hit the Hungry Lynx for 70 damage
The Hungry Lynx hit Iris for 67 damage

Iris was charging up for another attack, she could see it.

Willow pulled up another bolt, waiting for the right moment to let it go.

You hit the Hungry Lynx for 64 damage
The Hungry Lynx hit Iris for 70 damage
You hit the Hungry Lynx for 75 damage
Iris hit the Hungry Lynx for 143 damage

The lynx let out a devastating cry and crumbled to the ground, curling up as it died.

+267 XP

She went over to the lynx, taking out her butchering knife and leaned over the creature, pushing the knife into the belly of the lynx and butchering it.

You loot Lynx Pelt
You loot Wild Meat
You loot Leftover Animal Pieces
+20 XP Butchering

She shuddered as she stood up, still icky, then she looked at Dawn who was staring at her, his eyes big.

Meadow: And?

She could see some emotions play over Dawn's face before he replied.

Dawn: I've never seen a player like you before. It's...

That didn't sound so good. She shouldn't have done this. She was obviously not following the rules of this game and now someone found out that she was different. This never ended well.

> **Dawn:** This is cool. I didn't realise that you could even do magic without a staff or other weapon in your hand.
> **Dawn:** And that attack... You said you didn't have more than two attacks... But I've not seen that one before. What is it?

Sort of yay, for not getting reported to the game developers for doing something strange?

> **Meadow:** It's what showed up when I did the tutorial. I just went through the steps like I was supposed to as far as I know.
> **Dawn:** Yeah, you were supposed to do the tutorial, yes. Just, as far as I know, you can do fire or ice, not... What is it even?
> **Meadow:** I have no idea, it shows as %Element.
> **Dawn:** Impressive. Must be something that people haven't figured out yet. Cool.

He nodded, then stepped past her.

> **Dawn:** I'm mostly a healer, but these are my attacks.

He took his staff from his belt and pointed it at one of the lynxes, then he shot a ball of ice from it.

Dawn hit the Hungry Lynx for 248 damage

The attack took over two-thirds of the HP of the lynx in a single blow. Then he lifted the staff and flung it down and a cone of ice appeared over the lynx, falling down on top of it.

Dawn hit the Hungry Lynx for 324 damage

The lynx died, but Dawn didn't go over to it.

+67 XP

Meadow: You don't butcher them?

Dawn pulled a face, shaking his head.

Dawn: As soon as quests no longer required it, I
    stopped. Just... ick. No.

Willow shrugged. She didn't like it either, but it felt like such a waste to leave a perfectly good source of income right there, not doing anything with it, especially when the items from butchering seemed pretty useful.

Meadow: Right. Yeah...

It was of course a possibility... Just not one that had ever occurred to her as she'd been playing the game.

Dawn: I'll show you how to put stuff on the auction
    house, that way you can make quick money with
    those skins and the meat. Not a lot of people have
    the guts to keep butchering to a high-level skill,
    most people stay to mining and herbalism for out
    in the wild skills, they're less... gruesome.
Meadow: Thanks.

Yeah, she would probably enjoy it better if she could sell the items off at a good price. Like in DoE, the money she made here she could technically use in the real world, though she didn't want to chance transferring between the game and her BASE account just yet, just in case it would set off a bad alarm. But it would definitely be a good idea going forward, and the sooner she started saving up money the better.

Meadow: Now, how do I get more attacks?
Dawn: You should have a buff, a heal and two more
      attacks as your skills at this point. Usually, the
      attacks are either a cone, an AOE or a DOT.
Dawn: Mine were an AOE, the ice rock thing, and a DOT,
      I have a freeze attack, though I don't use it often,
      it's not the most useful for my style.

Right. So, she 'just' had to figure out what other attacks she could have? Figuring out the first one had been bad enough and she officially only had had a choice of two attacks back then.

Meadow: How do you know what to do?
Dawn: You kind of just do, I think? At first, I just kept
      waving the staff around, seeing if it made a
      difference.
Dawn: I did stumble into finding out that my buff is a
      speed up buff that way, which affects movement
      but also casting times and even cooldowns, so
      that was nice. But other than that, everyone just
      sort of does their own thing.
Meadow: Right.

This game was odd, really odd, and not really in a way she enjoyed... 'You sort of know' wasn't really a strategy that tended to work for her. She was a lot better when things were clear and had logical and distinct steps to go through.

Iris sat down next to Willow, leaning against her leg. She reached out to the little dragon, petting her on the head. How did someone do this without looking silly?

There was only one way, really...

She stepped forward, toward one of the other lynxes and held her hands out in front of her. A cone type of attack would probably make the most sense for a stance like this, right?

Dawn: You're not using your staff?

She took a deep breath. A cone type of attack required a focused energy in front of her hands and then pushing it out to the lynx. She took another breath, trying to connect to the sense of energy inside of her, like she figured out for her bolt, but while the energy inside her spiked a little, nothing happened. Maybe not a cone?

An AOE attack would be different, there were so many ways she could try to summon that. First, she needed to focus on the location she wanted the attack to take place. And maybe focus the energy there too? Like, instead of making it appear in her hands to shoot over to the monster, maybe somehow making the energy start there in the first place?

Somewhere in her head it made sense.

She envisioned the area of the attack and then, as she took a deep breath, she raised her arms from around her sides up, like she was lifting something, and suddenly the area she was visualising started to move under the lynx, bubbling almost and it went red hot, throwing up splatters of what looked like lava.

You hit the Hungry Lynx for 105 damage

Willow dropped her arms down, and the lava pool disappeared. The lynx wasn't dead, though, and it came running at her. But she suddenly couldn't remember how to do her normal attacks, too surprised by what just happened.

Did she really just create a lava pool? What the...?

As the lynx got really close to her, she pulled up her arms in front of her in defence, trying to protect herself, and instantly she was surrounded by a clear shield-like thing as Iris

226

roasted the lynx.

Willow came to her senses enough to shoot off one of her own bolts.

The lynx fell down, curling up. She'd defeated it. Then she knelt down and butchered it, taking the items. Trying to do something that was sort of normal in this game before she thought about what just happened.

She'd just... created lava, and then the shield?

She turned to Dawn.

Meadow: Did you make that shield?

She could still see the buff that went with it on the side of her view, now slowly fading away as the effect wore off.

Dawn shook his head.

Dawn: No, that was all you. Cool buff too, handy if you suddenly get jumped or something.
Meadow: Yeah.

That was intense, and very surprising, but she didn't know if she liked finding attacks out this way. As she glanced to the bottom of her view, she could see two more boxes on the line filled.

Lava pool
Seidhr ability
You make the ground beneath their feet so hot
that it's trying to burn them alive.

Barrier

There were still two boxes empty in the middle of them. Dawn said that there was supposed to be another attack and then a heal or something.

She now had five skills on the bar, her racial attack, the elemental bolt, the ability to summon Iris, an empty slot, the lava pool attack, another empty slot and then a skill called barrier, which was probably the buff she'd just pulled up.

Now she just had to figure out the rest of them...

Willow stepped back as a large wolf jumped for her, pulling up her barrier, and then throwing a bolt at the wolf. She'd been playing with Dawn for the last hour or so, defeating creature after creature, levelling up a little faster than she would normally have been able to do.

They were now fighting level 14 monsters, even though she was only level 10, but with Dawn at her side, they were able to get through them pretty quickly.

About ten minutes ago, she'd found out her other attack skill. She'd tripped as she'd stumbled back trying to dodge one of the wolves and as she'd been waving her hands, trying to hold onto something, the wolf had gotten tangled in spooky vines, putting a bleed DOT on it. She'd still fallen on her ass, and it had hurt pretty badly, but at least she'd found the other attack. That had been something, for the bruised behind and ego.

She'd also realised why she'd never really figured out any of the extra attacks before. She'd been playing it pretty safe

228

when it came to how to fight monsters, only fighting the ones who were a little separate from the rest of the mobs and well within her level range, so there was never any reason to really push herself.

Now she was actively trying to find them, they came quite easily.

Dawn: You in for another zone up?

They were walking along a path to the next zone and Willow checked the time of the outside world.

Global time: '42 - 05 – 26 23:46

Local time: '42 - 05 - 27 00:46

System: Body stats on food and sleep are low

It was already past midnight and she'd obviously missed dinner today. Great...

Meadow: I've got to go, I need to sleep.

She'd been inside HF all day and no matter what, she needed to log off for a couple of hours so she could get some sleep.

Dawn: Oh, okay. See you tomorrow?
Meadow: Yeah. Sure. Sounds like a plan.

It wasn't like she had much else to do, and she still had to progress in this game, or at least find some way to get clue as to how she could help Soleil and Violet and the others...

Meadow: See you tomorrow.

You are now logged out of Helheim Fallen Online

She wasn't so worried about her location this time as they were standing in the road on a pretty safe spot, and as she took off her VR headset, she sighed. That had been one intense session, way too intense.

But she also wondered why the game hadn't told her the time yet, or that she was supposed to have dinner hours ago...

Something odd was going on, this hadn't happened before in the years since she'd had her BASE implant, it would always give her notifications, it hadn't not done it before...

What was up with that?

20

Under the Cover of Night

Willow walked over to her delivery box, wondering why her BASE notifications weren't getting through in HF, when she saw that one of the chats required her attention, the low red glow pulling her attention. She opened the chat as she took the box with her dinner from the delivery box and put it down on the table.

> **Sage:** Willow, where are you? Are you here?
> **Juniper:** Willow?
> **Sage:** Hey, where are you, Willow?

Her heart started beating faster. Was there something wrong?

> **Willow:** I'm here, what's going on?

She kept her eyes on the chat as she opened the dinner box and found some rice, curry and grilled vegetables. Not exciting, but the curries were usually pretty nice in flavour. So it wasn't too bad either.

> **Sage:** Where were you? You've been gone all day.

> **Willow:** Just playing a game. What's going on?
> **Sage:** You're okay?
> **Willow:** Yeah, I'm okay. Just tired and hungry.
> **Juniper:** Good.
> **Juniper:** You gave us a scare, you didn't reply and with
> Violet…

Willow nodded, though she knew they couldn't see it. She'd been playing HF all day while she'd asked her friends to look for blitzed accounts in DoE. She asked them to do such a scary task and then she went radio silent for hours on end. Of course they'd become worried.

> **Willow:** Sorry. Are you okay? Anything going on?
> **Juniper:** Not much. Been keeping an eye on the game
> and the forums but there isn't much chat about the
> thing.
> **Sage:** We finished the boat, though.

Now Willow really felt bad. The guild had needed her help with that, both her and Violet's, and she'd totally flunked out on them these last days.

> **Willow:** Sorry I didn't help more.
> **Juniper:** You've got more important things on your
> mind. We know. It's okay.
> **Sage:** Yeah, it's okay. We just wanted you to know, so
> you could come check it out any time.
> **Willow:** Thanks.

She was going to have to, she couldn't just dump this all on her friends. They'd been playing together for years, they'd worked so hard to get to the stage where they could do things like making guild boats. And now she was failing them, like she was failing Violet and Soleil.

She started eating, not sure what else to tell her friends. Not sure if she could explain anything. She'd been playing HF all day and was no step closer to figuring out what had happened to Violet or any of the other blitzed accounts, what was really going on in the game or why people went missing in the first place. She was no use, she really was no use to anyone. She was failing everyone.

A lump formed in her throat as she closed her eyes. Why did she think she could do this? She'd been enjoying herself today, playing with a new person in a new game, while her friends were waiting for her return. She was supposed to be focused on saving Violet and finding out what happened to her. But all she'd done was play videogames and enjoying herself...

This wasn't right. It really wasn't.

The side of her view started colouring green, shaking a little, signalling she got an incoming call. She switched her attention to it and 'Rotnem' came into view. Soleil? Why was she calling?

Willow picked up, her heart beating fast again. "Yes?"

"Willow." Soleil sounded off, though she couldn't exactly figure out how.

"Soleil?" What was going on?

"Yeah. Good. I was afraid you'd be asleep already. I just—" Her voice was rushed, but then she stopped.

"What's wrong?" Soleil knew not to call Willow unless it was really needed and Willow knew that Soleil also hated calling someone.

"Can we meet?"

"Now?" It was the middle of the night, that wasn't really a time to meet up normally.

"Yeah. I can get you out of there. Just... I think we need to meet up right now." There was something in Soleil's voice that

Willow really wanted to place, but the only thing she could think of was a combination of panic and determination.

Because of where she lived, and her age, Willow couldn't get out of the garden of the 'low sensory' building after ten in the evening. Not that she normally would want to, she'd barely been out of here during the day since she moved in, let alone in the evenings, that just wasn't her thing. But there were still systems in place that would prevent her from doing it.

"It's not just the getting out of here... My BASE notifications are going to complain about me staying up too late soon." And if it started to do that, it would notify the people in charge of this place and then they'd call her in for an examination and she'd get a talking to about taking better care of herself. It was a bother. It had happened before when she'd been ignoring the notifications a little too much while grinding a new raid with the guild. She didn't want to have to do that again.

"That's no problem either. You're talking to someone in charge of those notifications." There was almost something like entertainment in Soleil's voice. "I can override all of them. Don't worry. We just... We need to talk."

"Okay." It sounded urgent enough, and she knew that they couldn't openly talk about what they were doing while using the BASE system. "Where do you want to meet?"

"At the gate? And as soon as you can get dressed?"

"What?" Willow stood up, going over to one of the windows at the front of the building, but after she unlocked the regular window view, she couldn't see anyone at the gate.

"Don't try to look." It was like Soleil knew what she would do. "I'm not standing in view. Just, come over to the gate, yeah? I'll get us out of here."

"Okay. I'll be right down." She disconnected the call and then looked over to her dinner. She was still hungry... But maybe she should get dressed properly first, that was kind of more important here.

What was going on with Soleil? And why did Willow have a bad feeling about this? Why did she have a bad feeling about this meeting or trip or whatever Soleil was doing?

Willow carefully took another spoonful out of the bowl as she walked through the grounds surrounding her building. She'd figured that since the curry and rice had come in bowls and everything anyway, that she could just as easily take it as a to-go meal. Especially since it was cold by now.
She walked over to the gate, still not seeing anyone there.

Then someone stepped out of the shadows. Soleil! She waved Willow to come closer to the gate and Willow did so.

"Eating?" Soleil looked at the bowl in her hands.

"Accidentally skipped dinner." Willow shrugged. "How are you getting me out of here?"

"That's no problem." Soleil stepped closer to the console next to the gate and, after a couple of moments, it opened, and she came through it.

A memory popped up in Willow's head, something from earlier this week. "Hey, were you here at like four in the morning a couple of days back?"

"No." Soleil frowned. "Did you see someone?"

"Yeah." Willow shook her head, it had probably been nothing anyway. But there had been something strange about the person, like they had been purposefully looking for her there. "Yeah... Never mind. You were here for a reason, I presume?"

"Yep." Soleil sighed and held out a manual device towards Willow. "Going to change a few bits of code, just a moment."

Willow waited, still eating the curry. There wasn't much she could do otherwise anyway.

Then Soleil stepped back. "Okay, check your coded thingie. What do the notifications say?"

Coded thingie? One, Willow made that piece of code years ago, it was handy. Two, Soleil wasn't technically supposed to know about it, was she? Willow frowned at Soleil, but then pulled up her time and notification app.

Global time: '42 - 05 - 27 00:16

Local time: '42 - 05 - 27 01:16

System: All Good

"All good?" Willow raised an eyebrow at Soleil. She'd never seen that notification before. Although, maybe that was because she was always getting nagged about something by the system…

Soleil flashed her a grin. "It works, that's all that counts." Then she shrugged. "But we need to get going now. There's somewhere we need to be."

"Okay. You want to tell me what or where?" Not that it would probably stop her from following Soleil, but some clue would be nice. Especially since Soleil was dragging her out into the night even though Willow should be going to bed instead.

"Not really." Soleil's eyes went up to the cameras at the gate and Willow knew that whatever it was, it had something to

236

do with the stuff they were working on. Somehow taking her out of the building in the middle of the night was okay, but discussing whatever was on Soleil's mind wasn't? That was strange.

"Okay. Lead the way." Willow shrugged.

"Good." Soleil nodded, and started walking out the gate.

Willow followed her, wondering for a moment if she was going to be stopped or would get any annoying notifications to stop, but everything in the BASE system stayed quiet.

They walked down the road, which was totally deserted, nobody walking around, not even those automated delivery systems were rushing from here to there like they would do during the day. It was strange, seeing the city quiet like this, asleep. Even the commercials and other things that would normally visually scream at her with the best new things she should be buying were now dimmed or off. It was like people had stopped existing, like they'd been wiped out. Then Soleil stopped at a small self-driving car.

"This is mine." She looked a little awkward. "We're going to a place where you've probably not been before. I don't want you to be scared or be afraid of the people there, they're not dangerous." That didn't sound good, and neither did the look in Soleil's eyes as she said it.

"Where are we going?"

"The slums." Soleil's voice dropped, and she looked away, to her hands, but not in Willow's direction.

"The slums?" That's where Violet lived. Her heart started beating faster. "Why?"

When Soleil looked up again for a moment, there was no question or humour in her eyes. "You know why."

Willow nodded, she knew why. And just the thought made her hands shake and her heart beat faster. "Okay." Her voice was barely over a whisper. "Okay."

Soleil nodded again, and then opened the car door, getting inside. Willow opened the door on her side and got in too. Soleil was bringing her to where Violet lived. Violet who may or may not actually be alive anymore... Soleil was bringing her there for some reason, and the way Soleil was looking, it may not be the hopeful reason that Willow's heart had been rooting for.

This day may still turn into the worst day of her life yet, and she didn't feel very dramatic thinking that either.

Their surroundings changed the further they got to the northern side of the city. Willow lived in a quite affluent neighbourhood on the southern side of the city, the area was beautiful and there had been a real effort to make it a comfortable place to live. There were even gardens and small parks, although nobody ever used them anymore as it wasn't 'cool' to sit around in your own garden when you could be sitting on some exotic beach in the VR worlds.

But as they passed the city centre, going up north even further, the style of the houses became rougher, not as cosy or comfortable as she was used to seeing. And as they kept going, the houses turned into large buildings, flats, on and on.

No, they weren't even flats, they were almost buildings designed purely for storing people in. Each one had a 'convenience machine' on one corner of the building, allowing people to buy cheap food and drinks at any time of day, then most of the middle of the ground floor was dedicated to delivery boxes and on the other end there was a machine which would allow people to convert game money to real money or the other way around without it immediately being connected to their own accounts.

It felt so impersonal, so bare. This was the storage of humans on a scale she hadn't imagined before. This was beyond dystopian, this was merely 'human storage'.

Everything was a dark grey and, especially in the cold light from the street lamps, she could see how uninviting this place was. She couldn't imagine ever living here, but she also felt like she now understood better why so many people escaped into the fantasy worlds of the VR games. Anything was better than facing this day in, day out...

But the car kept going, the buildings around her kept getting worse and worse. Not just in condition or construction, but also in what they offered. Soon the money exchange and the convenience food machines were gone from the corners of the buildings, now only sparsely squished between the grey blocks and many of them didn't even seem to be working anymore, their lights off and some had their fronts violated.

Later on, even the delivery boxes were gone from the buildings, and Willow's heart got heavier. Nothing set apart the first block of 'human storage' from the next. They were all the same colour, the same size, the same everything. And each and every one was falling apart.

This was... She'd never realised that places like these existed in her own city. This was what she imagined poor countries looked like, not neighbourhoods not even an hour drive from her own place.

"What are you thinking?" Soleil's voice jolted her, but her tone was soft, caring, like she already knew what was going through Willow's head.

"I... I didn't think it could be this bad. I didn't realise the slums were so bad."

They were now coming into an area in which only every other street light worked, the streets themselves had holes in places and so many of the houses had wood in front of what should be windows. The word coming up in her was 'desolate'.

"Yeah, it's strange the first time you see it." Willow looked at Soleil, but Soleil only looked ahead of them. "The place where your friend is supposed to live is... definitely not as good as where you live."

Willow nodded. She may not have realised it when Violet talked about where she lived before, but she could see the world of difference between where they both lived now, and she felt bad about not realising this sooner.

Willow had whined about being locked up in that 'low sensory' building, but it was like a princely castle in comparison to where Violet lived. She felt so stupid for ever complaining to Violet. It felt wrong, she felt dirty for ever thinking that what she had was bad at all.

Then the car stopped in front of a large flat. It was larger than the ones around it, and it even looked decently maintained, but that didn't take away from the fact that it looked about ready to fall apart.

"We're here." Soleil's voice was grave.

This was where Violet was supposed to live, Violet and kids like her.

If Violet was still alive, that was.

21
The Ordeal

Willow looked up at the building where Violet was supposed to be living, not getting out of the car yet, not knowing what to do. It was all so sudden and she'd never even imagined something like this ever happening. Ever seeing Violet in real life, or visiting her or something.

"How did you find her?" It was the one thing Willow needed to know. How did Soleil find Violet when they couldn't track blitzed accounts?

Soleil let out a slow breath, looking out over the street, she seemed nervous. "You know that I've been keeping an eye on you for a long time. That included knowing who your friends were. Because of a few things I knew about Violet, I could track her through a couple of different systems, and finally found this place."

"Systems?" That didn't sound good.

"Did you know that Violet's parents refused to take her back in after she got out of jail for stealing?" Soleil's voice was careful.

Willow nodded. At least, Violet had given her the short version, but it came down to the same. She got caught stealing and that meant she didn't live with her parents anymore. Willow hadn't really worried about the how or why connection between the two, because it wasn't an uncommon story, it happened all the time. Parents didn't want to have to deal with kids who were 'unruly' or otherwise inconveniencing them, and instead those kids were sent to places where they would work for companies, doing data or computer jobs that nobody really wanted to do because they were boring, and they'd have a place to live. It was a common story.

"After she got out of jail, Violet was sent here, and she's apparently been living here for the last couple of years. As far as I could find out."

Tears started to form in Willow's eyes, suddenly really realising what it meant when Violet had called herself a 'sewer-girl'. She'd known that Violet didn't have it easy, but she never considered what 'not easy' had meant in reality, in the real world. "I had... I had no idea it was this bad." Willow's voice wobbled. Violet had always appeared so cheery and full of joy, but how much of that had been true if this was where she lived?

"Do you want to meet her? See if..." Soleil's voice quieted until nothing. *See if she was still alive.* See if Violet wasn't actually the dead woman the police had found.

Willow nodded, opening the car door but stopping right in her tracks. The air here was filled with the fumes of the exhausts from the big factories that were just on the other side of this area. She put her shawl over her nose and mouth and stepped out of the car.

Maybe Violet was here. Hopefully she was here. Hopefully she was still alive.

Willow put one foot in front of the other and slowly walked over to the door. There was a list of names next to the door, all with their own buttons, probably the people who lived here. She let her eyes go down the list, and finally found Violet near the bottom. Willow pushed the button next to Violet's name before she lost her courage, before she'd over think it and would run away.

A quiet ringing came from near the button, and she quickly pulled her hand back. Violet should have been able to hear that, right?

But the seconds passed and nobody answered.

Willow pushed the button again. She didn't care if she was waking Violet up anymore, she needed to make sure that Violet was okay, that she was alive.

That she wasn't the girl who...

A lump formed in Willow's throat and she turned around to the car. Soleil was still looking her way, but her eyes had already lost all hope. This wasn't going well, at all. Willow pushed the button one last time, longer this time, just to make sure.

But nothing happened, at all.

This wasn't right. This wasn't what was supposed to happen, at all. Violet was supposed to be here, she was supposed to open the door and this was supposed to be all over. Not like this.

Willow's heart became heavy and she started to get sick to her stomach.

Violet wasn't here. She wasn't. The chance that the woman the police found, frozen to death, was Violet just grew exponentially. It could really be her. She could really have lost her friend, and Willow didn't know how to deal with that.

Willow stumbled to the car, putting her head against the roof as she dry heaved.

The girl she'd played so many games with hadn't just gone missing, she could be dead too. She could very likely be dead...

Willow had to sit down, her head spinning, everything in her head going to mush.

This was bad, really bad. Really, really bad.

She closed her eyes, tears sliding down her cheeks, her body shaking as she quietly sobbed.

What was the use anymore? Why would she keep trying now?

She'd lost her friend. Violet was gone. Really gone. And all because…

"Willow?" A voice sounded from a little away. A voice she knew so well, but she had to be imagining it... Right? It couldn't be.

Willow looked over to the voice, to the figure standing out against one of the few street lights which were still working. *Violet?*

"What are you doing here?" The figure came closer, and as she became more visible in the light from the other side, Willow could see her better.

The girl's hair was a pale purple, braided into cornrows, her skin a dark brown which seemed to have almost an unhealthily ghostly hue in the poor street lighting, but what pulled Willow in most was the way the girl was almost smiling, a smile she'd recognise anywhere, even though she definitely looked surprised.

"Willow?" The girl knelt down next to Willow before glancing at Soleil for a moment.

"Violet?" Willow's voice was so quiet that she didn't even know if the girl could hear her.

"Yes. I'm Violet." The girl nodded and slowly reached out.

Willow's heart started beating much too fast but she reached out to Violet too and took her in her arms. Violet was here. She really was. She was alive.

She was really alive.

They were quiet for a while, just holding each other. Willow was so glad that Violet was safe, that she was alive. She didn't even know how to explain how happy she really was.

Then Violet loosened her grip. "Why are you here?"

"To—" Willow swallowed. "To make sure you weren't dead. They found..." She shook her head, not sure she could talk more.

"Ah." Violet's voice was quiet. "Ah, yes. I just... I couldn't get to you sooner. I'm sorry. I just got back from leaving a note at your place to tell you not to worry about me. I knew you'd worry." Violet's rubbed Willow's back, soothing her.

"What?" Willow pulled back a little. She'd done *what*?

"Yeah. I couldn't do it sooner." Violet pulled a face. "Trying to get work when your BASE account is blitzed isn't particularly easy, so I wasn't able to leave you a note again. You really thought it was me?" There was emotion in Violet's voice, and Willow nodded. "I'm so sorry. You must have been so scared. I wish I'd had another way to tell you that I was fine."

Willow shook her head. "It wasn't your fault. They did that

to you. You got... They..." Willow didn't know what to say anymore. The words wouldn't work.

Violet looked up at Soleil and then she nodded. "I think we need to talk. Explain a few things, but not here." She shook her head. "Let's go somewhere we can talk in private. I know a place nearby." She carefully tugged on Willow's arm and they both stood up, but Violet kept her arms around Willow, giving her comfort. Being close to Violet felt as good in real life as it did when they were in the VR world, maybe even better, though that could be because of how relieved Willow was that Violet was alive.

Willow looked around the area again, remembering how she'd felt realising Violet lived here. "And I'm so sorry, I didn't know..." Willow shook her head. "I had no idea."

She felt Violet's arms tighten around her. "It's okay. I know that you didn't know about me living here. I never intended for you to find out, especially not like this." Then Violet stepped back a little, smiling carefully as Soleil also came to their side of the car. "Let's go somewhere a little more private and talk."

They walked a few blocks, mostly through small alleys, until they reached an 'internet cafe'. Willow thought that these places had died out when the BASE platform was implemented over a decade ago, and everyone could connect to the internet from their mind, never needing an old-school computer again.

** *All BASE functions like AR and social
contacts are disabled after this point* **

Violet had really meant it when she'd said a location that

was more private.

Violet walked them past rows and rows of computers with a black chassis with brightly lit panels in them, just like the one Willow used to play on when she was a little kid. And it surprised her that a lot of computers were actually in use right now. It felt strange, like she'd been transported to a time three or four decades ago, maybe even longer.

When they passed a bar, Violet waved at the guy behind it. "Three lemonades, please." And she walked on to one of the round tables at the back with some very old-looking chairs around it, all wood and almost saloon-like.

When they sat down, Willow looked around again. This whole place was a mix of old technology and a saloon-type style, like you sometimes saw in old Western movies. Sure, both things were considered 'old', but Willow thought it was a strange combination anyway. Supposedly one of these was a few centuries ago and the other just a couple of decades.

"Why did you order lemonade?" Soleil asked and Willow also turned to Violet, who only smiled.

"Because you don't want to order any of the alcoholic drinks here. And I'm not so sure you'd appreciate some of the other non-alcoholic slum drinks they serve. The lemonade is basically the only thing without a load of caffeine or alcohol in it." She shrugged, leaning back as if she was totally at home here, and Willow wondered if she was. If this was where Violet spent most of her days if she wasn't playing videogames.

The guy from behind the bar came over with three glasses with clouded-yellow liquid in them and a jug with more of it. "Got you the good stuff."

"Thanks." Violet flashed him a grin. "You still owe me

though."

The man grumbled as he walked off, but they seemed friendly together, no matter Violet's words or the gruff way the man acted.

Violet put the glasses in front of them. "Be warned, it can be a bit more sour than you're used to." Then she leaned her elbows on the table, looking between them. "Willow, I know, but who are you?" Her eyes were on Soleil, a serious look in them. "Not that I'm not grateful that you helped her come here, but still. I don't think I know you."

Soleil nodded. "I get it, you're protective. I'm Soleil. I worked at the same department at the same company as Willow's dad did a couple of years ago. I met Willow when she was really young, and I've kind of kept an eye on her since." Soleil reached out and took a sip from the glass of 'lemonade', pulling a face before putting it back down. "You weren't kidding about the sourness."

Violet shook her head. "It's hard to get a lot of clean drinking water here, so the lemonade is a little more potent than people from outside this area are used to, usually." Then she eyed Willow before looking back at Soleil. "If you've kept an eye on her for so long, why did you bring her here? You know that it's not safe here, you could have checked on me on your own. Why did you feel the need to bring her here?" Violet's eyes changed, and Willow could hear the pain in her voice. Why didn't Violet want Soleil to bring her here? Why was she so against it?

Willow couldn't let Violet think bad things about Soleil, not when Soleil had been helping so much. "Because I had to know. I couldn't..." She looked at her hands, tears forming in

248

her eyes and she wished she could just type, not having to actually speak now as she felt her voice get all stuck inside. She opened her mouth, but the words stopped coming. She was caught again, the words were there but they wouldn't come out. She was caught in her head again, locked in.

Violet's hand covered hers, her touch warm and comforting. "I'm not angry with her. It's just... She's putting you in a lot of danger. Making you leave the building you live in in the middle of the night, coming here... It's not safe."

"I know." Willow put one of her hands over Violet's, holding it. "I know very well. We know about the... the thing going on…" Could she say the word? But as she looked up, she saw realisation dawn in Violet's eyes.

Violet spun to face Soleil. "Oh, *hell no*. What are you getting her all wrapped up in? What are you doing all that for? Why?"

"Because she can help. She can look through the code. She can do things. She can help fix all of this." Soleil sighed, looking down. "It's not like I did this lightly."

"I *wanted* to help. I want to help to stop people going missing." Willow leaned forward, trying to make sure Violet understood how serious she was. "We want you back."

"Do the others know?" Violet frowned.

"No. They don't know what we're doing. They're not involved. They just..." Willow sighed. "But they do know what happened to you."

"Right..." Violet looked at her and then at Soleil again. "Apart from 'checking if the slum girl is still breathing', why *are* you here?" She looked so serious now, not the friendly person Willow had known for so long. "I'm tired. Willow should go back home. So I don't want to deal with excuses right now."

"You're the only..." Soleil didn't say the word, looking around her nervously. "The only person who had been, you know, who I knew how to track."

"*Blitzed* person? The only *blitzed* person you knew how to find?" Violet raised an eyebrow. "Are you serious?" She let out a laugh, but there was no joy in it.

"Yes." There was a defensiveness in Soleil's voice, but she also seemed confused.

Violet made a move with her arm to encompass the whole room. "There are multiple people in this room alone who have been blitzed in the last weeks. If you want more people for your little experiment, pick someone. They'd probably *love* to help you, someone from the very company that made their accounts unusable in the first place. Go ahead. Choose any one of them. But leave Willow out of this. Leave me out of it." There was no joy in Violet's voice anymore, and she looked ready to walk out right now, or kick them out of here, either was possible.

Willow's mouth dropped open as she looked around.

Multiple people in this room had blitzed accounts? How did that happen?

How widespread was this thing? How many people had gone 'missing' without anyone noticing it? And how many were connected to HF?

What was *really* going on?

22
Going Old-School

"What?" That was Soleil, her eyes darting around the room. "Are you sure?"

"Yes." Violet shrugged like this was the most common thing in the world. "In my building alone, there are five people who have been blitzed in the last weeks."

"Why?" Soleil shook her head. "Why?"

Violet shrugged again, her eyes serious. "How would I know? You're the one who's from the big company that takes care of these things. Why don't you tell *me* how people's accounts are getting all messed up and we can't even do simple things like buying food anymore because we have no way to get to our bank accounts? Why don't *you* tell *me* how this can happen?"

Soleil blinked, and Willow could see how she was struggling to understand what she'd just heard. This couldn't be easy on her. Soleil had no idea about the scale of all of it, that much was obvious. Soleil had been sending Willow into HF, she'd had contacts all over the place, trying to get a grip on what was going on, but she honestly had no idea about the real scale of the blitzing, *if* all of these things were even connected.

"I have no idea what to say." Soleil's voice sounded small, odd for the strong person she normally seemed, and Willow saw Violet's face fall immediately.

Violet let out a dismissive sound. "It's not like we don't have our ways here. We're not dying of hunger or anything. The woman the police found was unlucky, she'd already had bad health and then had gotten locked out of her house in just her sleepwear. But most of us don't have the whole house decked out in BASE platform security. The connection to the system is too unreliable here. And we have our own ways of taking care of our own. But we've lost all our savings, everything that we need to live a somewhat normal life here. All of *that* is gone." She frowned. "Nobody here has ever heard of this before, blitzing on this scale. It's unheard of. And it seems that this hasn't just been blitzing, people's accounts are gone, damaged, they can't just get fixed like before."

"It happens, though? Blitzing? I thought it was some urban legend." Willow stared at Violet. "Are you sure?"

Violet shrugged. "Yeah. Sometimes. Someone pisses off someone higher up the food chain and suddenly they can't get into anything anymore. It also means that lots of people here don't have legal jobs, exactly... It's not illegal, but legal is something else. It's how we grew up here, it's how we survive." She looked a little sheepish. "That's reality here. Blitzing happens. Just not on this scale."

Soleil nodded, and Willow could see her think.

But it wasn't just the blitzing itself that bothered Willow.

"Can you at least buy food and pay your rent and stuff like that?" She wanted Violet to be safe and taken care of first and foremost. She couldn't imagine leaving Violet here and not knowing that he was going to be okay.

Violet nodded, her face softening as she eyed Willow. "Yeah. I can buy food, and I've found a new job. It's just... the hours are a little more inconvenient than they used to be before, but at least it's closer to home now. So that's a plus. And no more annoying system bugging me about my 'optimal sleep times' and everything." Violet shrugged again, like these things didn't matter much, but then she frowned. "But not being able to talk to the guild... That's harder. It's very lonely not being able to talk to everyone. It's not the same without you all."

"We miss you. I miss you." Willow felt her tears come on again. How did she keep getting all cry-y like that? Although, stress plus exhaustion plus finally seeing her friend probably had something to do with it.

"I miss you guys too. How is Mira?"

"Bigger. Though I've not seen her much recently, I've been..." Willow eyed Soleil. "I've been playing HF."

"What?! *No.*" Violet turned to Soleil. "Please, tell me she's joking." Her voice dropped, sounding a little out of breath, but her eyes were wide with panic. "You can't have..."

"It's okay." Willow tried to get Violet's attention, to make her stop staring at Soleil like that. "It's okay."

"It's *not* okay." Violet stood up, still staring at Soleil. "Are you serious? Is *she* serious?"

Soleil looked away. "She is. She's playing HF."

"Get her out of there. I'll do whatever you need, but get

her out of there. Get her *out* of that game." Violet's voice wobbled, and Willow saw tears in her friend's eyes, her friend who she'd rarely ever seen upset like this.

"I need to be in there. I can't help otherwise. There is no other way." Willow hated seeing Violet upset, it made her own tears almost spill too. "We need to find out what happened, why the blitzing even takes place. We can't if we're not—"

"There has to be another way." Violet shook her head. "Has to be. That game... It..." She shook her head more. "I'm sorry. I have to go. I can't do this." Violet started walking off, her shoulders slumped, her whole stance defeated. She wasn't just hurt, she was scared, really scared. And if Willow knew one thing, it was that Violet didn't scare easily.

When Willow tried to follow Violet, Soleil grabbed her arm, holding her there.

"What?" She had to go after Violet, she had to explain what was going on better. Had to!

Soleil quickly let her go, surprise in her eyes at Willow's sharp tone. "Nothing. Just... I'm sorry for bringing you into all of this. She's right, you know? I've put you into too much danger already..." Soleil shook her head, then averted her eyes.

"I don't care. I want to help her. I want to help the other people who got blitzed. I want to *stop* this. But now... I need to..." She looked after Violet again, who just went through the door, the sound of the door closing reverberating in her chest. "I need to go after her." Willow's heart was hurting, and she couldn't let things end like this, she couldn't let Violet just walk away. She had to help her best friend, no matter what. Because that was what friends did, they helped each other when they were hurting or in trouble.

Soleil inclined her head, almost a nod, but Willow knew that Soleil understood. She rushed after Violet. She had to tell her why she was doing this, she had to tell her that they were trying to help.

As she left the cafe, she looked around the dark street, the sparse streetlights reflecting on the wet concrete, throwing her off as she was trying to figure out what way to go. Then she saw Violet walking away, her shoulders hunched up high in her thick jacket, her whole stance broken. Then she ran after her.

"Violet." Willow was so close to her, but didn't grab Violet, giving her space, giving her a chance to ignore her, to still walk away. "Please. Hear me out." Her heart pounded, the sound so loud she wasn't sure that Violet couldn't hear it either.

"Why?" Violet turned to her. "Why would you put yourself in danger? Why?" Violet's voice wobbled and Willow wanted to reach out to her, but couldn't, not yet.

"To help. I want to stop this. I want to stop people going missing. I want to stop whatever is going on. I…" She wanted her friend back.

"You really have no idea, do you?" Violet shook her head, her voice broken, her jaw setting in that stubborn-angry way again. "We're not *missing*. We're right here. Like we've always been. Right *here*."

"But your BASE account is gone. Nobody can contact you. Nobody can even figure out who you are. Nobody has any idea about who the missing people are, or where they are."

"There are no 'missing' people, Willow, just people whose accounts have been ruined. And, *someone* in HF knows who we are." Violet's eyes went hard, angry. "Someone in HF is

255

targeting very specific people, and somehow they know people's BASE and personal ID, or we wouldn't be able to get blitzed in the first place. *Someone* is targeting people who are on the beta key list of HF, and it's getting worse." How did she know this? But more importantly, she'd obviously not heard about some of the other things that had happened in the last weeks.

"It's not just HF anymore." Willow swallowed hard, taking a deep breath. She hated telling people bad things. "People have gotten blitzed playing DoE and other games too now." She looked away, somehow not wanting to tell Violet, but still feeling like she had to. "It's not just HF anymore, it's spreading."

"Crap. Are you sure?" Violet sighed as Willow nodded. "Why? Why would they do that?"

Footsteps behind them made them look around, Soleil came walking up to them, looking serious. "I've got some ideas. And I think I've started to understand a little more from the things you've been telling us. But you're not going to like them."

"What is it?" Willow hated the way her voice sounded so feeble.

"Violet, you said that people here don't always do legal things, right? So most of the people here have a criminal record?"

Violet nodded.

"What if *that* is how people are selected? It explains why there are so many of the blitzed people living around here. Lots of people here have come in contact with law enforcement in not-so-good ways." Soleil didn't sound happy about figuring this out, but yeah, it wasn't really good either. "What if they somehow cross-check people on the HF beta list with people who have come in contact with the law?"

"How? And why would they do it?" Violet didn't sound entirely convinced, but she also didn't seem that surprised.

"I don't know. That's the part that makes no sense. They totally destroy blitzed accounts, more severe than any blitzing I've seen before, totally gone. You can't even backtrack the accounts anymore in the games people have been. They're totally wiped. But there seems to be no real reason for it. It's like, even though we know *who* are getting targeted, there still doesn't seem to be any clue as to the *why*."

Willow nodded. It made sense, in some stupid way. "And now what? What are we going to do with this? Are we going to tell anyone with a criminal record to not log onto the game? It's too late, they're already on the beta list. And they're not just getting blitzed in HF, they're getting blitzed all over the place. You can't log out of your BASE account, and there is no way to get off that beta list anymore. So, now what?"

"I have no idea either. I'm sorry." Soleil shook her head.

That question seemed to have gotten them all stumped.

What now?

What were they going to do with this information, *could* they even do something with it? They had the *who* but still no *why* or *how* and those were a lot more important when it came to figuring out what they were going to do next.

They may have gotten a better idea about the current situation, but that didn't seem to help much going forward.

They slowly walked back to Soleil's car, everyone lost in their own thoughts. When they reached the car, Willow looked at Violet. She wished she could do something for her, something real, something useful. Then she realised that there was something she could do for Violet, something that would at least let them chat again.

"Do you have a way to connect an old-school computer to the net at your place?" Willow eyed Violet.

"An old-school computer?"

"Yeah, like they had at the cafe?"

"Maybe? I don't know, I've never checked. Why?" Violet seemed a little curious now.

"I've got a computer at home. It's old, really old, but maybe we can get it to interface with a text chat or something?" She eyed Soleil, who shrugged. "That way we can at least stay in touch."

"Probably. It sounds like something to try out." Soleil nodded. "And I should have some bits to connect it, if it requires extra cables and such."

"Really?" Violet blinked, slowly smiling. "Are you sure? Those things are rare. How would you get your hands on one?"

"I've got my dad's at my place right now." She saw Violet shake her head resolutely. "I can get my hands on another one later, but you've got nothing left. It's the least I can do."

"Are you sure?" Violet reached out and pulled her close. "You have no idea how much this means to me. Just... Can you stay safe? Please? I don't want you to end up like this too." Her voice was low, and Willow nodded.

"But I can't stop playing HF. I'm sorry. I need to find out what happened. Now we have some idea of how people are chosen, we need to find out what is happening, why they're doing this." Willow tightened her arms around Violet. "Please, trust me on this."

"I do. I trust you. You know that." When Violet pulled back, Willow could see how serious she was. "I trust you."

Willow nodded again, her heart heavy. "If we can get the computer working for you, at least we can talk again. We can do something. That's good."

"Yeah." Violet smiled a little, then she looked over to Soleil. "If I can get it to work, I want in on whatever you're doing. I want to be right there, I want to know what is going on and how I can help too. I'm right here, close to other people who have been blitzed, I can get you the information you need. Just let me in on this."

Willow looked back at Soleil, who nodded. "Sure. We'll figure something out. And I'll see about maybe getting some help down here, see what we can do about those who have been blitzed. Any help they may need."

"You can do that?" Willow was somehow surprised by the offer.

Soleil shrugged. "I can see about trying it. I have no idea if it actually works. Maybe, maybe not, but this isn't right, and you shouldn't be getting in more trouble because someone somewhere is being a controlling ass. I can try it, that's all I can promise."

Violet nodded. "Still, thanks." Then she looked more serious. "It's five days until the official release of HF. If we can prevent putting more people in danger by somehow getting the word out about what HF is doing or something. I don't know, maybe it helps?"

"That's what I'm hoping for too." Willow sighed. If she could prevent more people from getting in trouble, that would mean everything to her. "I'm just... I'm glad to see you're okay. I was really scared. We were all scared."

Violet nodded, her eyes soft. "I know. Tell the others that I'm okay. And tell them about what you've figured out, about the criminal record thing. Just... Just to protect them."

"Will do." Willow nodded. "What are your work hours at your new job? That way we can drop off the computer, right?" She looked at Soleil.

"Yeah." Soleil nodded. "If you know your hours, we can drop by whenever it's convenient."

"What's the time?" Violet looked at her.

Willow pulled up her little program in AR. "It's three in the morning." No wonder she was so exhausted, she'd been awake for almost a whole day.

"I've got work in about five hours, a twelve-hour shift. And then another shift from about midnight to six in the morning." Violet sighed like this was frustrating, but somehow she was used to it. "I know, not technically allowed, but I don't have a BASE account anymore, so they can break the rules all they want because there is no reliable way to track what hours I'm really working."

Willow looked at Soleil, a panic starting in her chest. They had to do something, and soon too, because this wasn't right, really not right.

"We'll come by between nine and midnight tomorrow." Soleil nodded. "And I'll see about getting you a few other old-school things. Maybe a handheld phone or something like that. It would mean that people can actually contact you and it works as a clock and alarm too."

Violet nodded. "Thanks. That's been… a little out of my price range currently, if I can even find someone selling them."

Willow hugged Violet tightly. "Take care. Stay safe."

"You too." Violet's voice was thick, but Willow tried to ignore it, because it made the tightness in her chest worse.

She'd learned so much tonight. So many things she never really wanted to know, but they'd also learned new things that should help them.

But in this all, she was still wondering why people would do this. Why would they hurt people by blitzing their accounts? What was their end goal?

What was the purpose of all of this?

23

A Glance Behind the Curtain

Willow curled up in bed, totally exhausted, but her head just wouldn't slow down, thoughts still rushing through it, one after another after another. When she'd returned home, Soleil changed the notification on her BASE notification system back, and now it insisted that she really had to go sleep. But how could she? How could she sleep like this? How could she sleep knowing all that she knew now?

She opened the chat with the others from the guild.

> **Willow:** Violet is safe, I saw her. She's doing okay. She told me to tell you not to worry.

Then she closed the chat, the others were probably asleep and she should be too. But she had no idea how she even could.

Willow took a deep breath and put on the VR headset. Maybe playing some memory videos would help her get to sleep, maybe that would calm her brain down a little.

She opened the part of the BASE platform where her

memories were stored. From one of the first days she had gotten the BASE implant and her excitement at the AR options, to going to school, for the few days they'd put her in a small VR classroom before deciding to give her private classes anyway, to playing games with her friends and even when Mira had been born in DoE. But tonight she was looking for a very specific memory.

She pulled it up, this one was from when she was quite young still. It was from the first time she'd been part of a raid, with Violet, Juniper, Sage and Opal at her side. They'd been such noobs, but it had been so exciting and scary at the same time.

Willow let out a long and slow breath as she played the video from the start, from right when they appeared inside the raid dungeon. There were people all around them, she remembered there maybe being fifty or so people at once, which was a huge amount of people for her at the time. Then she relaxed as she let the memory flood over her, let the past make her forget her present.

Her own memories of the time were a little different from what the BASE platform actually recorded, but the two combined were probably the best experience ever.

She dozed off, finally calming down enough after days of worrying about Violet. But now she knew where Violet was, now she knew that Violet was safe, somewhat, and that she was going to try to get her back into the digital world by giving Violet her old computer. Now she could finally let that worry go. She had a plan, she had something to focus on, and that had rarely ever felt this good.

When she woke up again, the memory had stopped

playing. The VR world around her was dark, but as it registered her waking up, there was a message in front of her.

It's unhealthy to fall asleep with the VR headset on. Please take it off and rest

She shrugged. Well, she was going to do that anyway, but more because her neck felt strange from the way she'd been asleep. The VR headset was designed to be comfortable to wear in bed, but you had to be on your back, it wasn't really designed to be comfortable when you were on your side, which is how Willow preferred to sleep.

As she sat up in her bed, she checked the chats. Her friends had woken up earlier and there were some messages from them, most of them happy about knowing Violet was okay, but nothing that required her immediate attention.

So, instead, she went on the hunt for her breakfast, which should have arrived by now. It was ten in the morning, she hadn't slept that much, she'd come back into the house between four and five, but if she didn't get up now, she would probably sleep for the rest of the day, which was a bad idea when they were on a deadline, like the release of HF being so close.

"Time to get to work," she whispered to herself.

She grabbed her breakfast from the delivery box, and this time she saw the note that Violet had left behind for her as it fluttered to the floor. She put the box on the floor and took the note. The paper was different this time, white and not as sturdy, it was even a little dirty.

She folded it open.

Dear Willow,
I hope you're okay and safe.

264

I wanted to let you know that I'm still here, I'm
   alive. The woman you heard about on the
   news is not me.
I'm sorry I can't write a longer note, I'll try to
   leave another one soon.
Please, take care of yourself. I'm doing good.
Love,
Violet

It was just a short note, but it felt good to hold it, making sure that last night really happened, that it wasn't a dream.

Violet was safe. She'd been blitzed, but she was alive and well, and that was the most important part of all of this. Willow smiled a little. At least it made her feel somewhat better, knowing that Violet was okay. Although, now she knew where Violet lived she was worried in other ways, but those were things she could focus on next, it wasn't that urgent.

Willow put the note in her pocket and picked up the box with breakfast, putting it on the table and opened it. Just some sandwiches, apparently they weren't feeling very fancy today, luckily.

She sat down, folding down the sides of the box and moving everything to the sides, trying to decide what to put on her bread first when a red notification started blinking fast in the corner of her view.

As her attention was pulled to it, a message popped up in the middle of her view.

***Daryl Hill, Helheim Fallen Online's
creator, speaks out about accusations
levelled against the company over
people going missing on their watch***

What?!

Was this real? Had she just walked into an alternate reality or something?

She accepted the invitation to open the video stream and then opened the chat she had with her friends and the one with Soleil.

> **Sage:** Are you all seeing this?

They'd posted it just a moment ago, right as Willow had gotten the notification too.

> **Willow:** Yeah. Unreal.

Then she switched to the chat with Soleil.

> **Willow:** What happened? What are they doing?

The video stream didn't show much right now. The camera filming this was positioned in a large room in some fancy building. There were reporters everywhere, just milling about, like they weren't really sure why they were there either. On one side of the room there was a large stage, the backdrop of it the Helheim Fallen Online logo and a simple stand at the front of it. There wasn't anyone from the company there, though.

> **Rotnem:** I have no idea, nobody knew about this. Everyone at work is watching too. Are you in the stream?
>
> **Rotnem:** Everyone here is confused about what's happening.

That didn't sound very comforting. If even the people at BASE, the main company that designed the whole platform that games like HF were played on, had no idea this was going to happen, then who did? Was this something HF's company had planned beforehand, or was this impromptu? Because both would be a bad sign for very different reasons.

She switched to the other chat.

266

Right then, a group of people in expensive black suits came from a door on the left side of the room. They walked to the stage, a few sat down in two short rows of chairs on either side of the stand, and a young man walked up to the microphone on the stand. Finally, two broad guys stepped off the front of the stage and stayed there, looking impressive, probably bodyguards or something.

The man on the stage was maybe in his mid-twenties, but he had the charisma of someone who was used to using his words to get people to do his bidding. He looked over the room, patiently waiting until everyone had quieted down.

"Welcome, and I'm sorry that this is such short notice. As most of you know, I'm Daryl Hill, the creator of the most anticipated VRMMORPG game of this decade." He looked over the reporters, his eyes seeming to rest of every person here for just a couple of moments, the look in them intense. He was almost controlling the crowd with just his stare. "I wish that I could stand here and talk about the successes we've had leading up to the release of Helheim Fallen Online, which is coming out in just five days. Instead, I'm standing here because there have been some unsettling and persistent rumours about my game. And I would like to assure you that the game is perfectly safe and people shouldn't be worrying about buying or playing it in the future."

"Why do a press conference about the rumours when they're not true?" Someone in the group of reporters yelled the question before Daryl could say more.

Daryl glared at the reporter for a moment, before taking a

deep breath and turning to the whole audience again. "I'm standing here because I feel like I need to personally talk about this. Helheim Fallen Online is in no way connected to the 'disappearance' of our loved and law-abiding fellow humans. These are only rumours, spread by people who would like to see this game fail, or worse, to see a game which has taken a great team of artists and programmers years of hard work to make cancelled. To my knowledge, the issue of people going missing while playing is something that multiple games have been struggling with in these past weeks. I've not heard of any sightings of what some people are calling 'blitzed' accounts in Helheim Fallen Online. I have no idea why Helheim Fallen Online has been targeted specifically for these rumours, but I'm saddened by these people's actions. I want to extend my deepest regrets to the people who have lost their accounts or otherwise have not been able to play the games that they love because they were targeted by a malicious group of people, but Helheim Fallen Online is not that group."

He looked so serious and honest, even though Willow was convinced he was lying through his teeth. She knew that at least some people inside the HF headquarters were aware of some issue within their own game, but that either hadn't reached Daryl, which was unlikely but possible, or he was forming his sentences really carefully as to not say things that weren't true, also possible, especially as a pr move.

Because, yeah, as far as she knew there hadn't been any sightings of blitzed people in HF reported, at least not on the forums, even though Willow had seen one blitzed account inside the game herself, but she'd not shared that with HF or on the forums. The 'no reports' part was, in a way, true. And so was the fact that other games had been affected too, though, only after reports of people logging onto HF with a beta key and going missing had started popping up, not before, as far as she knew. So that could have been a deflection tactic or just testing the reach of whatever they were doing.

"I'm sorry for the people who have lost their friends and are convinced that Helheim Fallen Online has been the cause of this problem. But there are always people who are struggling with their mental and emotional health. Changes, even good ones like getting accepted to play in the beta of a highly anticipated game, can trigger a negative stress reaction for those people, which can lead to rash actions. But the choices that people make while they are unwell have nothing to do with our game. There is no risk to healthy and honest players to play Helheim Fallen Online. None. Helheim Fallen Online is still the biggest and most anticipated VRMMORPG of this decade, maybe even of this century, and it will not let itself be bullied into anything less than a spectacular release day." Daryl inclined his head. "I won't be taking any questions. Thank you and have a good day." Then he walked off the stage, the rest of the people in suits following him.

The room fell into stunned silence for a few moments but then got noisy, and people seemed to be more confused now than they were before Daryl came onto the stage.

Willow stared at the empty stage until the live stream cut out and she was back in her apartment again.

No way. That was... *No way.*

The chat with Soleil blinked insistently.

> **Rotnem:** Did you hear that?
> **Rotnem:** He's covering his ass, something is definitely
> up.

Willow: Yeah.

She had to come back to herself for a moment. It was hard to believe that someone would be so... purposefully hurtful to people. It was hard to understand that this really just happened. But the language Daryl used gave her shivers and it just felt so *wrong*. So...

She didn't know how to describe it.

Willow switched to the chat with the other people from the guild.

Willow: Meet me in VRHome.

Sure, she could talk to Soleil. Figure things out, try to understand things by talking to someone who was so much deeper into all of this. But right now, she just needed her friends, she needed to feel connected to them, know that they were there.

She went to her bedroom, her sandwich with ham abandoned on the table in the kitchen, and put the VR headset back on.

There was a notification about over-use of the VR headset, but she ignored it, swiping it away, and dove right into the VRHome.

When she arrived, Sage was already there, their eyes serious. "Hey." They stood up, coming closer. "Are you okay?"

She nodded, the movement jerky as she was still so fizzy inside, bubbles of anger and frustration popping inside her. "Yeah." Though even her voice didn't sound right.

Moments later, both Opal and Juniper showed up too. All eyes were on her.

She took a deep breath. "I saw Violet last night. She's safe. But..." She shook her head. How could she even explain it?

How could she explain this bad feeling inside?

She turned a full circle, looking at everything she'd collected in this room over the years, letting all these memories calm her down, letting the familiarity soothe her. Everyone stayed quiet, waiting for her to talk again.

> **Willow:** I think that HF's release day is going to be
> dangerous for a lot of people.

She blinked, fear rushing through her now she'd said the words, well, typed them, but she couldn't take them back anymore. There were things she could step back from, but this wasn't one of those...

They were in real danger. People like Violet, but probably a lot more people, if Daryl's words were anything to go by. His speech was as much about the things he hadn't said as the things he had said. And the words he had used chilled her.

'Law-abiding', 'struggling with mental and emotional health', 'healthy and honest players'. They already knew that the people who had gotten blitzed during the beta weren't what everyone would consider 'law-abiding', so what would that mean for the other groups of people he spoke about?

For a game which promised to 'change the gaming landscape forever', those were some very dangerous words. Because cutting out whole groups of players would definitely be 'game changing'.

24
Rumours

Even though the thought of going into HF scared her even more now, she still logged onto the game. While she'd been talking to her friends in VRHome, her thoughts kept going back to Dawn. If Daryl's comment about law-abiding people was anything to go by, people with disabilities were next on his list with targets, and while she was at risk, so was Dawn.

She immediately went to her friends list when she logged on, checking if he was there, but his name was listed as 'offline'. Which, while inconvenient, was in some ways also a good sign, at least his account was still there, his name was there, so he hadn't been blitzed yet.

She hugged Iris, the small dragon a little bigger again. Though, it would take a long time before she was big enough for more than just some hugging. Iris could potentially also make a great mount if those tiny wings on her back actually had a use, they did look promising. That was, if Willow would be able to play this game for long enough to get there...

"Okay, little one, let's get some quests done and fry some monsters." She pulled up her quest log and saw that she had to kill a lot of lynxes for a quest. That one she easily could do on her own.

As she started to pay attention to her surroundings more, the field she was standing in, the lynxes and wolves walking around in it, she realised that something was off. There there wasn't anyone around, which wouldn't have been strange in the previous zone, but it was odd here. Sure, she'd logged out in the middle of nowhere basically, but there were suspiciously few people in this area at all, no matter where she looked. None, to be precise. And there were usually some people grinding mobs around here.

There *were* people online, right?

She pulled up a list of online players and saw thousands of names. So, check, there were players online. But most of them were listed as being in the capital, not around the other areas...

That was... odd, definitely. Was it because of the announcement? Because she'd never seen things like this in other games before. What was going on?

Hmm.

Willow motioned for Isis. "I guess we may want to check what's going on there too." Normally, she wouldn't want to hang out in the capital too much, everything overwhelmed her much too easily. But with the announcement earlier today, right now was probably a good moment to try and face that annoyance.

She started walking, ignoring the mobs as she passed them. She'd much rather go questing, but she wasn't in this game to just play it, she was here to find information. And going to the capital right now was doing what she was here for.

As she came closer to the city, she saw more and more people, all walking to the capital, just like her. She stopped, taking a deep breath, and then went into her settings. She'd been muting all the other players' chatter, but now that she was trying to actually find information, she probably should turn it on again.

Around her, the other sounds of the game, like the wind and animals, also got a little louder, but most of all, she could hear voices. Not words and sentences yet, but she could hear the voices of people as she got closer to the city.

"Did you see it too?" A guy somewhere ahead of her said to someone. She couldn't see if it was to one of the people around him or if it was through some voice system, like a call or something, since she hadn't actually looked into that part of this game much yet. But these things were possible in DoE, so why not here? Though, there didn't seem to be a reply, before he spoke again. "I know. I was surprised too. Why would he go on stage and insist things like that when there isn't anything to the rumours in the first place? I don't get it either."

She kept following the now growing group of people. All around her, people seemed to be having the same conversations, wondering why Daryl had gone on stage, why he'd spoken out if the rumours were false and if there was maybe more behind it. But none of that explained why so many people were all going to the capital. It didn't even seem like people were really wondering about it like she was either... They were just following the others or something.

It was... curious at best, not a good sign at worst.

Everyone seemed to be on their way to the big city square,

and as she got closer to it, the voices around her grew louder, slowly starting to overwhelm her, and she was about to turn the volume down, but then something caught her attention.

"I heard that there is something special going on in the square. Did you see it yet?" A girl sounded surprised.

This time there was a response from someone else. "Yeah, there is someone standing there saying that he's Daryl, the creator, you know. And that if the game was really as dangerous as some people were saying, that he wouldn't go into the game himself. I think it's a stupid idea." The other girl sounded almost bored. "You know, if he'd just ignored the rumours, people wouldn't have worried, but now he's just doing it himself. First the press conference and now this, if it's even him, it just makes him seem guilty of something or like he can't handle a little competition or whatever. None of the other games have responded like this."

"Yeah," the first girl spoke again. "But those games don't have a lot of deleted posts about missing people right on their forums... Did you see it? People are even sharing screenshots of the forums to show that posts are getting deleted or altered. They copied the posts about friends going missing, and suddenly the posts would be gone or changed and stuff like that. It's really... It's not good PR, he should realise that, right?"

"I know, right? If he really is the creator of this game, then why isn't anyone stopping him from doing something like that? It's silly. He's just making it worse." The second girl didn't sound convinced that this was all a good idea either.

And Willow agreed with her, there was just so much going on, so many things that either didn't fully add up or that were strange in other ways... But if the girls were right, then Daryl could really be inside the game right now. She should probably go check it out.

Willow pushed through the masses, her size and strength now definitely an advantage. She could at least see where she was going.

Then a message popped up.

Dawn has come online

Dawn: *Hey, where are you?*

He was pretty fast.

Willow made her way to the side of the street, out of the way of most of the pushing, and then replied to Dawn.

Meadow: *I'm in the capital, something is going on here, I got curious.*
Dawn: *Cool. Want me to come your way?*

She looked around. Did she want him to come here? She could potentially use his help, since he seemed to know a lot about the game, but then, she also knew that he could already be in trouble by just being in this game in the first place.

This was doing her head in... Why were things so complicated? The help he could offer was winning over her need to protect him.

Meadow: *Sure.*

She sent him a party invite, which he promptly accepted.

Meadow: *Find me on the map.*

Then she pushed through the crowd again, trying to get closer to the square so she could see things there. People around her were still talking about both the press conference and the player who could be Daryl, or not be Daryl, apparently either option was enough to get the gossip spinning out of control.

276

When she finally got to the square, she looked around. It was so much more empty here than it had been in the streets she'd just struggled through. Which was unexpected. While the streets had been filled with people, packed, somehow the square almost looked normal, no people pushing at each other or anything. It was a little more busy than usual, but it wasn't that much. Odd. Definitely odd. Like people were just trying to get near here, but didn't want to actually be here.

Then she spotted something.

> **Meadow:** Didn't you say that there was only one other
>   known player who also had a dragon as a fylgja?
> **Dawn:** Yeah. Only one player. Who is also almost max
>   level. Why?

Willow looked at a guy who was standing on top of some boxes surrounded by other players, waving his hands, talking to the group of people gathered around him. At his side was a dragon, a red one, and it was much bigger than Iris, but there was no doubt that both of them were based on the same base model.

Dragon, check. Almost max level, this guy was at level 45 and the level cap was 50, so check.

> **Meadow:** I may have found him.

Her stomach dropped. The only other player with a dragon fylgja was also the one player she hadn't really been looking forward to meeting, Daryl, HF's creator, the man of the hour.

She stepped back behind some crates out of the view of the other player, waiting for Dawn. She didn't really want to meet Daryl and if they were the only two people with dragons for fylgja, he would definitely notice her.

If she had to collect information on what he was doing and if his company was doing something bad, she kind of didn't want him to know about her.

Definitely not.

Dawn stepped in front of Willow, looking her over, frowning a little. He'd shown up in the city pretty soon after she'd arrived at the square, though he'd taken a while before he'd gotten through the crowd and found her in her hiding spot.

Dawn: What are you doing here?

Willow shrugged a little, now feeling silly for being stressed out about Daryl seeing her.

Dawn: That makes no sense.

He looked over to where Daryl was still talking to the people around him, and then to the streets that were packed full of people but very few of them actually dared to go into the square.

A lot of players were trying to spot Daryl for a moment, but barely any of them really seemed to want to talk to him, as they all kept their distance.

Which seemed a little odd, the guy was basically a celebrity simply for creating this game, but at the same time, from the whispers she'd heard while walking through the crowd, people didn't trust him. Real Daryl or not, they didn't trust the guy, and apart from some 'celebrity spotting' they didn't really seem interested to talk to someone who they didn't know if they could actually trust.

Willow motioned for Dawn to follow her and started walking down a street, navigating them to the frozen lake. As long as the ice ship wasn't arriving any time soon, which would bring people and supplies from some other big cities in the game, it would be pretty calm there.

When she first came to the city, she'd wondered how the docks could be so busy, but Dawn had shown her the ice ship. It was huge and one of the few ways of transportation in this game. It was used to transport players but would also transport items for the marketplace to players who were in other parts of the world. Like everything, even trading was fairly slow in this game.

She jumped off the docks and walked along the edge of the lake for a while, finding a comfortable spot to sit down while she was going to try to figure out how much she could tell Dawn.

> **Dawn:** What's going on?
> **Dawn:** You've been acting strange…

She wished she could trust the game integrity, that she could tell Dawn everything, explain everything that was going on, but, like the forums, she expected that most of the conversations in this game, verbal or in chat, were logged and checked on a regular basis. But she had to take this chance, Dawn seemed like a nice guy and he didn't deserve to be kicked out of the game just for not being 'normal' the way some people defined 'normal', the way Daryl apparently defined 'normal' for the players in this game.

> **Meadow:** What do you know about the missing people
>   rumours?

Dawn shrugged, looking a little lost on her question.

> **Dawn:** I've seen some posts on the forums about it, but
>   it always seems a little strange that in this world,
>   at this time, people would just stop existing, that
>   they can't be found anymore.
> **Meadow:** Why?

Dawn: There is always a trail, there is always someone
    who can find you. We're all living more digital than
    analogue these days, there will be a trail, even if
    you're kicked from a game.
Meadow: Not if they delete that data too.
Dawn: From every server that you've connected to,
    ever? That sounds unlikely.
Meadow: There are ways.

Willow had heard enough about this blitzing going on that she knew that nothing and nobody would be safe if they got in the way of whatever was going on.

This stopped Dawn, who now looked more seriously at her.

Dawn: What do you mean?

His frown deepened, and she could see the doubt in his eyes, the ways he was weighing this information against how much he trusted her.

Meadow: It's real. People, the flesh-and-bone people,
    aren't going missing, but their digital data is all
    corrupted. The rumours about 'missing people' in
    the BASE platform are real.

Dawn stared at her, his mouth open, stunned, then he slowly shook his head.

Dawn: Why are you telling me this? Why me?
Meadow: Because I think you should know about it, at
    least, some of it.
Dawn: You're not making much sense.
Meadow: I know, I'm sorry. I wish I could explain it
    better, but just know that it's real. It's really real,
    and people in HF headquarters know.

He frowned, and then nodded.

Dawn: But why me?
Meadow: Without trying to be alarming, it could happen
    to you too, when HF goes live for real.

Dawn: You're talking about the press release?

Willow nodded.

Then an odd BASE notification got through her system.

Soleil is at your door

What? At her door?

Oh! In her apartment.

Meadow: I have to go. I wish I could tell you more right
now. Just... I wish I knew how to keep you safe. I'm
sorry.
Meadow: I'll try to be back as soon as possible.

She swiped up the menu and logged out of the game, not waiting for Dawn's reply.

You are now logged out of Helheim Fallen Online

She sat up in bed, pulling her headset off and putting it aside. Now that she was back in the real world, she could hear the doorbell as it rang loudly.

She stood up, jolted by the sound, and as she walked over to her door, still frowning, she eyed the red blinking at the side of her view. She opened the message at the same time as she opened the door.

In front of her was Soleil, looking freaked out and stressed, her eyes red and wild.

At the same time, Willow saw the messages in the chat.

Sage: Willow, message me when you see this. I've
found something.
Sage: Willow? Please?
Sage: Willow?
Opal: Sage? Sage, where did you go?
Opal: Willow! Come to DoE!
Opal: Willow!

The last message from Opal was from just a few minutes ago.

Her heart started beating fast, and she felt a little sick. What was going on now? What had Sage found? And where were they?

A bad feeling settled in her stomach, and she swiped to the side, pulling up the participants of the chat. Sage was now listed under Violet, both with the same message next to their name, neither were connected to the BASE platform anymore.

No way.

No way.

This did not just happen!

But the way Soleil was looking at her, her even being here... It didn't bode well.

Oh, no...

No, no, no, no.

Tears streaked down her cheeks as she stumbled back, grabbing her couch for support. This was not happening!

25
Seizing the Sword

Willow shook her head, sitting down on the couch and staring up at Soleil. The look in Soleil's eyes… She wasn't here for a fun chat, and it was much too early for her to come pick her up to go see Violet. Soleil already knew something bad was going on. She already knew.

Soleil slowly stepped inside, closing the door behind her, and then sat down next to Willow, not saying anything yet. After a while, her fingers moved in the air, and a notification showed up in Willow's view.

> **Rotnem:** We need to move quickly, we can't wait too long.
> **Willow:** Move quickly?

She didn't know what Soleil was talking about.

> **Rotnem:** If we want Sage's account data, we need to get to their account before it backs up and we lose the access forever.

Of course, the data from Sage's account would get

thoroughly corrupted if they didn't get to it soon enough. And if that happened, they wouldn't be able to track Sage down, find out where they lived and maybe even help them. Plus, Sage also had information for them that could maybe help them out…

Willow nodded, standing up, going back to her bedroom in a daze, Soleil following her.

"I'm so sorry." Soleil looked at her, her eyes sad. "I'm really sorry."

Willow just nodded at her, not sure what she could do about it right now, not sure how to answer. She hadn't just lost one friend to this blitzing, she'd lost two by now, and she didn't know if or when she'd lose more.

She put the VR headset on and immediately connected to DoE.

You are now logged into Destruction of Elysium

She materialised in the middle of the living room of the guild house. It was eerily quiet around her.

Then a message appeared in the guild chat.

Opal: We're out back.

Willow made her way to the back of the guild house, going outside, and she didn't need any more clues about what was going on as there was a distinctive black glitching blob right at the back of the house's garden.

Sage!

Willow: Are you sure it's them?

It could technically be anyone, it didn't have to be Sage.

Opal landed at her side, probably having jumped from the roof, where he tended to hang out.

Opal: I saw it happen.
Opal: We were talking and they just disappeared.

Oh, no! Somewhere she'd hoped it hadn't been true, that it had just been Opal's guess.

Willow: How long ago?
Opal: Just a few minutes.

Okay, so the system shouldn't be backed up yet. *Shouldn't* being the critical word here.

She went into the BASE chat she ran with Soleil, glad that in DoE she had access to it, unlike in HF.

Willow: Can you track an ID? I'm here.
Rotnem: I'll send a mod your way, I already notified
      someone to stand by, and they will be there soon.
Willow: Okay.

And if they could get to Sage's ID, then what would they do? They could probably try to find Sage some other way, but more than just finding out some basic data about them would get complicated, right? If they didn't know their BASE ID then they couldn't get more private information anywhere else.

Willow walked over to the blob that now represented Sage. In HF she could see the broken code of a blob, but she didn't have that type of access here in DoE, sadly enough.

An elven woman walked into the garden, looking at them and then at the blob. "You're with Rotnem?"

Willow nodded. "Yeah. We… This is our friend. Please, help." Even conversations confused her now.

"I'll see what I can do." The woman walked over to where Willow was standing and pulled out a tool and seemed to 'scan' the blob.

Willow couldn't see what was going on on the screen of the tool, but she didn't like the way the woman was frowning.

"And?" Opal came closer too, moving carefully.

The woman looked at them. "We're right on time. I can get the ID, I will send it to Rotnem immediately. I'm so sorry about this."

Opal shrugged.

But Willow's chest hurt too much to think or even want to consider what had happened, what Sage had found out that someone blitzed them like this. Violet had said that sometimes people would blitz others just to get back at them for something. But the fact that Sage had said that they had information for Willow and then ended up a blob, kind of made the source of this blitz very obvious. There wasn't anyone but the people at HF responsible for this.

The woman looked at her. "It will be okay. I'm getting Rotnem the data, and then we can find out where they lived and get them help. It will be okay."

Willow shook her head. "It will never be okay." Why did everyone keep telling her that? Everything had changed, for the worst.

She couldn't do this, she couldn't deal with this. Willow walked out of the garden into the fields behind the house, trying to gather her thoughts. Trying to sort everything.

> **Rotnem:** Where are you going? Aren't you coming back?
> **Willow:** And then what?
> **Rotnem:** We can find Sage.
> **Willow:** There isn't anything I can do right now.
> **Willow:** All my friends are disappearing. I just bring
>   more problems.

"Willow?" Opal's voice came from behind her.

She turned around, finding her friend looking at her with worry in his eyes, and that made the pain in her chest only worse, her tears so much closer to the surface.

"How can we help? What can we do?" He almost whispered the words as he stepped closer.

"I don't know," she whispered back, finally voicing her fears. "I have no idea. There is no plan."

She'd thought that if they found another blitzed account that she would know what to do next. But it wasn't just another person, Sage was blitzed. Sage, who she'd known for years. Sage, one of her closest friends. Slowly, everyone she loved was taken away from her, and she didn't know what to do anymore. She was paralysed by fear.

Everything was too overwhelming, too much pulling on her when she had no idea what she could even do anymore. Her brain seemed to be stretched way too thin, about ready to snap.

First, Violet. Now, Sage.

Who else was she going to lose before this was all over?

When Willow came back to the real world, Soleil was still sitting at the side of her bed, waiting for her to return.

"Hey." Soleil's voice was low, weary.

"Hey." Willow nodded, sitting up and putting her VR headset aside. "I'm sorry."

Soleil shook her head. "Don't be. I can't imagine the things going through you, how hard this is."

"Any news?"

Soleil nodded as she stood up. "We were able to track Sage's BASE ID to their personal ID, and someone I know is going over to their place right now."

"Can we go too?" She wanted to see Sage, she wanted to hold them, make sure that they were really okay.

Soleil shook her head. "It's too far away. It would take four hours by plane just to get there. I'm sorry. I too wish that we could."

Willow nodded. She wasn't always so lucky as she'd been with Violet, apparently. "And now?"

"I'll get a notification about Sage soon. For now, all we can do is to try and figure out what to do from this side of things. How we can connect HF to the disappearances."

"Yeah." She sighed. Like that was so easy. It felt like everything she was trying to wade through when it came to HF got more complicated every time she looked at it. Every answer just brought more questions and it was overwhelming her.

Soleil touched the top of her head for a moment. "I think I've got an idea."

"What idea?" Her head was just going around in circles, not really getting anywhere, so anything was better than that.

"Your friend in HF. Dawn, right?"

Willow nodded. "What about him?"

"Can you get him to help you out?"

"How? I don't know anything that he can even help me with. He knows about HF's lore and game, but not much else. And I don't want to put him in more danger."

"I know. But if you can get him to help you level up, maybe he'll be able to help in other ways when you actually go face whatever it is that you need to face when we do find out what to do." Soleil let out a short breath, smiling just a little bit. That had been a long sentence to say in just one go.

"That doesn't sound like much of a plan." Willow raised

her eyebrows at Soleil. It was basically the plan they'd been running since the start. Plan: just whatever as long as they're not standing still.

"It's better than sitting around not knowing what to do. If you trust him enough, you could even tell him a little about what's going on." Soleil's voice was caring, soft.

"I already did… Somewhat." She sighed. "I've told him a few things about what is or may be going on, but then you were at the door and I couldn't tell him more."

"Okay…" Soleil kneeled in front of her. "Then, go back. Having at least one other player at your side in that game is going to be useful. It may even just let you get distracted from what's going on out here."

"And what happens when you find something? When you hear about Sage?" She didn't know if it was such a good idea to go out of reach right now.

"I'll let you know if we find out anything. And I'll also come back here later so we can bring Violet her computer together. But for now… I think it's better if we stay on plan, which means, you need to level up more." Soleil looked serious.

"Yeah…" Willow let out a low growl. "I guess."

"You can do it. It's just for a few hours. We should know more later tonight." Soleil tried to smile a little. "I'm going to go, see if I can get some of my own stuff done. I'll let you know more as soon as I have it."

"Okay." Willow put her headset on again. "I guess I'll see you later."

There was still this tension in her stomach over Sage and over not knowing how to go forward. But Soleil's plan made sense, she was going to have to level up as much as she could, if only to make sure she had more power when she had to face whatever or whoever.

She logged back onto HF, and as she materialised in the world, she was still at the edge of the frozen lake, though Dawn wasn't anywhere in sight…

Willow wandered through the city, going from NPC to NPC, running a couple of 'walking from person to person' quests, handing them in, grabbing new ones. She didn't really feel like fighting anything, and the quests were here anyway. Easy XP when she was waiting around.

Dawn has come online

Dawn: Hey.
Meadow: Hey.

What was she going to say now? What could she say after what she told him earlier?

Dawn: What happened? You suddenly logged off.

How could she tell him? How much did she trust him?

Meadow: A friend was in trouble. I had to take care of a
    couple of things.
Dawn: Are they okay?
Meadow: Hopefully. I don't know yet.

And now she didn't know how else to explain it to him, what to tell him. She handed in the final quest in her log with an NPC and then looked around. What could she do next?

Dawn: Do you want to kill some mobs?
Meadow: Sure, where?
Dawn: Meet me at the front gates, we'll go there
    together.

Willow started walking, pushing through the city. The heavy crowds were gone now, everything back to normal, like nothing had happened this morning. Like Willow's life hadn't changed even more, just in a handful of minutes.

When she reached the gates, she barely recognised Dawn, he was wearing thick armour and held a huge sword in his hands.

He smiled when he saw her.

> **Dawn:** I thought that trying out a secondary class would be a good idea for you right about now.
> **Meadow:** A new class?
> **Dawn:** Yeah, you can choose a secondary class when you reach level 12. What would you like?

Willow looked Dawn over, at how strong he looked like this, at how fierce he almost looked, even though he was still cutely elven. She guessed that elves never really looked rough, no matter what class they played.

> **Meadow:** Something warrior-like?

Dawn nodded.

> **Dawn:** I can get you that. Berzerker?

Willow nodded. Sounded okay.

Dawn opened a trading window with her and filled it with a huge sword and some gear for her level.

She accepted the trade and the items appeared in her inventory.

Then she equipped the sword and the gear, her whole body getting heavier instantly. Her level didn't reset to the start, she kept her level, only now she was differently geared up and she didn't have any spells anymore apart from the racial attack. Even Iris was now gone, bummer.

But if she couldn't get her frustrations out some other way, she could at least get it out this way, by using her body. By stretching her musles and hitting things.

She rolled her arms and shoulders, getting used to her new class.

Meadow: How did you know?

Dawn shrugged, grinning a little.

Dawn: You looked like you could use a way to get rid of whatever was going on in your head, right?

She nodded.

Dawn: Follow me.

They walked down the path, back to the starter zone, but they didn't cross the bridge, instead walking up to the wolves there.

Dawn: Go ahead, attack them.

The wolves were still a couple of levels above her, but that didn't stop her. She grabbed her sword with two hands, lifting it before she made a couple of swings. She wasn't used to playing warrior classes, but it couldn't be that bad, right? Just more physical than a caster?

Then she took a couple of steps towards the nearest wolf, who automatically targeted her.

She let out a loud yell and swung the sword, landing it on the wolf's head.

You hit the Hungry Wolf for 170 damage

If she couldn't let her frustration out some other way, she could at least try it this way.

26
Call from the Unknown

Willow looked at her dinner, not really feeling like eating. She should really eat something though, since she barely had anything today. Between waking up late and then seeing that press conference by Daryl and then Sage going missing…

Stuff had been a little crazy in her head, and eating had sort of gotten lost in all of that. But being hungry and having to get things done were not a good combination. If she was hungry, she got grumpy, and when she was grumpy her brain didn't fully function, and she'd lash out at people. And that was bad, very bad…

She had to eat now though, since Soleil would come by to pick her up to go to Violet's place soon. Drop off the computer and a few other things so that Violet wouldn't be totally locked out anymore, and she didn't really feel like bringing her dinner with her in the car again.

Today, dinner was boiled potatoes, some broccoli and something that was probably chicken breast or something, at some point in time anyway. It was, in other words, bland and boring. Some of the dinners they would give her really didn't appeal to her at all, and somehow there was this big thing about 'giving her what she needs' but then as long as she didn't get full-on panic attacks they would give her the grossest food that they could give her. Frustrating.

As she shoved a bite of 'chicken' into her mouth, she scanned through the messages on the DoE and HF forums, checking if there had been interesting posts today while she'd been off doing other things. But even though people everywhere were talking about the press conference, a quick glance didn't give her anything new about what was said or real useful theories about what Daryl meant by his words.

Apparently, some people were insisting that the specific words that Daryl had used were 'just his way of talking', while others were freaking out about people going to be round up and shipped off because they'd been in jail… Neither was very useful. And none of the people in these discussions seemed to really grasp that the 'disappearances' really were connected to HF like they'd been saying on the forums and that they hadn't been random and that Daryl had just told them in exactly what way the blitzing worked.

So, apart from once again realising that the world really was filled with people who had no idea how those with money thought about those who didn't have as much money to spend or those who they deemed 'useless' to society, like they usually thought about her. There didn't seem to be any new information that she could use to figure out what to do next. None.

Too bad.

She felt like she was running out of options, out of avenues of how to find new information, or on what was going to happen. And that didn't leave her with a good feeling at all.

She wanted to fix this, she wanted to stop Daryl from potentially blitzing a whole load of new people, just because of his deranged ideas.

Then a call came in. Soleil.

Willow accepted the call. "Hey." She was tired, but she knew she had to go on for a while longer.

"Hey." Soleil sounded just tired as her. "I'll be there soon. I'm on my way."

"Okay." Willow stabbed at her food a couple of times. "Any news?"

Soleil was silent for a few moments, but when she spoke again, her voice was quieter. "Yeah. They found Sage, and… Yeah."

That didn't sound good. "What is it?"

"You're probably going to want to talk to them yourself. There are some things that even I don't know how to explain."

"Bad things?"

"Depends on your definition of 'bad'. Honestly. There is 'good news', but it's being overshadowed by the implications of it and… Yeah, Sage will explain it better."

"You're being confusing." Willow pushed the plate away from her, really not feeling like eating any of this right now. Then she grabbed her jacket, put it on, and went out the door. Soleil still hadn't said anything. "Soleil?"

"Yeah, sorry. Was just reading something. Ehm… We're going to have to set up a call with Sage so that they can explain everything themselves. But right now… I don't have much else for you."

"What *can* you tell me?" Willow went to the food machine at the base of the building, getting herself a spicy beef wrap and a simple tomato and cucumber salad. That seemed much more appealing to her right now, much more than the potatoes and other bland food she still had upstairs.

"Sage is part of a group who have found something in HF that can explain what's been going on, but it's going to be hard to fix, and I don't know how safe it will be." Still with the confusing things.

"Will it ever be? Safe?"

"No, I guess not." Soleil sighed. "Are you ready to go?"

"In a moment, I still have to get the computer downstairs and everything." She went back up the stairs, to her apartment, putting the food near the door so she could grab it on her way out.

"Okay. See you in a moment."

"See ya." Willow disconnected the call and went over to the box with the computer. She'd opened it before, but never did much with it, too preoccupied with the blitzing and the people going missing and the trying to get her friends back. It just hadn't seemed like a good use of her time to actually play with it.

She took the coding books out of the box, that would at least make it a lot lighter, and it wasn't like Violet would need those.

Then, as she was reorganising everything in the box for easier and safer transport, the bell rang.

The trip to Violet's place seemed a lot longer this time, now that Willow knew what they were going to do, and now she actually looked forward to seeing Violet again. The box with the computer was in the back of the car, they had to carry it down together because it was so heavy, but they managed it, even though it hadn't been easy. And now they were just waiting until the car got them to where they had to be.

Willow looked out the window, her eyes going over all the different buildings, her mind somewhere else entirely. Then she opened the chat screen.

> **Willow:** ??
> **Rotnem:** What is it?
> **Willow:** Where does Sage live?
> **Rotnem:** Not in the slums. If that's what you're worried
>   about.
> **Willow:** Where?
> **Rotnem:** I don't know if it's okay if I tell you, so I can't
>   right now.

Soleil had already said that it was hours away by plane, but not in which direction that would be. So Willow still had no idea. She kind of wanted to know where Sage lived, if only to figure out what she could do to help them.

> **Rotnem:** Sage is fine. They actually have an old-school
>   computer to connect to the net, and we should be
>   able to talk to them soon.

"Talk to them?" Willow now looked straight at Soleil. "I can chat with them, voice chat?"

Soleil nodded. "We're just waiting until Violet is here too, that way we can all talk at once. Keep everyone in the loop at the same time."

Willow sighed. They still had quite a way to go before they would reach Violet's place, and now she had to wait until they were there before she could talk to her Sage. But at least she *could* talk to them, that was a good thing. Right?

She closed her eyes as she leaned her head against the cold window. Maybe she could just nap for the rest of the trip, just sleep for a little while so that she wasn't so exhausted when she actually saw Violet and spoke to Sage later. The movements of the car were soothing, the light humming from the electric motor a steady sound to focus on, her brain slowing down.

Then she startled as someone touched her arm.

"Willow?" That was Soleil, and she realised that the car was no longer moving. It had stopped. And they were at Violet's place. Okay…

"I'm here. Awake-ish." She felt drowsy, she must really have fallen asleep really deep.

"Good. You may want to go ring the bell." Soleil pointed at the building.

"Yeah." Willow got out of the car, the biting cold night air waking up her up more, and went over to the building. She rang the same bell as she had before, somewhere in her heart still scared that Violet wouldn't be there, that last night never happened.

A crackling sound came from a speaker near the bell. "Hello." That was Violet's voice!

"Hey, we're here." Willow smiled, breathing a little easier, her brain now starting to get fully awake.

"I'll be right down." The light crackling from the speaker stopped, and Willow stepped away from the door, waiting on Violet. Then the door opened, and Violet burst out, a huge smile on her face. The next moment Willow was wrapped in Violet's arms. "You're back."

"I'm here." Willow didn't know what else to answer, just glad to see her friend again and enjoying the closeness. Then she remembered what happened to Sage and that Violet didn't know anything about what happened today yet. "We need to talk. Stuff has happened."

Violet let go of her, and when Willow looked at her, Violet seemed worried. "Bad?"

Willow shrugged a little. "Sage found something, and then got blitzed. Pretty bad?"

Violet's eyes grew. "What?! Are you serious? Are they okay?"

"They're okay. Soleil was able to set up a call with them, but she wants you to be there too." Willow started going to the car, tugging on Violet's arm a little, but then let go. Too awkward.

They got back into the car, Willow sitting in the front and Violet in the back.

"Hey." Soleil nodded at Violet.

"Hey." Violet nodded back. "Thanks for setting this up."

"Yeah. Of course." Then Soleil hit a couple of buttons, and the inside of the car changed, turning Soleil and Willow's seats so that they were all sitting in a sort-of circle towards the middle of the car. "Ready?" Soleil looked at Willow.

Willow nodded. Was she ready to talk to Sage? Of course she was.

Soleil hit a couple of buttons in the air, and a module in the middle of the car lit up. In her AR view, Willow could see two portraits, one of a guy about the same age as Soleil, and one with just a generic grey person outline thing. Under the man was the name 'Aster' and under the empty portrait it said

'Sage'.

When Willow glanced at Violet next to her, she remembered that Violet probably couldn't see anything special now.

Soleil handed Violet a headset plus microphone contraption, which Violet easily slid on. "That way we can all hear each other easier." Soleil tapped in the air again. "You two ready on the other end?"

"I'm ready," said a lower male voice that Willow didn't recognise, probably Aster.

"I'm ready." This time Willow did recognise the voice. Sage!

"Hi Sage." Willow couldn't help her grinning.

"Willow, hi! I heard that Violet would be there too?" Sage sounded the same as they always did, calm and collected, like everything was normal.

"Yeah, I'm here too." Violet smiled, her eyes closed as she leaned back. "I heard you were making problems while I wasn't looking?"

"Depends on what you call 'problems', I was trying to figure out what was going wrong and get you back to playing with us again." Willow could hear the grin in Sage's voice.

"And that's why we're all here now," Aster spoke up. "Sage here triggered something that not only kicked them out of the system but also a couple of others who had been there with them."

"Others?" Willow didn't like the sound of that.

"Yeah…" Sage didn't sound so happy anymore. "Ehh… Remember that I talked about blitzing? Well, I found out about that from some place online, and a couple of us from that place got together, and we started hunting around in the code of HF… We may have found a few things that those in control of HF didn't like us to see… We got caught and then kicked out of the system. And then blitzed, of course, for good measure."

"But you were talking to Opal when you got blitzed." Willow frowned, that was what Opal had said anyway. And the blob in the garden of the guild house was supposed to be Sage…

"Oh, I was. I'd hoped that I may have escaped them when I went into DoE, and then I remembered what you said about needing a blitzed account to track something, if you could. So, I thought that if they were going to blitz me anyway, I could just as well be that link that you used for that." Sage made it sound like the most normal thing in the world. They'd been caught hacking into a game and after they'd been kicked out they made sure to go to a place where Willow knew where to find them so that they could still help, even if they'd lose their account and everything they'd ever done in BASE.

"What did you *do*?" Violet didn't sound very happy either.

"Well…" Sage sighed. "Like I said, we went hunting in the code, just to see if something seemed off. And we found a couple of lines of code that weren't supposed to be there. Code that requested the Personal ID of a player from the main server, pretending that it was just some innocent piece of code… The code kept trying to throw up errors or something to catch account information that HF never should be able to have access to. Basically, bad."

Willow looked a Soleil, she'd shown Willow pieces of code that did exactly that before, when they'd met for the first time. So it hadn't been just a one-off, and now some game was exploiting a flaw that very few people had found before. That couldn't be a coincidence…

Soleil looked at the unit in the middle of the car. "How much did you find out about what it does?"

"We found that HF runs player profiles through some sort of closed-off system while you're in the introduction video and if it does get an error, it will, ehh… *flag* your account. Which we suspect means that you're going to get a blitz. The thing is, this code can also be used stand-alone, so they can run BASE IDs through it without the need for the person affected to actually be inside the game. The strange thing we found though, is that it's in some system that is connected to HF, but doesn't seem to really part of it, as if it's not meant for players, just for some specific people, but it's still part of the game and it's still a game area. It was kind of confusing and strange."

Well, that explained how they could blitz the people who'd never even played HF, they only needed the BASE ID and could run it.

"Can we see it?" Willow would love to see the actual code, just to see how it worked. Coding was an interesting art, but also because this was just… evil.

"I've got the code. I was able to swipe it before we were found out," Sage replied. "It's stored offline, they can't get to it. We'll have to find a way to let me send it to you soon."

"And now what?" Violet looked interested. "Can we go after them? Kick their ass? Stop this all from taking out even more people?"

"How would you like to get a new BASE account?" The smirk in Sage's voice was unmistakable.

Violet's eyes went wide as she stared at Willow.

A new BASE account? Was that even possible? Could they really get Violet and maybe even Sage a new BASE account?

Because if they could, that would mean that they'd be able to play again… And maybe even help out.

27

What Friends Do for Each Other

Willow looked between Soleil and Violet. Was this true? Could Sage really get Violet a new BASE account? And what would that mean for them playing videogames together or what would that mean for all the other players who had gotten their accounts blitzed?

"Really?" Violet's voice was surprised.

"Really. But it's going to be expensive. Very expensive."

Willow looked at Soleil, whose gaze was dark. "You can buy new BASE accounts? Is that true, Soleil?" Because that meant that they could have gotten Violet a new account sooner...

Soleil shrugged, her gaze not lightening. "Sure. There is a black market trade in BASE accounts, so I'm not surprised. But if you get caught with one..."

Yeah, the chances they would be taking with that would be significant. Trading in black market accounts didn't seem like the safest thing to do or the best thing when you could probably be banned or something for doing it. But they didn't really have another choice, did they? Violet and Sage's original accounts couldn't be used anymore anyway, Soleil already knew that.

"I can get us new accounts, just say the word." Sage was calm, but they were very serious.

Violet shook her head. "I don't know. I don't have any money in my accounts right now, I don't have any accounts. I can't pay for it myself."

If money was the issue… "We have the guild funds. And the boat, that will bring in a pretty penny." Willow shrugged. What other use would they have for them if a large part of their guild wasn't even there?

Violet didn't look very happy about that. "But what about trading? What about making money long-term?"

"I don't think any of us want to play if you two can't join us." Willow reached out to Violet, taking her hand. "You're all part of our guild. We can make the money again, but we can't get new friends like you two so easily." She squeezed Violet's hand a little. "I'll talk to the others. Just say it."

Violet's eyes closed, but she nodded just a little. "Okay." Her voice was quiet.

"Good! I'll start looking around." Sage suddenly sounded much more upbeat.

"I'll just pretend I didn't hear any of this," Aster spoke up, Willow had almost forgotten he was there with them.

"Me too." Soleil raised an eyebrow at both of them. "I don't think it's the best idea, but it's not like we've got many other options right now. I'll see about a more legal solution as soon as this whole mess is over."

"Thanks." Violet grinned at her.

"Now, we've got a computer to install and a few things to set up so that Violet can join you in your antics again. So I think we should go do that now. Hopefully we'll talk to you two soon, under better circumstances." Soleil started clicking around in front of her again.

"Talk to you soon!" Sage called out.

"Later," Aster said.

"Soon!" Violet nodded, looking a little happier now.

"Talk to you later." Willow looked away from the hovering cards to the computer stashed in the back of the car, and from the corner of her eye, she saw the cards disappear.

Soleil started to move. "Time to get a few things done. I can't keep messing with Willow's BASE messages, we'd both get in trouble, so I need to get her home preferably soon-ish."

Willow nodded, not liking that idea, but she knew it was true.

At least, with Sage's new information, they now had something to go on with their plans, instead of going in blind constantly.

Maybe Sage getting blitzed wasn't the best thing, but at least they'd found out something very useful and important. Something that they'd needed, they now had the code of what triggered the blitz.

Now they just needed a way to disable it.

Willow and Soleil didn't stay long at Violet's place. After they'd set up the computer, they configured a chat for Violet that could interact with a specific type of old-school chat that could still be accessed from the BASE platform. Then they set up a chatroom with Violet, Sage and Willow in it. Willow was going to get the others into the chat later, after they knew for sure that the others were on board with the plan. When they left, Willow fell asleep in the car, she was that exhausted.

After Soleil had brought her up to her apartment, she'd looked at Willow with a sad look in her eyes and she'd apologised, although Willow didn't really have any idea why. She was too tired to think straight, so she'd have to ask Soleil again in the morning.

When Willow had finally gotten to bed, she'd fallen asleep fast. So exhausted. Little sleep the night before, and then being all over the place all day, and then finally going over to Violet's place late... Yeah, that wasn't really good for her energy.

When Willow woke up the next morning, there was a notification already slowly blinking at her. Before she did anything else, she opened it, her heart beating. A notification could mean anything at this point. But it was just a simple message from the BASE platform.

Helheim Fallen Online goes live in 5 days! Have you bought your pre-order copy yet?

Was it there to taunt her, or was this a normal message that everyone who signed up for the beta keys got? She didn't know, but it still annoyed her.

Five days until they went live meant that the new beta keys would be sent out in two days... If they had to get into HF to fix this, they had two days to make sure that the others from the guild also got into HF. And two days to make sure that

Violet and Sage could buy new BASE accounts to do that…

Willow stretched and sat up, going to the living room and throwing the plate of food from last night away before picking up breakfast.

Then, as she made a sandwich, she opened the chat with the members of the guild who were still left.

> **Willow:** Opal? Juniper? You there?

She started eating, enjoying some quiet time because the rest of the day was going to be really busy, she already knew that.

> **Opal:** Yes. I'm here. Any news?
> **Willow:** Yeah. Just… Not going to be fun.
> **Opal:** I don't care. Is Sage safe?
> **Willow:** Yes, they're safe, and they had a plan, but
> they're going to need us for it.
> **Juniper:** What's the plan?
> **Willow:** Meet me in DoE in ten minutes, I'll explain more
> there.

That way she could finish her breakfast and get dressed before she dove back into the VR world.

> **Opal:** Sure.
> **Juniper:** I may be a couple of minutes late, but I'll try to
> be there as soon as possible.
> **Willow:** Thanks.

They had no idea what she was about to ask them. But there was only so much that she could do on her own, as a guild they were a lot stronger, and had a lot more resources.

Willow finished her sandwich and then changed into clean clothes before she made herself comfortable on the bed. Then she opened the chat with Violet and Sage.

> **Willow:** I'm about to ask the others. This will work out. I
> promise.

Then she went to the chat with Soleil.

Finally, she put on the VR headset, ready to get things done. No matter if she'd have to do it on her own or if they were going to work together. One way or another, she was going to make sure that Violet and Sage would be back at their side soon.

You are now logged into Destruction of Elysium

As Willow materialised in the guild house, she looked around, at all the things they'd collected over the years. At all the things she had in her account, everything they'd fought so hard for to gather. And now they were going to give it all up. She was going to ask the others to give it all up too… And she'd still do it, even without Opal and Juniper, she was going to do it.

Willow opened her marketplace screen and pulled up her current inventory. So many things would have been sold at a higher price if they had more time to make this happen. But they were going to need the money soon, very soon.

*You're selling 19 Linen Cloth for 457 coins each, 8,683 coins
in total*

*You're selling 19 Linen Cloth for 457 coins each, 8,683 coins
in total*

As she went she split the stacks up into amounts that were easier to sell off for a slightly higher price. There was a perfect stack size and pricing amount for everything. You could sell larger stacks off for a slightly lower price faster, but a medium or small size stack could sell slightly higher because some people really didn't want 99 or 100 pieces of something at a time. So she put up a range of stack sizes so that she could hopefully sell them off as soon as possible.

You're selling 99 Linen Cloth for 449 coins each, 44,451 coins in total

You're selling 99 Linen Cloth for 449 coins each, 44,451 coins in total

You're selling 49 Flax for 386 coins each, 18,914 coins in total

While she was loading all she had onto the marketplace, Opal and Juniper both came online too.

Opal: Willow?

She went to the garden, where Opal was, and soon Juniper too.

"I spoke to Sage and Violet last night." She spoke, because she didn't want there to be too much of a trace of what she was about to tell them, audio felt better for that.

"And?" Opal looked at her, a little surprised.

"Sage found something… It points to a systematic thing in HF, and they said it could probably be fixed from inside HF." She took a deep breath.

"Okay?" Juniper raised her eyebrow. "And?"

Willow licked her lips before she spoke the next words. "If we get enough money together, we can get Violet and Sage new BASE accounts. Hopefully. So that they can come back and help out too."

"How much?" Opal frowned.

"I don't know. A lot, that's all I know." Willow didn't look at them, instead looking at the ground. "I'm going to sell everything I have here. Between getting Sage and Violet new

BASE accounts and them not having accounts to even pay for their rent and everything else right now. I'm going to sell everything off here. I just wanted to let you know."

"Willow…" She felt Juniper's hand on her arm. "I'm right there with you. Of course. It's just not the same without them."

"Me too." Opal also stepped closer. "We've played together for years now. You're almost closer than family to me. And if going into HF and fixing whatever Sage found will make sure that we all can keep playing for years to come. Of course, I'm joining you."

Willow nodded, a tightness in her chest. "Thanks. Thanks so much."

She opened the chat with violet and Sage.

Willow: They're in.

Then she looked up at her friends. "Thank you, for everything."

"Of course." Opal grinned, then he pulled a face. "You're going to want to sell the boat too, I presume? And the house?"

Willow nodded, still not very comfortable with the idea herself, but they had to do it. "Everything. Every last bit of it."

The exchange rate to credits for DoE wasn't very good, but it was all they had right now, at least, it was all Willow would be able to contribute.

"And I'm trying to get us all into HF for the next beta batch. I know that it's scary, but I'm going to need you, we're all going to need you." She kept her voice low, fear still in her heart. She had no idea how she was going to make this work. How she was going to defeat a game from the inside out. But with her friends at her side, she could try and make the best of it.

They had two days to sell everything they had in this game off and try to get Violet and Sage new accounts and also get all four of them into HF… It wasn't going to be easy, but it was the only thing they could do. It was the only plan they had.

Sell everything they had.

Get Violet and Sage new accounts.

Get all four of them into the new batch of beta keys of HF that was going out in two days time.

Find the weak spot in the game.

Fix the piece of coding which was targeting people to get blitzed.

It sounded so simple…

Right…

III
Return

28
The Road Back

Willow stood in the middle of the capital in HF, waiting for Dawn to join her. Her stomach was all in knots, because she had no idea how Dawn would react when she told him her plan. But she had to try. He'd been helping her out a lot and she wanted him to know what was going on in HF because if things went wrong, he'd be affected too. So she had to try and ask him.

She could really use a second player to help the others when they'd get their beta keys in a couple of hours. Sage and Violet didn't have their new accounts yet, but they should be getting them in the next few hours or days, hopefully. Which was sort of the downside of their plan... a lot depended on 'hopefully'.

Hopefully everyone could get the beta keys. Hopefully Sage and Violet could get their new accounts in time. Hopefully they wouldn't get blitzed again when they logged in. Lots of hopefully.

For the last few days, Willow had been selling off everything she owned in DoE, just hoping that she could scrape together enough money for Violet and Sage. And last night, finally, they got the news about the amount of money they'd need to get them the new accounts.

They'd had enough, everything added together, after they'd sold the house and the boat. They'd had enough, but just barely. Luckily, there was still money coming in from auctions that hadn't run out yet, so they'd have a little bit of a buffer after this was all done. But Willow's bank account looked frighteningly empty, which was why she really hoped that this was all going to work out. She didn't want to imagine things going wrong anymore, not now.

Dawn has come online

Meadow: Hey!

She wrote the message as fast as she could, trying to push away her anxiety.

Dawn: Hey. Missed you online, what happened? Work got you all wrapped up in it?

Even now he seemed to sort of think that she had a job or something… Yeah, she was going to have to explain that to him at some point.

Meadow: Helped a couple of friends who were in trouble.

This time the message back took a while longer.

Dawn: The same trouble we talked about last time?

She'd sort of told him about the blitzed accounts, but she wasn't sure how much he really believed her.

Meadow: Yes.
Dawn: Oh.

Meadow: I need your help…
Meadow: My friends and I need your help.
Dawn: In what way?
Dawn: I don't know how much I can help without…

He was scared, of course he was scared. Everyone would be scared having to decide between helping out someone they barely knew and putting their account in danger or their account being in the same danger if they didn't help…

Meadow: I just need someone to help train my friends when they get their beta keys later today.
Dawn: How do you know?
Dawn: No. Don't answer that. Helping training them sounds like it should be fine. But I can't get involved in anything illegal.
Meadow: No worries. I'm not asking that. Just that I need someone who has a little bit more knowledge about the game to help power level them. I can't do that on my own.
Dawn: I can do that. Sure.

Her heart skipped a beat, and she felt a lot lighter suddenly. He was in, he was going to help them.

Meadow: Thanks!
Dawn: We should probably go to the starter zone then, wait there for them?
Meadow: Yeah, I was thinking that.

Because on foot… It could take them a while before they'd arrive back at the encampment.

Meadow: I don't suppose there is a faster way than walking?
Dawn: No. You're not actually supposed to go back… just forward.

Yeah, she'd suspected as much. She hadn't seen any easy ways to travel around here yet, apart from the boat, which she wasn't able to get on yet anyway because she was too low level.

Meadow: Let's go then.

They started making their way to the gate of the capital, ready to get back to where it all began.

Willow really wanted to keep checking in with her friends, making sure everything was going according to plan. They'd guessed that if they got the beta keys from someone within the company, that they would probably be safer from the blitzing code thing than getting a real one. Hopefully.

> **Dawn:** I was wondering... You got here late, not with the rest of the batch of beta players. Did you get 'help' coming in here too?

Could she really trust him? She kept wanting to trust him, but she just didn't know if she should. They'd been having fun together, sure, but there wasn't anything that said that she could trust him with information like that without him going to the mods or devs with what he knew and ruin everything.

> **Meadow:** Maybe? Would it matter?

Dawn kept walking, but she could see him think, the way he frowned.

> **Dawn:** Maybe. Would my opinion matter?
> **Meadow:** Only if you report me to the game creators.

That made Dawn smile a little.

> **Dawn:** No. It doesn't matter to me. It just means that a couple of things are making more sense now...
> **Dawn:** So, your friends, what are they like? Are they as easy going and enthusiastic as you are?

Willow grinned, totally ready for a change in topic.

> **Meadow:** They're a lively bunch. They can be a handful, but we've known each other for a long time, played a lot of games together.
> **Dawn:** That's nice. Friends like that aren't easy to find.
> **Meadow:** You can borrow mine sometimes.

She meant it too. Dawn had been great while they'd been playing here, so if everyone got along well, he was welcome to join them whenever.

Dawn: Thanks.

Then they fell into silence, just walking down the road. There weren't a lot of people here, they were mostly on their own. Willow watched her surroundings change, forests appearing at her sides, the trees covered in ice and snow.

This was really getting back to where it all began.

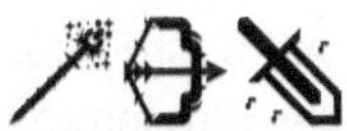

Now that she was more familiar with the game, she saw the world in the starter zone a little differently, less overwhelming. The first thing that she noticed was that the encampment wasn't its own instance, which she had considered as a possibility before, but that it had simply been empty because everybody had already left. Then she noticed that the captains who had given her the first quests now had levels above their heads, something she hadn't seen before.

Meadow: We can attack the NPCs here?
Dawn: Apparently?

He saw him look around too, his eyes going over to the captains and then to some of the other NPCs they could see from here.

Meadow: Is that new or does it not show up when
you're too low level?
Dawn: I've not heard about this before, but the game
doesn't really think about players going back to the
lower zones, so either is possible, we may have
just unlocked it at some point during levelling.

Willow shrugged. Yeah, but it did give her some interesting

ideas.

> **Meadow:** It means we could potentially kill them. Just
> hunt and main them.

Although, the NPCs were still more than ten levels above even Dawn. And that ignored the fact that there were a lot more NPCs than just the two of them as players… So, for now, this was purely theoretical.

> **Dawn:** Don't even try… Not looking forward to getting
> killed off. I'm not even sure we'd spawn around
> here if we did…
> **Dawn:** Or that we'd put a target on our head that will
> mean they will keep trying to kill us off…

Hmm, interesting ideas. She hadn't even considered that.

> **Meadow:** Don't worry, I'm not doing anything.

She pulled up her timer, checking how much longer it would take for the people with beta keys to show up.

Global time: '42 - 05 - 30 09:39

Local time: '42 - 03 - 30 10:39

System: Good morning

About twenty more minutes before the keys would drop… She sighed, then looked around and leaned back against the fence a little while off from the captains.

Twenty minutes until the beta keys were handed out, but they'd still have to wait on everyone actually getting through the character creation before they'd show up here.

> **Meadow:** BRB.

She swiped the menu up.

You are now logged out of Helheim Fallen Online

She checked in on the chat with her friends.

> **Opal:** How long before the new accounts come in?
> **Sage:** No idea. Sorry.
> **Juniper:** And what if they're not on time?
> **Willow:** Then we're going to have to do this on our own
> until they can get in.
> **Violet:** Willow! Aren't you supposed to wait for us in the
> game?
> **Willow:** Just wanted to mention that Dawn is willing to
> help out, please be nice to him.
> **Sage:** Aren't we always?

Willow narrowed her eyes, even though of course nobody could see it.

> **Willow:** Just be good.
> **Willow:** I hate waiting.
> **Opal:** Tell me about it, at least you get to play while
> waiting, we're just sitting around.

Then she checked in with Soleil. But Soleil hadn't responded yet to the message she'd sent this morning asking if everything was in place. She either was still asleep, or didn't have any updates. Either of which Willow couldn't do anything about. Then she went back to her friends.

> **Willow:** I'm going back into the game. Just find me
> there. Don't scare when you see me. I'm Meadow.
> **Willow:** Good luck everyone.

She was still as nervous as before, not having calmed down at all.

She really did hate waiting.

You are now logged into Helheim Fallen Online

She appeared back in the same spot she'd been in before, Dawn at her side.

> **Dawn:** Anything?

She shook her head. It would have been nice if there had been something new she could share with him, but there wasn't anything new. It was just waiting, a waiting game.

Nothing more. It was HF's move first, sending out the new keys.

The first new players started to appear a little while off. First, just two or three at a time, but then the influx went faster. Each of the players had their own newbie pet, the ugly little almost gremlin-like creature that was so annoying and boring.

But it was also kind of fun to see all the new players show up, she'd not seen anyone go through that same frustrating start as she'd been through. There was something compelling about the different choices people made about who they were going to play as. And since people knew so little about what each race or class could do, apart from the most basic class type conventions, it was mostly going to depend on their favourite play styles, or their creativity or experimentation as they logged on.

There were a lot of elves and humans walking around, as she'd expected, since it was the same when she was in the city. Then there were the handful of jötnar and draugar.

She noticed that there were very few dwarves walking around though. She'd thought that those would be more popular than the undead draugar, with their bright red-orange beards and their stocky build. Although, as she looked at a few of them, without fail, all of them were wearing loincloths and little else… Warriors, mages, hunters, all of them. *Hmm.* That may be one of the reasons so few people played them… She'd seen some dwarves before in the capital, but every piece of gear after the starter gear at least covered the private bits of dwarves better. But players couldn't see that when they chose their starter race, of course.

She tried looking for her friends, sort of knowing what to expect from them, but they could always surprise her. They'd done that before.

She remembered Juniper choosing to play as a tank-warrior golem in some strange freebie fantasy VRMMORPG they'd tried about a year back. Juniper was about as far from a tank player as could be. But that hadn't mattered much as, about three hours in, it had bugged out on them, forcing them to start a character all over again. So they'd dropped it and went back to DoE.

Then, a decently tall dwarf with a huge hammer slung over his shoulder came walking up to them. The name above him said 'Opal'. Of course, well, that wasn't unexpected at all. Opal, the berserker dwarf. She should have known.

Willow invited him into their party and Opal immediately accepted it.

> **Opal:** Hi!
> **Meadow:** Hi.
> **Dawn:** Hi. You must be one of her friends?
> **Opal:** You could say that.

He grinned, the beard moving, and it looked kind of funny. She'd seen Opal as a human warrior before, but a dwarf, especially a half-naked one, would be exactly what he'd like. Especially if he could make other people uncomfortable looking like this.

Then an elven lady with a bow came over, waving. Juniper.

She also invited Juniper into their party.

Meadow: Hey! Any news?

Juniper shook her head, frowning a little.

Juniper: Nothing. They hadn't gotten anything before
we jumped in.

Willow nodded, her heart heavy. Would they be able to pull it off with just the four of them, or did they really need Violet and Sage too? It would be good to have Sage at her side, especially since they knew so much about coding. It would have been a real help for whatever they were going to have to do.

Dawn: You should probably go do the starter quests,
and then we can all go out together for the other
quests.
Opal: Can't we just go and kill stuff?
Meadow: Do you have attacks on your bar?

She watched as Opal checked his interface, his face falling.

Opal: Oh.
Meadow: Yes.
Opal: FINE.

He took Juniper's arm and then they went off to the captains together, getting the quests they would need.

Dawn looked at her, smiling.

Dawn: Yeah, the game has a pretty strict linear start, I'd
forgotten about that.

Willow hadn't forgotten about it, because it had annoyed her so much when she first started playing. It was just so annoying and there was no need for it. Like everything else in this game, there were just decisions that made no sense, but still somehow ended up in the final game.

She wondered if some people who made this game even knew what people liked best about playing MMORPGs, but probably not. Such a strictly linear progression at the start of the game was definitely not in line with things that people tended to appreciate most. Loads of players loved to just go kill a few things before they started the quest lines, but that wasn't possible here.

As she watched the new players, some of them started to look more and more frustrated with the UI and other things, before resignation set in and they would follow exactly what the ugly starter creature told them that the game wanted them to do. Grumbling the whole way.

Then a new message showed up in her chat, this one not in the party chat, but a private message.

Sage: *We're in.*

29
A Sizable Surprise

Willow looked over her group of friends. Everyone had been able to get into the game, they were finally complete again. They were finally all together in the same game.

Violet had chosen a female elven hunter, beautiful and deadly, like Juniper, and Sage was a human mage, which surprised Willow a little, Sage tended to pick unique races when playing, but now picked the most plain race there was, although, their fylgja was a huge bear, which was interesting in its own way.

But, all in all, they turned out to be a colourful bunch of players. Everyone had finished the starter quests around the encampment, and they were about to go out into the world to kill some wolves.

> **Violet:** Anything we have to watch out for?
> **Meadow:** Make sure you don't get sneaked up on from
> behind? But that's kind of useless right now…

Violet grinned her way and Willow grinned back. Yeah,

well, as a solo player, that was kind of a worry.

Sage: That wolf?

They pointed at one of the wolves standing a while off. Everyone else went into their attack stance as Sage's bear Arthur and Opal ran at the wolf, almost as if they were trying to outrun each other.

Arthur hit the Dire Wolf for 32 damage
Opal hit the Dire Wolf for 40 damage

Then the range attacks also hit it as the wolf focused on Sage's bear.

Juniper hit the Dire Wolf for 36 damage
Sage hit the Dire Wolf for 24 damage
Violet hit the Dire Wolf for 35 damage
Opal hit the Dire Wolf for 41 damage
+ 2 XP

And then it fell down, curling up with a low moan. Next to her Willow saw Juniper's face fall, as she watched the movements. If Juniper thought that was bad…

Meadow: Butcher it, Opal, you need the meat for the
quests.
Opal: How?
Dawn: Grab your butchering knife, and make a cut down
the belly of the wolf. Put some pressure behind it.

Opal knelt down on the belly side of the wolf and Willow winced, knowing what was about to happen. He took the knife out of his inventory, running it over the belly of the wolf, like he would do in DoE, but nothing happened, and he looked up at them, frowning.

Meadow: Push harder, you really have to cut in.

Opal raised an eyebrow, but then really put some strength behind it, the knife disappearing into the stomach of the wolf as he cut it open. The guts and blood flowed over his hand as he did so and his eyes grew as he finished the slice, a mixture of curiosity and apprehension on his face.

Next to her, Juniper retched and she could even see Sage turn away from what was going on, looking a little less sure about the 'hyper-realistic' gameplay that HF had been boasting about now.

> **Dawn:** You'll need a strong stomach for some parts of
>   the game.
> **Juniper:** Are you kidding me?
> **Opal:** Gruesome!

Everyone turned to him, and he shrugged.

> **Opal:** What?!
> **Opal:** This is wicked.

At least someone was enjoying themselves.

When Willow glanced Violet's way, Violet looked at it with calculated interest, and then Violet eyed her. Willow could almost see the numbers run through her head. Gross butchering skills meant few people would do it which meant more money from selling the items off.

> **Violet:** I suspect that not many people take on
>   butchering?
> **Dawn:** Not many, no.
> **Violet:** So it sells well on the marketplace?
> **Dawn:** You're obviously friends with Meadow...

Willow didn't need to hear his voice to know that Dawn didn't entirely mean that as a compliment. Violet looked at her, smirking. Of course they were.

Then Dawn let out a sigh, looking between them.

> **Dawn:** Yes, meat and leather sells pretty well. Few
>   people have the stomach for this day in, day out.
> **Opal:** Cool! I think I'm starting to like this game.

Juniper shuddered.

> **Juniper:** Not me. Tell me there is something cool about this game that has nothing to do with blood and guts…
>
> **Meadow:** There is, don't worry.

There was a whole cooking and alchemy skill that Juniper would enjoy, especially some of the more curious items an alchemist could make, like bombs. As Willow had seen on the marketplace when she'd been browsing it earlier.

> **Opal:** Next wolf!

Maybe he was a little too enthusiastic about this?

Well, at least the quests would be quicker to complete now they were playing as a team instead of on their own. Things like killing a certain amount of wolves would be much faster, but the gathering quests could still take a while. There was always a payoff in these things.

> **Meadow:** Next wolf.

She pointed ahead, laughing. She felt at home again, surrounded by her friends.

She felt like everything was right again, even though everything was wrong, so wrong.

Willow threw one of her elemental bolts at a goshawk as it came flying for them.

You hit the Goshawk for 126 damage
+ 3 XP

And it crumbled at her feet into a pile of feathers and odd angles. It wasn't much use for her to really join it, the XP she got was only minimal, but that didn't matter. She just had to do something, she didn't want to stand around not doing anything.

That was boring, and she wasn't here for boring stuff.

Getting through the starter quests did indeed go a lot faster than when she had been on her own. There weren't as many new players around them anymore, as they'd progressed through the content a little faster than most, so they got a bit more freedom as to how many creatures they could fight at a time, fewer of them were now being killed by other players. It also meant that they wouldn't be bothering other players as much. Win-win.

Willow stopped as they reached the area where she'd found the corpses of the maimed NPCs before.

Meadow: I want to show you guys something…

She started walking to the area, slowly moving as the corpses came into view. They were exactly the same as last time. Thrown about the place like they were dolls someone had gotten tired of playing with. Rotting and decomposed dolls…

Meadow: This is actually for a quest you'll either get
soon or have already picked up.

She couldn't exactly remember the order, but they should be needing this for a quest soon-ish. She watched as the others looked over the corpses, the recognition of the different playable races and classes setting in.

Juniper definitely didn't look very happy, turning a little green…

Meadow: But what I really want to show you is a little
further along, this is only part of it.

She walked along the edge of the tree line, and at her side, Iris began to growl again, as she had done before. Then they turned a corner and stood in front of the enormous cave.

Just looking at it gave her a strange feeling in her stomach, a mixture of excitement and dread. Sage's bear began to growl too, its detection range a little more limited, probably because it wasn't a creature with a ranged attack, instead it only had melee attacks.

> **Violet:** What's in there?
> **Meadow:** Something… odd.
> **Meadow:** Keep your eyes open.

She started to walk into the cave, first her eyes going to where the blitzed player had been, hoping that it was gone by now. But as they approached the location, she saw the black blob again. The blitzed player was still here, days after she'd first found them.

> **Dawn:** What the?!
> **Dawn:** Is this…
> **Violet:** Yes, the remnants of a blitzed account.

It hadn't been cleaned up yet, which meant that they were probably not even aware it was here. Which could be alarming or comforting, she didn't know.

Willow saw Violet come closer, her expression grim, her hand slowly sliding into Willow's. And then a new message showed up, but not in the chat, in a private message instead.

> **Violet:** *I'm so sorry this all happened. I can't believe you've been fighting in this world all on your own, just to find out what was going on.*
> **Meadow:** *Thanks. It's been… Soleil has been trying to help as much as she could, but this is…*
> **Violet:** *Yeah…*
> **Violet:** *I wish I could have been there. I wish I could have been at your side, helping you out. It's unfair that you had nobody around.*

Violet squeezed Willow's hand a moment before she let her go.

Yeah, out of everything, one thing she'd really missed was

having Violet here with her. Willow wasn't much of a fighter, but Violet was enough of a fighter for the both of them.

> **Sage:** Where does the cave go?

Willow looked on.

> **Meadow:** I can show you, but you may want a strong-
>   ish stomach for that.
> **Dawn:** Really? This actually goes somewhere?
> **Dawn:** I just thought that it was a cool thing to explore.
>   It gets really dark at some point and I assumed
>   that there would be a wall by then, so I stopped.
> **Dawn:** But there really is more back there?
> **Meadow:** Yep.

As she started walking again, Violet slid her hand into Willow's and walked next to her, Sage close by on her other side, and the rest behind them. She wasn't sure if it was safer or more dangerous to go in there as a group, but they would find out soon enough.

The cave darkened until it was pitch black. They walked in the absolute blackout for a good couple of minutes before it slowly became illuminated with a red-orange glow and the torches showed up on the walls soon after. The sounds of the trolls became louder as they walked on, even with Willow's lowered settings. It took them a couple of minutes before they reached the end of the cave, the sounds now loud and strong.

Willow pointed up.

> **Meadow:** If you climb up there you can look in. You may
>   want to keep your pet back tough.

She didn't need to look into the troll's cave again, the memories of the first time she'd seen them still clear enough in her mind, but the others all climbed up to the window.

> **Dawn:** Wow.
> **Opal:** Scary! Big!

Well, yes. Definitely that. The trolls were impressively big, that was for sure.

A private message showed up.

Sage: *Come up here, I need to show you something.*

Willow looked up at Sage, who was frowning, looking really worried now. That was no good…

She climbed up to the window, right next to Sage. Sage put their arm around her shoulder and then pointed to something at the back wall.

Sage: *That symbol is an early version of the HF logo.*

What? She looked at it again, but it didn't look familiar to her in the slightest.

Meadow: *Are you sure?*

Willow eyed the trolls. Their status bars still showed them as way too high level for her to beat, and maybe they would always show that, no matter what level she got to.

That was a worrying thought.

Sage moved a little, holding up a screen in front of them. Willow recognised it as the same screen she got from the mod's potato. She grabbed her own potato and then held up the X-ray vision to the cave. The trolls looked just like regular monsters, nothing strange there, and the code for them didn't reveal much. They had a lot of HP, and they were weak to some gaming elements, but that was about it. What was much more interesting was the way her screen showed there to be much more coding and things going on around the symbol than just the texture on the wall that they could normally see.

Meadow: *What do you think it is?*
Sage: *I have no idea, but it looks interesting.*

Willow tried to scan the code with her eyes, and then

moved the screen lower, to the empty space underneath the symbol. There was a door hidden below it. A door to somewhere else, a part of the game that was closed off from the outside, she couldn't see anything beyond just the front right now.

> **Meadow:** *You said something about a special area in the game where they could run code and things? Closed off from players but still somehow available from within the game?*

She felt Sage nod.

> **Meadow:** *The door leads to a hidden area, I can't see anything about it. And since it's guarded by trolls that will probably scare off anyone coming close enough to even try to take a second glance.*

Like it had scared her off the first time around. Willow looked at her friends.

> **Meadow:** Dawn, can you see the level on the trolls?

He was still almost twenty levels higher than she was, so it was worth a try. But Dawn shook his head.

> **Dawn:** Nothing. Just generic too high level symbol.

Willow looked at the trolls through her screen again, trying to find the actual level of them. The trolls were level 99. The highest level anyone in the game could currently be was just 50. So this was in place for a specific reason, to make sure nobody passed them. That scared her but also gave her some courage, that meant that they definitely had to check out what was going on behind that door. If they were protecting something, then it had to be important. Important enough for them to try to find out.

> **Meadow:** Okay, let's get back out of the cave.

Because just being here, while the trolls were eating NPC parts for their meal and just walking and sitting around, it didn't make her feel much safer. She had the feeling that if they got too close, they would still pull aggro on them. And they were nothing against the trolls as they were now.

Everyone carefully made their way out of the cave as quickly as possible. Then they rushed past the butchered NPCs. They only dared to breathe again after they'd left all of that behind.

Willow was the first one to burst out laughing, all the tension draining from her body. They must have looked ridiculous, sneaking around like that, trying to be as fast as possible without being heard or for some other way to trigger the trolls or whatever else could be in that cave.

But they had learned something new.

Sage had been right. There was a hidden area in this game, an area they couldn't just reach because it was guarded by mobs that should not be able to exist, at least, their levels were well beyond the range that should be possible right now.

Was that an abandoned area that they'd developed and then just forgotten about, or was there more to it? Was it an area that wasn't supposed to be found? And who would need something like that? Who would use it?

Why would they leave something like that available in the game? And was there a different reason for the blitzed account in the cave than just being caught up in the blitzing because of having a criminal record?

The place had creeped her out before, but now… It left her with even more questions, and not a good feeling about what they had to do to answer them.

30
Power Levelling

Willow took off her VR headset as she sat up in bed, sighing. Together with Dawn, she'd been training the others for hours now, trying to get their level up and to get them used to the mechanics in HF.

Juniper didn't seem too impressed with the butchering and some other more gruesome elements of HF, she was much more squeamish than the others, which Willow had known. And Sage and Violet seemed to have the same reactions to the game that Willow had had mostly, icked out by some things while still enjoying other parts. Only Opal really seemed to enjoy everything in this game. But then, he was into the gross stuff. He'd always been like that. When he wasn't playing DoE, he was usually hanging out in the most gruelling and gory horror games he could find, so she shouldn't have been surprised really.

Willow opened the chat with Soleil, who'd left a couple of messages.

> **Rotnem:** Beta codes have been applied to the available
> accounts, waiting on the others.
> **Rotnem:** It seems Sage and Violet are there with you?
> Are the new accounts working out?
> **Rotnem:** Is everything going well in HF? Just checking
> that there are no issues. Don't want to leave you all
> on your own if there are.

The final message had been from three hours ago. Oops.

> **Willow:** I'm good. Everyone got into HF fine, we've been
> helping them to power level so that they're not so
> far behind us.

The message from Soleil was fast.

> **Rotnem:** We?
> **Willow:** Dawn is helping me. I thought that two people
> who could explain the game would probably better
> than just one. Especially since I don't actually know
> much about it…
> **Rotnem:** Good, I'm glad to hear that.
> **Rotnem:** Anything else going on? Found anything new?

Willow hadn't sorted her thoughts enough yet about what she'd seen in the cave, especially not what it could mean for what they were going to do. How the trolls would fit into everything and the hidden doorway…

> **Willow:** Not yet.
> **Willow:** Still trying to find more clues.
> **Rotnem:** Let me know when you find something.
> **Willow:** Will do.
> **Willow:** Thank the person at HF for the beta keys and
> the mod tools for me, will you?
> **Rotnem:** Will do. Good luck to you.
> **Willow:** Thanks.

She was going to need it.

She stood up, definitely in need of something to eat right about now. There were so many things going on, and she needed to clear her mind a little. Everything was slowly falling into place, but she had no idea as to what that place was or how everything slotted together. She had a lot of puzzle pieces but no clue as to how many there were supposed to be in total and if she had enough of them to even get a rough idea of that...

There was a plan slowly forming in her mind, but it didn't have a shape yet.

Luckily, they had a couple of days left to figure it out. So hopefully, when the time came, there would be an actual plan to work with.

Two days until the release of the most anticipated game of this decade, Helheim Fallen Online!

Order your copy now!

Two days to solve the issue of the blitzed accounts. That wasn't much.

Sure, Sage had given her some good ideas about the code and the programming from what they'd found before they got blitzed, but that didn't really give her enough to go on, really.

Two days.

Two days to power level her friends. Two days to find the place where this code that selected people to blitz and actually blitzed their accounts was located. And two days to make it all stop.

It felt like she still had some time but at the same time no left time at all. When she'd started, there were ten days until release, now there were two days left, and she felt like she'd barely made any progress at all. She'd lost and then gained her friends. She'd gotten her ass handed to her in the game a good number of times. And then she'd found out that there was much more going on in the background of the game and the coding than any of them had suspected.

Dawn: Meadow!

Willow's vision blinked for a moment as a hungry lynx jumped onto her.

> *The Hungry Lynx hit you for 65 damage*

Jikes.

> *Opal hit the Hungry Lynx for 132 damage*
> *Sage hit the Hungry Lynx for 111 damage*
> *+25 XP*

The lynx curled up at her feet. Dead. She stepped aside as Sage came over and butchered the animal.

They were still trying to power level, and even Willow had gained a few levels by now, just from how much content they'd been working through.

It was like they were a machine. Find mobs, kill mobs, butcher mobs, round up items and other things from the area, and then move to the next area. They were running a couple of areas in a system, moving to the next one when they'd killed all the mobs off, instead of waiting for the respawns. That way, when they came back to the area, there would be new mobs to kill.

> *Iris hit the Hungry Lynx for 238 damage*
> *Opal hit the Hungry Lynx for 119 damage*
> *Juniper hit the Hungry Lynx for 98 damage*

Willow looked around, finding Sage's attention on a different mob than the others were working on. She held up her hand, pulling up the %Elementbolt and throwing it at the other lynx, just as Sage also attacked it.

You hit the Hungry Lynx for 135 damage
Sage hit the Hungry Lynx for 80 damage
+25 XP
+25 XP

The notifications came in fast and steady. She barely even had to look at what was going on, just helping everyone out by attacking whatever the others were fighting too.

You've reached level 18!
+4 Strength
+2 Dexterity
+6 Intelligence
+5 Wisdom
+4 Endurance

Iris has reached level 18!
+6 Strength
+4 Intelligence
+ 6 Toughness

She pulled up her character screen to check what her stats were by now.

Name: Meadow
Race: Draugr
Class: Seidhr
Level: 18
Health: 405
Mana: 394
Armour: 38
Strength: 83
Dexterity: 32

Intelligence: 114
Wisdom: 87
Endurance: 72

Fylgja:
Name: Iris
Race: Dreki
Level: 18
Strength: 113
Intelligence: 85
Toughness: 116

She was making good progress with her levels. Although, she had no idea how useful that would be in whatever they were going to face later on. No levels would matter if they were going to take on those trolls, but that still didn't mean that they wouldn't face more reasonable creatures after that.

They'd all agreed that trying to get as high level as possible would probably be their best bet for whatever they were going to face. Too low level wouldn't be useful at all, no matter what. But getting at least a little bit better geared up and having a good range of attacks available to them and a couple of options to protect themselves would make any battle easier.

Or it would make them feel more confident that it would be easier, which in this case was about the same. Never underestimate how much confidence influences a battle, if they felt like they could do it, chances were, they would find a way to do it.

At least, that was the idea. That was about all the plan they'd come up with in the last day.

Sage: Meadow, we're moving.

She looked around, realising she kept spacing out today, and that wasn't good. She'd not slept much last night, her brain constantly going over what they were going to have to do, what they'd done in the last couple of days and all sorts of things like that. The ability of her brain to come up with multiple, in some cases odd, solutions was great. Her brain deciding to do that when she was trying to sleep and had to be active again the next day wasn't so great…

She felt a weight around her shoulders and then Violet pulled her against her.

A private message popped up.

> **Violet:** *What's wrong? Are you upset?*

Willow shook her head.

> **Meadow:** *Just tired. I wish I knew how or if we'd be able to solve this.*

If they couldn't 'fix' the code, then, as soon as the game went live, it would start picking out players who the creators of HF had decided weren't 'worth' it to let into their game and would blitz their accounts, as they'd done to Violet during the beta. Willow wasn't looking forward to that prospect, and it was giving her a lot of stress.

> **Violet:** *I know. Have you heard something from Soleil yet? Does she have something we can use?*
> **Meadow:** *No. Not much. She's waiting for news from us.*
> **Violet:** *Right.*

Then Violet started pulling her along to the rest of the group, who had started to kill off some wolves.

> **Violet:** *All we can do is try to prepare for the worst.*
> **Meadow:** *True.*
> **Violet:** *We're going to make it happen. I know we will.*

Violet flashed her a smile and then pulled on her bow,

shooting a wolf before she put it away again and jumped onto the creature holding two daggers and finishing it off in a flurry of attacks.

Willow couldn't help but smile, but then she turned her hand and healed Violet for a moment.

Violet had still managed to get hit by the wolf twice. If Violet was going to survive in PVE on her own, she really had to consider her own squishiness when it came to fighting monsters. Sure, right now, Dawn and Willow healed her when needed, but that wouldn't keep happening, especially if they were going to play this game more after all the problems were over.

But first, they had to make sure that they *could* keep playing this game…

The group had moved to a zone that Willow hadn't been in yet. With the six of them together, they were able to take on monsters who were a good number of levels above them instead of having to stay around their own level zone.

In this zone, they had to fight big brown bears. They looked similar to Sage's fylgja, but the most significant difference was that they were definitely not as friendly, well, that, and the crazed look in their eyes. Apparently, in the normal storyline, that would have brought them into this zone, it would have been explained that they'd been poisoned by the ones invading Helheim, to turn against the creatures that they used to live in peace with. Fun, very fun.

Opal hit the Crazed Bear for 166 damage
Juniper hit the Crazed Bear for 141 damage

The bear fell down, curling up and letting out a loud death groan. Opal butchered the bear with significant skill and didn't look unhappy with the items he got from it.

Then, next to her, Juniper fell forward, a bear on her back. *What the?!*

Willow pulled up a bolt and threw it at the bear as quickly as she could.

Juniper was finally able to crawl from under the bear, more than three-quarters of her health gone in a single strike. *Jikes.*

Willow tried healing her as fast as she could, as Dawn helped too. They had not expected that to happen.

That was… That was definitely not something they'd expected to happen. They thought that they'd been safe, but apparently, a bear had spawned behind them, and they hadn't realised it. Fighting mobs way above their level helped with the XP gain, but it also meant that everyone was a lot more squishy if they did get hit by one, especially classes that weren't made for melee combat much.

> **Juniper:** Wow. That was scary.
> **Opal:** Tell me about it. I suddenly saw your HP go from full to almost gone. I thought that you'd gotten hit by a system bug or something, not just a bear.

When Willow looked at they others, everyone looked spooked. They'd been flying through the content easily, but this was the first time that they realised that things weren't that easy in this game… That even in a group they could get surprised.

> **Sage:** Pay more attention, people. We don't want anyone to suddenly drop out on us.
> **Sage:** I don't feel like waiting on some people who need to run back here from the respawn point.
> **Opal:** Yeah.
> **Dawn:** Yeah.
> **Violet:** Definitely.

Willow looked behind her, the area where the bear had spawned was only small, it was just the path they'd taken into this location plus a little extra, but even in that space had been a spawn point. They shouldn't have been this reckless when they stormed in.

> **Juniper:** Next one!

She'd obviously recovered from the shock, ready for more. Then Juniper pointed at a bear a little off but waited with attacking it until Opal, Sage's bear, Iris and Violet were already on their way to attack it first. Then, with a satisfied grin, she pulled the arrow on her bow back and let it fly, hitting the bear right before the others reached it.

Willow grabbed Juniper by her shoulder and pulled her to the side, hoping to get her out of range of whatever may try to maim her from behind next. Willow wasn't going to let anything sneak up on them again, not now.

Just as the others killed the bear, a new one spawned not too far off. And as Willow pointed at it, Iris ran for the mob, getting in close range, before firing her cone of fire. The others now also saw the bear and went for it, just as Willow used her AOE spell on it.

Iris hit the Crazed Bear for 253 damage
You hit the Crazed Bear for 208 damage

Opal: Meadow! Why?

As she looked his way, she saw that the heat of the AOE kept Opal from attacking the bear too. It may not do any damage to him, but that didn't mean that the heat of it wasn't uncomfortable.

Meadow: Sorry?

Opal shook his head and grabbed his axe with two hands before he yelled and jumped at the bear, letting the axe cleave into its side as he came down. He didn't seem particularly upset by Willow's actions, especially with the way that he cleaved the bear to pieces.

They were a good team. If there were any group of people who could help her save the world, or at least their world, it would be this group.

31
Final Attempt

***Only 8 hours until Helheim Fallen
Online goes live.***

Do you have your copy yet?

The message hovered in front of her as Willow woke up, before it faded away like it had never even been there.

She'd had a strange sleeping pattern for the last couple of days when it came to the time of day that she woke up, although it was all still guided by the BASE platform, so no issues there. But since the system had been a lot more lax than usual, somewhere in the back of her mind was the sneaking suspicion that Soleil had something to do with the relaxation of her system rules as of late…

She sat up, stretching as she took calming breaths. Eight hours until HF went live, that meant it was already late in the afternoon of the previous day right now. A little late for breakfast or whatever, but she had to eat something before she dove back into HF.

She'd only slept for six hours, but they didn't have more time to waste. They'd all gone to bed when the others had reached level 20, a nice round number. They'd spent as much time as they could levelling up their characters, trying to get their hands on the best gear they could get and from here on out they were going to have to trust that things would go well.

They had eight hours. In those eight hours, they had to get back to the trolls' cave, get the trolls out of the way and then make their way through whatever was on the other side of the hidden door.

Willow pulled up her timer, the same one that worked inside HF, since they were really running against the clock today. Then she opened the code for it, and added a few new lines of code at the bottom.

```
time_t TimeLeft = Countdown(2042-04-02
00:00:00);
cout << "Time to midnight " << TimeLeft;
```

As she compiled the code, the timer refreshed and at the bottom of the list was now the time until the release of HF visible.

The time until midnight tonight, the time until everything would go wrong unless they did something about it.

Time to midnight 07:23:23

There was no way to get around it anymore, and she knew that everything, a lot of players' gaming and accounts, would depend on what they were able to pull off today.

As she took her box with breakfast/lunch/early dinner, she eyed the chat with the guild. There should probably be more people awake by now.

She sat down with the box, opening it to find a variation on the standard 'sandwich with cheese, ham or sweet fillings' in the form of bagels instead of regular bread. She wasn't so sure about it all. Like she needed to think about things that were different than normal today, like she needed 'different', it only threw her off. She eyed the box, not entirely sure what to do.

Then she got a notification for a call, only, instead of a single person, it said 'guild'. *Uh, oh.*

She accepted the call and immediately heard Violet. "I'm not saying that, I'm just thinking that this is a bad plan."

"No, it's not." That was Opal. "It really isn't."

"Morning, or afternoon, people." Willow plucked at the bagel, and then opened a small cup of jam, dipping the piece of bagel in it, before popping it into her mouth. Bagels made pretty good dipping objects, better than trying to cut them open and get stuff on them because that always made a mess.

"Willow, tell Opal that he can't go and distract the trolls while we slip past them." Violet was way too active for Willow's brain. She'd just woken up, she didn't need yelling.

"He can't." Willow sighed, dipping another piece.

"See?!" Violet sounded triumphant.

"Because I'm going to do that." Hey, it had been her plan, she just hadn't wanted to reveal it quite yet.

"What?!" That was all four of them, she could hear Sage and Juniper too.

"I've got a plan. And we're going to make it work. Now, I'm eating breakfast, I'd like to do that in quiet. I'll see you all in HF soon." She disconnected the call, then quickly put all communications on silent so they couldn't disturb her while she prepared herself before diving into HF.

350

She had a plan. Before bed last night, this morning, she'd looked online, and she'd found the one weakness of trolls, a weakness that she could remember was also in the coding for the trolls in HF. For all the things that they'd changed in how Helheim worked in comparison to old Norse Mythology, this was one thing that they'd apparently kept in place.

And the guild was going to use it to their advantage.

Willow shook her head as Violet and Opal kept glaring at her. They were standing right outside the first encampment in HF, waiting on the others.

When she'd logged on earlier, she'd still been on the outskirts of the capital, but they'd agreed to find each other here, instead of waiting around there since they had to be near here to get to the trolls anyway.

Dawn, Sage and Juniper were still on their way, and she wasn't going to spill the beans before then. Mostly because she was pretty sure that they'd all disagree with her plan.

 Meadow: I'm not telling until everyone is here.

She pulled up her timer.

Time to midnight 04:49:25

Just under five hours. It had taken them more than an hour to even get here, the walk between the capital and the encampment really was quite long. But she was going to wait on the others before revealing her plan, no matter what.

 Opal: Why can't you say just something?
 Violet: You're not going in on your own. You're not a
   lone wolf.
 Violet: Nu-uh.

At Willow's smile, Violet narrowed her eyes at her.

> **Violet:** You saw something. Sage showed you
> something when we were at the trolls, and you
> know something about them that we don't.
> **Meadow:** Maybe…
> **Opal:** Arg!

Just then, they saw Juniper come down the road, sprinting, closely followed by Dawn, and not too long after also Sage. The whole group was here. Now everyone was here, she could tell them the plan.

And, no matter how much they would object to it, they had no other way to pull this off. They had one chance, and this was it.

They didn't have enough time to come up with a new plan.

This was their one shot.

Time to midnight 04:03:56

They stood in front of the cave, Opal and Sage both glaring at Willow. The others just looked confused at them.

> **Opal:** No.
> **Sage:** No way.
> **Meadow:** Yes.

The one weakness of trolls was that they couldn't deal with sunlight well, so, the most sensible plan was to try to get the trolls out of the cave, pull them into the sunlight and hope that they would either get severely weakened, or, closer to tradition, they may even turn into stone. Either way, they would be out of the cave, and it shouldn't be a problem for them to either get rid of them or just walk past hem.

Only, Willow's plan included something like her being the

352

one to aggro the trolls to get them out. And while the others agreed on the general plan, that part they didn't agree with.

> **Dawn:** You're too squishy to be tanking them.
> **Meadow:** We don't have a tank.
> **Sage:** We have pets. We can use our pets.
> **Meadow:** And then what? What if they kill them?
> **Dawn:** Then we summon them again.
> **Dawn:** We're not giving up a player just to get past the trolls. Because you won't survive it, no matter what you're thinking.

It made sense, but it still didn't feel right to do this. It felt wrong to sacrifice the pets just to get past some trolls. It didn't feel right…

Violet stepped next to her, her hand strong on Willow's arm.

> **Violet:** Opal, Juniper and I wait here. We'll be safer here outside. You three go inside.
> **Meadow:** Are you sure?

She looked at Violet, who had a fighting spirit in her gaze that Willow could appreciate, even though she hated the feeling of putting anyone in danger.

> **Juniper:** Go. Get those trolls.

Willow nodded, making Iris follow her, and she stepped into the cave. Moments later, Sage and Dawn were there too, their pets at their sides. They could make this work, right? They should be able to.

> **Dawn:** I'll get Aya to attack them first. She's got the longest ranged attack, so we can hopefully kite them for a while before they take her down.
> **Sage:** Then Arthur next, he's the tankiest pet we've got, he can take some hits, hopefully.
> **Dawn:** And Iris can finish it off. Hopefully, she can get to the end of the cave, she's got a good ranged

attack with her fire too, so she doesn't have to get
too close.

Willow nodded. It made sense, and the basic plan was still hers, but this was a lot more scary because it put a lot more people in danger. Not just the pets, but Dawn and Sage too.

Meadow: Yeah. Yeah.

They all stayed quiet until they reached the end of the cave, standing in front of the huge door. Now they had to get the trolls out of there…

Dawn climbed up to the window and, at first, Aya followed him, but then she flew back to the door, slipping through a crack at the side, small enough for a tiny bird like her.

Dawn: Ready?

Willow and Sage started walking back, Arthur and Iris close at their sides.

Meadow: Ready.
Sage: Ready.

Dawn jumped down, reaching them before he made a movement with his hand.

Dawn: Go!

He started running, and they quickly followed him.

There were loud noises behind them, the trolls screaming as they were attacked by the tiny bird, then the door opened with a bang, and the trolls came storming out, yelling.

The loud footsteps kept following them, sometimes pausing for a moment as the trolls would let out sounds of frustration. Probably as they attacked Aya, or were slowed down by her attacks.

Dawn: Sage!

354

Sage's bear stopped running at their side, falling back, and now becoming the target of the trolls.

Aya was down. Way sooner than she'd expected, they hadn't even gotten that far yet. They'd made it maybe 1/4 through the cave.

They were now in the total darkness area. The only thing around them was total blackout darkness and the sounds of the trolls following them not too far behind.

Sage stumbled for a moment, a light flash shooting from their hands, probably a quick heal onto their bear.

Sage: 50%

They were getting close to the lighter part of the cave again, they were over halfway now.

Willow looked behind her, the trolls even more creepy and ugly in the low lighting, accentuating their strange facial features, making them even scarier than they seemed in their cave.

Sage's bear ran closely in front of them, clawing at the trolls' legs if they lost too much attention on him. It seemed that even though the level of the trolls was much higher than the game would allow, their attacks weren't that strong. They had a very high HP, but not much attack power. But it was still more than they would be able to handle for long stretches of time.

She watched as Arthur's health bar slowly went down. Sage healing it but then the trolls would attack him again, the HP dropping faster as Sage was running out of mana.

And then… Arthur was gone.

Sage: Meadow!

Willow made Iris attack the trolls, hoping that they would

make it to the end of the cave now. She put Iris back on follow for a couple of seconds, before swapping her to aggressive, switching between the two so that Iris would kite the trolls.

She could see the aggro that the trolls had on Iris, it was scary to watch. But they were following her, just as they'd planned.

Willow had to constantly cast healing spells on Iris, trying to keep her health up high enough. While Iris was mostly out of range because she didn't need to be within melee range to do damage, some of the hits from the trolls would still reach her. They just had to keep her topped up enough…

She could see the end of the cave.

They were getting so close now!

Next to her, she Sage and Dawn also threw healing spells at Iris.

They were getting really really close now, Willow could hear some of the sounds from the birds and other creatures outside of the cave. Not much further.

She looked ahead and stumbled over something on the floor, which made her crash to the floor. It tripped up her healing cycle and Iris' health dropped dangerously low.

No! No, no!

That was not happening.

She shot out her hand, healing Iris again.

But it was too late.

She couldn't do anything else anymore, her mana depleted, her healing spell still recharging, she was defenceless now.

The trolls caught up to Iris, their giant fists connecting with the small dragon, her health dropping to zero, and Iris fell to the ground. *Dead.*

Then the trolls' aggro was on Willow. She was Iris' creator, Iris belonged to her, so now Willow had the most aggro of the group.

She scrambled up, running to the end of the cave. She had to get the trolls to the end of the cave before they could hit her, she was too squishy for them.

She had to get the trolls into the sunlight before they could hurt her, or kill her, which was more likely.

Willow felt the tension in her body, she could feel how she was pushing her own body to the limit just to get to the end.

She'd never run like this before, she never had to. But there was always a first for everything.

Then, someone pushed her aside, making her fall over again, sliding away. And as she rolled away, she saw how the trolls hit Opal, just as they stepped into the sunlight and turned to stone.

But even as the trolls turned to stone, something even worse happened to Opal.

He blinked, looking at her, his eyes going wide, and then slowly, his form began to lose colour before it lost its shape, turning into a puddle. His code disintegrating and turning into a black blob on the floor.

No!

Willow opened her mouth, a low keening escaping her.

No way!

Opal was gone. The trolls had just broken his code. They'd somehow blitzed his account and the guild couldn't do anything about it. Opal hadn't done anything wrong. He'd saved her.

But he still paid the price.

Opal still paid the price.

They'd lost one of their team.

They'd already lost their strongest melee fighter, and they hadn't even gotten into the next stage of the plan yet…

No way!

Willow felt tears on her cheeks as she wrapped her arms around herself.

How many more people were they going to lose before they made it to the end?

And apart from their characters in this game, how much else were they going to lose if they failed?

How much would this cost them?

32
Crossing the Bridge

Violet pulled Willow up, making her stand on her feet. Violet's eyes were dark, filled with emotions, though she wasn't crying. They all knew what this meant for what would happen down the line. The level of danger had now been set.

If they lost, even a little, they would be out, this was an all or nothing situation. There was no going back.

Time until midnight 03:23:35

Juniper: Try to summon your pet.

She stood in front of Willow, her face unreadable.

Willow hit the pet cast button on her bar, but nothing happened. It was greyed out, but her mana was low too. Maybe that was the problem… Only, a sinking feeling in her stomach told her it wasn't.

Meadow: Can't yet.
Sage: Me neither.
Dawn: Still low on mana.

Violet handed her a mana potion, pushing it into her

hands, her gaze determined now.

Violet: Drink this. Then we start moving.

Willow nodded. They had to keep going.

Waiting out here wasn't going to solve anything. It wasn't going to make things better. And she had no idea how long the trolls would stay in their stone forms, or if there was a respawn rate on them or something. They had no information, they were going in blind and without any guidance.

Meadow: Let's go.

She took a sip from the potion Violet had given her, pulling a face. It tasted sour, so sour. But at least that seemed to clear her head somewhat, which she could really use right now.

They had to get moving. They could worry about Opal later, they could worry about what happened to him when they had gotten back out. When they knew they were safe.

She knew that Soleil had said something about keeping an eye on her friends, and when Sage had gotten blitzed, she'd also known pretty quickly. So, no matter what, Soleil could probably find him and get to him.

Their only task was to keep going. Because Soleil could deal with trying to get back a handful of players, but she wouldn't be able to do much when it would become hundreds or thousands of blitzed accounts. That was a totally different scale of problems.

Sage and Dawn were also drinking from a mana potion as they walked down the same cave as they had ran out of not too long ago.

Back into the cave, hoping that they would be able to get through the strange door before they were caught by new trolls or whatever.

The 'house' where the trolls had been living made her feel like she was nothing but a doll. Everything was so much bigger than she was and walking through it was something totally different than standing outside and looking in through the window.

The scent of the cooked meat was pretty nice, apart from the fact that this was supposed to be meat from NPCs who were the same races as that they were. This wasn't supposed to be 'nice' meat at all, but the game had done pretty well with the scent of the roasted meat. Priorities, right?

They walked up to the bare section of wall Sage and Willow had seen from the window, right under the old HF logo. Willow pulled up the X-ray vision screen, looking at the wall with it.

There it was, a door which they couldn't normally see in the game, but it was visible when she stripped the layer of texture with the view.

She reached out, and as the tips of her fingers grazed the hidden door, a shock like an electrical current went through her.

At the same time, a dark wooden door with a heavy metal ring connected to the latch appeared in front of them, like it had always been there. The outline all bright and shiny, inviting, like it was some sort of magical object or an interactable item for a quest.

Turn back.

Willow swallowed hard. Of course, it made sense that the game creators would try to stop them. Random players walking into this area and finding hidden doors and things, probably wasn't their plan.

But she grabbed the metal ring, turned it, and then pushed the door open. The space behind it was pitch-black, like it didn't exist, and even as she hovered the scan over it, nothing appeared.

Okay… From here on out, they were going to be forging ahead on hope and conviction only.

She looked back at the others.

Meadow: Keep going?

Everyone nodded. Then Sage reached out to her and took her hand.

Sage: Let's try not to lose each other.

Willow nodded and watched as Sage took Dawn's hand, and Dawn took Violet's hand, who took Juniper's hand. Then she stepped into the darkness, into the black. Trusting that there would be something on the other side to catch her.

Everything around Willow had disappeared, even the ground seemed to not exist as she kept walking somehow. Until she stepped onto a solid surface again and with each step she took,

362

more light came back.

They were in a cave of some sort, but definitely not the same as the one they'd just left. This cave looked like it was much further below the surface, the walls around them stretching out far and wide, and she couldn't see the bottom of the cave anywhere.

She could see a bridge in front of them, and more things that looked like bridges going from the walls to a spire in the middle of the cave. Everything here appeared like it had been built around the spire, around a single core.

Sage: Meadow…

She looked back, and everyone stared at something on her back. Willow reached behind her and grabbed her staff. She never used the thing so she'd almost forgotten about it, but now the end of the staff glowed, like a torch in the darkness around them, making it easier to see each other. It wasn't the light of a fire, or some digital light, but instead the gem on top of the staff glowed from the inside out.

Meadow: Wow.

That was cool, and interesting. She looked at the weapons of the others, and Dawn and Sage's staves also had a light at the end, while Violet and Juniper's weapons were still the same. Cool trick for casters, definitely.

Then she tried to summon Iris again, wanting her with them while they walked through this cave, but even though her mana was fully recharged again, the spell for it was still greyed out. That wasn't good. Sage and Dawn shook their heads, they couldn't summon anything either.

So, not only were they down one player, their pets also had been affected by the death at the hands of the trolls.

Not good.

Willow sighed, looking to the spire in the middle of the cave. If they had to go anywhere in this place, it was probably there.

The spire's light fluctuated, a constant brightening and darkening, like a heartbeat.

Time until midnight 02:57:25

Had it taken them that long to get back through the cave and out here? Really? *Wow.*

The door behind them had a red-ish outline against the otherwise dark wall. They would worry about how to get back out of here when they'd finished what they came here for. They had to go forward first.

Willow took a couple of steps towards the bridge, each step giving her more courage.

They'd passed the trolls, they could face anything.

Together, they could face anything.

Hopefully.

As Willow could see more of the cave, the world around them looked almost like they were walking between the roots of a huge tree, and they were travelling over one of the roots to the core. Roots which were curling up around each other, which curled and curved, hanging from other roots until they were big enough to latch onto the outside wall.

It was almost like they were in some way at the roots of the big mythological tree Yggdrasil. Like they were on their way to the core of the tree.

A while ago, flecks of light had started to fall around them.

Just small specks, creating some light in the large space. It was almost like they were specks of dust, but when Willow tried to catch one, it disappeared without a trace, leaving nothing behind. Like nothing had been there in the first place.

It was odd and a little uncanny but at least the light helped with seeing more of their surroundings. Not that there was much 'more' to see, just more roots going off in every direction, but it felt safer.

They'd been walking for over an hour, and Willow felt like they hadn't gotten closer to the spine-spiral-core-thing at all. That didn't bode well…

Suddenly, there was the sound of crackling, like a bad monitor, and ahead of them, the air rippled like heat above a hot object or an old-school monitor with cable connection issues.

Willow stopped, and she felt the others behind her do the same.

> **Juniper:** What's going on?
> **Meadow:** No idea.

But it couldn't be good.

> **Meadow:** Wait here.

She looked behind her for a moment, making sure that they would do what she asked. Then she walked up to the pulsating air, holding out her staff in front of her.

As her staff touched the air, it flashed, and a female giant appeared on the bridge.

The name over her said 'Modgud', and her level wasn't visible. *Not good!*

Willow stepped back a little, hoping to get out of immediate reach.

Modgud: You're not supposed to be here.
Meadow: We want to pass.
Modgud: You cannot pass. Go back.
Meadow: We are going to pass.
Modgud: What is your purpose?
Meadow: We want to fix something broken in this
    game.

Hey, no matter if the thing could interpret that or not, she didn't think the actual words mattered.

Modgud: You cannot go on. Return, or I will have to
    make you return.

Yeah, no.

Willow carefully walked backwards to the group, keeping her eyes on the female guardian.

Meadow: Any idea?
Sage: Push her out of the way? I don't think we can
    fight her.

Willow agreed with them on that, they wouldn't be able to kill her. This monster was way too high level for them to defeat, that was for sure.

Meadow: Is that a plan?
Meadow: Try to get her off the root, don't get too close.
    Try not to die? We don't know what will happen
    then.

It could be that any attack from the guardian could blitz them, or just the final attack that would kill them. But after the trolls, they weren't going to take any chances. *None.*

Juniper: yes.
Sage: Yes.
Dawn: Yes.
Violet: Yes.
Meadow: Let's do this!

The guardian didn't have any aggro on them, but they

could attack it, which allowed them to get their first attack in first.

She held up her hand, just a simple bolt would have to do for a start, she didn't have too many other attacks that were true damage attacks.

She let the bolt go, targeting the right side of Modgud's chest, around her, Sage's firebolt and Dawn's icebolt were joined by arrows from both Juniper and Violet.

You hit Modgud for 221 damage
Sage hit Modgud for 173 damage
Dawn hit Modgud for 309 damage
Juniper hit Modgud for 250 damage
Violet hit Modgud for 246 damage

All of the attacks hit the guardian, but her HP didn't budge.

Yeah, definitely way above where they could defeat it within the time they had.

The guardian came charging towards them.

Willow and the others threw anything at her that they could come up with. Dawn used his speed buff on the whole group so that they could attack facter. And Willow and Sage threw attacks, binds, AOE, anything.

Just to stop Modgud, to slow her down.

Willow moved her hand in a way that was reverse to

pulling up her normal shield, and as she did so, an energy wall shot up before the guardian. Which did seem to slow it down for a moment, but it was draining her mana fast to keep it up.

Oh, what a great moment to find out about a new skill… Cool, but she wasn't exactly sure that it was useful for very long.

At least it slowed the guardian down, letting them catch their breath for a moment. They moved back, trying to put more distance between them and the guardian.

They had to get past her, but that wasn't easy, apparently. Modgud kept pushing them backwards and this way they were only getting further and further away from where they had to be.

Dawn: Her leg, try to get her leg from under her.

Yeah, that made sense.

Willow pulled up an %Elementbolt, focusing on the guardian's leg and foot, if they could make her trip, maybe it would help more.

Meadow: Go!

She threw bolt after bolt, as fast as she could. The light from everyone's elemental attacks and the other things thrown at the guardian's feet almost made it impossible to keep looking at where she was throwing. The flashes were so bright.

The guardian stumbled for a moment, but then started walking towards them again.

No good. No good. No good.

Dawn: Keep going.

He stepped next to her, and when her eyes shot to him for a moment, there was a strange look in his eyes.

He had a plan, and she wasn't going to like it. That was for sure.

Dawn: Keep going.
Meadow: Keep going!

She threw everything she could into the attacks, swapping between every attack, AoE and debuff she had, just to keep the guardian off-balance and to stop her from coming too close.

A single private message was all she got as a warning.

Dawn: *I'm sorry. Good luck.*

Then he rushed towards the guardian, in his hand he held a bomb that was about to go off. She'd seen the bombs on the stalls in the markets before, and she knew that alchemists could make them, but she hadn't known that Dawn had taken one with him. What had he expected to do with it?

No!

Meadow: Down!

She let herself fall to the floor, watching as Dawn grabbed onto the guardian's side, the bomb still in his hands.

Then two things happened. As the guardian took hold of Dawn, crushing him to death, Dawn started to disintegrate, as Opal had, and at the same time, the bomb went off, blasting the both of them off the bridge.

No way! No!

No!

The darkness after the flash of light made that Willow couldn't see anything anymore for a while, the darkness and silence now overwhelming and made of shadows and panic.

She had no idea if it had really worked, and if it hadn't, they would all be vulnerable right now, but she also couldn't see or hear anything to check what was going on.

The world was made of total silence and darkness.

The quiet before the storm, but what storm?

33

The Man Behind the Creation

They'd lost Dawn.

Dawn was gone.

He'd sacrificed himself so that they could keep going, even though he barely knew them. He'd still sacrificed himself for them.

Slowly, the cave came back into view, the sounds around Willow slowly coming through.

She hadn't been ready. She hadn't been ready for Dawn's surprise attack. She'd known Dawn as someone who always thought before he did something, not as someone who was rash. But even he could surprise her.

Violet: Willow?
Meadow: here.

She carefully moved, looking to her other side and finding everyone staring at her, looking lost. Nobody had expected this.

Meadow: Is everyone okay?

Sage: HP is regenerating.

So, sort of a 'yes'?

Violet was closest to her, as she tended to be. And she reached out, taking Willow's hand, holding it tightly.

It was down to the four of them. Just the four of them, and they all looked as lost as Willow felt.

Time until midnight 01:34:24

They were running out of time. They had to get to the spire, and they still had a long way to go.

Meadow: We have to keep moving.

This wasn't going to be the end, and they had no time to waste just sitting around.

She pushed herself up, letting her eyes go over to where the guardian had just been and where Dawn had blown himself up with the bomb. The floor was still scorched, but even that was now slowly fading. The game updating the effects of the blast and slowly fading the soot and other residue it had left behind. The results of what happened soon gone. Like it had never happened.

But inside her, it hurt. It hurt so much. Losing Opal, and then losing Dawn. They'd all known that it wouldn't be safe, they'd known that when they said that they would help her out. But had they ever realised that they could lose their account and everything with it by helping her out? Did they ever consider that?

Someone wrapped their arms around her shoulders.

Violet: When we finish this, we'll make sure that they're okay.

Willow nodded, hoping that Soleil at least knew how to track Dawn down. Willow hadn't known him for very long, but she still hoped that Soleil could find him… Hopefully.

Then Sage and Juniper wrapped their arms around Willow and Violet too, everyone pulling tightly. And for a few moments, Willow allowed herself to feel connected to them, to feel safe. Before they had to move again and hope that they could keep other people safe too.

Meadow: We need to fix this. We need to stop this blitzing from happening.

They'd lost two friends to it today. Nobody deserved that. Especially if it wasn't for anything more than having a record or a disability. Nobody deserved to have their life ruined over stuff like that.

Willow carefully climbed from under the others, looking down at the group.

Meadow: Let's go.

They still had a rong road to go, and time was constantly ticking away, never stopping. They couldn't rest now.

The others also stood up. And when Willow looked to the spire, it did seem a little closer than before, but that may have just been her imagination…

Willow started walking and the others followed her, all silent.

There wasn't much they could talk about now. There just wasn't much they could do. And no matter how beautiful or interesting her surroundings were, it all felt like nothing when she couldn't share it with all the people she loved. When she couldn't share the joy with everyone, when the only thing she could feel was frustration and anxiety.

She'd never been one to wish for one of those 'the world rests on your shoulders' kind of stories, but somehow, she still got here, and got handed that role all the same…

Because she had realised what the implications would be of one game blitzing people for stupid things and other games picking up on it. If one game could do this, other games would start doing it too, especially if nobody stopped them. And, sure, not everyone would be playing HF, but if enough other games started doing this, it could be a totally different issue.

In a sad way, if it came out how serious this blitzing and missing people really was, people would stop trusting the BASE platform and unit and the people who worked on them, and that also wasn't good. BASE didn't deserve to be broken down just because some people abused a bug or vulnerability and were doing bad things to people.

She had to fix this, for everyone.

Time to midnight 00:36:46

They were finally getting close the spire, and the closer they got, the more Willow got an unsettling feeling in her body. Like shivers of cold going through her, even though the air around her had been getting warmer. It was a strange experience, it was… She didn't know how to explain it. There was something odd going on, definitely. And it wasn't a good type of 'odd'.

Sage: There are no guards.

Yeah, that was the other strange thing. They'd encountered the trolls, and then the guardian, but now they'd gotten so close to the spire, they hadn't run into another guard or system to keep them from getting closer yet.

As it stood now, they could just walk up to the spire and do whatever they wanted, no questions asked. And no matter how simple that would be, Willow was sure that that wasn't the purpose here. She was sure that it wouldn't be that easy at all. Something would be in place to prevent that from happening.

Somewhere, she wished that this place would have given them one of those 'dungeon counters' kind of things. One of those lists of how many bosses or monsters they had to kill before they got to the end of the dungeon. That would have been cool, and actually useful.

> **Juniper:** What are we going to do?
> **Juniper:** When we get there, I mean.
> **Meadow:** I'm going to go into the code and, together with Sage, I'm going to fix the part of the code that allows this program, or this company, whatever, to do the blitzing.
> **Sage:** Sound simple enough.
> **Violet:** Which means that it won't be.

Yep, because that was always how things went. They may seem simple but always turned out to be much more complicated.

At the end of the bridge-root-thing that they'd used to walk here from the door they'd used as an entrance to the cave, there was a platform around the spire.

Up close, the spire was definitely bigger than she expected, even with ten people, hand in hand, they wouldn't be able to span around it. It was impressive, that was for sure. And now they were so close to it, they could see that there was a constant data stream running through the lighter part of the spire. Continuous data being collected and exchanged, though it could just be a visual overlay of what was going on behind it, but that still didn't take away how impressive it looked and that this was the location they needed.

Willow walked closer to it, stepping onto the platform. Her

eyes going over the monitors lined up on most of this side of the spire. Over the random bits of data being shown on them. Over what was basically the brain of HF, right in front of them. It was impressive, and in a geeky way, it was beautiful how form and function were combined into this thing. How the idea of the tree of Norse mythology was used as the data centre of HF. Pretty cool.

"Over here!" Sage called out, and Willow turned to them, surprised to hear their voice. Sage was pointing at a specific monitor, a few over from where Willow was standing.

Willow went over to them, looking at the code that Sage had pulled up on the screen. In some ways, this looked similar to some of the code that Soleil had shown her before, it was trying to collect data that they weren't allowed to be able to get to…

"You're not supposed to be here," someone said behind them, and Willow immediately twisted around. Daryl, Helheim Fallen Online's creator, was standing not too far behind them.

"Well, you're not supposed to hurt people." Sage stepped partially in front of Willow, crossing their arms in front of them. "Why are you blitzing accounts? These people have done nothing wrong."

Daryl shrugged, like Sage was asking him a useless question. "They also haven't been doing anything good. Just because you breathe doesn't mean that you should be welcome everywhere. Existing does not give you the privilege to just demand to go wherever you want."

"You're hurting people. People are dying because your program locked them out of their BASE accounts." Violet stepped next to Willow, her eyes on Daryl.

"That hasn't been proven, or I wouldn't be standing here. That's just an exaggeration. If they could prove that my game did that to people, the police would have done something about it." Daryl took a step towards them. "Now, get away from my program. This isn't yours. This isn't for some kids to just do what they like with just because they're some special snowflakes."

"I don't think so." Willow stepped closer to Daryl, looking at him head-on. "You're going to take the code which checks the BASE accounts with personal IDs against government records out."

"Or else?" Daryl looked at her with the glint of a boy who'd never heard the word no in his life, at least not a no that he couldn't turn into a yes by bullying or bribing people.

"Or else we'll take it out ourselves." What did she have to lose?

If the code was in place at midnight, her account would be blitzed, if Daryl did something to them, he'd probably blitz them too, this way they at least still had a chance.

"You're too late." Daryl waved his hand and in the middle of the air, above them, a timer started counting down. Bright red letters and numbers, floating in the air, covering everything in a creepy red glow.

Time until Helheim Fallen Online goes live 00:30:26

Willow quickly checked her own timer, just to make sure that he wasn't messing with them, but it showed the same thing.

Time until midnight 00:30:13

They had half an hour to fix this.

Ten days of trying to figure out what was going on now came down to thirty minutes.

"What are you going to do? What do you think you *can* do?" Daryl dared them. He looked at them like he'd already won.

But if there was one thing that Willow had learned, it was that nothing was certain until after the moment that it happened, or it failed, either way. They still had a chance.

"We're going to fix this. We are." Willow pulled up her %Elementbolt, hovering it over her hand.

She'd gotten quite good control over her attacks by now, which was cool, because she felt badass like this. Like some mage from a cool anime or something, although, she did still look like an ugly undead, but that didn't stop her from imagining how awesome she must look now, in her head anyway.

Daryl's eyes flashed with surprise as he pulled a similar type of bolt up. "You're not supposed to be able to do that. You're not supposed to be able to get that attack."

"Because it's yours? This bolt, which has no official name?" A special attack, just for him? Was he that childish?

"Yes." He was so sure.

"And I'm not supposed to be able to have a dragon fylgja either?" Which would explain why Dawn had been so surprised by her dragon and why there hadn't been other players with one. This was starting to sound a little silly though.

"You're not. It should be hardcoded that your account can't get them. They're not for regular players."

Oh, well, that made a lot more sense. Thanks, person who was helping them at HF headquarters, apparently Willow hadn't just gotten some mod tools, her account had some perks that she wasn't supposed to be able to get to normally at all. Curious…

"Get away from the spine." Daryl reached out next to him and a dragon spawned right there, his hand now on the shoulder of the creature, above it showed the name Topaz. And although Willow still couldn't summon Iris, it was pretty cool to see what Iris would one day grow into, *if* they were going to survive this.

"Or what?" Violet stood next to her, an arrow on her bow, pointing straight at Daryl.

"Or I'll make sure that you do. By any means." He pulled up not one %Elementbolt, but four at the same time in his hand, and Willow wondered for a moment if she'd be able to do that one day…

Then he threw the bolts at them, being able to control each one separately. They all jumped to the side, not wanting to get hit.

At the last moment, Willow put up a shield, just to be extra sure that the bolt wouldn't hit her, but the shield only seemed to absorb the bolt and the next moment the button for her shield attack had also greyed out on her bar.

Oh, no. No good. Definitely *not* good.

Daryl could make attacks, and probably people, disappear like what had happened before with their fylgjur when the trolls killed them.

"Don't let his attacks hit you. You will be blitzed." Willow got back on her feet, looking at the spire behind her.

Daryl had blown up some of the monitors around it, making them useless, disabling them.

The timer above them kept counting down, a steady decline of the minutes and seconds.

Time until Helheim Fallen Online goes live 00:28:02

They had to get rid of Daryl before he destroyed the whole setup around the spire and before he got rid of them…

They would have no chance to save this game otherwise…

34

Countdown until Midnight

Willow dove to the side as she threw another %Elementbolt at Daryl, trying to at least get him to move back away from them a little.

You hit Daryl for 226 damage

Her attacks were hitting him, but they didn't do much damage at all, at least not to his HP. This guy had inflated his HP to far above normal, there was no way that he'd have this much HP when he was just level 45. There was no way, especially not since he was a squishy mage, like her.

Violet hit Daryl for 251 damage
Sage hit Topaz for 175 damage
Juniper hit Topaz for 247 damage

They kept moving, never standing still, always making sure that they got out of the way of whatever could harm them.

This was no way to play a game. This was no fun. Diving away or death really wasn't a fun game type. They were just four DPS classes, no real healer, no melee character who could tank for them. Just, four DPS classes of which two were actually pet classes too, so their damage output was already low…

"You're not going to win this." Daryl shot another range of attacks their way, some %Elementbolts, quickly followed by a fiery blaze.

Willow and Violet got out of range of them as quickly as they could. Luckily, they had a good amount of experience fighting raid monsters in DoE, so they were pretty quick on their feet if needed.

"There is no law against having a system in place about who can and cannot play my game, they can just play another game."

"It *is* a problem when it destroys people's whole BASE account. When it corrupts all their data." Violet shot a volley of arrows at Daryl as she shouted at him.

"You're exaggerating. The system simply makes sure that people who play this game are at least contributing to society, it just locks the rest out. That's all." As he was verbally fighting Violet, Willow could get some good attacks in, and Daryl stumbled back a couple of steps. "See? This is what you get when you cater to snowflakes. Everything is the end of the world for you people."

Did he really not know what his game was doing? What the system was doing to accounts that it targeted?

He really seemed to have no clue, the way he was self-righteously arguing them. He may have stupid ideas about who was supposed to play his game, but he didn't seem to be wanting to actually ruin people. Sadly enough, that was exactly what his game was doing, though.

"And if a few more games would put this in place, even better. Gaming is a privilege, not a right. If you can't work, maybe you shouldn't be playing games all the time either, but do something else useful with your time instead." He shot a new round of attacks at them.

Violet was able to avoid being hit by one by holding her bow up in front of her, but the bow disappeared into nothing, and Violet quickly pulled her hand back.

Uh, oh.

She glanced up.

Time until Helheim Fallen Online goes live 00:22:43

No.

They couldn't argue with his man, not anymore. Maybe if they were in the outside world they still could. But in here… In here they were running out of time, and he could ruin their lives with a single reckless attack. On top of that, he seemed to have no idea about the real damage that his game was doing.

Willow had to start taking chances, because they were quickly running out of options.

Meadow: Get him away from the monitors, get him as far away as possible.

From the corner of her eyes, she saw another attack coming her way, it was too close to dive away so she pulled the big wall-shield up. Which, after absorbing the bolt, also disappeared from the attacks in her bar. She was now out of shielding options. Not good.

They had to make sure Daryl didn't destroy more of the station, because they couldn't do anything without it. Even though Daryl could probably fairly easily replace it after they were gone… But after it was gone, *they'd* be out of options…

That was not a pleasant thought.

Willow moved her hand up, engulfing Daryl in her lava AOE, which seemed to make casting harder for him, the constant stream of low damage interrupting his actions.

You hit Daryl for 299 damage

Good.

As she watched his HP, it was finally starting to move down a tad, even ever so slowly starting to not be entirely full anymore.

This wasn't going to be easy, they already knew that, but at least it may actually be possible, if the time hadn't been ticking away.

Violet kept throwing knives at Daryl, since she knew that getting close to him would be a bad idea, and she was out of a bow.

How were they going to defeat him without getting wiped themselves?

They didn't have much time left, the clock above them kept reminding them of that fact, slowly ticking down, as time tended to do, but way faster than Willow was comfortable with.

**Time until Helheim Fallen Online goes
live 00:18:59**

They had to do something serious, something radical. They

384

had to find a way to get away from Daryl long enough to come up with a plan.

Willow tugged on Violet's arm, pulling her along to the back of the spire, as Daryl's attacks kept flying around them. At least they had one advantage, Daryl didn't seem like the best shot... Most of his attacks were sloppy and only in their general direction.

"What's the plan?" Violet took a couple of deep breaths, looking back over her shoulder, at the attacks that were still coming.

"We need to get to a computer. We have to." Willow looked the other way, hoping that Sage and Juniper could also make their way over to them. Hoping to find some safety for even a little while.

Then Sage came into view, Juniper close behind, but closely behind her was Daryl's dragon.

It opened its mouth and was about to use a flamethrower on Juniper when Violet sprinted away from behind Willow, her blade out. She cut open the dragon's throat in one neat slice, right over the jugular. And the next moment it fell down at Violet's feet.

Critical hit!
Violet hit Topaz for 1673 damage

That was one down.

Willow had expected that the dragon would also have inflated HP, but maybe it couldn't do much against an attack like this? Maybe brutal kills like slitting their throats wouldn't be something they could recover from, no matter their HP.

As Violet stood up, ready to get back to Willow, Willow watched as four bolts came right at Violet.

A scream escaped her as Willow could see Violet realise what was going on. She watched Violet trying to get out of the way of the bolts, but it was too late. She had been able to avoid two of them, but the final two hit her both.

Violet's body lost all colour and started to go putty, her character being reduced to a black blob. A black blob for Violet while Topaz' dragon body fell apart in light sparkles, a normal death of a fylgja.

They'd lost Violet.

They'd lost Violet because she protected Juniper.

Now they were down to the last three players. And any attack from Daryl that hit them could cut into their rankings even further. They may be outnumbering him in pure numbers, but the man was like a god here while they were mere ants.

Willow looked at Sage, met their eyes, and then they both looked at Juniper. How were they going to do this?

"You have to get to the monitors." Sage's voice was rushed.

"You're the one who knows what the code looks like. I can't do this myself." Willow shook her head. It was such a mess in her mind, everything cluttered.

"You can. That's why Soleil believed that you could do this." Sage looked at her seriously. "You have to."

"Incoming." Juniper pushed them to move, and they started running to the other side, out of range of Daryl's attacks again. "Keep moving." Juniper kept pushing them.

Willow looked behind her and Daryl definitely didn't look so happy anymore, not now they'd taken out his pet.

"Willow, hide there. We will distract him!" Sage pointed at some computer parts that were almost like a slight barrier around the base of the spire. "Hide."

"How?" Daryl would see her move there immediately.

Sage flung something behind them, and then a lot of smoke billowed up. Sage apparently had an interesting AOE attack, they hadn't shown it before, but it also wouldn't have been that useful in normal fights, not when they had a whole group of people who were attacking the same creature.

Now was a great time for it though.

Willow could barely see enough to know where she was going, but that didn't matter, she knew the general direction she had to go and walked as fast as she dared. She just had to find the computers.

When she ducked down, the smoke had started to come down, and she saw that Sage and Juniper had kept running ahead, now much further away.

Daryl stopped for a moment, looking around, probably trying to find her, but Sage and Juniper were able to distract him by attacking him. He may have a lot of HP but getting hit was still annoying for him, and he probably didn't want to accidentally lose to them either.

Willow looked on for a few moments, hoping that Daryl wouldn't notice that she was somewhere totally different, but he seemed distracted enough.

Then she slowly crawled to the monitors, trying to find one that hadn't been too damaged. It took a few tries, but then she found one that responded when she hit a few keys on a keyboard.

She quickly looked behind her, but Daryl was still distracted.

Willow types a few keywords, trying to figure out where

she was supposed to be looking for the files, sorting through all the mess in her head, but nothing seemed immediately obvious.

She glanced up to at the timer, the red light a constant reminder of its existence.

Time until Helheim Fallen Online goes live 00:10:36

They were running out of time.

She tried to remember what Sage had shown her before, what part of the code that it had been in, but it didn't come to her easily. Damn.

She didn't do well under stress. They knew that! Why was she the one doing this?

"Willow!" That was Sage's voice and, as she quickly ducked down, the monitor above her shattered into a million pieces.

It seemed that Daryl had also noticed what she was doing… There went that plan.

"You're going to keep trying?" Daryl's voice sounded amused for some reason. Like this really didn't influence him at all, like he really was in the right.

"Of course." Willow glanced past the small wall of computer parts that she was hiding behind for a moment, and then threw her creepy binding vines thing at Daryl. It didn't hit him, but it at least made him move as he was trying to avoid them and that gave Sage and Juniper more time to attack him.

Now they were split up, Sage and Juniper on one side and Willow on the other side of Daryl. Which they could use to their advantage, but it also meant that Willow wasn't so safe behind her wall now. She'd become an easy target.

They should really have come up with a plan before they

came in here. But since they had no idea what they could expect or what was going to happen, they just went in… No plan, nothing. That may be biting them in their asses now.

Violet was the one who had the better plans, not her. Violet and Sage were the real strategic planners, Willow just did the numbers, she just worked out the best way to optimise the plans that the others came up with. She wasn't the one making them, usually.

Smoke started streaming around her, and while Willow couldn't see anything going on in front of her, neither could Daryl see her, which was good. She ran along the row of computers, staying as low as possible.

Above her head, more monitors blew up, Daryl obviously realising their plan… But he couldn't see her, so he just threw the attacks in her general direction since destroying the computers was of no consequence to him.

When the smoke cleared, Sage and Juniper had moved back too, and Willow was now standing near where they'd come onto the platform.

Daryl was now closest to the computers and she could see the way he looked at them. If he could destroy the computers, they wouldn't be able to do anything anymore…

She could see the moment Daryl realised that too, that if he destroyed all the computers, this would be over. He would have won.

A surprised yell left her. No way!

No way!

All three of them reacted at the same time as they rushed towards Daryl, trying to throw as many attacks at him as they could.

Daryl split his four bolts up, one to the computers and three at them.

They were able to avoid the bolts, but just barely. Willow could feel the heat of one going narrowly past her arm, and Sage lost their staff, which they quickly dropped.

Another set of computers blew up.

If this took much longer, they wouldn't be able to fix anything, nothing. Everything would be over.

The red numbers taunted them.

Time until Helheim Fallen Online goes live 00:04:44

Then, as Willow used her lava pool on Daryl, Juniper jumped forward, one of her knives in her hand, and she knocked him over, jabbing the blade into his chest, pushing on as they hit the floor.

It wasn't much damage in comparison to Daryl's HP, but with the blade still inside his chest, it didn't stop there, the health bar now steadily draining.

Daryl froze for a moment, stunned. Then he struggled, letting out another bolt into Juniper's chest, taking her out.

Juniper's form drained of its colour, starting to dissolve. She'd known it would cost her her life, but she'd still done it.

390

Juniper had still gotten close, just to try and take Daryl out. And it may have worked.

But the bolt into Juniper's chest was all Daryl could do anymore as his HP was starting to get critically low. Between the blade still inside him and the lava AOE that he was on, he was getting constant damage, quickly draining him.

He must have realised it too because in a last attempt, Daryl shot out more bolts towards the computers, trying to destroy them, trying to stop whatever they were doing one last time.

Sage didn't even seem to think as they jumped in front of the bolts, protecting the computers.

No! No way!

But as Daryl's form fizzled away, like a regular character death, not getting blitzed like the rest of them, the attacks on Sage also dissolved. And while Sage's code started glitching, weird visual artefacts sprouting from them, they were still here.

Time until Helheim Fallen Online goes live 00:02:09

"Go!" Sage pointed to the computers and Willow ran for them, trying each keyboard she found, trying to get one of the screens to light up.

Then, as the final computer finally lit up, she let out a sigh of relief.

Time until Helheim Fallen Online goes live 00:01:33

She looked at Sage, but they held out their hands, the forms of them constantly glitching. No help there.

She needed the code that compared the BASE IDs against the official system. After a few tries, she found the entry under

'Account viability'.

Time until Helheim Fallen Online goes
live 00:00:54

Willow checked the piece of code she needed, trying to decide how to disable just a small piece of it, how to get the one bad bit out, just the checker. But as the seconds kept ticking away, she did the one thing she could think to do.

She selected the whole piece of code and deleted it. All gone.

If the game errored because of it, that would be fine, but she had no time to put a good piece of code in place. She had no time to repair it.

The whole formula that compared the systems and would throw the 'tag this person' error up for blitzing was now gone.

Time until Helheim Fallen Online goes
live 00:00:15

She had no idea what would happen next.

Willow looked at Sage, who was staring at her, their eyes filled with relief and fear. Then she wrapped her arms around them.

Time until Helheim Fallen Online goes
live 00:00:00

And the game went dark.

35
Return To the Ordinary

Willow's heart was trying to get out of her chest as her eyes darted around her bedroom.

What had happened? Had she been blitzed? Had she been kicked out of the system? Had it worked?

Had they fixed the 'bug'?

She almost jumped as two calls in BASE came in, one from Sage and one from Soleil. She accepted them both at the same time, merging them into a single call, so glad that at least some people were still there and that her account hadn't been blitzed.

"Willow!" Sage and Soleil said in unison.

"I'm here." She stood up, her hand on her chest, trying to make her heart slow down. She needed to move her muscles, the high tension still in them. "Where are the others?"

She could hear Sage's sigh, but Soleil answered instead, "They got blitzed. I've got people going to their locations as we speak. Just to make sure they're safe and to give them all the help they may need. They're going to be okay."

"And Dawn?" She had to know that he was safe too because they wouldn't have made it without him.

"Got someone onto him too." Soleil's voice was much calmer than she felt.

"And now?" Willow eyed the headset she'd just taken off, not sure she wanted to dive back in immediately. But she also felt like she may have to.

"My account is glitching. I'm not sure it's safe for me to go back in now. I'll have to see if I can fix it." Sage sounded exhausted, and Willow felt exhausted too. Like she'd been awake for days instead of just over eight hours.

"How will we know that it worked?" It didn't feel 'finished' yet, not until she was sure.

"We wait and see. It will probably be all over the net and over the news if it didn't work." Soleil's answer wasn't what she wanted to hear.

But before she could say anything else, there was knocking on her apartment door.

"Wait a moment." She went over to her door, opening it carefully, not exactly sure who to expect.

In front of her stood Violet, out of breath, her eyes wild. She must have come over here as soon as she'd gotten blitzed, because there was no other way she could have gotten here so quickly otherwise.

"You're okay." Violet's face split into a grin, then she wrapped her arms around Willow, who wrapped her arms around Violet too.

On the call, Sage and Soleil must have been getting a little confused, since they wouldn't have been able to hear the knocking on the door or Violet's voice.

"I'm going to hang up, Violet is here. Let me know if you need me. You can reach me via chat." Then Willow disconnected the call.

Of course, she was glad that things seemed to have worked out for some of them, but right now, all she really wanted was to be close to someone she knew. She needed to feel safe and she needed to be held, she needed real world physical contact with someone, preferably Violet.

"Did it work? Who was there at the end?" Violet eyed her, taking a step back, she seemed worried, an edge to her voice.

"I think it worked. Sage and I were the last ones left. Juniper gave her life to stop Daryl, to help us. Sage's account is glitching, but not blitzed. Which, I guess, is a good thing." Willow went over to her kitchen to grab herself a glass of water, not wanting to look at Violet too closely.

The sight of how Violet had died and the pain that had shot through her still too fresh on her mind. She took a few gulps of the water, before she felt Violet closely behind her, waiting patiently.

"I'm scared," Willow whispered. Of all the times, now the adrenaline was gone, the fear was finally settling in.

Violet's arms snaked around her, supporting her before she collapsed to the floor, all her energy gone, all the stress having eaten away at her and she couldn't keep herself up anymore. This was beyond exhaustion.

Things were okay, weren't they? They were done now?

Violet guided her to the couch and gave her the stuffed hippogriff, before crawling onto the couch with her. "You did it." Violet's voice was quiet. "You did it. Thank you."

Willow shook her head.

She hadn't done it alone, they had all done this together. 'We did it.' She wanted to say the words, but they didn't come out. Without her friends, she wouldn't have been able to get as far as she had. She wanted to thank Violet for being there, she wanted to tell her how much they'd all helped.

But her eyes were too heavy, and she couldn't stay awake anymore. That would have to wait until later.

Her body was checking out, her brain too, and Willow disappeared into a dreamless slumber.

When Willow woke up, Violet was tapping away on a mobile phone screen, sending a message to someone.

"Morning." Willow sat up, rubbing her eyes. "What's the time?"

"You've slept for about an hour or so. It's not been that long." Violet smiled at her, then showed her the small screen. It was the chat she had running with Sage and Violet and the others, but she was still too bleary-eyed to be able to read it. "Sage says, no mentions of blitzing yet on the forums. As far as we know."

"Good." Willow nodded. But she also knew that there was one thing she still had to do. There was one way to test if that was really true.

She had to log into the release version of HF herself.

Willow slowly stood up and could feel Violet's eyes on her.

"You're not going to test it yourself right now, are you? You're too tired, BASE won't let you in." Violet also stood up, following her.

"I have to. And BASE won't complain. I've got a shortcut for that." She opened the chat with Soleil.

> **Willow:** I need you to set my BASE status so it doesn't kick me out of the system when I log on.
> **Rotnem:** Are you sure?
> **Willow:** Yes.
> **Rotnem:** Okay.

Then Willow looked at Violet. "At what point were you blitzed when you went into HF? Did you get to the character creation?"

Violet shook her head. "Nah, I never got there. It happened almost instantly. I downloaded the game, went in, and suddenly I was kicked out again, my account fried. It probably didn't even take seconds."

Willow nodded. "Okay." At least she knew what to look out for.

She still had enough money over from selling all the things in DoE to get Sage and Violet new accounts that she could buy her own copy of Helheim Fallen Online now. And no matter how many problems they'd had inside HF, ignoring some of the strangeness of its creator, the game was actually pretty good. Or maybe she'd just gotten used to playing it.

She sat on the bed, putting the VR headset back on. Then, as she made herself comfortable, Violet took her hand, giving her courage.

Willow connected to the BASE platform, appearing in the platform game store. There, right in front of her, was a copy of HF she could buy.

She clicked on it, the credits deducted from her account, and the game downloading onto it instead. The version she'd been playing was a separate install, though she had no idea why.

It was probably connected in some way to the fact that she'd gotten it through a fake beta code and that it didn't even show her as playing HF when she was in the game.

As soon as the install was in her account, she opened it, and was dumped right into the opening video, with no way to skip it…

Oh, joy.

Willow had no idea what she'd expected, or what she'd hoped for. But when she finally opened her eyes, she was standing in the character creation screen again, her being a blank slate. Nothing there, nothing at all.

But the most important part was that she was *here*. She was in the game, she hadn't gotten blitzed, and she was actually playing. Or about to anyway.

Her deletion of the code seemed to be working. It had stopped the blitzing and the corruption of the accounts. At least, that's what it looked like right now.

They did it. They'd done it. They'd made sure that the code wouldn't hurt anyone else.

Willow quickly created her character, exactly the same way as last time. She actually enjoyed playing a draugr seidhr, and even with a new installation, she wasn't going to change that.

Now, she just had to come up with a new name for this character.

She reached out to the door, which asked her about her name.

Sigrun

She smiled as the door opened and she was transported

398

into the frozen world of Helheim, surrounded by other players.

Surrounded by hundreds, if not thousands of new players, all playing HF for the first time. She was greeted by noises and voices, people talking all over the place, people joking around and interacting with each other.

She couldn't help her own smile at seeing this. She hated big crowds, and really didn't enjoy being in them, but this crowd was a good thing. This crowd meant that the game was still working, and that people were able to play.

Around her, she could hear a couple of people complaining about the linearity of the game that they were playing. Well, she did hope that the people working on HF would make a couple of changes in an upcoming patch to that, even if just to take these things out, really… It had never been a good design idea.

She accepted the starter quests. And as she was about to log out to get back to Violet, she'd gotten all the proof she needed that the deletion of the code had worked, she received a private message from someone.

> **Sage:** Willow?
> **Sigrun:** Sage?
> **Sigrun:** You're already in?

She thought that they would have had to wait for a while longer to come back in. That they didn't think that it would be safe with their glitching account just yet. Had they fixed that so soon?

> **Sage:** I'm not the only one.

Willow received a party invite, which she accepted. Then, at the side of her view, the names of her friends all showed up.

Violet

Sage

Juniper

Opal

Dawn

Sigrun

Sage: Soleil made a good deal for us when she bartered
for new accounts for Violet and me.
Sage: Oh, wait a moment.

Then a seventh name showed up in their group.

Rotnem

They were all in the game now. They were all in HF, and
they were all safe.

Rotnem: Would you like your old character swapped
over to this account, Sigrun?

Willow grinned. As much as she'd be interested to try and
play this game again from the start, it really wasn't for her. She
hadn't been looking forward to getting through those starter
quests again, especially not after basically having done them
twice in a week.

Sigrun: Yes, please.
Rotnem: One moment.

Willow's world went black for a couple of seconds, before
everything brightened again and she was back to her normal
player self. Her normal draugr seidhr self. All the skills on her
bar worked again, and she could even summon Iris.

Meadow: How?
Rotnem: The information you gave us got us a lot of
leverage, and I was able to get a few people to look
the other way about you know, character creation
and accounts and such.

But if this was possible, and Violet had been at her side

400

since she got back out of HF. What?

Meadow: Violet, you knew?
Meadow: When you let me get back into the game, you already knew?
Violet: Not exactly, but we had set this up in case you wouldn't get blitzed immediately.

In case she wouldn't get blitzed immediately? They were waiting until she tested the game? She had been the test subject? After everything they'd been through?

Meadow: Even Dawn?
Dawn: Your friends are inventive, and a little scary.
Meadow: That's why they're my friends.
Dawn: I'd guessed as much.

That was the same thing as he'd said to her before, that her friends were a little scary. But she guessed that he knew that from experience by now since he'd seen how 'scary' her friends really were.

Since she was no longer a low-level character, she walked out of the encampment.

Meadow: Where is everyone?
Violet: Just up the road. Waiting for Rotnem to finish her starter quests.

Willow smiled, yeah, of all of them, Soleil was now pretty far behind them in level. Although, she suspected that that wouldn't be for very long. Soleil always seemed like someone who would make things happen, no matter what she needed to do to get there.

Like she'd been sure that Willow would be the one to be able to save this game, and she had…

After hanging out with her friends for a couple of hours, too relieved that everyone was okay, Willow had finally gone to sleep.

Willow had crashed in her own bed, while Violet had gone to sleep on the couch in the living room.

It had already been close to sunrise, but she really needed her sleep.

There was just so much that had happened in the last day that she was totally exhausted and she had no idea what the world would look like when she woke up again. When she would no longer have this looming thing over her head of her friends going missing or being missing, or anything like that.

When the world would be back to 'normal' in some way. It sounded strange, but that was actually what it would be.

'Normal.'

Whatever that meant.

When Willow finally woke up again, and got out of bed, she found Violet sitting on the couch, playing a game on her VR headset, totally unaware that Willow had woken up and come into the living room. And, with a smile, Willow sent her a message through the BASE chat system.

Willow: Morning.
Violet: Morning. I'll be right there.

Violet's body didn't move in all of that, totally still while Violet was in the VR.

Willow went over to the delivery box to pick up the breakfast container. Hopefully, there would be something good in it because she was starving. She'd kind of forgotten to eat while everything was going on. And that was a bad thing… Forgetting to eat was one of her biggest problems…

She put the box on the table and opened it, finding

402

nothing special. Just normal sandwiches today, with a pretty good range of toppings and such. But it was all back to normal, all back to how it was supposed to be in her life.

She wasn't sure if she should be disappointed that there was no special breakfast for her to celebrate having saved thousands of people from a horrible fate, or glad that everything seemed back to normal…

Then she opened the notifications from the Helheim Fallen Online searches that she'd been using for months. The notifications she'd already seen blinking when she woke up.

She'd just ignored them because she didn't want to deal with any drama before she'd been awake enough.

Helheim Fallen Online: biggest game release of this year, maybe this decade

Daryl, creator of Helheim Fallen Online, questioned by police in connection to woman who died after her account was blitzed

Daryl, Helheim Fallen Online's creator, taken into custody by police over large-scale account blitzing scheme

Helheim Fallen Online, the record highs and lows of the first day of release

Helheim Fallen Online, out for eight hours and already famous and infamous in equal measures

Willow looked at the headlines, smiling a little, her heart starting to feel lighter.

Things were going to be okay.

Things were going to be fine.

This nightmare was now behind them.

They'd done it.

They'd saved the game, they'd saved the players, and now things would stop being so overwhelming anymore.

Right?

36
Mirror

4 months later

Willow leaned back on the grass in the warm evening sun, her legs over the edge of the cliff, Violet at her side, and behind her, the rest of her friends were milling about.

They'd finally gotten enough money together to buy a guild house in Helheim Fallen Online. They were only a small guild, so it hadn't been that easy to get the funds. But with three people who had little problem butchering and harvesting items from creatures, and finding out that in HF, like a lot of strange things in this game, cooking required some actual skills to make the food, it had gone a lot faster than they'd initially expected it to go.

Sure, the low level potions and cooking recipes were simple, but as they'd reached higher levels, they'd actually needed some actual cooking skills to complete the food. And since few people still had those skills, higher level food also sold really well on the marketplace.

Helheim Fallen Online had boasted about 'realistic' and 'hyper-realistic' elements to their game in their promotions. And sure, there were quite a few of those things, but the choices of what elements they'd made 'realistic' and what elements they'd just taken from the most basic RPG and MMORPG games were a little… odd.

Not that Willow minded much. She had a strong enough stomach to deal with the butchering, especially after getting better at it in the last months, and she could cook, but she'd never thought that her cooking skills would actually be useful inside a videogame. Another win for 'odd ways her life connected together'.

But between all of them, they'd found that they had a lot of people who already had real-life skills that they could apply to this game or just strong enough stomachs to deal with the more gruesome elements that others didn't want to deal with. Which had definitely accelerated the speed at which they could afford a guild house, especially considering it was in a very beautiful and competitive area.

That didn't even take into accounts their new obligations, which had been eating into a lot of their time to play HF…

"Violet! Willow!" Sage dropped down on their knees behind them, wrapping an arm around their shoulders. "I know that you guys like looking out over the lake and all, but we could really use your help back at the house. The living room isn't finished yet and some of the rooms still require their settings to be finalised." They laughed, and Willow looked back at them, not able to stop her own smile, her heart light.

"So, what are *you* doing here then?" She raised an eyebrow

at Sage before she got up. "Fine, I'll go be useful. But you have to come do some dungeons with Violet and me this weekend. Deal?"

"Deal." Sage grinned.

Then Willow looked around, finding Dawn on the roof, looking out over them and she waved at him. She had a suspicion that he was hiding there from Sage. She really should explain to him that that wouldn't work. Sitting on the roof was about as common a location to hang out as the living room was, at least for her friends. But for now, she'd let him believe otherwise.

> **Meadow:** Hey!

She hadn't seen him come online.

> **Dawn:** Hey! Great view! Top spot!
> **Meadow:** I know, right?

She grinned, too happy and comfortable to not share it with everyone.

> **Rotnem:** It would be an even greater view if *some
>   people* would help with setting up the garden sets
>   and the other things you've been making or
>   collecting these last months…
> **Rotnem:** Who went on a spending spree?

Nobody responded to that. They probably all had been… Too excited not to?

> **Rotnem:** At least someone come help me out?
> **Violet:** Fiiiine.

Then a small dragon came rushing over, jumping on Violet and pushing her off the cliff into the water below. The dragon jumped after her.

Willow laughed as she looked at them.

With a recent update, HF had added autonomous pets to

the game, and they'd been able to get the personality coding from Mira over into HF, as a dragon this time. Which was cool.

AI personalities could be so complex, and they'd felt really bad for leaving Mira behind in DoE. So they moved her over to this game. With their friends and all their other things here, it didn't seem like a good idea to leave Mira behind in the other game. It seemed unfair.

> **Opal:** Your dragon ate the meat again.
> **Opal:** Seriously! Do something about it!
> **Juniper:** I don't think you can blame her, that meat did
>   look really good.
> **Opal:** It was!

Willow laughed. They'd all gotten so used to playing together. Dawn and Soleil had easily fit into the rest of the group. And even though there had been times where the game had seriously grossed some of them out, even Juniper seemed to have gotten over her ickyness of things.

Although, that could also have had something to do with the way she'd fought Daryl off... She seemed to have overcome her objection to blood and gore in a few instances when she'd stabbed him.

They'd all gotten on with their lives and their games pretty easily after everything that happened, though Willow still sometimes woke up in sweats, scared that she'd lost her friends again. But those nightmares had gotten better too lately.

Daryl, on the other hand, and some of the other people high up in the chain of Helheim Fallen Online, hadn't gotten off so easily.

Not only did it come to light that they had code in their game which could blitz accounts and on top of that a discriminatory sequence which would trigger it to work on very specific people. But slowly, the investigation had ballooned into even more.

It turned out that most of that code had come not from Daryl himself, but from the engine that they built the game in. It had been a 'super powerful' and 'brand new' engine and gaming companies had been really excited about using it.

Daryl really had believed that the code was simply there to stop certain players from coming in, he may have had some gross ideas about who should or shouldn't be allowed to play his game, but he'd never meant to blitz people's accounts. It also came to light that certain people around him, people with actual knowledge about coding, unlike Daryl, had been aware, but they either hadn't cared or had actively tried to hide what was going on from him. It seemed he hadn't surrounded himself with the right type of people. But none of that mattered to the law, easily trusting people he shouldn't have trusted wasn't a defence when the accusations were this severe.

After the problems with HF came to light, the company which had created the engine had disappeared. When the police and BASE had tried to find out what really had happened, anyone connected to the company was gone. No trace of them, at least, not that they'd found yet.

It was scary to think that there were people out there who really meant for the code to be used this way, to harm people over the most innocent of things. But when their destructive code in the engine had been found, the company didn't want anything to do with it anymore, and they'd fled.

It made Willow feel like she'd always have to be cautious when trying new games now, because there would be no way to know if the same code may be in other games too. She could try to keep an eye on the engine certain games used before she tried them, but that wouldn't help when the creators could make a new one, just as bad or maybe even worse, and she wouldn't know. It scared her.

Of course, this meant that Soleil had been making long days at BASE, trying to figure out what they could do to make BASE safer and how the destructive code could have been implemented in the first place. Previous blitzing had been done in ways that you needed to find someone's personal ID the old-school way, like actually getting into their homes or getting your hands on their ID, but this bug or connection was able to get to it even though it shouldn't have been. Which was really worrying.

Soleil hadn't been the only one hard at work since HF came out four months ago and it became known not just what Daryl had been planning with it, but also who were the ones who figured it out and fixed the problem.

Willow and Sage had been offered jobs at BASE in the new department that did a more thorough examination of the code of new programs and games that were going to be launching on the platform.

Violet had gotten herself a brand new job in setting up a better way to deal with blitzed accounts and blitzing prevention, and ways to support people who had been blitzed. She'd roped Dawn into helping her out. There had been systems in place before, but none of those systems accounted for the extra struggles people who were living below the poverty line or who were disabled had to deal with when trying to get their accounts back, or back up. And with this new type of blitzing, the old system had needed a real overhaul anyway.

Opal and Juniper had both been on the forefront of creating and vetting new content for HF. Opal because he loved the game so much and Juniper because even though she'd overcome most of her squick, she still wasn't the 'perfect' HF player, and that made her a good resource for the game, apparently.

They'd been trying to keep their names out of the news and out of the media as much as possible, especially their in-game names, as they really wanted to play HF like the other players and not be flocked to as soon as they even appeared online.

Which hadn't been easy, and Opal had apparently used his charm on someone at HF as they'd been taken off the 'online' roster for the other players to see and their names showed as someone entirely different to anyone who wasn't on their friends list. Just to protect them, really.

Fame was fun, but not when it wouldn't allow them to play and experience this game they way they wanted to.

They'd all been really busy with life for the last months and were now finally able to get a good evening of gaming in together. They'd been exploring the game in small groups as much as they could, running some dungeons, finding new hidden skills. All the fun things. But it had been a long time since they'd all been able to play together like this.

So, tonight was the perfect night for it.

Willow walked into the guild house. In many ways it was different from what they had in DoE. For one, the style of the house and the game were totally different, Greek vs Norse mythology mattered a lot. But there were also things in which they were the same. Like the way the living room had been laid out, with a couple of big couches, and a huge fire where Willow loved to sit at with Iris and Mira.

She could see herself become comfortable in this game too, just like she'd been in DoE. She could see this become her second home, much better than the place she actually lived in, of course, but also the place that she shared with the people she loved the most.

There were a few things that they still had to change or work on in the house, it was very much a work in progress. But it started to feel like home again. It started to feel like the place where she would always be looking forward to spending her time. With her friends, with the people she shared her life with.

Soleil wrapped her arm around Willow's shoulder.

> **Rotnem:** What are you thinking?
> **Meadow:** We did it.
> **Meadow:** We changed lives.

She heard Soleil laugh.

> **Rotnem:** That, you've certainly done.
> **Rotnem:** Many lives.

The future of Helheim Fallen Online wasn't certain yet.

They'd kept the game online even though the accusations against people in charge of it had been severe. There were new people running it now, and they were under constant scrutiny from the government and BASE and tens of other organisations, all making sure that everything kept running smoothly and that there were no more problems with player accounts. But it still wasn't certain if the game would stay running, just because there was so much controversy around it.

Sure, the advertisements had been right. This definitely was the game of the decade, but it wasn't clear if that was because of the game itself or all the controversy around it.

For now, Willow and her friends kept playing it, it was their place, their online home. But that could always change, digital life and the cycle of games went very fast these days.

In the last couple of weeks there had been rumours about a new type of gaming. A blend of virtual and augmented reality that was so sleek, nobody had seen it before. It drove the BASE implant technique to new heights, and it promised a seamless experience in VR and AR gaming together. It promised that even when players couldn't go fully into VR, they could still feel like they were, while in AR. It was impressive.

Willow had seen a few short videos of it, and it definitely looked sleek. Only she wasn't so sure about the way it would work, at least not for games. But the thing she'd been most interested in from the 'new experience', as it had been called, was that it boasted the ability to regulate sensory imputs in AR like she could do in VR. No more only partial blocking of sounds or images, but full control over what she would be able to experience. That had definitely been the feature she'd been most curious about.

Violet barged through the door, laughing as she played with Mira. They were both dry again after their splash in the lake. The 'wet' debuff didn't stay on very long. Then Violet looked at Willow and Soleil, grinning.

> **Violet:** What are you standing there for?
> **Violet:** Opal wants us to get some new meat since Mira here ate most of it. And he insists that it's no real summer barbecue without roasting some meat.

Violet reached out to Willow, who took her hand.

> **Meadow:** I'll come help.

She then took Soleil's hand, who didn't fight back either.

As soon as they left the house, Violet started sprinting to the nearest patch of forest, Willow and Soleil closely behind her.

This was what Willow loved about games the most. Playing together with people who understood her. Playing together with her friends.

And she'd rather forget that all of this had almost been gone. All of this had been nearly taken from them by some strings of code.

They'd nearly been gone, their lives ruined.

But they weren't. They'd stopped that from happening.

Only, to do that, they'd all changed, sometimes in invisible ways, because of all the bad things they'd gone through.

Some of those changes had been good too, the connections between her and her friends had gotten stronger, and that made that Willow didn't think about all the bad, just the good.

She'd gotten her best friend back. She'd made new friends. And while life would never be the same again, she couldn't exactly cry about it, because for the first time ever, things seemed to start to look up for her.

She wasn't just 'Willow, the autistic girl', she was now 'Willow, the unlikely hero, still autistic and still a girl, but with a better future'. And she could definitely live with that.

+100 real-life levels on the cool scale

SHOUT OUT!

SHOUT OUT to my amazing partner who has been having to put up with me blabbing on about Willow and her adventures for months and who was even so kind to help me out with some of the more nitty-gritty coding things so that I'd keep it truth-y, even in a semi-fantasy setting.

SHOUT OUT to my younger brother whose notes on an earlier draft made me laugh so hard and whose conversations about our different experiences as gamers and his knowledge about some parts of the health care system helped this book become much better.

SHOUT OUT to the people on the LitRPG Forum, and especially their Discord server, where they seem to not only put up with my oversharing of my process of writing (and editing in the final days) but also somehow trust me enough to put me in a position of power as a mod! You guys keep me sane!

SHOUT OUT to the people of the GameLit Society where I've had many an interesting discussion and I learned a lot about the genre.

SHOUT OUT to my Royal Road and Tapas readers! Without

you I don't think this story would have gone as well as it did now. Seeing the story (and the reading stats…) grow as each chapter came out helped me through some really hard times.

And SHOUT OUT to you, reader, for buying the book and reading it! Without you I wouldn't be able to keep writing!

About E

E is a player of games, a lover of numbers and stats and a creator of words and worlds.

They spend most of their time writing in a variety of genres and any of the rare time left over they spend painting or playing Warhammer (that Ork Kill Team as a first army wasn't the best choice…), playing FFXIV (cute cat girls, what else is there?) or Cities: Skylines (best city builder made in years!) or reading books (words need to go into the brain too, not just out).

www.ingramcontent.com/pod-product-compliance
Lightning Source LLC
Chambersburg PA
CBHW030057310726
48970CB00004B/1044